TRAITOR

DUNCAN FALCONER
TRAITOR

sphere

SPHERE

First published in Great Britain in 2010 by Sphere

A CIP catalogue record for this book
is available from the British Library.

ISBN HB 978-1-84744-119-5
ISBN CF 978-1-84744-118-8

Typeset in Bembo by
Palimpsest Book Production Limited,
Grangemouth, Stirlingshire
Printed and bound in Great Britain by Clays Ltd, St Ives plc

Papers used by Sphere are natural, renewable and recyclable
products sourced from well-managed forests and certified
in accordance with the rules of the Forest Stewardship Council.

Mixed Sources
Product group from well-managed
forests and other controlled sources
www.fsc.org Cert no. SGS-COC-004081
© 1996 Forest Stewardship Council
FSC

Sphere
An imprint of
Little, Brown Book Group
100 Victoria Embankment
London EC4Y 0DY

An Hachette UK Company
www.hachette.co.uk

www.littlebrown.co.uk

To Paul Whittome
One of the toughest men I have
the honour of knowng

1

Stratton dropped a tea bag into a mug and filled it with boiling water from a kettle. He pulled up the sleeves of the tatty old rugby shirt he wore and scraped some diced carrots from a board into a crockpot of meat and other vegetables. As he added some of the water a sound outside caught his attention. He brushed a strand of dark hair from his face and looked through the window. A pheasant, flapping its wings to negotiate the tall hedgerow bordering the back of the garden, landed on the grass, which was coated in thick frost.

Stratton took a piece of bread and quietly unlocked the back door, opening it just enough to toss out the crust. It landed close to the bird which looked at it. The sudden chirp of a mobile phone in the kitchen spooked the pheasant into flight.

Stratton shrugged as he watched the bird crash over the hedge. 'Sorry, mate. I tried,' he muttered, closing the door. He picked up the phone from the breakfast table and pressed the receive button. 'This is Stratton.'

'Mike here.'

'Morning, Sergeant Major,' Stratton said, as he stirred the crockpot. 'Don't tell me that rubbish car of yours has broken down again and you need a lift.'

'No. I'm at the office . . . and I need you in here asap.'

Stratton checked his watch. It was still early. 'Okay.'

'And put your supper in the fridge. You might be eating out tonight.'

The line went dead.

Stratton looked at the crockpot. Things had been fairly busy of late but despite the current cold weather he hoped he wasn't going anywhere hot and sandy this time. He was growing tired of the Middle East and of Afghanistan in particular.

He unplugged the pot and placed it in the fridge. 'Tomorrow, hopefully,' he said to it.

Stratton walked into his bedroom and took off his shirt. His strong back bore several livid scars, a couple of them looking as though they'd been made by bullets. He pulled on a clean T-shirt followed by a thick fleece and walked to the hallway, taking a well-worn leather jacket off the coat hook. He paused at the front door to feel his pockets, checking that he had his phone, wallet and keys. Satisfied, he left the house.

Stratton slowed the open-top Jeep on the approach to the heavily guarded SBS camp in Hamworthy, near Poole on the Dorset coast-line. At the entrance barrier he lowered the scarf wrapped around his face and handed the armed soldier his ID.

The soldier placed the card in an electronic reader and Stratton punched in a code. The man handed back the ID, raised the barrier and Stratton drove through the centre of the camp, the icy wind pulling at his tousled hair. The place was like a ghost town and had been pretty much since the invasion of Afghanistan. He turned into the headquarters car park to see half a dozen cars, just one of them covered in frost. He wasn't the only early bird to arrive that morning. He climbed out and headed towards the main administration building, a squat two-storey modern struc-ture. Half a dozen mud-caked men in shorts and T-shirts came running across the rugby field that stretched to the far perimeter of the camp.

'Hey, Stratton!' one of them called out on seeing him. 'A minute, guys,' the man said to the others who seemed happy to take a breather. He headed over to Stratton. 'No workout today?' he asked, out of breath, his face pink, steam rising from his head and powerful shoulders.

'No time for such luxuries, Chaz old mate. Some of us have to work for a living.'

'No kidding. I'm enjoying my first quiet week in ten months.'

'You've nothing on at the moment?' Stratton asked, fishing.

'You're looking at the entire standby squadron,' Chaz said, indicating the others. 'Six of us for the whole world.'

'Overworked and understaffed.'

'When has it ever been anything else, mate? Maybe I'll catch you for a beer later on. Blue Boar around seven sound good?'

'If I don't turn up it's nothing personal.'

'Roger that. Okay, lads,' Chaz called out. 'Let's finish with five times up the ropes, hands only, no touching the ground on the bottom. Take care,' he said to Stratton as he set off after the others.

Stratton felt a twinge of guilt at not having done any physical exercise that morning. He had been looking forward to a long run, these being his favourite conditions for a cross-country jog: the air crisp and bracing, the icy ground crunching underfoot. Tomorrow, he promised himself, then wondered immediately if that was wishful thinking.

He made his way past the large chunk of Gibraltar rock that served as the SBS's memorial to fallen comrades, a brass plaque with many names inscribed on it affixed to its face, and pushed his way in through the HQ entrance. A soldier behind the reception counter gave a nod as Stratton swiped his ID card across a keypad that unlocked an inner door.

'Morning,' Stratton said, walking through the spacious empty lobby. He skipped up the stairs, went around the internal balcony landing to a corner office and paused at an open door to look inside.

A well-built grey-haired man in a plain uniform sat behind a desk by a window. He was reading something on the computer monitor in front of him.

'Morning, Mike.'

Mike glanced up as Stratton walked into the room. He hit a couple of keys to close the screen, picked up a file and got to his feet. 'I think you'll like this one,' he said as he came around the desk. 'Hasn't been done in over thirty years.'

'What hasn't?' Stratton asked, eyeing him.

'Think Buster Crabb,' Mike said, tapping his nose and winking. He walked past Stratton and on out of the office. 'They're waiting for us in the ops room.'

Stratton followed along the landing, pondering the comment. Crabb had been an MI6 operative who'd disappeared while on a top-secret dive to investigate a Russian warship during the Cold War. Some believed he'd been a spy who'd taken the opportunity to defect. Others thought that Spetsnaz divers had killed Crabb while he'd been in the water under the destroyer. No doubt MI6 had the true account on file inside its vaults and might one day release it. Or not. Stratton took Mike's point to mean that it was an underwater task, quite possibly against the Russians. Crabb had never returned home. That bit stuck in Stratton's mind.

The two men headed down the stairs and across the lobby to another and more narrow set of steps, which descended to a large black steel door. Mike punched a code onto a keypad. The internal lock clicked and he pulled the door open easily on its heavily sprung hinges.

Stratton followed him into a small space hung with curtains of thick black cloth. With the door closed behind them Mike pushed the curtain aside to reveal a brightly lit spacious operations room. Maps, charts and flatscreen monitors covered the available wall space, providing all manner of global environmental, political and conflict data. Seated at a table and sharing a pot of tea were the

SBS commanding officer, the operations officer and a civilian whom Stratton recognised.

'Ah, Stratton,' the CO said, taking a sip of tea. 'How are you today?'

'Fine, thank you, sir.'

The white-haired CO, although tall, had a mass to him, the result of younger days when he had regularly occupied a place in the navy's rugby team second row. The scrum experience clearly influenced his manner, which was straightforward. 'I think you know Mr Jervis,' he said.

'Yes, sir. Good to see you again.'

'You too, Stratton,' Jervis said. He was not your typical London military-intelligence suit. In fact, neither did he dress like one. He looked scruffy compared with his colleagues in MI6. And he had a voice to match, coming as he did from the East End or south-of-the-river London – or so rumour had it. But Jervis was head of the intelligence organisation's operations wing for a reason. Some referred to him as the brilliant mongrel – not to his face, of course, although maybe Jervis wouldn't have minded the nickname as much as he might have made out on hearing it.

'You know, I just realised something,' the CO said. 'Is Stratton in date . . . for diving? Didn't you get shot in the chest a couple of years ago?'

'And the rest of it,' Mike muttered. 'He's in date, sir. He'd better be. He's still getting paid for it.'

'I should think so too,' Jervis said, looking at Stratton and wearing one of his rare smiles. He was referring to a task he had run earlier in the year at a certain undersea prison. The other men in the room obviously knew of Stratton's frequent loans to MI6 for specialist operations, in particular the CO who was required offi-cially to 'sign him off' from time to time. None were privy to the missions themselves although there were always rumours. All had heard something about a deep-sea operation involving Stratton and the Yanks but that was about it.

'Oh yes,' acknowledged the CO, who knew a little more than most. It was sometimes an odd position to be in, both for Stratton and the CO, when the subordinate knew more about what was going on than those further up the hierarchy.

The CO glanced at Stratton. Something in the look gave Stratton pause for thought. It was the way the man looked away as Stratton caught his gaze. That was most unusual for the CO.

'Right,' the CO said. 'To business, then . . . David.'

The well-groomed young ops officer stood, smoothed his jacket on his slender frame and stepped lightly over to two large widescreen monitors. He touched the base of one. A satellite image zoomed in on the Black Sea, veering to the north of the mass of water and pushing in further to hold a position a few hundred thousand feet above a large harbour, its entrance at the centre of the screen.

'Sevastopol,' the officer announced. 'Principal base for Russia's Black Sea fleet. This is a ship-hull recording job. For the past few decades Six have carried out this kind of thing using robot cameras,' he said, nodding to Jervis. 'That's not going to be possible this time.'

The screen image zoomed in closer, following the main channel into the harbour and heading south along a finger of water. After a few moments it paused and focused its bird's-eye view on a naval ship moored stern-on to a jetty, several other vessels parked tightly either side of it. The ops officer touched the adjacent monitor and it displayed several close-up shots of the same vessel taken from the jetty itself. It was battleship grey and had the feel of a military craft yet it was void of armaments: no rocket platforms, no deck ordnance. Instead the design was stealth, the angular superstructure bristling with dishes, antennae and other complex-looking communications-technology features.

'The *Inessa*,' the ops officer said. 'For the aficionados among us that was the name of Lenin's mistress . . . It's Russian navy.

We're not entirely sure what its precise purpose is. It may have more than one. There's evidence to suggest it's a mother ship for submersibles, manned and unmanned. Other evidence indicates it's a surveillance ship. Mr Jervis believes it is far worse. The *Inessa* may aid in the delivery of chemical and biological weaponry . . . Our task? To photograph the underside of it.'

The CO gave Stratton another glance, which the operative did not return though he could sense the man's eyes upon him. The CO was far from being a dramatic type and Stratton wondered what his concerns were.

'And why can't the technical people do this?' Mike asked.

'Technology may be advancing every day,' Jervis said. 'But it will never replace human input.'

A moment's silence followed for them to digest that small pearl of wisdom. They waited to see if Jervis, the most senior person present, had anything to add to his own comment. He sat there impassively.

'The *Inessa* has so far defeated all attempts to visually record her hull bottom,' David continued. 'She has a device on her underside that MI16 has euphemistically termed a disrupter, a powerful combination of sonar, electronic jamming, microwave and sound waves. Two recording devices used against it already in operations have yielded nothing. In fact, the disrupter wrecked their electronics.'

'For the purpose of this briefing,' the CO interrupted, 'which, as you know is recorded, I should mention something we talked about before Stratton's arrival. I understand we don't know what this disrupter will do to a man?'

'That's right,' the ops officer said, glancing at Jervis.

'Much the same thing, I expect,' Jervis said in an off-hand manner. 'This will be our first attempt, so no one really knows.'

The soldiers in the room all had the same thought – Jervis was a cold bastard. The others glanced at Stratton for any reaction since it was pretty obvious who the man was intended to be.

Stratton's gaze flicked to Jervis who was studying the screen images. The operative switched to Mike who could offer nothing more than a sympathetic raise of the eyebrows. The CO looked at him and again Stratton chose to ignore it. There always seemed to be something in each operational task briefing that caused angst. Experience had taught him to keep quiet until the end when he would have the full picture.

Jervis finally spoke. 'In our attempts to understand this unique system we've discovered occasions when the device is switched off,' he said. 'Our boffins at Sixteen believe that operating it in shallow water causes a bounce effect that would be detrimental to the equipment on board the ship itself.' Jervis nodded for the ops officer to continue.

'The ship never sails anywhere except in deep water in order to keep the disrupter operational. The *Inessa* is also obliged to turn off the disrupter in Sevastopol harbour because of the density of sonar surveillance and security systems in operation. Those same systems prohibit us from mounting an effective surveillance task while she's in port. The *Inessa*'s disrupter is therefore kept in the standby mode until the ship has left the harbour. The captain can turn it on as soon as he has passed the mole. He appears to make a habit of taking the vessel as close to the northern mole as he can. The seabed there is less than a metre below propeller depth. The logic seems to be that if he can't use the disrupter until the ship's clear of the mole he'll opt for the shallowest point. The turbulence created by the vessel is too great to position a robot. A team of Spetsnaz shadow the ship and they have been seen inspecting the shallows after she has passed this point. They appear to take every precaution. We believe the only solution is to send a diver in, someone who can react quickly to a changing situation, record the data and get out of there before the Spetsnaz arrive.

'We have carried out a survey of the seabed, where the *Inessa* likes to pass,' the ops officer went on, touching the screen, which zoomed in to an area just beyond the end of the mole. 'It's uneven, made up of large rocks. MI16 has come up with a harness that can be bolted to rock. Theoretically, a diver should be able to attach himself to the harness and operate a recording device while the vessel passes overhead. When it's gone he disconnects and gets out of there.' The ops officer looked around at them. 'That's the task in general detail.'

'What tests have been carried out with this harness and recorder?' the CO asked. 'Has anyone actually tried this before?'

'I had a moment with the chap from MI16 who's here,' the ops officer said. 'I understand they've carried out several satisfactory trials.'

The CO looked at Stratton. 'What do you think?'

Stratton tried to visualise the operation. 'It'll depend on the kit, sir. There'll be a lot of turbulence. But if it's been done . . .'

The CO turned back to David. 'Did he describe the precise conditions in which they tested the equipment?'

'Apparently one of them wore the harness in its intended role while a Royal Navy frigate passed overhead,' the ops officer replied. 'With the same clearances as may be expected in Sevastopol.'

'They actually trialled it using one of their own?' the CO asked, impressed.

'So he said, sir.'

'Why don't we just get *them* to do it?' Mike quipped, with a smirk. No one laughed, though Jervis smiled thinly.

'The Spetsnaz are as much of a concern to me as the turbulence,' the CO said. 'This is a job for a soldier, not a scientist.'

'We have some useful underwater toys,' Mike offered.

'And so have the Russians,' the CO countered. 'This chap from Sixteen. Did he bring the kit with him?'

'Yes, sir. He's waiting upstairs,' the ops officer said.

'How long have we got before we mount this operation?' the CO asked Jervis. 'I'd like Stratton to have a practice run if possible.'

'You won't have time for any of that,' Jervis said. 'We believe the *Inessa* leaves harbour tomorrow night or very soon after. Your man would have to be on target by then and every night until it does depart.'

The information only added to the general discomfort among the specialist soldiers.

Stratton had a question. 'Do we know if the Spetsnaz conduct recces of the shallows before the *Inessa* passes the mole?'

'They're part of the *Inessa*'s crew,' Jervis replied. 'They satellite it whenever the disrupter's in standby mode and go aboard once it's operational. I've heard nothing about them recceing ahead but I'll see if I can confirm that and get back to you.'

'What about a team, sir?' Mike suggested. 'Give Stratton some back-up.'

'Too risky,' Jervis replied. 'I can't afford to have a crowd operating in that area. The Russians are highly sensitive at the moment. There's talk of conflict with the Ukrainians over the port lease. The Russians are due to leave in a few years but they don't want to. I want just one man. The kit's already on its way out there, anyway . . . one man's kit.'

The CO glanced at Jervis, once again thinking what a cold-hearted bastard he was. He looked at Stratton. 'I'm going to leave it up to you, Stratton. We really don't have anyone else up to the task at the moment,' he added, suddenly feeling as manipulative as Jervis.

Stratton nodded thoughtfully. 'Let's take a look at the kit.'

'Okay,' the CO said, getting to his feet. 'I'll leave you to it. Get back to me asap.'

Jervis stood and buttoned up his jacket. 'I'm going back to London. I'll need to know within the hour if it's a go or not.'

'An hour?' the CO echoed, surprised. 'And if we can't?'

'I'll find someone who can,' Jervis said. 'You're not the only specialists in town, you know.'

'Hereford couldn't do this task,' the ops officer jumped in.

'I know,' Jervis said. 'Watch your backs, fellers. There are some areas where you've got competition. That goes for Hereford, too. Good to see you again, Stratton.' Jervis pushed aside the black curtains and left the room.

'Who could he be talking about?' David asked.

No one had an immediate answer.

'There's a lot of specialist units cropping up,' Mike said. 'Twenty-odd years ago the SAS took the Iranian embassy because no one else could. Today the London Met could handle it just as well. I don't know who else does water, though – not to our level.'

The others couldn't think of anyone either.

'Take a look at the kit,' the CO said to Stratton. 'Let me know your thoughts soon as you can . . . within the hour.' The CO left the room.

'Be a feather in your cap,' David said to Stratton as he followed the CO.

'What do you think?' Mike asked his friend.

'What does that actually mean?'

'What?'

'Feather in your cap?'

Mike shrugged. 'I'll look it up . . . Let's go meet this boffin from Sixteen.'

The two men walked across the SBS HQ lobby to an office on the ground floor. Inside there was the usual paraphernalia and no admin staff had arrived yet. A smart though casually dressed man stood on the far side of the room, looking out of a window to the frozen rugby field beyond. He turned and smiled politely as Stratton and Mike came in. He appeared to be the same age as Stratton and was slightly taller, clean-cut and athletic. He looked the highly intelligent type.

'Phillip Binning, is it?' Mike asked.

'Yes. Phil, please,' Binning replied in a refined English accent. The two shook hands.

'This is John Stratton. He's going to be using your harness and recording device,' Mike said, adding under his breath, 'or not.'

Binning smiled again as he looked at Stratton, studying him with interest. When he shook Stratton's hand he did so firmly. 'I've heard of you,' Binning said. 'You have an impressive reputation.'

Stratton wasn't sure how to reply to the comment.

Mike spared him the trouble. 'Can you talk us through the kit? We don't have a lot of time.'

'Sure,' Binning said, going to a large black canvas bag on a table. He unbuckled a pair of straps, unzipped it along its length and pulled out a black lightweight metal frame wrapped in heavy-duty nylon strips that he unwound before deftly unfolding the frame and locking its joints into position. 'This is the harness that will hold you to the sea floor. Its operation is quite simple. You use a bolt gun to drive bolts through these holes here, here and here,' he said, indicating five small flat tongues welded to the corners and centre of the frame.

'Looks basic enough,' Mike said.

'The best things are, aren't they?' Binning replied, with a condescending look. 'I understand the seabed in the target area is sedimentary with large igneous-boulder deposits. Some of the boulders are granite, some are obsidian. You must bolt the frame to the granite boulders. Obsidian will not hold the bolt configuration. Can you tell the difference?'

Stratton shook his head.

'Well, you'd better learn before you go,' Binning warned. 'Otherwise you could find yourself going through the props.' He removed a gunlike device from the bag and offered it to Stratton. 'The bolt gun. Light, isn't it? It's off the shelf with a few modifications. Very clean reload features.'

Stratton looked over the commercially manufactured gun. It seemed straightforward enough. He put it to one side. There would be time to familiarise himself with it later.

'The harness is a quick-release system . . . legs, hips, chest and head.' Binning picked up the frame and turned it over. 'It leaves your arms free to operate the recorder.' He dug out a sturdy plastic-moulded waterproof box, unfastened the lid and took from it a complex-looking device that looked like a set of adapted night-vision goggles. 'This is the recorder . . . it obviously fits over one's face,' he said. 'You simply turn it on, look at the hull through the optics and the device will do the rest.' He took a file of printed paper out of the box. 'Here are the operating details. You'll need to read them thoroughly before you play with it. One word of warning, though. This button here arms the device . . . yes, I did say arm. Once it's activated, when you remove the memory card here – which is all you need to bring back with you once you've completed the task – the recorder will self-destruct. It's not a big bang or anything like that. It releases a chemical inside that destroys all the hardware. Very important. We don't think the Russians have anything close to its sophistication and we don't want them getting their hands on it.'

Stratton held the device and scanned the first page of the instructions. He put them both down, more interested in the harness. That was the part his life would depend on.

'Any burning questions?' Binning asked.

Stratton picked up a bolt and placed it through one of the holes on the frame.

'You'll need all five in place to ensure stability,' Binning advised him.

'How do you release the frame afterwards?' Stratton asked.

'Good question,' the young scientist said. 'The eyelets detach from the frame itself,' he said, demonstrating how.

'You're still left with the bolts in the rock,' Stratton pointed out.

'It's the best we could do in the time we had. All I can suggest is that you cover the bolts with stones. I understand the value of the information gained on this operation will not be compromised by the other side knowing we have it. Only complete deniability was on the wish list.'

Stratton wasn't overjoyed. Masking an operative's presence on target reduced the risk of pursuit. But he didn't expect a scientist to think like an operative so he kept his criticisms to himself.

'It's all pretty straightforward,' Binning added.

'I'm glad you think so,' Stratton muttered.

Mike scrutinised the scientist. 'Who did the live trials on this?'

'I did.'

'How many?'

'Five runs in all. On the last two the propeller was barely a metre above me.'

Stratton looked quizzically at the scientist who was wearing a cocky grin.

Binning picked his coat up from the back of a chair. 'Why don't I leave you to look it all over?' he said. 'I'll be outside getting some fresh air if you need me.' He paused at the door to look back at them. 'If you don't feel up to it, I'll do it.' Then he went out.

Stratton and Mike looked at each other, both wondering the same thing: was Binning Jervis's alternative underwater specialist?

'Couldn't be,' Mike said.

Stratton shrugged. 'Jervis is a civvy as well, remember. That means he thinks like one.' He went back to the equipment.

'What do you think?' Mike asked, holding up the frame and testing its strength.

'It's not a great plan,' Stratton mused. 'I hope the infil and exfil are tighter.'

'Does that mean you'll do it?'

Stratton was well aware of his own natural inability to refuse practically any operation, especially an unusual one. And as always he justified the decision by telling himself that he could pull out if things did not go to plan. But then, he wasn't very good at doing that either. Other factors came into play in this case, though. The high-intensity work he had been busy with of late had become mundane. It was relatively simple. The weather and terrain of Afghanistan made the tasks challenging and their nature, either hits or observation posts, made them highly dangerous, yet they had become repetitive. The diving task sounded different. And it had something else that Stratton prized: he would be doing it alone. That gave the job a high score as far as he was concerned. If he passed on this he could be back in Afghanistan within the week. 'We'll give it a go,' he said.

'I'll let the team know,' Mike said, heading for the door. 'The detailed briefing will be in about an hour. You'll have to be on the road by midday.'

Stratton nodded, despite a distant concern tugging at him.

'You're a total tart, aren't you? You can never say no,' Mike said as he went out.

Stratton picked up the recorder's operating instructions and began to read them.

2

The operative walked along an empty beach in near-darkness, his breath misting with each exhalation. White and gold lights from distant boats and a far-off shoreline glinted on the water. A light wind toyed with the harsh hinterland grass, the sound it made giving way to the lapping waves and the noise of his boots crunching the sand beneath, breaking the grains bonded by frozen moisture.

Stratton pulled up the collar of his jacket against the biting cold. The temperature must have been in the double minus digits now that the sun had dropped out of sight. He kept away from the water's edge, walking close to the scrubland to reduce his silhouette.

The end of the northern mole that formed one side of the entrance to Sevastopol harbour lay less than a mile up ahead. The harbour's illuminations had been quite visible when Stratton started out, in particular the bright red intermittent beacon at the far end of the northern mole and the green one on the tip of the southern one. A gentle bend in the coastline had put them out of sight for the moment. He did not expect to see either one again until he was in the water.

He checked the glowing face of the small GPS in his hand. The directional arrow had been pointing directly ahead when he'd first stepped onto the beach after leaving the rental car outside a quiet bar. Over the last dozen or so metres it had begun to turn towards the dense vegetation.

When the arrow pointed at a right angle to the shore Stratton stopped and took a moment to look around. He could not see another living soul. The sounds of the wind and the surf seemed to grow louder.

He sat down at the edge of the sand and looked out over the water, as if taking in the stark scenery. The bell of a distant buoy clanged somewhere across the black, shimmering water. Stratton felt conscious of the possibility that someone was watching him. Whoever it was would not be obvious. But he had reason to feel confident that he was not being monitored – not by the Russians, at least. Someone had followed him from the airport that afternoon to the small villa where he was staying. When he went out an hour or so later he identified his watcher, an old man who looked like a schoolteacher. The tail appeared to be quite good, not looking at Stratton even once. The watcher worked for MI6 and was not so much keeping tabs on the operative as looking for others who might be. Stratton had been warned to expect a friendly shadow. If the man had followed him along the beach there was no sign.

Stratton leaned back and eased himself into the scrub. He was most vulnerable now. He couldn't play the tourist card if security forces interrupted him. Once he'd made contact with the equipment he would be screwed if they found him. Stratton didn't hesitate.

Once he was completely hidden he turned onto his front and crawled through the tall grass. A check of the GPS indicated a waypoint five metres away. Stratton slithered into a tiny clearing and towards a patch of freshly disturbed earth. He dug at it with his hands. It did not take long to reveal a black canvas bag similar to the one Binning had brought to the SBS HQ.

Stratton unbuckled the straps and unzipped the bag. Clouds shielded most of the starlight but he could identify the familiar contents by touch: a dry diving bag, a complete set of diving accessories, a Lar 5 bubble-less rebreather primed and ready for use, lightweight body armour, a bolt gun and the now familiar frame and harness system. He took two final items from the bag: the electronic recorder inside its protective plastic casing and a P11 underwater pistol in a plastic holster. The sole weapon he had been permitted fired just as well on land. With only six rounds and no reload, its main advantage other than being able to fire underwater was a good one: because it had no moving parts and fired the slender tungsten darts electronically it was a truly silent weapon.

Stratton checked his watch. He had ample time to get ready. He took off his boots and coat and rolled out the rubber diving bag, a one-piece outfit with a long waterproof zip that ran across the back from elbow to elbow. He eased his feet all the way inside to the thin rubber booties on the ends of the leggings and pushed his hands through the wrist seals. The roomy bag could accommodate his clothes, including a thick woolly fleece to protect him against the cold temperature of the water. Before pulling his head through the neck seal that had been dutifully powdered by whoever had packed the equipment bag, he tucked his boots into the diving bag, placing one either side of his thighs, and wrapped his coat around his abdomen.

After ensuring that the zipper across his back was pulled firmly home he began ferrying the equipment out of the scrub. Whoever had packed the kit had had the good sense to include a nylon belt with numerous lines attached to it in order to tie the various pieces of equipment to his body.

Stratton secured each item to its line before sitting down to slide on the fins. He pulled on the body-armour waistcoat, buckled it tight, slipped the breathing apparatus over his head and fastened the sides. He felt like a tortoise. He strapped the bulky P11 pistol to his thigh and, after attaching the strap of the face mask to the back of his neoprene hood, he pulled on a thick pair of gloves.

He was good to go.

Getting to his feet, he picked up the frame, bolt gun and recorder and walked backwards into the water. He did not pause and waded into the gentle waves. As the water reached his waist he dropped onto his back and finned away from the shoreline, the equipment dangling beneath him on the lines. The icy water took the weight of the bulk. It seeped into the neoprene hood and gloves but his body heat soon warmed it. The water tasted salty, with a hint of fuel.

A hundred metres from the shore, invisible to all except the most sophisticatedly equipped, Stratton turned to head parallel with the beach. He finned at a pace that he could sustain for hours, looking up at the clouds. A star or two was visible through the occasional gaps.

It took half an hour to come level with the beginning of the mole. The slight current had worked against him. With the drag effect of the load, had he finned with less vigour he might have simply maintained his position. He still had plenty of time. The *Inessa* was not expected to leave her jetty for another hour or so and he would receive a warning when she did.

He studied the top of the brightly lit concrete mole as he finned along. It appeared to be deserted. A vessel went past a few hundred metres out to sea. It reached the main channel between the moles and went into the harbour. There appeared to be a steady stream of traffic moving in both directions between the ends of the two structures, with a good half-mile between each vessel. Stratton altered direction and gradually closed on the base of the northern breakwater.

The lights on top of it shone right into his face as he approached the massive concrete mouldings. He moved into the shadows of the parapet that ran around the top some thirty feet above him and manoeuvred himself inside a niche that had been formed by the breakers. Stratton carefully secured the equipment and settled in the lapping water.

19

He felt uncomfortably warm but he knew from experience that within minutes of sitting still the cold would start to penetrate his dry-suit and clothing.

Every now and then a heftier wave from a passing vessel threw him about despite having taken several minutes to cover the distance from the ship. Unlike the *Inessa*, none of the ships would risk coming too near either mole. The green light on the southern one flashed in the darkness.

The vast harbour hardly looked its size from where Stratton was. Most of Sevastopol's street and building lights along the water-line were obscured. It was impossible to see the narrowing channel that led into the harbour proper without climbing to the top of the mole. He settled in to play the oh-so-familiar waiting game.

If the *Inessa* did not depart that night, Stratton would have to be back at the villa before first light and then return to the cache the following evening to repeat the whole process. This could go on until the Russian vessel did eventually leave. He wasn't looking forward to that option at all. The longer he remained on the ground the greater the risk of exposure and of being detected. The task didn't concern him as much as the time he would have to spend in the villa during the day and especially his need to sleep for part of it. That alone could arouse suspicion.

Voices drifted down to his ears and he shrank deeper into the cranny. They could only be coming from the top of the mole. Men's voices, at least two, speaking in Russian. The sound was clear, as though the men were leaning over the parapet.

Stratton felt a sudden vibration by his right ear. The signal originated from a small receiver tucked into a pocket on the side of his hood. It was a GSM and GPS Sim-card device that could be activated from a cellular phone. There were three distinct vibration patterns: one to order him to abort completely, another to abort for that night only and the third to indicate that the *Inessa* was departing. He received the third signal, sent by an observer stationed where they could see the vessel or at least the finger of water that it would need to pass along to reach the main channel and the harbour mouth. Stratton had somewhere between fifteen and twenty minutes to get into position.

His adrenalin level rose and he eased his head from cover to look above. He could see two figures partially silhouetted against the night sky. The men moved along the wall and Stratton quickly turned on the gas bottle at the front of the diving apparatus. He pulled on the face mask, put the mouthpiece between his teeth, opened the flow valves and took several deep breaths before exhaling the gas through his nose to clear the device of excessive nitrogen. He craned his neck to look up again, the action made more difficult by the breathing apparatus. The men appeared to have gone further round the mole and out of sight. Gathering his equipment and looking and feeling like some kind of aquatic gypsy, Stratton moved away from the breakers and slipped below the surface.

Every step of the operation except the next one had been somehow quantifiable. It all depended on a handful of bolts remaining in their holes in a slab of rock. Deep down Stratton hated relying on single physical bits of apparatus – the rings that secured a man under his parachute, for instance, or the karabiner and line that kept him from falling to his death when he was climbing. It was a visceral complaint. Stratton could control the inner conflicts. They did not alter his reliance on such devices. But the concerns remained, components of his fear that were probably essential to his success.

Visibility was reasonable, at least ten metres, better than average in his experience. The rubber suit grew tighter as he finned, gripping his arms and legs as the air inside compressed. He looked at the needle of a luminous compass attached to his wrist.

The concrete mouldings gave way to huge boulders. Stratton followed them until they abruptly ended and a flat shale seabed stretched into the gloom. He had swum too far. The *Inessa* would pass closer to the mole, above the boulders. He turned back to look for a place to set himself up.

He inspected the boulders as he moved over them. They all looked like granite. The only obsidian ones, as far as he could tell, were some smaller rocks between the larger gaps. He had taken Binning's advice and studied the differences between the two rock formations. Confident at the time, he was less so now that he was on task and in darkness.

Stratton found what appeared to be a choice location: a broad, almost flat boulder, although it lay at a slight tilt. It was not big enough to accommodate the entire frame but another, slightly smaller boulder beside it looked ideal to take the overlap. A check of his wristwatch showed he had around eight minutes before the earliest moment the *Inessa* could arrive, if the calculations were correct and the GSM signal had arrived as soon as it had been sent. The bolting and harnessing of the frame could be completed in a couple of minutes or so, according to Binning's trial-timing average. Stratton could not afford to waste a second. He quickly undid the straps and locked the frame's joints into position.

After loading the bolt gun Stratton positioned the two holes at the top of the frame over the boulder, checking to ensure that the rock was solid and that the bottom corners, where his feet would go, rested on the adjacent slab. Satisfied that it was well positioned, he pressed the bolt that protruded from the end of the gun firmly into one of the top holes, pushing down on it to release the automatic safety lock. He pulled the trigger. A powerful jolt slammed the steel bolt through the eyehole and into the rock. When he removed the gun he gave the frame a tug. The bolt was firmly home.

He reloaded the gun and slammed the next bolt into the opposite corner. In a couple of minutes he had planted all five bolts and the frame appeared to be rigidly in place. But another firm tug revealed a loose bolt at one of the bottom corners. Unperturbed, he loaded a fresh bolt into the gun and tugged at the loose one in an effort to remove it. It twisted around inside the rock but would not come out. A fierce tug on the frame didn't budge it.

Stratton felt reluctant to spend any more time on the faulty bolt. It would require far more force than he could exert to remove it. Typical of what he disliked about technology, and this was the simple kind, according to Binning. There was no tangible reason, that he could see at least, why any of the bolts should remain in position. It was clear how a screw worked, and even how a nail hammered into wood could hold strong. A bolt punched into rock, and not a very long bolt either, failed to inspire him with confidence.

A check of his watch revealed time quickly moving on and Stratton suddenly feared he might not have enough. He pushed aside any doubts about the frame, untied the gun from his belt and let it sink to the bottom. If the *Inessa* came at that moment he would fail. He sat on the frame, strapped both his legs to it as tightly as possible, and lay back to secure the waist and chest straps. Before fitting the head harness he found the recorder on the end of its line, opened the container, removed the device and activated it. He set the arming switch and checked the series of LED indicators. The system appeared to be functioning. He removed his face mask, letting it hang from the back of his hood, and placed the cumbersome device over his face, pulling the head straps tight. Exhaling through his nose into the optical compartment displaced the water inside it and he blinked quickly to clear his eyes. A brief adjustment of the lenses brought his immediate surroundings into focus. The device could penetrate low light as well as some of the murkiness, improving overall visibility. So far so good, he decided. He was still not quite ready.

The *Inessa* would make all haste to get out of the harbour once it had slipped its moorings. It had a speed limit of ten knots in the main channel but the captain was committed to turning on the disrupter and accelerating to a cruising speed of thirty-five knots as soon as he could. He would get out of the harbour as quickly as possible.

Stratton passed the strap that secured the device to his head over the top of the recorder housing, clipped it into place and tightened it. He could only move his arms now. He was firmly secured to the boulders.

As he stared into the hollow grey glow around him, he picked up a faint noise – the water was a more effective medium than air for relaying sound waves. The sound became a distant hum that grew louder by the second. It could have been another ship passing through the harbour entrance but Stratton felt somehow sure it was the *Inessa*.

The operational briefing had covered all possible contingencies including another vessel passing overhead, or close by, around the time when the *Inessa* was expected. Stratton's orders were to remain in position and record everything, no matter what it was. But it would be a pointless risk for another vessel, even one close to the *Inessa*'s size, to pass that close to the mole. The *Inessa*'s captain knew the precise depth of the boulders where he intended to pass above them.

The deep hum intensified and divided into several tones, a collection of dronish whirring and high-pitched spinning. And something else joined the mix. It was more physical than audible. Stratton could feel it in his temples: a significant pressure wave produced by powerful turbines.

The boulders began to resonate as the pressure waves explored the gaps between them. The metal frame tingled against Stratton's skin.

He tipped his head back in the hope of catching sight of the vessel as it broke through the gloom. He couldn't see it despite the horrendous noise and intense shuddering that gave the impression the craft was already upon him.

A dark shape suddenly emerged from the greyness, heading directly at him. A dense broadening shadow followed it. Both were part of the same object.

The boulder Stratton lay on began to judder, its sand deposits agitating as if on the skin of a vibrating drum. The sound became almost deafening and the cutting edge of the vessel's bows crossed directly above him with a high-pitched seething sound.

Stratton's body vibrated along with everything else as he trained the recorder's optics directly above him, doing his best to keep the device steady. He felt the pressure on his chest increase as the tons of water displaced by the vessel pushed him down. The greatest danger was still to come – the propellers. He hastily tightened the strap across his head even more and gripped the sides of the recorder, holding it firmly against his face. His brain felt as if it was being puréed inside his skull.

As the vibrations increased the keel flattened out at either side of Stratton like a vast dark pitted ceiling that he could reach if he stretched out a hand. He felt insignificant beneath it. A short drop and it would erase him as if he was an insect.

The straps of the harness grew tighter as the pressure forced him upwards towards the *Inessa*'s hull, the propellers like a massive vacuum cleaner hungrily sucking in anything ahead of them. Shale and debris whirled around, spinning in the vortex. Stratton groaned as the harness bit into him. A square recess, like a dark doorway into the hull, shot past his vision. Another larger opening followed. Stratton was beyond evaluating anything other than his own ability to survive.

The lower corner of the frame snapped free. The whole frame wriggled and creaked as if it was threatening to buckle. It jolted even more brutally and the bolt on the opposite corner broke away too and Stratton's legs jerked up towards the hull. He could do nothing to control it.

The turbulence reached a screaming crescendo as the propellers closed on him. Shale and stones spun around as if inside a blender. The frame rattled as the blades sliced through the water, growing closer by the millisecond. This had suddenly become the craziest stunt he had ever agreed to. The propellers seemed to be lower than his head and would smash against the boulder. Then they were above him, the turbulence unbelievable as the huge blades carved through the water inches past his face.

A second later they were through. But something dealt a vicious blow to one of Stratton's feet and he felt sure it had been severed. He felt no pain but he had seen men lose limbs in battle and not know it. The fin swirled past his head but he could not see if his foot was attached.

The *Inessa* was not done with him. The force of the water coming through the propellers was so intense that the frame's centre bolt now gave way, quickly followed by one of the top corners. It flipped him over, the frame bending against the last remaining bolt. Stratton stared down into the gap between the boulders.

Standing on the bows of the *Inessa*, two Spetsnaz commandos watched the swirling water churned up by the propellers. One of the men squinted into the darkness as he saw a rubbery black object surface in the frothing wake. It glinted for a second in the moonlight. He shouted to his comrade who aimed a powerful light towards it. The first man took a closer look through a pair of electronically stabilised binoculars. The object floated briefly before sinking out of sight. The soldier hurled a small buoy off the back to mark the position and talked into a radio. A semi-rigid speedboat was a few hundred yards behind the ship and he waved at it as he gave the coxswain instructions.

Four men were in the speedboat, two in assault swimmers' gear. They bit down on mouthpieces and breathed off their sets as the coxswain accelerated the boat forward.

★

The turbulence around Stratton died down as the *Inessa* cruised away. The cacophony subsided and the shale that had swirled through the water like the flakes inside a snow globe began to drift back down to the seabed.

Stratton unfastened the strap over his forehead. He pulled away the recording device and held on to it while he reached around for his face mask, fearing he had lost it. Thankfully, it was on the end of its strap. He pulled it against his face and exhaled to clear the water. Before Stratton did anything else he looked at the end of his leg. The fin had indeed been sliced away but just beyond the end of his neoprene-covered foot. A wave of relief swept over him. Another inch and he would have lost his toes.

Stratton moved up a gear, another imminent danger consuming his thoughts. The passing of the *Inessa* meant the highly probable arrival of Spetsnaz divers to check the shallows.

Stratton ripped away the remaining straps and pulled himself out from under the frame. A new sound halted him, a higher-pitched whine growing to drown out the distant drone of the *Inessa*. Stratton looked up at the grey surface for any sign of the new vessel. The sound increased; a powerful engine was heading towards him at speed. Would it keep going, or not?

Stratton watched as a darker patch moved overhead. The engine abruptly decelerated and two heavy objects dropped into the water. Stratton knew they were divers and that he was in trouble.

The recorder. He couldn't swim or defend himself while he still held on to it and therefore it had to go. The brief had been to bring the expensive device back if at all possible. But if not, he was to remove the memory card after ensuring that the device had been armed to self-destruct. At the time Stratton could not help thinking how ridiculous that order was – the latter part of it. If the situation was so desperate that he had to ditch the device he would hardly have time to ensure it was correctly armed. They should have emphasised the need to arm the recorder properly in

27

the first place, before its use. Another example of how procedures were so often formulated by those with little experience in operational implementation.

Stratton pulled out the memory card and let the recorder drop between the boulders. He tucked the card inside his wrist seal. The divers came out of the gloom, both finning hard in his general direction. Experience told him that he could see them because they were against a lighter background and that they could not see him yet. He remained still, his best bet – initially, at least. He was a lame duck anyway with one fin and having his back to the enemy while trying to swim away would just increase the disadvantage.

His hand went to the plastic holster at his right thigh and withdrew the P11 pistol from it. The weapon was only effective within ten metres. He suspected the Spetsnaz would have something similar and was thankful for his body armour.

Powerful lights flashed on in the hands of the divers, who swept the beams across the boulders. The intensity of the Spetsnaz divers' diligence indicated strongly how confident they were that someone was in the vicinity. Stratton could not see them clearly beyond the glare of the lights. He selected one of the beams, aimed a fraction to its side and touched the pistol's battery-powered trigger. The weapon barely jolted in his grip as it released a slender steel dart. He fired two more bolts around the lights. At least one must have found its mark because the light turned upwards as if its carrier had lost control.

The other beam caught Stratton and something struck him in the side of his chest, the impact absorbed by the body armour. Another blow followed quickly and slammed through the fibreglass housing of his breathing apparatus. If the missile had done any damage Stratton would soon know about it when he breathed in a mouthful of water – or of caustic acid from the carbon dioxide-absorbent powder.

The Russian diver powered headlong towards Stratton, shining the light into the operative's eyes, blinding him, and fired again. The shot slashed across Stratton's shoulder, his blood leaking into the surrounding seawater as two more darts missed him by inches. Stratton could not make out his target in the glare and in desperation fired the rest of his pistol's darts, one of which smashed the light. But the Russian had closed the gap and, out of ammunition now, he grabbed at Stratton with his hands. The Spetsnaz diver knew the fundamental strategy for underwater hand-to-hand combat: he went for Stratton's breathing apparatus. Apart from the obvious effect, ripping away the mouthpiece causes immediate panic, thus placing the enemy on the absolute retreat. Usually the first to do it is the winner. It was therefore fair for the Spetsnaz man to assume that as he managed to grab Stratton's low-pressure oxygen hose where it was attached to his mouthpiece, wrench it out of his mouth and rip it from his set, he had gained the upper and indeed decisive hand. His training had also emphasised ensuring a clean finish, which required maintaining control over the victim until he had succumbed to asphyxiation. He could not allow Stratton to escape to the surface. So the Russian kept a firm hold on Stratton and finned as strongly as he could to push him down between the boulders and hold him there until he was dead.

Stratton reacted in panic to his mouthpiece being ripped out. He fought with all his might to wrestle free from the other man's clutches, his single aim to get to the surface so as not to perish. But the Russian was not only more powerful than Stratton, he was on top, could breathe, and had both of his fins.

As Stratton twisted and wriggled in vain he slid from the side of the boulder. The Russian pushed him deeper into the crevice. Stratton stretched out an arm to push himself back up and it landed squarely on something immediately familiar. He quickly found the grip of the bolt gun, hauled it up, placed the muzzle against the Russian's ribcage under his armpit, pushed it in to release the safety catch, and pulled the trigger. The bolt shot through the man's lungs and aorta before punching its way out the other side, followed by a stream of blood and tissue. The fight instantly went out of the Russian and his body went limp. Stratton ripped out the man's mouthpiece, shoved it into his own mouth and sucked on it, drawing in the air.

The sound of the speedboat circling above reached down to him. Stratton removed his own flooded diving set, unfastened the Russian's and tossed it over his own shoulders. He took one of the man's fins and swam away, keeping low to the bottom.

The compass helped him head straight out to sea away from the mole for a few hundred metres before changing direction back towards the cache. The icy water leaked in through the dart holes in his suit but he had to ignore it. He surfaced once to check he was on the correct bearing to his start point and then not again until he could look out of the water with his chest still on the seabed. After ensuring that the beach was deserted and that he was facing the spot where the cache was hidden, he pulled off the fins and got to his feet. The water in his suit filled the leggings as he hurried into the bushes.

Stratton remained still for a moment to acquaint his ears to the surrounding sounds. He had to move fast and get as far out of the area as soon as possible. He would also have to contact his people to let them know what had happened in case a change in the exfiltration plans was required.

His shoulder suddenly began to burn. The wound had stopped bleeding but it would need a few stitches. All things considered, he had got off lightly.

He felt under his wrist seal and removed the memory card. All in all the operation had been a success, from his point of view. That was one more job he would never do again. Bloody bolts and rocks. If those boys in MI16 wanted to do it, they could have it.

Stratton dumped all the equipment back in the black bag and hastily covered it. Whoever had buried it originally would be back to clear up, probably before dawn. His clothes were pretty much soaked through, but he had a change back in his room. He pulled on his shoes and after a brief scan up and down the beach stepped onto the sand and made his way along it. He combed his hair with his fingers, pressing out some of the water. He would take a quick shower to wash out the salt and then get on the road.

Stratton's thoughts turned to something more pleasant – the crockpot in his fridge that he was looking forward to heating up and digging into, and the glass of wine to go with it.

3

Stratton walked through Customs into the arrivals hall at London Heathrow Terminal Five wearing his battered leather jacket and with his holdall slung over one shoulder. He scanned along the line of faces waiting for arriving passengers, recognising Ted's large head lurking at the end of the line.

'How's it going, Ted?' Stratton asked as he came over to the driver.

'I'm grand, Stratton,' the man replied in a Belfast accent. 'This way,' he pointed, indicating a set of glass doors that led outside. Ted was a regular Royal Marine who had been attached to the SBS for half a dozen years. The dependable type, he took his job as driver to the unit most seriously. 'Did you have a good trip?' he asked, giving Stratton a knowing glance that suggested he was privy to the intimate details of the mission, which of course he had no clue about.

'I did,' Stratton replied, with a wink.

'You look fine, so you do,' Ted assured him. 'It's good to have you back in one piece again.'

As they made their way through the hall, Stratton saw a man he thought he recognised walk in from outside. The man looked strong and burly and was wearing a heavy parka with a fur-lined hood. His long jet-black hair was unkempt. Most notably he had a limp: the mobility of his left leg was restricted as he moved to get on an ascending escalator. He looked older and heavier than Stratton would have expected him to be after the couple of years since he'd last seen him. Stratton might not have recognised the man at all had it not been for his disability.

'Jordan!' Stratton called out above the cacophony of the hall.

The man, carrying a backpack, turned his head. He glanced in Stratton's direction before looking back up the escalator.

'Jordan!' Stratton repeated. This time the man did not respond.

'That Jordan Mackay?' Ted asked. 'That is 'im, ain't it,' he decided quickly.

Stratton dropped his bag at Ted's feet. 'Be back in a minute,' he said, setting off towards a flight of stairs to the departure level where Jordan was headed.

'I'll wait right here for you,' Ted called out.

Stratton ran up the stairs and paused on reaching the top landing. The man was limping briskly across the not too crowded hall. 'Jordan,' Stratton called out again after significantly closing the gap between them.

This time Jordan looked directly at him, appearing surprised as he stopped to face his old friend. His initially blank expression turned into a slight, vaguely tense smile. 'Stratton.'

'How are you, my old mate?' Stratton asked, holding out a hand.

Jordan shook it firmly, appearing to warm to the meeting, if somewhat reluctantly. 'I'm fine.'

'You look well,' Stratton offered. 'A little heavier around the middle, perhaps,' he added to remain honest.

Stratton suddenly suspected that Jordan had heard him call his name the first time but had wanted to avoid their meeting. In truth, Stratton shared some of that reluctance himself but would not succumb to it. His feeling of guilt formed an effective psychological barrier between them but a strong sense of old loyalty had pushed him through it. Despite Jordan's unease, he did not regret meeting him.

'You look tired,' Jordan said. 'They still working you every hour God sends?'

33

'Is it any easier being a civilian?'

Jordan shrugged. 'When you're off the clock nobody bothers you, at least.'

'There's something to be said for that. You off on holiday or work?'

Jordan hesitated. 'North Sea,' he answered finally. 'I'm a dive supervisor.'

'On a platform?'

'One you know well enough. The Morpheus.'

'Crawled all over that a few times, haven't we? How does it feel? I mean, working on it as a civvy.'

'I'd rather land on it by chopper on a nice sunny afternoon than climb it from the ogin in a Force Twelve in the middle of the bloody night.'

They laughed at the memories, Jordan enjoying the moment more than he felt comfortable with.

'Pay's better, too,' Jordan added. 'That's all that counts these days.'

Stratton maintained a smile. Jordan had never used to be interested in the money beyond providing for his basic needs. It was obvious what was missing in him. Stratton looked into Jordan's now soulless eyes and could only remember the good times – his hearty laughter at even the poorest of jokes, his tenacity as an underweight prop on the rugby field, always giving as good as he got. That was long before he'd got the duff leg that had ended his career in the SBS.

Jordan looked at his watch and glanced over his shoulder towards the check-in counters.

'I've got to get going too,' Stratton said. 'It was good to see you. Do you ever get down to the reunions?'

'Nah. Maybe one day. Too soon for me.'

Stratton understood. 'Where you living now?'

'I'm in the middle of moving,' Jordan said, stepping back to end the conversation. 'Maybe I'll surprise you in Poole one day.' He gave Stratton a wave and turned away.

Stratton watched Jordan cross the hall. The sight of the man limping caused him a fresh pang of guilt. He couldn't help wondering what things would have been like had that fateful day never occurred. Jordan would without a doubt have remained in the SBS, as well as staying one of Stratton's firm friends.

Stratton turned and made his way back to Ted. The two of them went out to the car park.

'How is he?' Ted asked.

'Seems fine.'

The driver nodded. 'Real shame about his leg.'

Stratton glanced at the driver, who gave nothing away. Jordan's injury had been officially judged as an operational acceptability but a lot of people believed it had been Stratton's fault.

It was still dark outside when the operative got out of bed the following morning, feeling the aches and pains from the underwater battle. Stratton's shoulder throbbed a little and he removed the bandage to reveal a clean, stitched wound. He picked a heavy sweatshirt up off the floor, pulled it on against the cold and walked into the kitchen to make a brew. He opened the fridge, took out the crockpot, inspected the contents with approval and plugged it into a socket.

A flapping sound. He looked through the window in time to see the pheasant bowl in over the snow-coated hedge. Stratton quietly opened the back door and threw out some bread. The bird see-sawed over to the crust and took a peck at it just as Stratton's phone rang. The pheasant took flight.

Stratton sighed as he looked at the phone. 'Some things are just not meant to be,' he muttered and put it to his ear. 'This is Stratton on his day off. How can I help?'

'It's Mike.'

'Morning, Mike,' the operative said. The kettle boiled and clicked off.

'I need you to come in.'

Stratton sensed the urgency in his voice. 'Is this an unplug-your-crockpot-and-come-in call?'

'No. You can leave it plugged in this time.'

'It's not urgent, then?'

'We need to have a conversation. But not over the phone.'

Stratton poured boiling water into a mug. 'Okay. I'll see you in a bit.'

The phone went dead. Stratton dumped his tea bag in the bin, added some milk to the mug and took a sip, wondering what it could be about.

When Mike saw Stratton in the doorway of his office an hour later his expression matched his earlier tone. 'Come in and close the door.'

The sergeant major took a moment to decide how to introduce the subject. He would have been utterly direct with just about anyone else. But Stratton was not only an old friend, he was a thoroughbred in the business and although not a prima donna he demanded a level of respect. 'The op in Sevastopol . . . when you dumped the recorder, did you see if it self-destructed?'

'Is that a joke?' Stratton asked. He already had an idea where the conversation was going.

'The Russians found it, apparently. The self-destruct device didn't work.'

'I'm sorry to hear that,' Stratton said. 'Anything else?' He went cold. It was obvious the blame-shifting had begun.

'Yes,' Mike answered. This would be even more difficult. 'The memory card was blank.'

Stratton stared at the man. All the effort and his own near-death experience had been for nothing. London must be going mental.

'The boffins at MI16 are saying that the device was in perfect working condition when you received it and that it failed to record or self-destruct because you didn't turn it on properly.'

Stratton's hackles rose and he leaned forward, his dark green eyes narrowing. 'I don't give a monkey's backside what those pricks say. My post-operational report gives specific details of every step I took. I turned it on. I armed it. I used it. I removed the memory card.'

'No one's suggesting that you're lying.'

'No. Just that I'm a wanker.'

'Come on, John.'

'Then why am I here?'

'Your report *does* reveal that you didn't follow every step precisely.'

'How's that?'

'You didn't check to see if the device had remained armed after you removed the card.'

'What?'

'I said—'

'I heard what you said. I want to know where it's coming from.'

'The recorder's instructions clearly state that when the card—'

'Those instructions were written by someone who's never done anything except sit behind a bloody desk. If it needed double-checking in the middle of a scrap it shouldn't have been used in the field.'

'Okay, okay,' Mike said, holding up his hands. 'Don't have a go at me. I just want you to know what's being said, that's all.'

'By those tossers in Sixteen?'

'No. Not just by them . . . Perhaps someone is trying to discredit us.'

Stratton sat back, his mood still simmering.

'Everything's becoming specialised these days. There seems to be a new unit springing up for every type of task. Look how the surveillance roles have changed. Us and the lads in Hereford used to do it all outside London. Now that's been compartmentalised and we hardly get a look-in. SRR does it all. Maybe we're getting squeezed out of other specialised roles.'

'Mike, I don't give a toss. But I do when I'm blamed for screwing up when I didn't . . . What has London said?'

'Nothing yet. Calm before the storm, probably. The Russians probably think we completed the mission since they found the recorder without the memory card. I don't know if that makes it easier to go back in again or not.'

'I'm not doing that.'

'I think that's the point. They won't ask again.'

Stratton felt psychologically wounded. He would have liked them to ask him to go back in again, which would have proved their confidence in him. He would have refused happily.

'There's something else that's going to piss you off, I'm afraid. You're to spend a day at MI16.'

Stratton eyed him, his look asking the obvious question.

'Let's call it a bit of cross-training.'

'They're teaching me or I'm teaching them?'

'They're going to talk to you about the kit.'

'They're training me?'

'It's politics.'

'It's an admission of guilt.'

'It's a compromise.'

'How's that?'

'Perhaps you're going to help start up their operations side.'

'That's another joke, right?'

'It was when I said it. Now I'm not sure if it is.'

Stratton shook his head, displeased with the whole subject.

'We can't halt progress. Spend a day or two up there. Charm them. Don't let them wind you up. And don't fill any of 'em in.'

Stratton had a sudden thought. 'Tell me something. Be honest. Do people think I'm losing my touch?'

Mike averted his eyes, as if Stratton had hit on something.

Stratton read it like a poster on the wall. 'Is that what you think?'

'No. But I do wonder if you might be getting complacent. It's not so much that you've lost your edge as that the edge has lost you.'

Stratton could not deny that Mike might have a point. It would explain his feelings of late. It wasn't boredom, as he sometimes thought. But whatever it was, complacency could well be a symptom.

Mike leaned forward and softened his voice to hammer the point home. 'You've done more of these kinds of ops than anyone. You've flown too close to the sun too many times, my friend. Maybe it's time to be honest with yourself. I'll believe you if you tell me you're fine. But just take a while to think about it. You know better than anyone. Compare yourself, your enthusiasm now, with your glory days. And don't let laid-back and blasé become confused with experienced. We both know the difference.'

Stratton considered this. He didn't believe he was so far gone as to risk screwing up an operation. But his cynicism had increased over the years. And this wasn't the first time accusations like these had been levelled at him. Either way he couldn't bully his way out of it. If people thought he was losing it they had to change their own minds. He would not be able to do it for them. Even Mike obviously had his doubts, and he knew Stratton better than most. Stratton reckoned he had two choices. He could throw his teddies out of his pram and get all upset about it or he could toe the line. Perhaps he needed a new perspective on things. He didn't think that visiting those twats in Sixteen would help any. Yet something positive could come out of it. He might even be able to prove the recorder was faulty and not him. And London might look favourably on him for going up there. Better than moping around in Poole.

'When do you want me to go?' Stratton asked.

Mike wondered if it was an admission of some kind or if Stratton was just playing the game. 'You plugged in that crockpot of yours?'

'Yes.'

Mike smiled. 'Take a few days off, then. How's the shoulder?'

'Fine.'

'Go for a long run . . . a couple of long runs. I'll tell 'em you'll be up there first thing Monday morning.'

Stratton got to his feet and went to the door.

'Everyone has dips and bumps, Stratton. Don't take it so hard.'

'This isn't a rugby club, Mike.' He opened the door and walked out.

Mike had to ask himself whether he would give Stratton a call if a special landed on his desk tomorrow morning. For the first time he wondered if he would.

4

A white and red Super Puma Eurocopter thundered across the blue-grey waters of the North Sea into the Beryl Oil Field, midway between the Shetlands and the Norwegian coastline. Without a cloud in the sky the sunlight reflected off the sea like the glittering of a million crystals.

Eight people wearing dark green overalls occupied the two dozen cabin seats, spread about the craft as if they did not want to know each other. Of different races and complexions they all had one thing in common – they looked like thugs. At first glance they appeared to be typical roughnecks but a closer inspection revealed more sinister characteristics. Each bore some kind of scar or other mark of past hardship or hostility. An observer could have seen it in their eyes, too.

A robustly built man sitting in the frontmost passenger seat got to his feet, opened the cabin door and looked between the pilots through the windscreen. He had mousy hair cropped short, his European features disfigured by a pudgy, broken-looking nose. He focused his gaze below the horizon on the only solid object in view. From a couple of miles away it looked box-like, as though dozens of giant containers had been piled randomly on top of each other and balanced on four gigantic cylindrical legs that rose from the ocean. A bright orange flame burned on the end of a derrick high up and out to one side of the main structure.

The pilot glanced over his shoulder. 'We'll touch down in less than six minutes,' he said.

41

'Any problems?' the man asked, his accent from somewhere close to London.

'None,' the pilot assured him. 'We're looking good, Deacon – don't worry.'

Deacon ignored the man, stepped back into the main cabin and regarded his motley crew. They had been together as a team for almost two weeks and he was still not used to the sight of the strange collection of individuals. When Deacon had mentioned it to the bosses the first time he'd seen the assembled team they'd told him that it was intentional. Deacon never really understood why, beyond the obvious theatrical value, and he didn't enquire further. If they were as able as they were odd-looking he did not care. He was used to working with different nationalities, just not so many in the same team. 'We're approaching the target,' he called out above the sound of the engines.

Most of the others looked up at him, though not all appeared to understand fully.

'Five minutes,' he shouted, holding up five fingers. 'Comms check,' he mimed, reminding them that the five-minute warning indicated a prearranged order.

Each had a large bag. Those that had not understood Deacon saw the others opening them to retrieve a radio and earpiece and caught on, doing likewise.

Deacon produced a radio from his pocket, turned it on and placed an earphone with a microphone attached into his ear. 'One-two, one-two. If you can hear me loud and clear raise your hand,' he said slowly.

All of them put up a hand.

'Good. Final weapons check,' he said, holding up an old Armalite M-15 carbine and extending the short plastic butt that locked into place.

The others removed the weapons from their bags and did the same.

'Put one up the spout,' he shouted, making sure the gun's magazine was firmly in place before snapping back the cocking mechanism and releasing it to allow the heavy internal spring to slam a round back home.

The sound of several weapons being cocked.

'Apply the safety catch and put them back into your bag.'

Each man obeyed, except one.

Deacon walked down the aisle to the end row and stopped to look at a familiar enough sight that he could never quite get used to. It appeared to be a woman, or at least that was a possibility. She had the athletic build of a man – angular shoulders, thick neck and muscular arms and hands – yet her complexion and make-up belied this: her unblemished Indonesian skin cared for, her eyebrows plucked to form a thin curving line, a ring of pale blue pencilling around the eyes. She was adjusting her make-up using a small mirror.

'Queen?' he said.

She sighed and ignored him.

'Is that really necessary?'

She finished what she was doing, put the lipstick away and snapped the compact closed. 'I've been asked that all my life, Deacon dear,' she said in a rugged accent. She removed an M-15 from her bag and deftly pulled back the working parts. 'I think you asked me the same question that first job I did with you.' She let the mechanism spring back into place. 'The high-profile convoy from the Kuwaiti border to Mosul – remember?'

'Yeah. You were winding up the Iraqis.'

'They didn't know what the hell I was when we ran into the first ambush. They pretty much loved me by the end of the second one.'

'No one's doubtin' your fightin' skills. I just don't want you weirdin' out this lot. Some are a bit confused about you already.'

'They're only confused about themselves,' Queen said, applying the safety catch with her thumb and placing the weapon back in the bag.

Deacon shook his head and turned away, heading back to the front of the helicopter. The large red-headed Viking-like man he passed twisted in his seat to take a look at Queen. She pushed her breasts together and gave him a wink. He looked to the front again, his brow furrowed.

Deacon stopped beside a man with short spiky ink-black hair, his nose to the window. 'Banzi?'

The man looked at Deacon. He was Japanese, his serious expression distorted by a false porcelain eyeball bearing the Japanese flag instead of a pupil, the red stripes of the rising sun disappearing into the surrounding edges of the socket.

Yet another weird characteristic that Deacon could not quite get used to. 'You happy with the route to the power room?' he asked.

'Of course,' Banzi said in an abrupt manner. 'Make sure the Pirate does,' he added, jutting his chin with obvious contempt towards the man in the seat in front.

Banzi went back to looking out of the window and Deacon moved forward to the tall slim Somali seated in front, his expression blank as if in a trance. A deep scar ran from his chin, across an eye and into his scalp where it continued to the back of his head through short wiry hair. 'You happy with the route to the power room?' Deacon asked. The jet-black man did not respond. 'Pirate?'

He half looked towards Deacon and gave a solemn nod.

The man's lack of communication skills had begun to frustrate Deacon but he put it to one side. It was too late to do anything about it, anyway. He'd wanted to leave the Somali behind but the boss had insisted that he should remain with the team, assuring Deacon that he had extraordinary killing abilities. The Pirate's partner, the Jap, seemed reliable enough.

Deacon went back into the cockpit.

The pilot was on the radio to the oil platform. 'Roger that, Morpheus. Understood.' He gave Deacon a thumbs-up.

The Morpheus, one of the North Sea's biggest oil platforms, filled the windshield as the helicopter drew closer, its series of exposed decks like a massive denuded steel tower block. The main platform, at least half the size of a football field, lay covered by building blocks with workspaces in between and a huge crane on one side. The flame derrick stuck out a long way on the far side. The deck below, like a layer of a thick sandwich, was crammed tight with more box shapes, all the same height but with different widths and lengths. Below that was a collection of large pieces of machinery amid more storage structures. A large heli-deck, with its red circular target, came into view on its own level to one side and on top of the platform. They saw the brightly dressed standby fire crew on the side of the deck. As the helicopter came in they could see workers on the various levels. Deacon had never been that close to an oil rig before but he had studied the Morpheus's blueprints and knew pretty much all of its facilities and features.

He felt his anxiety levels rise. The days of waiting had suddenly become minutes. Deacon certainly hadn't done anything like this before. His career had begun with the 2nd Parachute Regiment and had been followed by three years in B Squadron, 22 Special Air Service. He'd missed the Falklands conflict by a couple of years because of his age but had seen some action in the first Gulf War – which was where he'd begun to head down the slippery slope. A combination of boredom with the military life and the discovery of how simple it was to make money illegally had altered his perspective. He had never owned anything of value because he had never been particularly attracted by modern comforts such as fancy cars or wristwatches. That changed a month before the end of the conflict.

Special forces customarily received solid gold coins to take on operations in the desert. They were part of their emergency survival equipment. They could buy assistance if an action resulted in a team member failing to make the pick-up or emergency rendezvous. Nomadic tribesmen, for instance, roamed much of the desert entirely ignorant or uncaring of the battles going on around them.

During Deacon's last operation, an observation post along with three other SAS troopers, he had decided to keep the gold. He made a joke of it to the others, just serious enough for them to go for it if they agreed in any way – they all had to be a part of the plan for it to work. He mused how it would be such an easy way to make some money, that they deserved to come out of the war with something – the gold Krugerrands were worth around five thousand pounds for each man. The others bit. They agreed to see it through to just before the point of no return. If it looked like they could get away with it they would do it.

They would claim that a threatening enemy presence had caused them to bug out of the position, and that the only escape route headed away from the rendezvous point. Despite them hiding out during the subsequent daylight hours, a group of nomadic Arabs had discovered them and had threatened to turn the patrol over to the Iraqis. They'd had a choice: they could either fight their way out, which might have been costly, or hand over the Krugerrands in exchange for freedom.

It felt sound enough to go ahead with. Deacon warned them that suspicions would be raised but if they all stuck to their guns they would get away with it. No one would be able to prove otherwise.

The point of no return would be when the time came to hide the gold and present the operational report. They would secrete the gold among equipment already packed for the return to Hereford.

And that was precisely what they did. The interrogators questioned the soldiers as a group and individually. They even tried to convince each of the men that another had cracked and revealed the truth. But the technique did not succeed. And despite practically everyone 'knowing' that the patrol had stolen the gold, no one could prove it, as Deacon had said, and so they were never charged.

Deacon quit the SAS and the military a few months before the invasion of Afghanistan. Had he known that the regiment was going to war again he would have changed his mind – he liked a good battle. He turned his sights on becoming a mercenary, advertising himself as a former SAS soldier now turned freelance 'military specialist'. He soon got all the battling he could handle: many of his subsequent experiences were more dangerous than any he might have had with the SAS. The oil platform task, as it was planned, would be nowhere near as perilous as some he had carried out during those years. By the end of the second Gulf War, big money, along with big risks, had become the norm for him. Running convoys from one side of Iraq to the other, and more recently along the Khyber Pass into Afghanistan, was the most dangerous mercenary work there was. In the half-dozen years Deacon had been doing it he'd lost seventy-eight men serving directly under him, most of them killed alongside him. Many others had been captured after failing to escape an ambush but they'd faced the same fate.

When the British military pulled out of Iraq and the Americans were preparing to do the same, Deacon wanted to try something else – along similar lines, of course, because he couldn't do anything different. He had no real idea what that was until the mysterious caller a few months back offered him the task of capturing an oil platform for more money than he had made during his entire time in Iraq and Afghanistan. He hesitated when he learned of its North Sea location: anything in the UK, Europe or the States would have given him pause. It meant taking on sophisticated surveillance and investigative technology and lethal-quality security forces. The money and an assuredly watertight plan brought him on board. Half a million US dollars had been deposited into a Cayman Island bank account in his name. Another half-million would follow on completion of his part in the operation. These people had serious money. The rest of the team were making less than Deacon — half his salary, reputedly — but still a fortune compared with what they were normally paid for far greater risks. The audacity of the escape plan sealed it. Deacon was going to enjoy this.

One thing alone bugged him. He couldn't figure out the true motive of those who'd given him the job. Many things about it didn't add up and he didn't know who the ultimate client was, which was not altogether a surprise. They were obviously expecting a serious return on their investment. Deacon didn't care enough to stress about it. He was going to make a cool million, tax free, doing something he really enjoyed.

The helicopter flared as the craft slowed and aimed its underbelly at the centre of the helipad. Deacon went to the main cabin door and, steadying himself against it, eyed his crew. All still in their seats, most looking out of a porthole. When the wheels bumped down all eyes turned to him. Like Deacon, none of them had done anything quite like this before. The Pirate came the closest. Apparently he had hijacked half a dozen ships in his time, including a supertanker. Deacon had to wonder what he had done with the money, if it was true. He thought piracy paid even more than gigs like this.

The shifty-looking Lebanese guy seated in front of the Viking had played a key role in the hijacking of an airliner, or so he claimed. Once again Deacon wondered if there had been any logic to the selection of this crew, or was being a hardened mercenary the only qualification required? Scary appeared to be

another criterion. They all looked pretty fearsome. That made
sense. North Sea oil platforms were generally populated by tough
guys and ex-servicemen, types more likely than most to have a
go at a terrorist. With fewer players in his team, Deacon needed
fearsome as well as armed.

The helicopter's engines changed pitch as the torque went out
of the rotors. Deacon turned the handle and pulled open the door.
The wind rushed inside along with the sunlight. Beyond the steps
leading up to the helipad, half a dozen platform workers waited
with packs and suitcases, part of the rig's hot-bunk routine, which
meant that with every new arrival there were departures. This
batch was going to be disappointed, as were the eleven original
members of the shift currently locked inside the bowels of a boat
somewhere off the coast of Scotland. They'd been surprised when
the helicopter had made an unscheduled stop alongside the boat
and even more so when Deacon had stepped into the cabin with
his assault rifle levelled to order them off.

Deacon stepped down onto the pad and walked towards the
exit stairway. One by one his crew followed.

As the line passed them the two standby fire-crew guys both
had the same thought: in their day they had seen enough brutes
climb in and out of the rig helicopter but never such a collection in one batch.

Deacon headed along the main deck followed by the Lebanese
thug and a large dark-skinned Bulgarian with a massive head
draped in a mop of brown hair. The Pirate and Banzi went
calmly to the edge of the platform and down a stairway. The
red-headed Viking, the tallest of the team at almost seven feet,
crossed to the opposite side of the deck and went down another
staircase, followed by the shortest team member, a growling
Scotsman with half an ear missing. It looked as if it had been
bitten off.

Queen alighted last and stood at the chopper's door, signalling to the waiting passengers to remain where they were. The firemen stared at the transsexual. Now they had seen everything.

The oil platform's control room was divided into two, the larger area tightly packed from floor to ceiling with electronic devices and machinery, the room hum constant. Some of the several technicians present were wearing ear protectors. Gauges just about everywhere measured every essential pressure, temperature, fluid level, voltage and flow rate involved with the running of the platform's production, life-support and safety systems. The smaller adjoining administrative room contained the platform's security and radio and satellite communications systems. A couple of flatscreen monitors displayed split CCTV images of various parts of the rig including the Eurocopter on the heli-deck, its rotors turning. A tall long-haired individual in green overalls stood at the cabin door with his back to the camera.

The Morpheus's security officer, sipping a cup of hot chocolate from a Union Jack china mug, sat at a small paperwork-covered desk jammed into a corner. He looked at the screens and saw two of the newcomers in green overalls and carrying bags come into view, walking purposefully along a deck corridor. Another screen showed two more of the men heading towards the main power room. An exterior camera showed the backs of three more approaching the entrance to the control room. One of them pushed a button by the door. A buzzer sounded in the room.

The supervisor put down his drink. Something about the images niggled him.

The handful of technicians in the main control room remained busy with various systems while the platform's general manager stayed seated in a corner. 'Is someone gonna get that?' he called out.

'Just a second,' an engineer yelled as he entered some data onto a console.

The security supervisor leaned closer to the monitors, looking from one to the other. The new arrivals hadn't booked in with the shift operations manager or checked into the accommodation complex, which was the normal routine. It looked most unusual.

The control-room door buzzer sounded again. 'Okay, okay,' shouted the engineer. He put down the recording device and reached for the access-control button on the wall.

The security supervisor watched the two men outside the power-generating room open their bags and take out weapons. At the same time the long-haired individual at the helicopter pointed a rifle at the firemen, who put up their hands.

'Don't open the DOOR!' the security officer cried.

Everyone in the control room stopped what they were doing to look at him jump out of his chair and into the room. The engineer's finger was already pressing down on the button. The door opened with a clunk. The security supervisor stared in horror at it.

Deacon walked in, brandishing his short automatic rifle, followed by the Bulgarian, who stood by the door. The Lebanese remained outside.

'Gentlemen,' Deacon announced, with a broad smile. 'I hope you appreciate from the outset that this is a no-win situation for you and that you won't do anything stupid. And don't feel bad about opening the door for us,' he said, looking at the security supervisor. 'This entire operation was not dependent on you letting us in.' He held up an explosive charge the size of a cigarette packet. 'I brought my own key, just in case.'

The rig's general manager pulled himself together and stepped out from behind his desk. 'What is the meaning of this?' he demanded. 'What are you doing here and what do you want?' The weapons in their hands gave him a pretty good idea.

'It's really quite simple, Mr Andrews. General manager, yes? We're taking over the platform.'

'What on earth for?' the GM asked, dumbfounded. 'You can't seriously hope to gain anything from this. It's ridiculous.'

'No need to go off on one now, Mr Andrews. My boys and I didn't just all meet up in a pub, 'ave a few beers and decide to knock off an oil platform for a giggle. I might sound a bit thick but I'm not. So respect that. Respect us. Respect the threat. Be good. And no harm'll come to you. But if you come the 'ero, you'll only piss me off. You've all been around this crazy world long enough to know that things like this can end in tears if it all gets bollocksed up.'

The GM remained stoic, along with the security supervisor. Several of the technicians looked about ready to piss their pants.

'Your emergency distress button is over there,' Deacon said, pointing to the wall-mounted red box with a small hinged panel on its front. 'I suspect you're itching to press it.'

'And I suppose you'll kill me if I try,' the platform boss said, jutting out his chin defiantly. 'I was in the Royal Air Force and my father fought in the Battle of Britain.'

Deacon raised his eyebrows. 'I love the RAF. The only military unit that sends its officers to war first. I won't kill you if you try. In fact, I *want* you to go ahead and press it.'

The GM glanced at his security supervisor, suspecting a catch of some kind. The security man had nothing to offer apart from a fearful stare.

'Go ahead,' Deacon said, encouraging the man. 'It's all part of the plan. *You* wanna do it. *I* want you to do it. So let's just do it.'

The manager remained anxiously hesitant, suspecting a trap.

'Go on,' Deacon urged.

The GM took a step towards the button, scrutinising the hijackers for any sign of a reaction. There was none. He took another step.

Deacon gestured for him to get on with it, looking at his watch as if he needed to be somewhere else. 'I don't 'ave all day.'

The GM clenched his jaw and decided to go for it, whatever

the outcome. He felt close enough to activate the alarm even if they did shoot him. He faltered just before pressing it in order to take a look and see if the large thug with the machine gun had it aimed at him. He did not. The GM gritted his teeth and depressed the button all the way. Seconds later a red LED light above the box began to flash, accompanied by a soft beeping sound.

Everyone remained still, waiting for the terrorist's next move. But the man simply checked his watch, looking as if he was impatient for something else to happen.

The phone on the general manager's desk rang.

'I expect that will be a response to your general-emergency activation,' Deacon said. 'You can go ahead and answer it.'

The manager remained uneasy. 'What do you want me to tell them?'

Deacon shrugged. 'Whatever you like. Start with what's 'appenin'. The truth . . . Go on, then.'

The GM brought the phone to his ear. 'This is Andrews . . . Yes. We . . . we have a situation. The Morpheus has been hijacked . . . Yes, that's what I said. Hijacked. Armed men arrived by helicopter and . . . well, it would seem they have control of the platform . . . No. No violence yet. No damage as far as I'm aware,' he said, glancing at Deacon. 'I don't know what's happening outside the control room but they appear to be quite serious . . . They're in the room, with me, here, right now. Their leader. They're armed.' He listened to a further question and looked at Deacon. 'What exactly is it you want?'

'The usual. A shitload of money or we destroy the platform. And if anyone tries to attack us we'll kill everyone on board.'

The manager was unbalanced by Deacon's casual manner. 'How much money?'

'A small percentage of the platform's value plus loss of productivity if it met with a disaster. Two billion dollars, US. Pretty cheap, really.'

The GM cleared his throat. 'They want two billion dollars,' he said into the phone.

'That's enough,' Deacon said. 'You can put the phone down now. We can get into the details with them later. They've got enough to be getting on with for the time being.'

The manager hesitated, wanting to say something that might be of use to the crisis-management team. But he could not, partly because of the possible repercussions and also because he could not think of anything to say anyway. It was all so surreal, all so quick. He placed the phone's headset back into its cradle.

'Good. That's that part over. Now for the next step. All outside communications sources will come under my control. I'll allow one engineer at a time in here to keep the place running. Same goes for engineering. What are you pumping right now?'

'We're at around sixty-three per cent of capacity,' the GM replied.

'You'll maintain everything as normal. You,' he said to the security supervisor. 'Turn off all your CCTV now. Go.'

The security supervisor walked quickly through the cluttered room to his office and turned off the cameras.

'Unplug the hard drive and bring it here,' Deacon ordered.

The officer carried the small heavy box through the room and held it out to Deacon, who took it.

'You try to turn on any of the cameras, I'll find out about it and you'll end up going for a swim without a life jacket. Understood?'

The security officer nodded.

'I like to run a pretty loose ship,' Deacon said, facing the GM. 'But don't get carried away with it. This is how it will play. As we speak, radio-controlled explosive devices are being placed at key points around the platform. If anyone makes any attempt to interfere with my operation, the charges will be detonated. If any of my men are attacked, the charges will be detonated. In a little while, when I tell you, you'll address your personnel over the platform intercom. You'll tell them exactly what's going on. You'll also make it absolutely clear that there are to be no heroics. Tell them the consequences as I've laid them out to you.' Deacon headed back to the entrance, pausing to look at the manager. 'Don't be fooled by my easygoing manner, Mr Andrews. I'm not the master-mind of this operation. But the people who hired me knew what they were doing. How many men do you currently have on this platform?'

The GM took a moment to think about it. 'A hundred and sixty-five,' he replied looking at the security officer for confirmation.

'That's less than the number of men I've personally killed in the last six years . . . Now. Everyone sit down and don't do anything silly or he'll shoot you,' Deacon said, indicating the large Bulgarian. The man looked up to the task.

A clatter of gunfire came from outside. A ripple of panic shot through the platform workers in the room. The Bulgarian, himself unsure for a second, levelled his weapon towards them.

Deacon stepped outside and onto the deck to see a man lying face down near the railings. He looked over at the Lebanese thug and his smoking weapon. 'What did you do that for?' Deacon asked calmly.

'He surprised me.'

Deacon crouched by the casualty to feel for a pulse at the man's neck. There was none. Blood dripped from the torso through the deck grilles onto the level below.

'You're paid to 'andle surprises,' Deacon said. 'I'm gonna deduct a hundred grand from your money. You step out of line again and all you'll end up with is your deposit. You got that?'

The Lebanese gritted his teeth but knew better than to argue. He had never met Deacon before the team had gathered at the safe house in the Shetlands fourteen days previously. Initially twelve team members had spent the days going over plans and each indi-vidual's role. But four of them had disappeared one night – they simply were not in the house the following morning. Deacon said they had been removed to a secure location until the operation was complete, but the Lebanese believed that Deacon had killed them. He knew enough not to cross the Englishman, not during the operation at least. Threatening to cut his wages had been a stupid error, though, and he could already see himself killing the man. 'It won't happen again,' he said.

Deacon had in fact wanted to dump him but the four that he had already cut were worse and he needed a minimum of eight to carry out the operation. That was the first thing he had complained about. But when the escape plan was revealed he understood. It was tight but he would have to make it work. 'You see that crane over there?' he said, pointing across the platform. 'Take this geezer and 'ang him on the end of the 'ook. We might as well get some use out of 'im.'

The Lebanese wanted to ask why but that was another thing he had learned about Deacon back in the Shetlands. He didn't like to be questioned.

'Get on with it, then.'

The Arab shouldered his weapon and dragged the dead man across the deck towards the crane.

The radio crackled in Deacon's ear. It was Queen. 'Hey, sweetie. The pilot wants to get going but he's nervous about the ditching procedure. He says there's a storm front heading this way.'

'There's always a storm front heading somewhere in the North Sea.'

'His orders are to ditch the chopper in the middle of the ocean a hundred miles from nowhere.'

'So?'

'He's worried about not being picked up.'

'You tell 'im this. If he fails to ditch where he's been told to, 'is biggest worry will come when – not if – I find 'im. If he doesn't ditch at the precise GPS coordinates he will not be picked up.

And even if he survives that, I will find 'im and kill 'im. Also, remind 'im that if he does not ditch at the precise location he won't get the rest of his considerable pay cheque. And I'll still find 'im and kill 'im.'

'Sounds clear enough to me.'

'And one other thing.'

'Yes?'

'Don't call me sweetie.'

A chirp sounding very much like a kiss came from the radio as Queen disconnected. Deacon frowned as he dug a satellite phone from a pocket, retrieved a number from the address book and hit the call button. It rang a couple of times before it was answered. 'Yes,' said a man's voice.

'This is Thanatos. Phase one is complete.'

The phone beeped as if it had completed some kind of electronic eavesdropping scan and a monotone voice answered. 'Understood. You can make the call to the British Ministry of Defence.'

Another beep indicated that the signal had been disconnected and Deacon turned it off and put it back in his pocket. The first phase had gone according to plan, apart from that Lebanese twat killing the worker. Then again, it added some gravitas to the operation. It had all been so polite and amicable otherwise.

The sound of the Eurocopter as it powered up its engines grew from the direction of the heli-deck and Deacon looked beyond the control centre to see the chopper rise into the air and turn away from the platform.

He looked to the control room to see the GM looking at him through the open door. 'One hundred and sixty-four,' Deacon called out, shrugging.

The Bulgarian closed the door.

Deacon looked down at the hard drive in his hand, walked over to the rail and tossed it over the side, watching as it flipped and caught in the wind on the long way down to the water. On the far horizon, beyond the crisp blue sea, slate-grey clouds were forming. The plan took into consideration the North Sea's reputation for harsh weather, but it could still prove detrimental to the operation's overall success.

He retrieved another stored number from the satellite phone and pressed the call button. 'Is this the Ministry of Defence? . . . Good. Me and some friends have just hijacked an oil platform in the North Sea. Who should I speak to?'

5

Gerald Nevins walked briskly down a broad staircase into an Elizabethan hallway. Its ornate wooden carvings stretched from the ground- to the second-floor ceiling. He touched the perfectly tied knot of his silk tie as if to adjust it but without doing anything of the kind. It was a characteristic reflex when he was deep in thought. Two suited aides came down the steps behind him, one tapping the keys of a BlackBerry while the other talked into a phone.

'All shipping within a radius of fifty nautical miles is being diverted away from the area,' one of the aides announced. 'Airspace is being cleared out to a radius of one hundred.'

'The submarine HMS *Torbay* will be inside the operational boundaries by this evening,' said the second. 'Admiral Bellington will command all forces. He'll be on board HMS *Daring* within the hour and then inside the ops area by early morning.'

'It's confirmed that the satellite-phone transmission originated on the Morpheus, sir,' the second added.

'Thanatos is Greek mythology,' the BlackBerry scrutiniser offered. 'The god of death.'

'What did you think he'd call himself? Kermit the bloody frog?' Nevins muttered.

'Voice is definitely English,' the aide continued, used to the sarcasm. 'London or close to. Ninety per cent certainty he's Caucasian.'

The three men headed across the marble-floored lobby towards a pair of solid-looking carved doors. The aide with the phone hurried ahead and placed his hand on a fingerprint scanner that unlocked the door. He opened it in time for Nevins to breeze through without breaking stride.

They entered a large operations room dominated by a huge screen that practically covered an entire wall from the floor to the high ceiling, the majority of its surface taken up by a live map of the North Sea – a hybrid of satellite imagery and colourfully illustrated enhanced topography. The Morpheus was indicated at the centre. Colour-coded reference numbers shadowed hundreds of other platforms and vessels, including the smallest fishing boats. Lines emanating from naval vessels extended across the map, indicating their tracks. Details of aircraft included their number, altitude and speed: most of them looked as if they were moving or turning away from the centre of the map. The screen's deep margins contained data on various meteorological and current events. The air was filled with suppressed radio conversations from countless sources.

A dozen men and women occupied the room, a few in civilian clothes but most of them in casual military uniform from all three forces. They sat in front of computer consoles, facing the large screen and typing or talking into wire headsets.

The command centre's operations officer, wearing a Royal Navy uniform and standing in the centre of the room looking at the screen, turned grim-faced towards Nevins as he approached, acknowledging his superior with a slight stiffening of the back and a nod. 'We'll have a satellite view of the platform in fifteen minutes,' he said while Nevins scanned the display. 'A Nimrod will provide a view in less than five.'

'Do we know who these damned people are yet?' Nevins asked as though it were all a great personal inconvenience.

'No. It still appears to be a purely economic event. The ransom demands remain focused on the oil company.'

'Arcom,' one of Nevins's aides interjected. 'They're at the top of the ownership tree, sir. Head office in Abu Dhabi.'

'Any previous?' Nevins asked.

'Nothing relative to this,' the aide replied.

'Shareholders?'

'Still compiling that one, sir,' the other aide said. He went to one of the consoles and with the briefest apology to the operator typed in some commands. 'A couple of red flags have already come up, though. Al Qatare Jalab Natar. Sim Basar Negal.' Faces matching the names appeared in the margins of the large screen. 'Both notorious money launderers for heavy Russian Mafia players like Valery Moscov and Boris Kilszin. Moscov's a political player but so far there's no plausible tie-in to this type of crime.'

'Winners and losers?'

'Still hard to say right now. We're waiting for the underwriters to get back to us with the details of the coverage. One of them did say, with unmasked pleasure, that the ransom was marginally within the first-level deductions, suggesting that the oil company will take the brunt of the hit.'

'Sir, I have a call for you,' the other aide interrupted. A Mr Kaan in Abu Dhabi. Says he's Arcom's crisis-team manager.'

Nevins frowned as he looked at his aide clutching the phone as if he was protecting his boss from it. 'He specifically asked for me?'

'Yes, sir.'

The operations officer looked at Nevins and raised an eyebrow. 'He's well informed.'

'Clearly,' Nevins muttered. 'I only moved from South-East European operations last month.'

'I can confirm that the call is from Arcom's executive offices,' said a young female technician operating one of the computer consoles.

'Shall I tell him you'll call back?' the aide asked, putting the phone to his ear.

Nevins took a few seconds to decide before holding out his hand. The aide passed him the phone.

'This is Nevins.'

'Good day to you, sir.' The accent was foreign but the words came across as well defined as any upper-class English that Nevins had heard spoken.

'What can I do for you, Mr Kaan?' Nevins asked.

A technician brought up something on her monitor and transferred it to the margin of the big screen: a photograph of a well-attired dark-skinned gentleman in his forties, with a finely groomed goatee. A biographical summary accompanied it.

'I suppose the question to begin with has to be: what are you going to do about our oil platform?'

Nevins scrutinised the information on the man with disdain. Kaan had spent two years at Eton before moving to Harvard to complete a law degree. 'Why, everything we possibly can, Mr Kaan.'

'I don't need to tell you that we have over a hundred and sixty people on board the Morpheus whose lives we are responsible for.'

'Many of them British citizens who I am responsible for . . . not to mention that the hijacking has taken place in our sovereign waters.'

'I fully appreciate that, Mr Nevins. Nevertheless, we will be the ones liable if harm comes to any of them. Can you give me an indication of your intentions?'

'Have the hijackers made contact with you?' Nevins asked, still reading the man's bio.

'Not yet. At the moment their dialogue appears to be directed towards your government.'

'What's your company policy with regard to the payment of ransoms?'

'We don't have one. We don't enjoy the luxury that governments have when it comes to sacrificing our personnel for political purposes.

62

We run a business. We will take the least expensive option. If that means paying a ransom it will be a strong consideration. We would appreciate you keeping us informed of your intentions since they will have an impact on that.'

Nevins finished reading the last paragraph of the bio. Kaan had been born in Dubai and was part of a wealthy family with connections to the ruling family. 'Who is your decision-making authority?'

Kaan did not respond.

'Who do you answer to?' Nevins asked.

'I'm afraid that has to be confidential, for the time being at least.'

'I see. Well, it's been nice talking with you, Mr Kaan,' Nevins said. 'Good day.' He handed the phone back to the aide and looked up at the screen. 'What are our options for taking it back?'

'Remove the battery from your cellular phone, please,' the operations officer said to the aide.

The aide almost dropped the phone in his speed to obey. The ops officer looked at the other aide who held up his cellphone with the battery already removed.

The operations officer redirected his attention to Nevins. 'Technically this comes under the Grampian Police.'

Nevins glanced at him, a confused frown on his face. 'Since when did the police have the capability to recapture an oil platform?'

'They don't. But every UK offshore structure now falls under the responsibility of its coastal police force. Our special forces are too thin on the ground and too overworked to maintain that role. It's all part of a programme to have Home Security eventually deal with all domestic issues, terrorist or otherwise.'

'Are you telling me that if I want to take the platform back by force I'm going to have to rely on a troop of constables?'

'Of course not. None of the forces are even remotely trained and equipped to carry out such a task.'

'This is clearly an SBS option.'

'The duty squadron in Poole has already been placed on standby. But they're severely undermanned. The majority of the service is currently in Afghanistan.'

'Isn't a squadron big enough to do the job?' Nevins asked.

'If it was up to strength. The current duty squadron has just six operatives.'

Nevins looked at him questioningly. 'The SAS?'

'They can only offer limited support to the SBS on a rig as complex as the Morpheus. I've requested that two SAS packets move to Afghanistan to relieve two SBS packets.'

'How long will that take?'

'Realistically, four days minimum but probably more. The SBS standby team could carry out the preliminaries – a technical attack, for instance – and put in surveillance while we're waiting for the assault teams to get into position.'

The ops officer was suddenly distracted by information coming in over his wire headphones. He looked up at the big screen where a red marker began to flash.

Nevins noticed it. 'What's that?' he asked.

'The Eurocopter that delivered the hijack team to the Morpheus. They've ditched.'

Nevins scrutinised the screen. 'I don't see any vessels in the immediate area.'

'There isn't another vessel for twenty miles.'

'Did they crash?'

'One can only assume so. Or sabotage. The storm front is still miles to the north.'

'Sir, the Nimrod has the Morpheus visual,' an operator called out.

They all looked at the big screen where a section displayed a long-range bird's-eye-view image of the platform.

'Thermals have picked up people on the main deck,' the operator continued. 'Close to a dozen by the helipad. Two people outside the control room.'

The image became grainy as it gradually zoomed in on the top section of the platform. It was clear enough to make out a figure moving in the open.

'They've identified something on the end of a cable. It's dangling from a crane. Looks like a body.'

On the screen the thermal qualities became more visible.

'It's cooler than the others,' the ops officer pointed out. 'I would have to say the person died not that long ago.'

Nevins's thoughtful frown returned. 'Is that storm front going to hit the Morpheus?'

'Without a doubt. It'll be in for a couple of days, too.'

'Something working in our favour, then. Let's get that SBS section into the arena. Have them ready to put in surveillance.'

The operations officer acknowledged and nodded to one of the operators.

'I'd better have a chat with the PM,' Nevins said, heading across the room to the heavy black curtains.

His aides followed him.

6

Stratton stopped the Jeep in a narrow lane lined by black leafless hedges. An icy breeze gusted as he studied the empty crossroads in front. He pulled the thick Afghan scarf down from over his mouth, removed one of his sheepskin gloves and pulled a map from between the seats.

The map showed a T-junction at the point where he thought he was, not a crossroads. On the far side of the junction a bereft-looking wooden signpost leaned at an angle. It was all very peculiar.

He considered backtracking but decided against it, confident that he was in the right place. The GPS would have confirmed it but this had become a challenge, if a minor one, and he was determined to solve it using map-reading and his instincts rather than electronics. It was Stratton's belief that people had become too dependent on modern technology and that it would eventually lead to the erosion of basic skills.

He put the engine into gear and drove into the junction to get a better look in all directions. The grid reference he had for the MI16 compound was less than a mile away in an unmarked piece of MoD land. No one at the SBS HQ had been to the place before and so there were no clear directions.

Stratton began to turn the wheel to go left but changed his mind, focusing instead on the unmarked lane that carried on straight ahead. He usually leaned more towards taking the route to discovery if he got the chance. On the other hand, now he had a convenient reason to turn around and go home. Not that anyone would have bought the excuse. A strong residue of doubt about the visit prompted his hesitation. Mike had tried to gloss over it as some kind of meeting of minds but Stratton had not entirely bought into that. Ultimately he didn't like people questioning his abilities and he would always challenge them. But after a couple of days to reflect on the subject, its importance had started to wane in his mind. It was all down to his level of self-confidence. Stratton rarely doubted his own operational abilities. He felt as if he was still in his prime. When he started to have genuine doubts he would know he was over the hill. By then he would be out of the business anyway. It didn't mean, though, that direct accusations, especially from those he did not respect, could be levelled at him without provoking a response.

He felt reasonably relaxed about it at that moment but he knew that could change if anyone at MI16 rubbed him up the wrong way.

Stratton accelerated the Jeep across the junction and into the unmarked lane. The tarmac quickly turned to mud. Bushes and saplings encroached from either side. The track soon became so narrow that the Jeep could barely squeeze along it. The thick undergrowth on either side was impenetrable.

A sign warned anyone using the lane that government property was up ahead and trespassers would be prosecuted. It was an encouragement to Stratton to keep going at least. At the top of a short rise the ends of a chain fence were visible at either side of the lane. The gate across the road was open. He carried on through and down a steep dip, then to the crest of another rise where the trees thinned out and the dense scrub gave way. A hut came into view on the edge of the track, a robust metal gate – this time closed – just beyond it.

Stratton half expected to find someone in the hut but there

was no sign of life. Just a metal box with a card slot. Stratton dug his military ID card out of a pocket and pushed it into the reader. The card came out seconds later, a green light flashed, accompanied by a gentle beep, and the heavy gate began to open.

He must have found the place. No turning back now. There was an element of adventure to this, at least.

He drove on through and the gate closed behind the Jeep. Up ahead the trees gave way to a wide, unfenced compound. An insignificant-looking place, at least compared with the organisation's daunting reputation and indeed with what he had been expecting. Enough for him to wonder again if it was the right location.

Everything about the compound looked as though it had been constructed during the last world war. An area the size of a football pitch had been cleared of trees, concrete had been poured and levelled, and a collection of long, narrow prefabricated bungalows had been positioned in neat rows. It must have taken all of a week to construct.

Stratton followed a path of faded white lines that turned abruptly through a gap between two buildings into a square. Parked to one side were half a dozen ordinary-looking modern cars, the only indication of human life somewhere nearby. Stratton drove into an empty slot and turned off his motor.

A sudden silence. Stillness. Refreshing until Stratton realised it was too quiet. He couldn't even hear any birds. He climbed out of the Jeep and looked around. All the windows in the identical buildings had been either painted over or boarded up. Despite the run-down look of the place there wasn't a speck of rubbish or debris. Stratton wondered if he had missed a sign that instructed visitors where to go or what to do. Or perhaps the super-duper MI16 organisation was unaware that someone had arrived at their secret facility.

Stratton would have loved to surprise Binning and his pals. That would take the edge off his resentment. Somehow, though, he didn't think he was going to be that lucky.

A small sign above one of the cabin doors announced rather mutedly ENTRANCE and he headed towards it.

As he was about to open the door he glimpsed part of an odd and until now hidden structure – odd insofar as it looked out of place date-wise. A few steps beyond the edge of the cabin a short steel staircase led to a modern helicopter pad. A fire-foam system circled the entire structure, looking as if it was automated. A concrete block on the far side had what appeared to be large metal sheets sunk at a steep angle into its face. They looked like sliding doors although there were no handles.

Stratton returned to the door with the entrance sign. The handle was shiny and well used. He opened the door to reveal a snug, sterile lobby. The rest of the building was partitioned off, the floor covered in fake tiled linoleum and the ceiling stained by leaks.

A gentle humming sound, like that of distant machinery, filtered in from somewhere. Set into a wall was a bland lift door, a single call button on the frame. Stratton pressed it.

The lift opened to reveal a space big enough for half a dozen people. He stepped inside. The door closed but the lift remained still. There were only two buttons and a card slot on the control panel. He pushed the lower button. Another humming sound came from above but he felt no sense of movement. Either it was an incredibly smooth mechanism, or something else was happening.

A series of stark blue LED lights, their bulbs hitherto invisible, rippled from the lift's ceiling to the floor.

'Remove the battery from your communication device, please,' a softly spoken computer-generated voice instructed.

Stratton took his BlackBerry from its hip holster and as soon as he removed the battery the voice thanked him.

'Remove your wristwatch, please.'

Stratton frowned and removed his watch. A metal drawer slid out from the side of the lift.

'Place all items in the drawer, please.'

Stratton obeyed. The drawer closed.

'Thank you.'

The lift began to descend.

When it came to a halt the doors slid open. Binning stood in front of him dressed in a pair of running shorts and a sleeveless sports shirt with a towel around his neck, looking as if he'd just had a rigorous workout. His muscular arms and legs presented quite the picture of athleticism.

'Stratton,' he announced, wearing a broad smile and acting like they were old friends. 'Good to see you again.' He held out a hand.

Stratton stifled his hostility and shook the man's hand. 'Hi,' he said, smiling slightly and wondering if Binning was a two-faced sod, thick-skinned, or had had nothing to do with the criticism that he had faced. He chose to believe the first option just in case.

'Sorry you were left to fend for yourself up there. I was in the middle of a fierce circuit when I heard you'd arrived. Do come in.'

'This box has my phone and watch,' Stratton said.

'Of course.' Binning pulled a card from a pocket. 'It's routine, I'm afraid. It's designed to detect electronic devices, weapons and explosives. We have no physical security in this place, no guards. Nothing's allowed in or out without clearance. I'm qualified at least to get you your phone and watch back.' He slid the card into the slot. A second later the drawer opened and he handed Stratton his items. 'So. I take it you found us without any problems. I would expect so. Man of your calibre. I see you like an open-top Jeep even in the middle of winter. Man after my own heart.'

Binning was certainly in a chipper mood.

'I don't suppose anyone warned you about this place,' the scientist continued as they stepped into a pristine white pentagon-shaped lobby, the ceiling low, a few chairs around the walls. 'I don't know the last time one of your people came up, and I've been here six years. Let's start with the canteen, get a cup of tea, warm you up a bit. Then we'll meet the boss. I think he'd rather show you around himself.'

Binning led the way into a broad curving corridor. It was a complete contrast to the dilapidated cabins above.

'How far down do you think we are?' Binning asked.

'Haven't a clue,' Stratton muttered, uninterested in guessing games.

'The ceiling is a hundred feet from the surface. There's supposed to be over three miles of tunnels down here but unless they've hidden some of them I think that's an exaggeration.'

One of the walls gave way to plate glass from floor to ceiling, an empty conference room beyond. Then a series of offices and data-storage rooms either side of the corridor. It was all very high-tech. The place sounded alive, a mixture of electronic humming and moving air.

'They built these tunnels at the same time as the buildings up top, a couple of years into the Second World War. Then it became some kind of government emergency evacuation centre in the event of a nuclear attack. That was sometime during the late 1940s, early 1950s. MI16 took it over twenty years ago. It has been completely gutted and modernised, of course.'

Binning pushed through a pair of swing doors into a canteen equipped with chairs and tables for a dozen people. The place had a row of food and drink dispensers, a handbasin with a soap dispenser and paper towels, and several hatches labelled for various types of waste that were set into a wall.

'We're very much a help-yourself organisation down here. Everything's self-service. All part of the security. You get used to it,' Binning said as he pushed a button on a machine that responded by dispensing a plastic cup followed by a jet of brown liquid. 'Tea, coffee, or something else perhaps? There are sodas, fruit juices, soup if you prefer.'

'Coffee, thanks. White, no sugar.'

Binning pressed the appropriate button but the machine did not respond. 'Of course, it's a bugger when something breaks down. It's like trying to pass a bill through Parliament to get a mechanic down here.' The machine suddenly responded. 'Do you know much about MI16?' he asked, handing Stratton the drink.

Stratton shrugged. 'Only that you make toys.'

'Yes, I do like that expression. War toys for war boys. We're essentially divided into three parts: research and theory, construction and development, and then testing and field trials. We have around a dozen staff down here, a dozen more low-key techs at another surface location. We work in quite a unique way, a sort of free-form system. Anyone can work on any project at any of the stages – within reason, of course. Can't neglect the boring jobs or crowd the interesting ones. One of my specialities is simplification. Much of the equipment we produce is far too technical to hand over to you chaps.'

'We're a bit thick, I suppose?' Stratton said, sipping his coffee.

'I wouldn't have put it quite that way,' Binning said, with a grin. 'You're soldiers, not scientists. But then again, it's not always easy or possible to make things user-friendly for everyone. Look how long it took to make the computer compatible with everyday users. We don't have the facilities, the manpower nor the time for that kind of compliance. Once we've built it, we need to get it in the field as soon as we can. Most of the things we put together three years ago are already out of date. A lot of them never even reached the field, at your level, because they were too complicated.'

Stratton found the coffee bitter. 'So who did?'

'I beg your pardon?'

'Who did take them into the field?'

Binning wasn't expecting the question. 'I don't think that's for me to say, really. Shall we press on?' He headed back through the door.

Stratton poured the coffee down the sink, placed the cup through the hatch marked 'plastic rubbish' and followed the scientist. As they walked, a casually dressed man in his late fifties stepped into the corridor. 'Hello, Phillips. This is John Stratton from the SBS,' Binning said.

'Ah. Right,' Phillips said, offering a hand while inspecting Stratton through his glasses as if trying to bring him into focus.

Stratton shook it. 'Hi.'

Binning did not hang around and moved on. Stratton caught him up. The scientist said in a low voice, 'We've got a few old fogies here. Surprisingly youthful team otherwise. That's all Jervis's doing. You know Jervis?'

'Yes.'

'He takes a lot of interest. Believes technology moves so fast that only younger minds can keep up with it. I'd be inclined to agree but I'm mindful of the fact that it probably means I'll be turfed out before I think I'm ready.'

They arrived alongside a large room beyond another plate-glass wall. A young woman in a slim-fitting jumpsuit and wearing protective goggles was operating a complex-looking piece of machinery.

Binning stopped to look at her with more than polite interest. 'Rowena Deboventurer,' he announced, as if there were a lot more to say about her. He tapped on the glass. She looked around at him, her expression blank as though he wasn't really there. She glanced at Stratton for less than a second before going back to her work.

'Whatever your first impression of her is, you're probably right,'

Binning said, smirking. He walked on. Stratton thought the young woman looked very cute.

Behind yet another glass wall lay a dojo-and-gym combination: on one side of the room was a collection of weights and workout machines, on the other a judo mat. A tall blond-haired man who looked about the same age as Stratton and Binning and was wearing a *karategi* was conducting a *kata*, each move focused, strong, crisp and decisive, his arms and legs lashing out in precise arcs at an invisible foe.

Binning watched with interest, nodding in approval occasionally as though acknowledging the accuracy of the strikes. 'Our intrepid boss. Jason Mansfield. A third dan in karate, brilliant nuclear engineer, and handsome to boot. Quite the perfect male, don't you think?'

Stratton wondered if Binning seriously expected him to agree. It just wasn't the sort of thing one bloke said about another where he came from.

'Rather an extraordinary fellow. Flunked his first degree at Oxford because according to him it was boring and failed to stimulate him. That was when we first met. People put him down even though he was playing with theories that most of them couldn't fathom. The underprivileged background didn't help. He did impress some of the professors with his theoretical designs but generally they saw him as a flash in the pan who would amount to little. We all did. Probably what drove him forward. Einstein never completed his first degree either. When Jason left Oxford nearly everyone thought he'd disappeared down some hole in the ground, myself included. But the next time he turned up he shocked all of his contemporaries. It was at CERN, the European nuclear research institute. After a PhD in particle physics he went on to become their youngest senior engineer. That probably means nothing to you but those are the dizzy heights even young geniuses dream about. Two years ago London recruited him to head up this place. Remarkable, don't you think?'

'Amazing,' Stratton said dryly, confirming Binning's suspicion that it meant little to him.

On the other side of the glass Mansfield came to a controlled finish, feet together, shoulders visibly relaxing. He stood with his eyes closed, slowing his breathing, allowing the tensile energy of his body to release itself. When he came back to normal consciousness he removed a towel from a rail and wiped the perspiration from his forehead. He noticed the audience. His face cracked into a grin and he bid them enter.

Binning pushed the door open. 'That looked pretty crisp,' he said. 'I still think you need to turn your hips out a little more on the second thrust.'

'Oh, really?' Jason replied, twisting his body suddenly and swinging the sole of his foot towards Binning. Mansfield's subordinate stepped to the side, tapping the foot down with practised ease. But Jason countered with his other leg, followed by an arm, striking repeatedly. Binning defended coolly, stepping back, to the sides, always under control. Jason's final punch stopped a fraction of an inch in front of Binning's nose, the arm not fully extended. 'Strike!' he shouted nevertheless.

'You're an animal,' Binning retorted. 'I wasn't ready.'

'You should always be prepared. Isn't that right, Stratton? You're the fighting professional here.'

Stratton forced a polite smile.

The man held out his hand. 'Jason Mansfield. I've heard a lot about you. Even Jervis hints highly of you, and he says nothing about anyone, and when he does it's never polite. So what do you say? Shouldn't a man be prepared at all times?'

'Sounds pretty exhausting to me,' Stratton said.

Jason saw the funny side. 'Which is your preferred martial art?'

'I don't have one.'

'You mean, no specific one?'

'I mean none.'

'What do you people practise down in Poole? A hybrid, I imagine. Mixture of various techniques. Ju–jitsu?'

Stratton shook his head. 'No.'

Jason looked unconvinced. 'Come on. You must do *some* kind of self-defence. How do you defend against someone coming at you – with a knife, for instance?' he asked, adding a mocking jab without actually touching Stratton.

'I'd shoot them.'

Jason grinned. 'What if you don't have a gun?'

'I'd probably run.'

'Oh. A dry one, he is, Binning. You'll get on well here.' Jason looked Stratton in the eye as though examining his very soul for something. 'Well. Has Binning shown you around?'

'Not really,' Binning said, jumping in. 'Thought we'd meet the boss first.'

'Let's head down to my office, then,' Jason said, rubbing his face and neck with the towel. 'We'll sound out one or two things. Then we'll show you the rest of the place.'

They headed further into the underground complex, reaching a four-way junction. Another glass wall revealed a conference room. Inside, two men were examining a complicated mathematical calculation on a whiteboard that included diagrams of some kind of device.

Jason put his head round the door. 'How's it coming?'

'We've broken it down into a couple of options,' one of the men replied.

'Okay. Once you're certain, bring it back into the theory room and we'll pick those options to bits.'

'Will do,' the man said and went back to the board.

They continued along the corridor. 'How's that retractor demonstration coming along?' Mansfield asked Binning, businesslike. 'We need that to go without any hitches.'

'We're all ready apart from the power plant. I'm told it'll be here at least a couple of days prior.'

76

'I need a guarantee on that. I don't want to see it plugged into a battery box. We must have the right power units. Otherwise it looks bloody amateurish.'

'Of course.'

At a door, Jason slipped his index finger inside a scan tube by the handle and the locking mechanism gently clicked open. They went into a rectangular open-plan room, the walls lined on three sides by whiteboards and computer monitors. It had been subtly divided, using movable partitions, into small clusters of tables and chairs, a couple of which were occupied by a handful of staff who were sitting in circles discussing something.

'This is the theory room,' Jason said in a quieter voice. 'Each new project has its own stance, its own position in the room, but also in an open forum that allows anyone with an idea they wish to contribute to do so. One person oversees what we call the subject but other than that it's a free-for-all.'

Stratton looked at the various 'stances', the boards and screens containing mathematical data and diagrams. It was all Greek to him.

When he looked back at Jason the MI16 director was watching him, an expression in his eyes like that of a master examining an uncomprehending child. 'Bit daunting for you, I expect . . . Let's go to my office,' he said, gesturing towards a smaller glass-partitioned space at the far end. 'Take a seat,' Jason said as they walked into the office. He sat in a comfortable leather chair behind the desk, a large portion of whose surface was a computer screen.

The warmth was beginning to make Stratton feel uncomfortable and he removed his leather jacket before sitting down.

'We run a pretty loose ship here,' Jason began. 'No scheduled meals or work times. It's up to the individual. We even have nap rooms,' he said, raising his eyebrows. 'The emphasis is placed on freedom . . . freedom to think, to express. The primary function is creation. It's bad enough having to live like rabbits in a warren. So we do our best to compensate with pitiful luxuries and distractions.'

One such distraction caught Jason's eye as he looked past Stratton.

Rowena was heading towards the office, no longer in the one-piece laboratory suit but in a short skirt that revealed a pair of shapely legs. Her gaze lingered on Jason perhaps a moment too long as she entered the room but her expression was still void of emotion.

'Rowena. Have you met John Stratton?' Jason asked.

'Yes,' she said, without looking at the guest and taking a seat in the other side of the room. She appeared aloof beyond rudeness as she pulled out a cigarette packet, removed a slender cigarette and lit it.

Jason smiled thinly as she blew a long line of smoke towards him. 'That describes Rowena to a T. Rude and rebellious. This is a no-smoking establishment. But she's invaluable, knows it, and so she gets away with everything.'

The young woman ignored everyone. Binning stared at her in private thought. Rowena somehow involved everyone and ignored them at the same time. She seemed to live under a cloud, contemptuous of everything.

'I asked Rowena to pop in because she's, well, a part of why you're here,' Jason said, looking at Stratton. 'I can't help feeling there's bad feeling between you and us. I'd like to move beyond it. I think there's been an overreaction to the hull-recording incident. It's quite acceptable that under such hostile circumstances an operative could forget to arm the self-destruct option—'

'I didn't forget to arm it,' Stratton said, surprised by his own sudden anger. It was a warning that his previous acceptance of the situation was a smokescreen that he'd created in self-defence. Deep down he still felt sensitive about the incident, at least where these people were concerned.

Everyone else in the room felt the sting of Stratton's glare although they did not appear to be unduly fazed by it.

Jason took a moment to compose his next words. 'The likelihood of the device failing to self-destruct after it was armed is very low. But obviously nothing is impossible.'

'Total crap,' Rowena snapped, looking at Stratton as if he was dirt. 'I designed the self-destruct system on that device. It's simple, functional, and the one that I prepared for the operation worked perfectly. And I'm not going to be blamed by this Neanderthal for some fictitious malfunction.'

Stratton got to his feet, barely able to hold on to his anger. 'I'm not taking any more of this shit.'

'Oh, grow up,' Rowena said, taking a pull on her cigarette. 'If you prima donnas only knew how difficult it is to dumb down designs just so you can use them you wouldn't be so damned arrogant.'

The other scientists in the theory room outside the office had stopped talking and were looking towards them.

'Easy,' Jason said, getting up and walking around the desk as if to get between the pair.

'I can see what's going on,' Stratton said. 'You eggheads screwed up and as far as you're concerned my coming here acknowledges that it was my mistake. Fine. You win. I came. Now I'll go. That recorder didn't work. You know it. I know it. It'll be our little secret.'

'You bloody coward,' Rowena retorted, standing now. 'You may have the guts to do the job but not to admit when you screw it up.'

'Please! Can we stop this?' Jason had raised his voice to match the volume of theirs and now he moved to the doorway to prevent Stratton from leaving. 'Let's all calm down.' He faced Stratton. 'There's no underhandedness going on here. I understand your feelings, both of you,' he added, glancing round at Rowena.

'I think I know how difficult it was for you to come here. You're an operative and, well, I expect that in your eyes we're nothing more than a bunch of white coats . . . and in the eyes of some of the people here you're no more than a mindless thug. I'm being perfectly frank because I want to be fully understood. I believe we're wrong about each other. I would like to see closer cooperation between us than there has been in the past. For our part we need to know more about how you think, react, analyse. That goes for all operatives and for you in particular, Stratton. You have an impressive record when it comes to thinking on your feet, reacting to life-threatening situations, solving problems under pressure. Yet forgive me if I sound insulting, but . . . well, you don't have a great education. Your IQ is average . . . don't get me wrong, please: I'm trying not to sound condescending. What I'm saying is, you have something that isn't easily quantifiable when it comes to IQ or physical tests. I want to know what that some-thing is.'

Rowena rolled her eyes and sat back down. 'No one ever heard of dumb luck?' she muttered.

Stratton realised he was grinding his teeth. Yet the woman had disengaged herself from everyone else, seemingly to concentrate on her cigarette.

A beeper sounded at Jason's hip. He unclipped the device and checked its screen. 'I would appreciate it if everyone just took a deep breath and settled down,' he said, moving back behind the desk.

Stratton picked up his coat and headed out of the office.

Jason frowned as he picked up a headset – a greater priority – placed it against his ear and touched the desk screen to activate a connection. 'This is Jason . . . I understand . . . Yes, of course. That's what we're here for.'

He put down the headset as Stratton reached the door. 'Stratton. I think you'll want to hear this. That was a call from London.'

Stratton stopped at the word 'London'. That probably meant the call had nothing to do with this rubbish. He looked at the scientist.

'Somebody hijacked an oil platform in the North Sea early this morning. They're holding some hundred and sixty-plus workers to ransom. An SBS team is on its way here to pick up the G43.'

'When will they be here?' Binning asked.

'They're in the air. Any time.'

'Is that all they need?' Now Binning was completely methodical – his job was to liaise with outside units who needed equipment.

'That's all they've asked for. But stand by for updates.'

Stratton released the door handle. He wasn't sure how the news directly affected him but felt he should stick around and see what developed . . . as long as that bloody bitch Rowena kept away from him.

A gentle yet persistent buzz filled the air and a small light flashed above one of the flatscreens on the office wall. Jason used a remote to turn it on. Several split-screens displayed various parts of the compound as seen through a collection of closed-circuit television cameras. He selected one of the views, enlarging it to fill the screen. The camera moved skyward where it picked up a helicopter.

Stratton looked at the screen. It was an SBS Chinook, unmistakable, like a thick, short sausage with rotors on either end. A letter and a pair of numbers flashed on the screen and moved to a corner where they continued to blink.

A voice crackled over speakers. 'India one-six, this is Whisky four-zero, clearance code Golf two-zero.'

The code the pilot had given matched the one on the screen.

'India one-six affirmative. You're clear to land,' Jason said.

'Roger that. Thirty seconds.'

Stratton suspected that Chaz and the standby team were on

board, probably acting as the advanced recce team preparing surveillance for an assault team, whenever the lads could get back from Afghanistan. He wondered why he had not received a call from SBS HQ. The visit to MI16 was not a priority of any kind. They'd certainly known about this hijacking before he had arrived. Maybe Mike had been serious and they were resting him.

He put the thoughts aside as the powerful helicopter closed in on the landing pad.

Rowena glanced at the screen as if she was only half interested.

'They'll no doubt be in a hurry,' Jason said. 'Better get down to the airlock and meet them as they clear.'

'You coming, Rowena?' Binning asked as he started out of the door.

'If there's anything you can't handle give me a shout.' She seemed pissed off with him too.

Binning chose not to make the half-expected answer and put her from his mind as he went out.

The helicopter settled onto the pad and the cabin door opened. Men in black one-piece fireproof suits climbed out. Stratton recognised Chaz.

The heavy angled sheets of steel that Stratton had seen began to slide open. A red light to the side flashed and a sign lit up stating 'ENTER THIS WAY'. The six men filed through the opening while the pilots and the crewman remained on board the Chinook. As the last man passed through the heavy steel door it began to close.

'I take it you know these men?' Jason asked.

Stratton was not ready to act as if all that had been said before had been forgotten.

'Shall we go down and greet them?' Jason asked. He walked off through the room. Rowena hadn't moved so, rather than remain with her, Stratton set off after Mansfield. It would be a relief to meet Chaz and the boys.

They headed along another gently curving corridor and soon arrived at a more dingy part of the complex. The concrete was unfinished, as if the construction budget had been exhausted. Exposed pipes and conduits ran across the ceilings, connecting the bare strip lighting.

They passed under an archway into an expansive room containing a cloudy standard-sized swimming pool. Their feet echoed in the cavernous space as they walked along its length. 'Testing pool,' Jason pointed out as if he was a tour guide.

Another steel door led through to a wide room where over-lapping sheets of rubber hung from ceiling to floor, which was covered in gravel. Around the room were distributed a dining table and chairs, a torn cord sofa, and two ragged armchairs – the cheap furnishings of an ordinary living room. Three men stood around the space in civilian clothes, two standing, one crouching. They didn't move. Sponge dummies.

Stratton noticed ammunition casings in the gravel as he crunched through it, bullet holes in the furniture. He was surprised. MI16 had a killing house.

Jason glanced back at him. 'When I got here it was a weapons-testing room. But I decided to make it more entertaining.' They went into what appeared to be a storeroom containing rows of metal racks and shelving stacked with a variety of mechanical and electronic parts.

A muted alarm began to sound. Jason stopped in his tracks and looked up at the red light flashing above a door at the end of the room. 'What the hell . . .' he muttered. He pushed through the door into a dull concrete bunker where Binning stood in front of a control panel, holding a phone to his ear. Above the panel was a small monitor filled with Chaz's irate face.

'You were told that all weapons and communications devices were to be left on the helicopter,' Binning said into the phone, sounding vexed. 'And under no circumstances were any pyrotechnics to be brought into the complex.' Binning looked at Jason and shook his head in frustration. 'One of the bloody fools brought something in. The vault has locked down.'

'We *didn't* bring anything in!' Chaz shouted in defence of himself and the others.

'Did you clean your equipment after your last training session or operational task?' Binning asked. 'I'll answer that for you. No. You didn't. You were warned that the system picks up the slightest chemical residue. If it has anything to do with explosives it reacts. You were told.'

Jason looked around at Stratton with an irritated glare. 'Don't these people pay attention to detail, damn it!'

Stratton didn't like his tone but let it go. The boffins were clearly under stress. 'What's the problem?'

'The security scanning system in the airlock is like the one you went through in the elevator,' Jason explained.

'And I put my phone and watch in a drawer and continued on down.'

'You weren't carrying any form of explosives. Without the clearance codes access goes into lock-down.'

'Then give them the code.'

'We don't provide them,' Binning said. 'London does.'

'Then send them back up to clear their gear,' Stratton suggested, looking between the two men.

Jason sighed heavily as he tried to calm himself. 'We can't.'

Binning explained. 'An unauthorised pyrotechnic invokes a Priority One protocol. It's classed as an SSB, a serious security breach. We can't override the system response and send them back up to the helipad. And neither can they carry on down to us.'

'Our security is automated,' Jason expanded. 'Designed for a complex without physical security. We have no armed guards. Therefore we have far more stringent precautions . . . Your men are locked in, and that's that.'

Stratton was getting the picture. 'For how long?'

'The vault can't be opened for twenty-four hours.' Jason was not apologetic.

Stratton automatically ran through the obvious implications.

Jason got the impression from his expression that it was the fault of MI16. 'This has never happened before.'

'Can I speak to him?' Stratton asked.

Binning flicked a switch on the panel. 'Go ahead.'

'Chaz? This is Stratton.'

'Stratton, what the hell is going on? They said we're stuck in here for twenty-four bleeding hours.'

'That seems to be the story, mate.'

'That's madness. We've got to get on.'

'I know. There doesn't seem to be a solution,' Stratton said, looking at Jason to be sure.

A buzzer went off on the panel. Binning touched a button. 'Binning here.'

'London's just called.' It was Rowena. 'The crisis response centre received an airlock-shutdown alarm.'

'Tell them it's under control.' Jason cut in. 'Give them our duress code, let them know we're fine. It was an error. The SBS lads brought something into the lock.'

'What a surprise,' Rowena said.

'Have London send the unlock code,' Jason ordered.

'We didn't bring anything into the bloody access!' Chaz shouted.

Jason looked at Stratton as if he'd been through that already. 'It will take twenty-four hours to get them out. Nothing can change that.'

'That's bloody ridiculous,' Chaz's voice boomed.

'You have to understand what this system was designed for,' Binning explained. 'Think of it like a bank vault that someone has tried to rob . . . the Bank of England, for instance. There are billions of pounds' worth of systems in here. But it's not just their financial value. Some of the devices would be extremely dangerous in the wrong hands. It would be catastrophic, in fact. There are foreign governments that would give almost anything to get hold of some of the items we have in here.'

'Yeah, but—' Chaz began to argue.

Jason was growing more irritated and cut him off. 'Let me put it another way. If this had been an actual break-in attempt, on a scale of importance to this country's security your oil-platform hijack would have equated to a handbag snatch in comparison . . . There's nothing more we can do. Deal with it. Good day to you.' He headed out of the room.

Binning gave Stratton a sympathetic look and followed his boss.

Stratton watched them go before looking back at the small screen. 'Sounds like you're going to have to sit this out for the next twenty-four, Chaz.'

'That's just friggin' brilliant!' Chaz shouted. 'We *didn't* bring anything in here. Their system screwed up!'

'I know exactly how you feel. What was the task?'

'Dropping in some new surveillance device that these guys put together.'

'When are the assault teams supposed to be getting in?'

'First packet in the next forty-eight hours. Two more to follow soon after.'

'Where's the forward mounting base?'

'Aberdeen initially. Then on board one of the assault ships. They're going to give us our RV within the hour.'

'Any task timings?'

'No. But they want to have the ability to assault asap. This puts us back big time. Someone's going to be pissed off in Poole.'

'I'd better let them know the bad news,' Stratton said as he realised what he was going to have to do.

'Sorry, mate.'

Stratton suspected that Chaz was going to get it in the neck. 'Make yourselves comfortable. I'll talk to you later.'

Chaz's frustrated look filled the small screen.

Stratton headed back to the main complex.

7

The wind whipped at Deacon as he walked down a set of metal steps beneath the housing deck that was sandwiched under the main deck. He stopped to look further down between multiple cross-struts at a couple of his men working below. 'How's it coming?' he shouted.

The Scotsman looked up, grimacing unhappily. 'It's coming,' he said as he fixed a thick malleable plastic pack horizontally to one of the massive supporting legs that reached down into the foaming grey water thirty metres below. The metre-long pack joined the end of a string of others fixed around the leg. The Bulgarian handed Jock another pack from one of several large plastic containers that the team had brought with them.

'That storm front'll be here in an hour,' Deacon shouted. 'That stuff'll need to withstand a good pelting.'

'You do your job, I'll do mine,' the Scotsman shouted back without looking up.

'Good enough,' Deacon mumbled to himself. His satellite phone buzzed in his pocket and he took it out to read the screen. He pushed the call button and put it to his ear. 'Yeah.'

'You are cleared to go to the next phase,' a rugged male voice said.

Deacon checked his watch. 'We're ahead of schedule, then.'

'The schedule was always meant to be flexible.'

'Will do,' Deacon said, unconcerned. He turned off the phone. 'How much longer will you be?' he called out.

88

'Ten, maybe fifteen minutes,' the Scotsman shouted.

'Head up to the control room when you're done. I need you to do that video feed.'

'Am I the only bastard with any brains in this outfit?' Jock shouted.

The Bulgarian paused to look at the Scotsman as he handed him another explosive charge.

Deacon knew that the man actually relished the responsibility. Jock was one of only two on the team whom he'd met previously. The first time had been in 2004 in the Green Zone US military hospital in Baghdad. Jock had had three bullet holes in him. Deacon had only had a piece of shrapnel in his leg. The Scot had been the sole survivor of an ambush on a six-vehicle, thirty-man convoy to Mosul.

A couple of hundred insurgents had hit them from all sides on the outskirts of the city. It had been a soldier's worst nightmare. They'd had no support, no air cover, no reinforcements and no hope. Jock's steel-plated black pick-up had been riddled with armour-piercing bullets within seconds and the next thing he remembered was running down the road back the way they'd come with a couple of colleagues on his tail. They'd all taken hits. The others had gone down but Jock had managed somehow to keep on going. Stopping would have meant death.

He wouldn't have survived had it not been for a local who'd happened to come out of a driveway. God only knew why the man had chosen that moment to go for a drive. Iraqis tended to put all survival judgements in the hands of Allah. Operating on full survival mode Jock had shot the man through the head, yanked him out of the car, jumped in and hit the accelerator.

Within a couple of months he'd been back on the convoy route. The man was part crazy, Deacon was certain of that.

Deacon headed back to the accommodation block and went in through a door and then another immediately after it that acted as an airlock. The doors closed with a bang behind him, slammed shut by the rising wind. 'Viking, this is Deacon,' he said into his walkie-talkie. 'I'm heading to the galley to set up the first media scenario.'

'Understood,' a voice came back.

Deacon pocketed the radio and walked along a narrow corridor of rooms, some with their doors open to reveal beds and closets. Bedding and clothing lay on the floor of the corridor as if there had been a hasty exit. There was no one here.

Deacon pushed through a door at the end, past vending machines, emergency firefighting equipment and signage, through a pair of swing doors on his left and then into another long corridor. Near the far end Viking and the Lebanese thug stood outside yet another door, carbines to hand, magazine pouches on belts around their waists, pistols in holsters on their thighs and radios dangling around their necks.

'Did you hear what I said?' Deacon called out as he approached.

The red-headed warrior glanced at his Arab colleague and then back at Deacon.

'Yeah, you,' Deacon said, looking at Viking.

'I answered,' Viking explained.

'So what are you still doing here? Go set up the bloody camera!'

The Norseman understood, grabbed his foul-weather jacket off a hook and hurried away.

'Viking idiot,' Deacon muttered as he pushed in through the door they had been guarding. The Lebanese thug jammed it open with his foot, his weapon at the ready.

Inside the large dining room a hundred and sixty-four platform workers minus those maintaining the rig's life-support systems sat on the floor, hands secured behind their backs with heavy-duty plastic cuffs. They were a variety of shapes and sizes, many of them big or just overweight, dressed in dirty clothes and looking dishevelled. Among them were the rig manager and the security supervisor. They all eyed Deacon, their expressions ranging from curious to self-pitying, from coldly calculating to angrily malevolent. The room felt uncomfortably warm with that number of bodies crammed into it and the smell of sweat and other body odours was almost overwhelming.

Banzi and Pirate squatted on the edges of the counter in opposite corners of the room with guns held easily in their hands. Queen walked between the hostages, offering water which he squirted none too accurately from a plastic bottle into their open mouths. He looked approvingly at one handsome young man and gave him an extra helping.

Deacon took a moment to look them all over before stretching out a hand and pointing to one after another. 'You, you, you, you, you, you. Stand up.'

The randomly selected six men looked from one another to Deacon, each waiting for the others to make the first move. Several of them looked concerned about their possible fate.

'Come on. Hurry up. Get to your feet,' Deacon called out.

'Piece o' shit,' someone grumbled loudly.

'Who was that?' Deacon asked, not particularly annoyed and even somewhat admiring of the man's spirit. He managed a smirk. 'You six selected men. Stand up and file out of the room. Nothing's gonna happen to you. The only shootin' we 'ave planned, for the moment at least, is a little TV show.'

'Lying bastard,' another voice called out.

The men still did not move.

'If you make it difficult for me, I'll make it difficult for you,' Deacon assured them.

'Gutless bastard,' another man muttered.

Deacon pulled out his pistol, walked over to the outspoken hostage and stopped behind him. The man was suddenly horrified about the outcome of the move. He had good reason to be. The hijacker slammed the pistol into the side of the man's head, almost knocking him senseless. The man fell onto a colleague, blood pouring from a wound across his ear.

'If you men don't stand up in five seconds I'll kill this gobshite,' Deacon snarled, placing the muzzle of his pistol an inch above the man's skull. 'And then I'll kill another, and another . . . If you think we went to all the trouble to hijack this bloody platform to be jacked around by its staff you must be on drugs.'

One of the men began to get to his feet, though he struggled to gain his balance with hands tied behind his back. It was more than this that hampered him. One of his legs was giving him trouble. The man was Jordan Mackay, Stratton's old mate. He gritted his teeth and dragged his faulty leg beneath him, making a determined effort to get upright.

Jordan breathed deeply with the exertion and set his stare coldly on Deacon.

Another five men got to their feet.

'Good,' Deacon said, stepping back through the hostages to the galley entrance. 'Now follow me.'

They paused in the corridor to await further instructions. 'That way,' the Lebanese thug said to Jordan, giving him a firm shove.

With his short temper Jordan did not appreciate the push but he controlled his anger and headed along the corridor. Deacon took up a position in the rear and followed the line of men.

The Lebanese led them through the swing doors and along to a staircase, which he climbed. He pulled on a foul-weather jacket, pushed open a door at the top and stepped into a narrow airlock that led to another door that required an effort to open. The fierce wind ripped into the structure, tugging and chilling the men in their jeans and T-shirts as they filed outside.

Jordan stopped once again, waiting for further instructions.

The Lebanese thug pushed him on, this time more aggressively. 'That way,' he snarled.

Jordan almost fell over and when he regained his balance he faced the hijacker, baring his teeth. 'Don't push me again,' he warned in a low, deliberate voice.

Jordan's impudence astounded the Arab, who slammed him in the gut with the butt of his weapon. The ex-SBS man doubled over as the wind went out of him, his face spasming. The thug wasn't finished with him and took a firm hold of his hair. 'You don't talk to me, ever.'

As Jordan pulled away the thug belted him across the face, sending him sprawling across the metal decking. The sea was visible far below through the grillework. Blood seeped from a cut on his mouth. He rolled onto his face, his hands tied tight behind his back. Using his forehead to support his weight, he brought his knees underneath him in order to stand up.

'Stay down if you know what's good for you,' the Arab growled.

Jordan ignored him and fought to get to his feet. He had never been a man to bend easily.

The Arab poised himself to deal Jordan another severe blow with the stock of his weapon.

'Easy, shit-for-brains. You need to chill out. No one dies unless I say so,' said Deacon from behind them. He looked at Jordan as the man finally managed to get to his feet.

Jordan was out of breath with the effort and the blow to his gut but his eyes found the Arab's and stared into them. The thug smirked at him.

Deacon felt like remonstrating with the idiot but knew that he couldn't in front of the prisoners. He had orders not to harm the rig's workers unless it was absolutely unavoidable, and if he did he would have to prove that there'd been no alternative. An unsatisfied client meant a reduction in pay. He had already lost one hostage to the Lebanese fool, which he felt he could get away with by docking the Arab's pay. The man was a liability, no question.

Deacon decided to use the situation to his advantage. 'I warned you people not to step out of line,' he said, addressing Jordan and then the others. 'We've already had one execution.' He pointed to the body swinging from the crane. A look of revulsion came over the faces of all the prisoners except one. Mackay's. 'Don't give me a reason for another. As you can see, my men are enthusiastic . . . That way.'

Jordan glared at the Lebanese hijacker before shuffling off. The others followed him across the deck towards the crane where Viking was setting up a video camera on a tripod.

'Stand in a line along here,' Deacon said, positioning them between the camera and the crane.

Some of the men began to shiver. Jordan refused to.

Viking looked through the lens. 'Put your hood up,' he told the Lebanese thug. The Arab reached for the hood at the back of his jacket and pulled it over his head. Viking struggled to adjust the settings on the camera with his oversized fingers. 'You,' he called out, pointing to Jordan on the end of the line-up while looking through the lens. 'Move a little over.'

Jordan did as he was told. The wind suddenly picked up and whipped at them all.

'A bit more,' Viking ordered.

Deacon moved beside him to view the scene. The Lebanese stood at the other end of the line, pointing his gun at the men aggressively.

'I like the shivering. Adds something. Abdul's got the 'ang of this,' Deacon muttered to Viking. 'Bet 'e's done this before.'

Viking grinned. 'They're good,' he said, holding the tripod to prevent the wind from blowing it over.

'Take a long shot of 'em. Pan from one side to the other and back again. End on the dead guy. Zoom in on 'im. That'll be a nice finish.'

Viking did so. 'That's it,' he said finally, standing upright.

'Take it to the control room. Jock'll meet you there. I want that on YouTube soon as you can.' Viking picked up the camera and tripod and headed away.

'And tell Jock not to forget to send a copy direct to CNN,' Deacon shouted.

Deacon looked out to sea at the blackening sky. The clouds really were building. 'Get 'em back to the galley. And Abdul – in one piece if you can manage that.'

Abdul removed his hood to reveal a disgruntled expression. 'Get going,' he said, aiming his remark at Jordan.

The line of men traipsed off the way they had come, the wind whipping at them. Freezing drops of rain began to fall. Deacon pulled up his collar and headed towards the control room.

The theory chamber was locked when Stratton got to it. He pushed a buzzer beside the keypad and after a pause stepped inside to find Jason, Binning, Rowena and two other men standing around one of the tables. He felt like he'd interrupted something.

'I should call Poole. They need to know what's happened in case London hasn't told them yet,' he said.

None of them replied. All of the scientists looked strangely conspiratorial.

'I need to use your phone,' Stratton said, taking a step towards Jason's office.

Jason held up a hand. 'Can I ask you to hold off on that for one moment.'

Stratton looked at him enquiringly. 'They need to know right away.'

'Another minute won't hurt . . . There's something we need to discuss.'

Stratton found the mood odd indeed. 'Why can't it wait until I've talked to Poole?'

'It'll be too late then.' Jason looked thoughtful, as if he was searching for the right approach. 'I'll get straight to the point. The task to the oil platform should continue, and immediately rather than tomorrow.'

'What's that got to do with you?'

'The SBS are not the only ones who can carry out the task.'

Stratton's brow creased as he realised where this might be going. Every scientist was looking at him, except Rowena, who sat in front of a computer terminal typing something on the keyboard.

'Do you want to explain that?' Stratton asked, not particularly keen to hear the answer but curious nonetheless.

'It's obvious what I'm saying,' Jason said. '*We* can do it.'

'You're joking, right?'

'I'm afraid not.'

'You must have your heads up your backsides. Do you think you can just climb aboard that chopper and do the task like you're the reserve team? For a bunch of geniuses you're pretty stupid.'

'You're right. We are all geniuses. Don't you think we'd work out how we could do it before we mentioned it?'

Stratton tried unsuccessfully to suppress a chortle. 'Why don't you guys go and have a pink gin while I make that call? Then we'll forget whatever madness you're thinking about.' Stratton headed towards Jason's office.

'You can't call out without a code,' Jason said.

Stratton hesitated a moment, then pressed on to call his bluff. He picked up the phone. There was no dial tone. He replaced the phone and looked back towards Jason. 'I suppose I can't walk out of here without a code, either.'

No one replied, making the answer an obvious one.

'Take a moment to listen to us, please,' Jason asked.

'It doesn't look as if I have much choice.'

Jason was determined to press on with his idea. 'Let me first ask you this. Why do you think we're not qualified to carry out the task?'

'I said I'd listen to you because I have to. I'm not going to humour you beyond that.'

'We're more qualified than you think,' Jason said with confidence.

Stratton's expression remained blank.

'The surveillance equipment they want to install on the platform, the G43, is a multi-purpose static surveillance system. We built it, making us more qualified than anyone else to install it. But your doubts about us would naturally concern our ability to actually get onto the platform. Let me tell you a little bit more about us. As far as fitness is concerned, we're all accomplished triathletes. Take Smithy there.' Jason indicated one of the newcomers. 'He came third in this year's Hawaiian Iron Man competition. Jackson here came eighth. Binning was fifteenth. I came a modest twenty-fourth.'

'With a pulled shoulder muscle,' Binning added.

'Pain is not an excuse,' Jason countered. 'Rowena came eighteenth in the women's competition. I wonder where you would've come, Stratton.'

'In the women's?' Binning muttered.

'No need for that, Binning,' Jason said. 'But you do have a point.'

Stratton couldn't have cared less about the insult. Some things were beginning to add up for him. 'This isn't a coincidence, is it?'

Jason's eyes narrowed as he wondered what Stratton meant by the remark. 'What isn't?' he asked.

'The varied skills you're accumulating. You're all pretty young when I was expecting most of you to be quite old. You keep yourselves fit. You have a killing house. I suppose you're all good shots too?'

Jason smiled thinly. 'I see what you mean. You're right. It's not a coincidence. We've been preparing for a more active operational role for some time now.'

'Since *you* got here,' Stratton suggested.

'Since *I* got here,' Jason admitted happily. 'Do you have a problem with that?'

'Why should I?'

'If you were in a position to, would you approve?'

'Probably not.'

'Would you be specific? Please. We'd all like to know. What are we up against?'

Stratton felt reluctant to answer.

Jason pushed him. 'Come on. You criticise, but without an explanation. I would respect your thoughts more than most.'

Stratton gave in. 'It's simple. You're not soldiers.'

Jason looked at the others. 'I happen to agree with him. I have said as much myself.' He looked back at Stratton. 'However, we can learn to soldier. But if, for instance, that surveillance device went wrong in the field, you couldn't fix it. You couldn't defeat a sophisticated alarm system with a couple of old cellular phones. I could go on.'

Stratton was growing irritated with the conversation. 'And you couldn't take part in the operation without London's say-so.'

'True.'

'Then what is the point of this conversation?'

'We could do it, though.'

'Because you can run, swim, ride bicycles and shoot a gun at a rubber target?'

'I accept that we lack the know-how for climbing the oil platform.'

'Which is only one of many reasons why London wouldn't let you do it.'

'Let's just play this through a little further, then I'll let you make your call. If we went together, you and us, that would give us all the expertise we would need to complete the task. That's my point right now.'

'That's it? Are we done? Can I make my call now? I'll keep this conversation to myself. No one would take me seriously, anyway.'

'What are you afraid of?'

Stratton sighed. 'If London called right now, gave you permission to go ahead and ordered me to go with you, I'd tell them to get stuffed. Okay?'

Jason was disappointed.

'I don't think he's going for it,' Binning said.

'CNN has just released some breaking news on the Morpheus,' Rowena piped up, scrolling through a web page.

Stratton looked up at the mention of the name. 'Morpheus?' he asked.

'The hijacked platform,' Rowena explained.

Binning looked over Rowena's shoulder at the monitor. 'Put it up on the screen,' he asked.

She hit a couple of keys and swivelled in her chair to face a flatscreen television on the wall across the room.

It came to life, showing the CNN newsroom and an anchorman talking about the hijacked oil platform. A picture of the structure filled the background. It had the attention of everyone in the room, including Jason.

The news anchor was saying that only moments ago video footage from the platform hijackers had appeared on YouTube. They were threatening to kill six workers within the next twenty-four hours if their demands weren't met.

The image changed. Six oil workers stood in a line on the windswept deck. The camera panned across their faces before zooming to a body hanging from the crane in the background. The picture was grainy, as if it had been processed for several generations.

Stratton stood transfixed, certain the man on the end of the line was Jordan. 'Is there any way you can play that back?' he asked.

Rowena typed something and the image began to rewind to the beginning of the footage and then played again at normal speed. Stratton watched intently as the camera panned to his friend once more.

In the live broadcast the news anchor was reiterating that the selected workers were to be shot within twenty-four hours if the hijackers' demands weren't met. The anchor cut to a man in a studio and Rowena reduced the volume.

A myriad of issues went flying around inside Stratton's head. But there was really only one that mattered. Jordan, an old friend, had been singled out for execution. The two men's relationship was a more complex one than that of mere former colleagues. Jordan had saved Stratton's life. Of course that was all part of the job: the teamwork, covering each other's back. Stratton owed his life to others in the SBS who'd fought alongside him over the years, as several owed theirs to him. But the situation with Jordan differed greatly. Jordan had almost died trying to save Stratton because of a decision that Stratton had made in the first place. Jordan would still be in the SBS – and as an active member – had it not been for that decision.

Things sometimes went wrong on operations, and when they did it was down to human error, equipment failure or interference from the gods. You went into the special forces knowing this. In fact you volunteered. You had to. The extreme risks and the inevitable failures demanded it. Those responsible for the mistakes were rarely dealt with severely. It could not be described as forgiveness, more a level of understanding, among the top brass at least. Yet the operatives were harsh on themselves as well as on each other. Those who failed colleagues could never forget it, even if others chose to leave it unmentioned.

Stratton had not failed Jordan officially, not according to the subsequent inquiry. Opinions among the operation planners and those who had been on the ground at the time differed depending on who you talked to. Justifiable or not, Stratton had never truly come to terms with the results of his decision. At the time he had stood by it as the best he could have done under the circumstances. That had not made the outcome for Jordan any easier to accept, particularly when the man had knowingly risked his life in order to comply with the order. Time could not heal the wound for either man. If any opportunity came along for Stratton to make amends he would grab it with both hands.

Stratton was well aware that the kidnappers could be bluffing, if not about the execution then about the timing. That was often the case and a part of the strategy of negotiation. But not always. Quick executions had sometimes proved helpful in speeding up the decision-making process in the kidnappers' favour. The group that had hijacked the Morpheus had already killed one worker. They had to be taken seriously.

Stratton felt a sudden jolt of fear: this could be his only chance to make amends. He needed to think it through – he couldn't afford to be rash. Time was the major factor. He just wouldn't be able to work out every phase. He'd have to go step by step until he got to the point of no return. By then he would hope to know if the risks of continuing were acceptable.

His first thought was to get out of this nuthouse and back to Poole as soon as possible. If the SBS were planning to act fast, another team would have to be put together and he would probably be the ideal person to lead it – if he could get there. But that would take time. And if they didn't have the manpower they couldn't mount the operation, which would put him in the wrong location. The planners might have to ignore the threat, wait for the time lock, and use the original team. Jordan would be screwed if they did.

Stratton wondered if he could find a way onto the platform alone – a private operation. Even a brief consideration of the idea led nowhere. He didn't have the right kit, for one thing. For another, he would never be able to get a vessel within fifty miles of the rig without being stopped by the Royal Navy. It might theoretically be possible in a small rubber inflatable, if he could carry enough fuel. But if the weather was anything like it usually was in the North Sea that plan could only lead to disaster.

Stratton looked around at the scientists as he pondered these choices and he felt suddenly horrified. Out of all of them, theirs seemed to have the best chance of success in the time-frame. Yet it was rife with obstacles.

London would not go for it, of course, so he would have to begin with subterfuge. The first step was to get on board the waiting helicopter and convince the crew to continue the task with the new team. But even if he could get them airborne, keeping them in the air and heading towards the objective was another big obstacle.

Unable to think of a solution, he moved on to the next major problem: getting this lot onto the platform. It would be putting them at too great a risk. These arrogant nutters were no doubt capable of much but learning to climb an oil rig for the first time in operational conditions was madness.

He had to be mental for even considering it. But as soon as he tried to put the idea from his mind, Jordan was there instead, looking at him, waiting for him to come and pay him back. That was one image Stratton could not delete so easily. The answer was to use what he had available to get as close to the platform as he could and then go it alone. If the scientists were crazy enough to try, he would use them to his advantage. How, he was not yet sure.

Jason realised Stratton was staring at him and with a strange look in his eyes. Binning saw the same thing.

Stratton went over the Poole options once again just in case he had missed anything. He imagined arriving in Dorset that night, and also the airlock opening to free Chaz. In both cases he heard

Mike saying he could not be a part of any team because he was not 'operationally fit'. The thought of it made him angry.

The only option that had any hope lay with the nutters. Even then, it didn't have much chance of success but it looked like it was all he had. He thought fast. Equipment. What did they need? MI16 had dry-bags, and the chopper would already hold nearly everything else they'd want in the team's boxes. One step at a time, he reminded himself. Up until the point of no return.

'I'll do it,' Stratton said.

The other men stopped talking to each other and looked at him.

Rowena turned in her chair to face Stratton, her eyes not filled with expectation like those of the others but with suspicion. 'What changed your mind?' she asked. 'Five minutes ago I'd have said there wasn't a snowball's chance in hell of you going along with it.'

'I don't particularly care,' Jason said, jumping in. 'We can't get the operation going without him.'

'You trust him so easily, don't you?' Rowena flashed Mansfield a look. 'You're really that naive?'

Jason resented the dig but respected her point and faced Stratton in the hope of an explanation.

'Tell us. Why the change of heart?' Rowena asked the operative again. 'It would have to be an exceptional reason. Let's face it, you'd need to be insane to even attempt the operation with this lot.'

Her directness required a response.

Stratton suddenly found himself in the most bizarre position of having to convince *them*. He ran his fingers through his hair as he pondered the answer. The truth was more convincing than any story he could come up with. He saw no harm in telling them. 'One of the men they're threatening to execute on the Morpheus is an old friend.'

'The one on the far end?' Rowena asked, remembering how Stratton had looked at that hostage.

'Yes.'

'That's it?' She did not believe him.

'I owe him my life. Call it an unpaid debt.'

Rowena studied him, still unconvinced. She turned back to the computer keyboard and began tapping away.

Jason appeared to believe him, whether from desperation on his part or not. 'You're serious, aren't you, about doing it?'

'I wouldn't say it if I wasn't.'

Binning's energy soared at the prospect of going on the adventure and he immediately began to plan ahead. 'Is there anything else we can bring? We have a few items that your service is unaware of that might be useful.'

Stratton didn't want them bringing anything else along. But neither did he want to dampen their enthusiasm. 'The final approach will probably entail a surface swim followed by a climb. Trust me when I say that climbing a caving ladder out of a heavy swell is not easy, even for you super-athletes. It's more technique than strength.' He needed to sound serious about taking them all the way onto the platform itself, regardless of his own reasons for going. 'I advise you to carry as little as possible,' he added.

The men began discussing various items of equipment and their pros and cons.

'What was his name?' Rowena asked, cutting through the chatter.

Stratton paused to consider the wisdom of saying anything else. 'Jordan Mackay.'

'Dates in the service?' she asked, typing.

Stratton had to think. 'I don't know how long he was in the Marines but he was in the SBS for about ten years.'

Rowena studied the screen, which displayed the faces of several men. She had scanned Jordan's features from the news report and was matching it to a database of SBS operatives past and present. A match came up quickly.

'He's telling the truth. The man on the Morpheus is Jordan Mackay, former member of the Special Boat Service, retired a year ago.'

'You're going to the oil platform to rescue a friend?' Mansfield asked.

'Did you think I was going for you?'

This didn't satisfy him. 'The surveillance system will be set up on the lower levels of the rig without anyone needing to go up top and become exposed. If you go in search of this man, you'll put the whole operation at risk.'

'I guess it's not perfect for either of us. I thought this was a chance for you to prove yourselves.'

'And for you too, perhaps,' Rowena added. 'After your last cock-up.'

Stratton clenched his jaw. The woman was an arse, to be sure, but he was not going to let her get to him this time.

'That's irresponsible, isn't it?' Jason asked, pressing the point.

'Look who's talking,' Stratton responded.

The scientist remained unsure. This was the opportunity he had been waiting for but the question was: could he achieve his aims under these conditions? 'How do we get on board the helicopter?' he asked.

There was a moment's silence while everyone took in the likely reality of the situation. It was a serious step in itself to try, even if they didn't get out through the door. If London knew they were even considering it they would not be amused.

'We get fully rigged and walk on board,' Stratton said. 'Leave the rest to me.'

'The crewman will know we're not the same team,' Smithy said.

Stratton had been aware of an air of nervousness surrounding the tall, skinny, pale-looking man. Now that they seemed to be going ahead with the task it was getting even more noticeable.

'Obviously,' Stratton replied. 'So we don't try and pretend otherwise. We tell them the truth.'

'Tell the crew that the SBS team are stuck in the airlock, you mean?' Jackson asked. Jackson was bigger than all of the others but none of the man's bulk tended to fat. He looked the type who liked to take supplements and press weights, and he did not look apprehensive in the least. He held Stratton's gaze.

'Won't they want to verify any changes with the operations officer?' Smithy asked, looking to the others for agreement.

'That's the bit we need to delay,' Stratton said.

Jason nodded his understanding. 'What's the lost-comms procedure?'

'They'll proceed with the plan,' Stratton replied.

Jason faced Binning. 'We need to block their comms.'

'That's easy enough,' Binning said. 'Would they go all the way without comms?' he asked Stratton.

Stratton shook his head.

'Then what do we do?' Jason asked.

'Baby steps,' Stratton said. 'Options may present themselves.'

'Rather like a trapeze artist releasing the swing without knowing where the other swing is,' Rowena offered.

'Welcome to my world. You sure you still want to play in it?' Stratton asked.

Jason had heard enough. 'Are we agreed?' He looked at the other four scientists.

Binning nodded. 'Most definitely.'

Smithy nodded.

'Yes,' Jackson said.

Rowena hesitated. The others waited for her answer.

Her stare was fixed on Stratton. It was him she was unsure of.

'We need you,' Jason said.

'Got to have a babe in the team or they won't make the movie,' Binning said, grinning.

Rowena eventually lowered her eyes and remained where she was.

Jason knew her well enough. 'We're all in,' he announced.

Stratton felt his awareness of the insanity of it all rising up in his consciousness once again but he suppressed it. 'Just one thing,' he said. 'I'm in charge, all the way. No arguments, deals, negotiations. I want that understood.'

Jason accepted the condition without hesitation. 'Agreed. You're the boss.'

Stratton checked the others to ensure that it was unanimous. There did not appear to be any objections apart from the unvoiced ones from Rowena who remained looking at the floor. 'How do we get up to the chopper?' he asked.

'Same way you came down,' Binning replied.

'Then let's get rigged,' Stratton ordered.

'Do you mind if I have a brief word with my troops first?' Jason asked. 'Kind of a pep talk, really. You're welcome to stay.'

Stratton checked his watch. 'One minute. Let's not keep the crew hanging around much longer or they may start making calls before we can get up there.'

Jason understood and faced his colleagues with some urgency. 'You too, Rowena,' he insisted.

Rowena got to her feet to join them, although a level of reluctance from her was still evident.

'Up until now we've only fantasised about going live, as it were . . . getting stuck into a real operation,' Jason began. 'There's a good chance it will now happen. Granted, it isn't because of our renowned capabilities but due to a series of unexpected events. Nonetheless, it could put us in the spotlight as a team of operators as well as the boffins we already are. But I want you all to be aware of the risks involved. This may be a surveillance task but it is the nature of this business that when things go wrong it can be costly. I want you all to be completely sure that what it is

107

you're about to attempt is dangerous and that it could cost lives as well as save them. Frankly, if you're not prepared to take such a risk for this opportunity you should not be embarking on this task. Am I clear?'

They all nodded.

'Are you prepared to carry on with this task with the understanding that some of us may not come back?'

They each nodded in turn as Jason looked at them, Rowena last. She made him wait.

'Good,' Jason said, straightening up. 'I'll take you to the equipment room,' he said to Stratton who was waiting by the door.

The storeroom was packed with special-forces operational equipment: a rack of hanging dry-suits, fireproof undersuits, a box of harnesses, boots, leather gloves and so on. 'You guys are well stocked,' Stratton said.

Jackson, a head taller than Stratton, was beside him, attaching a flare to a diving-knife sheath with a thick rubber band. 'We trial every piece of equipment we design for special forces and the other clandestine departments in the conditions in which we expect them to get used. That means having similar operational equipment.' He took his dry-bag and left the room to get rigged.

Stratton searched along another shelf. 'Do you have any karabiners?' he asked the figure in the next row. As he looked between the boxes he realised it was Rowena. She pushed a box towards him through the shelving, gave him a cold look and went out.

Stratton sat alone on a chair. He pulled off his boots, followed by his outer garments, and climbed into the one-piece undersuit. After putting on a pair of rubber-soled climbing boots he got to his feet, ready to go. He picked up the bag containing his dry-bag and harness and looked for somewhere to leave his civvies. He spotted an empty shelf at the top against the far wall.

As he reached up and shoved the bag onto the shelf he heard

someone talking softly on the other side of a door. He was about to step away when he recognised Jason and Rowena's voices. Something about the situation, maybe a defensive suspicion of this crowd, and also the lowered voices, stopped him from leaving. He moved so that he could see through the narrow opening. Rowena and Jason stood close to each other, unaware of Stratton's presence.

Jason placed his hands on the young woman's hips and wrapped them around her waist, pulling her against him. She rested her arms on his shoulders, her fingers entwined behind his head. Their lips came together and they kissed passionately, their hold on each other tightening.

It was the point beyond which Stratton felt uncomfortable.

He headed back to the theory room, where he bumped into Smithy.

'Hi,' Smithy said fumbling with the fingerprint analyser. 'I'm excited to be coming along.'

Stratton doubted that very much.

As they went in they saw Binning and Jackson in fireproof suits, looking ready to go. Binning held up a rigid laptop-sized plastic box. 'This is the G43 overlook device.'

'How will we block the Chinook's comms?' Stratton asked, interested in the more immediate problem.

'Same device,' Binning said.

'You can do that from here?'

'No. Nothing can transmit from down here except through the secure cabling. It's already active. Soon as we're through the screens it'll block all comms.'

Jason and Rowena walked into the room wearing firesuits and carrying kitbags. It didn't surprise Stratton that Rowena's suit fitted her shapely body very well. 'What else are we taking apart from the G43?' he asked.

'Nothing,' Jason replied. 'We've taken your advice and gone for lightness.'

Stratton nodded. 'Okay. Look after your kit. Make sure it works. In the middle of the North Sea in the dark when the chopper has left is not a good time to discover you have a leak.'

'We're ready,' Jason assured him. 'Let's go,' he said to the others, forgetting for a moment that Stratton was in charge.

As they walked, Binning came alongside Stratton. 'Do you mind if I ask you a question?'

Stratton glanced at the man he didn't think he could ever warm to. It was more than Binning's cocky, condescending attitude. The scientist had an underlying greyness, an indistinctness about him. Stratton couldn't put his finger precisely on it but it was ever-present. 'What?'

'The story between you and this Mackay chap who's on the platform. What is that?'

Jason overheard the question and glanced back as if he too was interested to know the answer. Stratton didn't particularly want to talk about it, not with this lot. 'It was just an operation in Afghanistan that didn't go to plan.'

'Rowena found a watered-down report on the incident,' Jason said. 'It implied that some bad decisions were made but did not lay blame. You were the team commander.'

Stratton suspected they were trying to wind him up. Yet a twinge of guilt rippled through him. 'If you're wondering whether or not it was my fault, the answer is yes, it was.'

'You made a mistake?' Binning asked.

'I made a decision. There are always choices in any operation. Sometimes none of them are any good.'

Stratton had never explained the incident in detail to anyone, other than in the clinical post-operational report he had written. He was suddenly attracted to the notion of telling the MI16 lot about it. There was no harm in them knowing. He thought back to that dark and dangerous night. 'It was in Helmand. We went into a village a few hours before sun-up to lift a guy, a warlord,' he said. 'He was a grower – heroin – and he'd kill anyone, coalition forces, locals, to protect his business. He paid off the Taliban, who also protected him.

'We knew where he was. A small army, three fifty, four hundred men, surrounded the house. Our surveillance showed they weren't very alert at night. Sentries slept at their posts. We went in on foot, walked right into the village. We took out anyone in our way . . . At the first sentry position half a dozen Taliban lay on the ground, sleeping. We killed them all. The next lot in our way were talking and smoking around a fire. We took them out, too. The silenced weapons we used weren't really silent. You can't hear the bullets coming out of the muzzles. But you can hear the machinery, the clatter of the working parts inside the weapon, pushing the next round into the breech before it fires. Click, click, click. That became our catchphrase for killing. Click-click. What are you doing tonight? Click-click. We did a lot of that over there.

'We went in through the back door of one of those mud-walled houses, a bungalow filled with the smoke from kerosene lamps. They were sleeping on the floor. People all over the place. We divided up and shot every one of them simultaneously, except in the end room where the target lay. We gagged him and he woke up and we bound his arms. Our Afghan guide told him we would kill him if he tried to raise the alarm. He understood.'

They had stopped walking now, a few steps from the compound's lift. Stratton had the scientists' attention.

'I went to the front door and looked out onto the street. We intended to walk on out of the village with this worlord. But men were up and walking about in every direction. We didn't know why. Maybe they'd found bodies. A couple of men approached the house. We let them enter and then we killed them. Click, click, click. But we couldn't do that all night. If one of them had managed to get off a round none of us would have got out of there alive. They would have hit us with everything they'd got, even if it meant killing their warlord. We could only carry so much ammunition and no one would have been able to get to us in time.

'I had two options, as I saw it. We could walk out of there and hope we didn't bump into anyone. Or we could call in our vehicles. That was Jordan's team. In the original plan he would pick us up beyond the village, when we were clear. But we had discussed the possibility of him driving through. The white Toyota pick-ups we used were the same as the Taliban used in that area. Convoys of them came through the village at any time of the day or night. We felt we could get away with it. A one-off. When I signalled Jordan he asked if we could get closer to the edge of the village. He could see movement on the road and thought he might be challenged. Once the Taliban got a look at the occupants of our Toyotas there would be a battle. I said no. He had to come in and get us. I thought he had more chance of success that way than us going to him.

'Jordan wasn't the type to argue, not in a situation like that. So he came on in – the three pick-ups, loud as hell, headlights cutting through the blackness. A handful of Taliban challenged them on the edge of the village but they pushed through. The Taliban didn't fire, they hadn't seen enough. Jordan kept on coming. Men walked out of houses as the pick-ups passed, or stood where they had been sleeping, wrapped in blankets. They always had AK-47s, as if the guns were part of their bodies.

'It was obvious it had to be a moving pick-up. We moved out of the house. A couple of Taliban came towards us. The warlord decided this was his best chance of surviving. We took the Taliban out. Click-click. Others came. We took them out. As the pick-ups arrived we ran to them and dived into the backs. The warlord began to scream, he could see we were succeeding. We shot him through the head. The op was over. We'd failed. It was survival time. It's not unusual. Not every op is a success. You can only plan for so much. You let go of the

trapeze a hundred feet above the ground and look for another.'
Stratton glanced at Rowena.

'The Taliban opened up on us. Our vehicles weren't armoured.
All we had was the dust we kicked up and the rounds we could
put down. Every vehicle got hit but somewhow we all made it
out of the killing zone. We lost one vehicle with a stalled engine
outside the village but everyone managed to get into another
Toyota. Two of my lads were hit – nothing serious. I didn't know
Jordan had been shot until we got to the air-extraction RV. He'd
driven without a complaint for twenty minutes until he lost so
much blood that he started to fall unconscious.

'He kept quiet, hoping it was nothing serious so that I wouldn't
get blamed for it. When he told me this later it was his only admission that he thought I'd made the wrong call. Within months he'd
been invalided out of the service.'

The lift doors stood open before them and they stepped inside.

'Do you still believe you were right?' Jason asked as the doors
closed.

'That's not the point,' Stratton said.

'What *is* the point?' Jackson asked.

'If you need to ask you wouldn't understand.'

The lift came to a halt and they walked out into the tacky
lobby. The others were dissatisfied with Stratton's answer. 'Was
Jordan a good operative?' Jason asked.

'Very.'

'Did *he* get the point?' Jason persisted.

It was an interesting question. That was Stratton's only complaint
about his old friend. 'You know how beekeepers deal with getting
stung? They can't blame the bees.'

Stratton left them to ponder the comment and he opened the
exterior door enough to look towards the helipad. The sound of
the helicopter's purring engines increased measurably. 'That thing
working?' he asked Binning.

Binning held the plastic case in his hand. 'I promise you it is.'

Stratton opened the door fully. 'Give me one minute.'

As the operative closed the door behind him it aroused Rowena's suspicions once again. 'Have you considered the possibility that he'll simply tell the helicopter crew what we're doing and bring this to an end?' she said.

'Don't you believe him?' Jason asked.

'Does he need us to achieve his mission?' she wondered.

'I think he needs us – for the initial stage, at least.'

'Want to bet he doesn't plan on taking us all the way to the platform, though?'

Jason opened the door enough to let the noise back in and saw Stratton walk up the steps of the helipad and out of view. 'We'll have to watch him.'

With the rotors unengaged only the hot exhaust from the engines bothered Stratton as he entered the Chinook. The relatively spacious cabin had a line of hammock seats halfway down one side, while on the other dozens of various-sized plastic moulded boxes were lashed to rings on the bulkhead. Taking up most of the centre of the floor was a reinforced fibreglass SBS mini-submarine that looked like a fat and stubby black cigar, rounded at the front like a revolver bullet. The propeller, at the rear, sat inside a housing designed to protect a diver from swimming into it. Directly behind the nose was the open cockpit with seats for pilot and navigator. A compartment behind that, separated from the cockpit by a grille, was just about large enough to accommodate four people. The craft had breathing umbilicals attached along the inside of the bulkhead with nozzles for six divers. With no doors in the cabin or cockpit, just gaps where the crew climbed in and out, the sub was termed a 'wet ride': it flooded fully when it was underwater.

As soon as Stratton saw the sub he had a fairly good idea what the SBS plan was. In the cockpit the pilots and the crewman were in a discussion about something. Stratton put down his bags, reached inside and tapped the crewman on the back.

The man looked around and broke into a broad grin on seeing the face he instantly recognised. 'Stratton. What're you doin' 'ere?' he asked, immediately wondering why he was wearing a firesuit.

'How's it going, George? You well?'

'Not bad. Not bad. Chaz didn't mention we were picking you up.'

'Who're the drivers?' Stratton asked, trying to get a look at the faces inside the helmets worn by the two guys sitting with their backs to him.

'Charles and Steve,' George said, tapping both men on the shoulders and indicating the new visitor.

Charles, the pilot, smiled a hello on seeing Stratton and Steve gave him a wave. 'What are you doing here?' Charles shouted.

'Complicated story,' Stratton said.

'Got a comms problem,' the pilot continued. 'We were in the middle of a sitrep from ops when everything shut down.'

'Can you fix it?'

'It's not us. I'm certain of that.'

'Maybe it's this complex. They have a lot of security here. Haven't you spoken to ops at all?'

'Told them we arrived.'

'Did they mention our situation?'

Charles shook his head. Stratton got a little closer. 'There's been a security breach inside the complex. One of the team tripped a lockdown.'

The pilot's gaze moved to look beyond Stratton at the bunch of new faces outside, all wearing firesuits and carrying kitbags. 'Who are they?'

Stratton glanced over his shoulder to see Jason and the others. 'What I thought you'd already know by now. Chaz and the others are stuck in a security vault for the next twenty-four hours. They took something into the complex that tripped the lockdown. London has given us the okay to continue with the task. These guys are up to it. Luckily enough I happened to be here.'

The pilot looked from his own crew to the newcomers. It was definitely an odd situation. 'I need to confirm this with ops.'

'Of course,' Stratton agreed.

'But I don't have any comms,' he reminded Stratton.

Stratton needed to help him along. 'We can't jeopardise the task,' he shouted above the noise of the Chinook's engines. 'I suggest we get airborne, see if your comms clear, then confirm it with ops.'

The pilot agreed. 'Get them on board and I'll wind us up.'

Stratton waved Jason aboard and the team filed into the cabin.

The entire crew gave Rowena a double take and George looked approvingly at Stratton.

Stratton moved his lips close to the crewman's ear. 'Careful, George, you're just her type.'

George suspected that Stratton was joking but a part of him hoped it could be true. Smiling, he faced the team as the engine noise increased and he indicated for them to sit in the seats. 'Buckle up!' he shouted and mimicked buckling the seat belts.

They felt at their sides for the belts. George was on his knees and in front of Rowena like a shot. He slid his hands past her thighs in order to retrieve the straps from beneath the thin nylon seat. She watched him but George was too thick-skinned to read her disdain. He went as far as to buckle it up for her.

'I've never seen a strap tighten that small before,' he said, raising his eyebrows and grinning.

Her look froze even further.

George stood up and took a step back. He walked around the mini-sub where Stratton was checking the boxes for the equipment they contained. 'Does she always look like that?'

Stratton glanced over at her. 'Yes,' he said.

116

George took it to mean nothing but then was unsure. He moved away to prepare the chopper for lift-off.

Stratton lifted a silenced H&K sub-machine gun out of a box to inspect it. The helicopter shuddered as it ascended. He looked through a porthole at the shrinking old compound. They'd done it. Now how the hell were they going to get to the coast, never mind get into the water?

8

The sumptuous penthouse offices of Arcom Oil looked out on a partially constructed cityscape: a forest of cranes and beyond them a sea of sand. Inside the spacious suite furnished with an unsubtle blend of expensive Arabian and Western fixtures sat four men, two of them Arab, two Eastern European.

The two Russians were both large and overweight, one of them was bald. One of the Arabs wore traditional if rather expensive Bedouin garb. His skinny companion wore a fine-quality Western suit. All four men were sunk into deep, comfortable leather chairs. The Arabs had cups of tea on small tables in front of them. The Russians had large glasses partially filled with ice on a single table between them, on which also rested an ice bucket that had a bottle of vodka pressed into the snowy shavings.

Two beautiful and busty young women in revealing evening wear sat on high stools at a bar at the far end of the room. They were talking quietly and comparing their nails.

The bald Russian looked at the face of the gold and diamond-studded watch he wore. But he seemed neither bored nor restless despite the lack of conversation. He leaned his heavy frame forward, reached for the bottle of vodka and filled a glass. He said something quietly in his native tongue to his colleague who nodded. The bald Russian filled his colleague's glass. They took a stiff drink under blank but somehow still disapproving gazes from the two Arabs and sat back, exhaling deeply with the effort.

A door opened and a well-groomed Arab in a smart Western suit walked in. It was Mr Kaan, Arcom's crisis manager, carrying a phone, which he held in front of him as if it were a chalice filled with God's blood. The skinny Arab snapped his fingers several times in the direction of the girls. After several sharp 'tsks' from the man the girls stopped talking, slid off their chairs and sashayed out of the room. Kaan placed the phone in a cradle on a desk, adjusted a speaker box attached to it, and touched a button. 'You can go ahead,' he said loudly. 'Say what you have to say.'

'The people from MI16 are on their way to the Morpheus,' a man's voice crackled.

The men remained expressionless. One of the Russians whispered something to his associate. The two Arabs exchanged a whisper as if in retaliation. The bald Russian gestured with his hands to the Arab opposite in a manner that asked if he had anything to say to the phone. The man produced a polite smile and shook his head. The Russian indicated to Kaan that they were finished with him.

Kaan disconnected the phone from the speaker, walked out of the room and closed the door behind him.

The four men looked at each other, waiting for one of the others to begin. The suited Arab spoke. 'We have reached the point where we must decide if we are to see this through, or abort.'

'We have not yet reached the point of no return,' one of the Russians pointed out.

The skinny Arab had not made himself clear. 'If we proceed to the next stage there may be no turning back.'

'He's right,' the other Russian agreed.

They all thought about it for a moment.

'Shall we vote on it?' the fat Arab asked.

'We didn't vote on the last decision,' the Russian who still had his hair pointed out.

'That's because we all agreed beforehand and a vote wasn't needed,' the Arab reminded him.

'What do we do if one of us votes differently from the others?' the bald Russian asked.

'We have already agreed that if it is not unanimous we abort,' the man said, making an effort to hide his mild frustration.

The bald Russian looked unsure. 'I thought that was only to begin with.'

'No,' his associate said, correcting him. 'It stands for every phase. This needs to be agreed by all of us. It is crucial.'

'So if one person votes no the whole deal is off,' the bald Russian summarised. The skinny Arab struggled to come up with a polite smile.

'Those in favour of continuing, raise a hand,' the other Arab said. 'Does that suit everyone?'

They glanced at each other and eventually nodded.

The bald Russian raised his hand.

The skinny Arab did the same.

The fat Arab followed.

The Russian with hair raised his hand.

All four broke into smiles.

The skinny Arab pushed a buzzer on his coffee table and a moment later the door opened and Kaan returned. 'Would you bring in the satellite phone and prepare to make a connection to Mr Deacon.'

'Are we going through to the next phase?' Kaan asked.

'Yes, we are.'

Kaan beamed. 'Excellent. I'll bring the codes.' When Kaan returned he placed the phone and a file on the table and reconnected the speaker. After dialling a number he placed the phone in the cradle. A beep announced that the call was going through. Seconds later it was picked up. The initial sound was like that of a wind tunnel.

A man's voice broke through the interference. 'Yeah?' he shouted as if he was outside in a storm.

Deacon was on the topmost deck of the platform, trying to find protection from the wind and driving rain among some heavy machinery. 'I can't hear you. Give me a moment,' he shouted.

He hurried along the deck, the rain lashing at him and whipping his hood from his head. He reached the control room and pushed in through the door into the airlock, shutting the first door behind him and the weather with it. Deacon remained inside the lock. 'Hello,' he said into the phone.

'Thanatos?'

'Yeah. This is Thanatos.'

'An identity code, if you please.'

Deacon took a second to select one of the many identity codes he had memorised. 'Jupiter's moon.'

'Good. You are instructed to proceed,' Kaan's voice came over the phone. 'I suggest you get a pen and paper if you don't have one to hand. We don't want this next phase to go wrong due to a faulty memory.'

'Right,' Deacon said, feeling his pockets. He pushed open the inner door, went to a desk and found a pen. Jock sat reading a newspaper. The only other person present was a technician working at a bank of electronic machinery. 'Go ahead,' Deacon said, ripping a piece of paper from a printer.

Jock looked up to see the nerd staring at the hijack leader. He picked a steel nut that was doubling as a paperweight off the desk and tossed it like a frisbee. It struck the man on the side of the head with a loud *clunk*, making him yelp. He looked over at the Scot, who made a threatening gesture indicating that he'd punch him if he did not get back to minding his own business.

Deacon wrote down the number and read it back to make sure it was correct. When he and Kaan were satisfied he turned off the phone and put it in his pocket.

He went to his bag that rested on the floor beside the Scotsman, took from it a small metal money box and placed it on the desk. The words WARNING: DO NOT OPEN THIS BOX WITHOUT THE CORRECT CODE had been written in bold letters on a piece of tape fixed across the keypad. Deacon removed the tape and studied a digital display, which he activated by pushing a button. He read the number on the piece of paper again and hit the first key.

'What's that?' Jock asked.

'My next orders,' Deacon replied, keying in the next number.

'Inside the box?'

'Yeah.'

'Why?'

'Because they don't want me to see them before I have to.' He pressed another key.

'Bit silly, isn't it, leaving your orders in a little box?'

'Not if it's got a stick of plastic that'll detonate if anyone tries to open it without the right code.'

Jock nodded, impressed. 'Nice. Wouldn't it also be a good way to get rid of you if they've changed their mind about the task? They just give you the wrong code.'

Deacon hadn't thought of that and gave Jock a look.

''Scuse me,' Jock said, picking up his newspaper and walking into the security office to stand behind a cabinet from where he could just about see his boss.

Deacon's finger hovered over the final key. If that was true, how had they planned to kill the rest of the team? He decided that killing just him would not make sense and so he pushed the key. Nothing happened. He could not help giving a small sigh of relief as he turned the handle on top of the box and raised the lid.

A lump of plastic explosive had been fixed to the inside of the lid. The detonator was wired to a battery and a small circuit board was attached to the keypad. An envelope rested in the bottom of the box. Deacon removed it and put the box into his bag.

The envelope contained a single sheet of instructions and a photograph of a man was stapled to a corner of the paper. The man was Jordan Mackay.

As Deacon read the instructions his brow creased into a frown. Jock stepped back into the room. 'I take it we're moving right along, then.'

'It would seem so.' Deacon put the envelope into his pocket. 'I'm going down to the galley.'

Jock watched him go and glanced at the technician, who was looking at him. When he saw Jock's hostile expression, the nerd could not get back to work quickly enough.

Deacon entered the accommodation block and wiped the rain from his face as he made his way down the stairs. He strode purposefully along the corridor, through a door and along another corridor towards the galley. The Lebanese thug slouched outside the entrance to the food hall. He gave Deacon a glance but no more.

'What you doin' out 'ere?' Deacon asked.

'I think some of them have shit their pants,' the Arab said.

Deacon pushed open the galley door and scanned the room. It smelled like a foul toilet, and the workers were crammed into every inch of floor space. Some of them appeared to be sleeping. Banzi, the Pirate and the Bulgarian were sitting on the long serving counter, guns across their laps.

'Why aren't you letting these blokes do their business?' Deacon called out.

'We are,' Banzi answered. 'Some of 'em couldn't wait. The she-he is making food for them now.'

Deacon scanned the faces of the hostages. He saw the one he was looking for. The man was staring straight at him. Deacon checked the photograph to confirm the man's identity, realising he was one of the men they had filmed on deck. 'You,' he said, pointing. 'Get to your feet.'

Jordan struggled to comply.

Deacon indicated the entrance doors. He stepped aside to let Mackay pass into the corridor. When the doors had closed behind them he said, 'What's your name?'

'Don't you know?' Jordan said coldly.

'I know *a* name.'

'Jordan Mackay.' He turned his back to Deacon and offered his bound hands. Deacon took a knife from a sheath on his belt and cut the plastic bonds. The Lebanese wondered what was going on.

Jordan rubbed his chafed wrists. 'Give me your pistol.'

Deacon looked at the man questioningly.

'You were given instructions about me.'

'They said nothing about you being in charge.'

'You were told to give me anything I asked for.'

'They said nothing about a weapon.'

'A weapon comes under "anything I ask for",' Jordan said, holding out his hand. 'You all have weapons. You have them for a reason. Give me one.'

Deacon considered the brief instructions on the sheet of paper. As the man said, anything meant anything. He reached inside his coat, took his pistol from its holster and put it in Jordan's hand. Mackay removed the magazine, pulled back the top slide enough to see the round in the breech and replaced it.

'So. What's your part in this?' said Deacon, curious.

Jordan levelled the pistol at the Lebanese thug's face and pulled the trigger. The deafening report of the gun reverberated along the corridor as the bullet went through the Arab's head and into the wall behind, followed by a spout of blood. His body went limp and dropped to the floor.

Deacon stiffened at the sight and sound but kept cool, wondering immediately if he was going to be next.

Jordan stuck the pistol into his trouser belt. 'You can have his,' he said.

The doors slammed open and Banzi crouched in the opening with his M-15 at the ready, his gaze flicking between the two standing men and the Lebanese thug's corpse on the floor. 'Is all okay?' he asked, confused.

'He was a wanker anyway,' Deacon said.

'Have you laid the charges?' Jordan asked.

'Yep.'

'I want to take a look.'

Deacon took the Arab's coat off a hook and handed it to Jordan. 'Let's go,' he said. 'Would you mind tossin' 'im over the side?' he called out to the Japanese mercenary. 'Weigh 'im down a bit so's he doesn't float where someone might find 'im.'

Deacon led Jordan into the accommodation block. Partway along a corridor Jordan stepped into one of the doorways. 'I need a minute,' he said. Deacon paused at the end airlock. A moment later came the sound of a toilet flushing and Jordan stepped back into the corridor, buckling up his trouser belt.

Outside the weather hit them like a brutal ambush, heavy pelting rain and powerful winds that twisted between the sandwiched deck and through the grilles above and below. It felt like a typhoon was assaulting the platform. The men leaned into the storm as they moved across an exposed stretch of deck to a flight of rain-soaked metal stairs. They held tightly to the rails to maintain their balance.

Deacon stopped halfway down the steps and crouched to

indicate the huge platform leg nearest to them. 'There's the first,' he shouted above the wind. Jordan continued past him onto the next deck. The wind and rain lashed at him as he limped across the griddled flooring to the massive leg. He examined the linear charge, wrapped in black plastic sheeting, and followed it around its entire circumference.

Deacon joined him. 'Is it okay?'

'Looks it,' Jordan shouted back.

'The other charges,' Deacon said, pointing.

Jordan leaned over a rail to look down between the lower struts. He saw a charge wrapped around a heavy link that held fast one of the dozen anchor cables that kept the rig in position.

'There are five more like that. Can you manage a ladder?'

Jordan frowned at the implication and walked over to a ladder welded to the side of the leg. He grabbed hold of the cold wet rungs with his bare hands, swung his legs beneath him and began to descend.

Deacon grinned, amused by the man's effort to prove himself. He rubbed his hands together against the cold, took hold of a rung and followed.

Jordan reached the lower deck. Here there were fewer equipment blocks and machinery to check the wind and rain, and the gale funnelled between the spars ferociously. He inspected one of the charges and eyed the others spread around the perimeter of the deck. He looked back to see Deacon partway down the ladder. 'You have the detonating control?'

Deacon touched down onto the deck and removed a yellow box the size of a cigarette pack from his pocket. Jordan wanted to ask for it. But from what little he knew about Deacon he could sense that the man wouldn't give it up. The bosses hadn't been clear enough about who was in ultimate command. Splitting the leadership in this way was not very clever and could cause friction when final decisions had to be made. Jordan decided not to make his play just yet.

He took in the vast oil platform above, below and around them. 'You think they're serious enough to do this?'

'I get the feeling they don't bluff.' Deacon wondered what Mackay knew. 'Is this just about ransom money or is it something else?'

Jordan wondered in turn how much the other man knew, if anything. 'I've got my piece to do, just like you. Other than that I don't know.'

'You're the platform expert?' Deacon shouted.

'Not exactly.' Jordan looked out to sea. 'They'll come at night.'

'Who?' Deacon asked.

'Those whose job it is to take back the platform. They might come in force, one heavy assault, or send in a recce team first.'

'When?'

'Depends on the negotiations . . . Soon . . . Days.'

Deacon had an idea who – or, at least, what – Jordan was. 'You ex-SBS?' he asked.

Jordon nodded.

Deacon smirked. 'We'll be ready for 'em. I'm going to place booby traps on all the stairs and ladders coming from below.'

'They won't come the way you think. You won't see them until they show themselves. If you're still on board when they get here they'll kill you.'

Deacon's smile melted.

Jordan reached for a rung and pulled himself up the ladder. Deacon watched him climb, suddenly feeling less comfortable. He sensed that Jordan might be a problem. The man had the air of someone who thought he was in charge. Deacon would take the first opportunity to let him know who really was.

The Chinook cruised at several thousand feet above the English countryside, keeping the city of Sheffield on its left as it headed towards the coastline at Scarborough. Stratton had gone through every operational trunk and the team's personal boxes to gather the equipment that he felt he needed for the task. It had been more an exercise to keep himself busy than it had been based on any great confidence that he would actually use it.

The crewman came over to Stratton and tapped him on the shoulder, looking concerned. 'Charles is getting stressed about the lost comms,' he yelled above the noise of the rotors and engines. 'What's weird is that none of us have even been able to get a signal on our cellphones.'

'What does he want to do?' Stratton asked, placing a magazine into a semi-automatic pistol. It was drawing close to that critical moment.

'Do you think something back at MI16 damaged our comms?'

'Ask those guys,' Stratton said, indicating the scientists still in their seats.

George glanced at them. Jason was looking at the ceiling. Binning was watching him and Stratton. Jackson was tapping the screen of a pocket computer with a stylus. Smithy was literally twiddling his thumbs and Rowena had her head back and her eyes closed. 'Doesn't matter if they can't fix it. We're going to have to land somewhere we can contact ops.'

Stratton had been thinking all the time about a way round this obstacle and had been unable to come up with an even remotely acceptable option. The only solution was the extreme long shot of the pilot taking things into his own hands and pressing on with the task. But that would have required a sudden madness in Charlie.

'If there's been a change in plans we won't know about it,' George explained.

Stratton knew he had to make some kind of effort, futile though it looked. He made his way to the cockpit, stepped inside and tapped the pilot on the shoulder. Charles looked around at him.

'Ops'll know that you have lost comms. The procedure is to continue with the task.'

'I understand that. The plan calls for us to put down on a ship north of the Morpheus. But a serious storm has overtaken the operational area. We have enough fuel to get to the ship and land on it but not for a return to the mainland. If the ship has moved and we have to turn back for the coast, we could be in trouble.'

Stratton had hoped they were headed directly for a sea drop-off. 'Could you drop us off a couple of miles from the Morpheus and get back?'

'The rig's closer to land than the command ship. But those aren't my orders.'

'It's one of the contingencies, though, isn't it? To go direct to water drop?' Stratton was guessing but it was an option he would have put in the orders.

'I can't make that decision. And neither can you.'

Stratton knew he had hit a brick wall.

'If we don't have comms by the time we reach the coast, I'm landing,' Charlie added.

Stratton nodded and walked away. He sat beside Jason. 'The pilot's going to land if they still have no comms by the time we reach the coast.'

'What are our options?' Jason asked.

'If we have any, I can't think of one.'

Binning began to look agitated. 'If it comes down to it, could we threaten the pilot?'

'You want to threaten to shoot one of the crew?' Stratton asked sarcastically, wondering about the man's common sense.

Binning realised it was a stupid comment but it was a sign of his growing frustration.

The crewman stepped out of the cockpit and walked over to the group. 'Scarborough's coming up,' he said.

Stratton looked through the porthole behind his head at the coastline below. The sea stretched to the horizon.

'We're going to head north to Aberdeen,' George informed them. 'Charles will put down at the forward mounting base there.' He headed back to the cockpit.

The news only served to increase Binning's agitation. 'We're screwed if he does that.'

Stratton had to agree. He could see it all grinding to a halt if they landed in Aberdeen. 'You'd better turn the comms block off.'

Binning was on the verge of anger. 'Is that all you can come up with?'

Stratton flashed him a look, finding his response odd. 'Turn it off,' Stratton ordered, a warning in his tone.

Binning clenched his jaw and looked at Jason for help.

'Turn it off,' his boss said resignedly.

Binning was alone and had no alternatives. He opened the apparatus's plastic casing, reached inside and flicked a switch. Stratton got to his feet and went to the cockpit door, taking a pair of headphones from a hook. He put them on and the voices in the cockpit came to life.

The operations room commander sat in his high chair staring at the giant screen showing the North Sea covered in its various information markers, with Morpheus in the centre. On the east coast of England, close to the Scottish border, was a moving object circled in red, the window next to it giving its details. The circle turned to blue and began to flash.

'Whisky four-zero is back on line, sir,' one of the console operators called out, informing his boss of something that he had seen for himself.

The ops officer pushed a button on his panel. 'Whisky four-zero, this is zero Charlie.'

'Zero Charlie, Whisky four-zero.' The pilot's voice came over speakers that were mounted around the room.

The operations officer beckoned to one of the aides. 'Tell Nevins we've got comms with the SBS team,' he said.

'Haven't a clue about the cause of the blackout,' the pilot continued. 'Strangest bloody communications breakdown I've ever experienced. Everything went offline. Even our mobile phones. Diagnostics picked up absolutely nothing.'

The ops officer frowned. 'What's the likelihood of it happening again?'

'Since I don't know what caused it, I have no idea.'

The ops officer looked over at his communications specialist who could only reply with an apologetic shrug. The door opened and Nevins walked in, his stare switching immediately to the screen.

Jason joined Stratton at the cockpit door, unhooked another pair of headphones off the bulkhead and put them over his ears. 'You're fifty minutes behind schedule,' he heard the ops officer say to the pilot. 'How's your fuel?'

'Plenty to get to the RV. I was idle while at India one-six waiting for the team change which took more than half an hour.'

Jason and Stratton braced themselves for the reply.

The operations officer frowned on hearing the words, as though he had missed something. 'What do you mean, "team change"?'

'The new team, sir. After Chaz's bunch got stuck in the airlock. They took a while to get geared up.'

The ops officer looked around at Nevins whose confused expression reflected his own.

'I received a report of a shutdown at Sixteen but no mention of any personnel involved,' Nevins told the officer.

The ops officer was now completely confused. 'I don't know what the hell you're talking about,' he said into the microphone.

The pilots looked at each other and the crewman turned to look at Stratton.

'Tell me precisely who you have on board your helicopter,' the ops officer asked.

'John Stratton, SBS, and five members of MI16, one of them a woman.'

Jason moved the headphones' microphone to his mouth and found the transmit switch on the cable hanging from one of the earpieces. 'Hello. This is Jason Mansfield, head of MI16.'

The ops officer was stunned to hear the strange voice boom over the speakers, as was Nevins.

'I am accompanied by Phillip Binning, Avis Jackson, Harold Smith and Rowena Deboventurer,' Jason continued.

'By whose authority are you on board my helicopter?' the operations officer asked.

'The original team violated a security protocol and got themselves automatically locked in a security vault as a result. The task is within our capability and so I decided to take it on. Naturally, I would have contacted you immediately but the communications failure prevented that.' At this blatant lie he gave Stratton a child-like look but he was still working on sticking to the task, desperate as that was.

The ops officer removed the microphone from his lips. 'Can someone pinch me?' he said. 'I don't believe I'm having this conversation.'

Neither did anyone else in the room by the look of their expressions.

The officer returned the mike to his mouth. 'I sometimes feel I could do a better job as England's scrum-half but I have so far resisted the temptation to rush down onto the pitch and take over. I'll ask you once again,' he said, raising his voice. 'What the hell are you doing on my helicopter?'

Jason put his hand over the mike. 'I think he's upset.'

Stratton was ahead of the scientist. He knew what would happen next and he wasn't looking forward to it. Yet his concern for Jordan, his failure to come to the man's aid, overshadowed the fear of punishment. He'd failed his old friend.

Nevins piped up. 'You tell that pilot he's to put that bloody kite down and then I want those fools locked up until we can get to the bottom of this.'

The operations officer was about to relay the order when Nevins stopped him. 'Wait. Give me that. I'll tell him myself.'

As the ops officer handed Nevins the microphone neither of them saw the large doors that led into the operations room open and a man walk in. Nevins was about to speak when he felt a hand on his shoulder, while another clamped over the mike, preventing him from talking into it. Startled by the sudden intrusion he wheeled around to see Jervis, head of MI6 operations.

'What the devil?' Nevins demanded.

'Let them go,' Jervis said.

'What?' Nevins was stunned.

'I need you to let them go,' Jervis repeated. 'I have the minister's backing on this.'

Nevins could not wipe a look of utter confusion from his face. Everyone in the room had frozen: some kind of power play was happening before their eyes. They could only remain still and watch to see what developed.

'I'll discuss this with you in your office,' Jervis said. 'Not here.'

Nevins brought himself back under control. He was an experienced man in the business, and knew Jervis well enough. The man

was a canny high-stakes player and something extraordinary definitely had to be going on for him to intervene in such a manner at
this level of the operation. And if the PM had given his support
there was nothing more to say, for the moment at least. But he
was also aware of Jervis's manipulations and ambition to set up the
boffin inventors as medium-level operatives. It was well known
within the secret service's inner circles. If he'd chosen this moment
to make his move, it was a bold one indeed. If it went wrong,
Jervis was toast. Far too much was at stake all around and Nevins
knew he could not afford to make an error either. He handed the
microphone back to the operations officer and acknowledged
the master mongrel's new grip of the reins.

'Tell the pilot to continue with the contingency RV,' Jervis told
the operations officer.

'The target drop-off?' the ops officer asked. He knew it was
what Jervis meant but the situation was so remarkable that he had
to confirm it.

'That's correct. Stratton is to lead the next phase of the operation. MI16 is his team.'

The ops officer knew he had just witnessed a remarkable event,
one far beyond his level, but he quickly recovered. He pushed the
transmit button. 'Whisky four-zero, this is zero Charlie.'

'Whisky four-zero send,' the pilot's voice crackled over the
speakers.

'Continue with the task. Proceed to the target-drop RV.'

'Sorry, sir. Did you say proceed to the target-drop RV?'

'That's correct. Maintain normal communications schedule.'

'Roger that,' the pilot said, glancing at his co-pilot and shaking
his head as if he'd missed something.

Jason could not believe it. 'What happened?' he asked Stratton.
'They were about to order an abort.'

'Someone important changed his mind,' Stratton said, as confused
as anyone else.

Jason removed the headset, hung it on the hook and walked back through the cabin to the others. They had no idea what was happening and looked at him as if they were waiting to hear the bad news.

Stratton could not begin to think of an explanation. But whatever had happened back in the operations room, it seemed they were on their way. He would only believe it when they were in the water and beyond the point of no return.

He walked over as the others gathered close to Jason to listen to what he had to say. 'It looks like we're going in,' Mansfield said, smiling.

Binning could hardly contain his relief. Jackson nodded, with the thinnest of smiles. Smithy looked pale – his nervousness that had been bubbling below the surface became more evident as he squeezed his hands together tightly. Rowena gave nothing away.

'London has acknowledged that we're up to the task and has given us the go-ahead,' Jason continued. 'They clearly recognise our potential. I'll bet my bottom dollar we can thank Jervis for this. We're on our way.'

He held his fist out in the centre of the group. Binning was the first to grab it strongly. The others piled their hands on top.

'Now we have to make sure this is a damned success,' Jason said emphatically. He looked around at Stratton. 'I hope you now share London's confidence in us.'

Stratton couldn't understand the decision, nor could he have argued with it even if he'd wanted to. His personal motive had not changed. The decision's major impact for him was how it affected his original plan to ditch the team when he got to the Morpheus platform and then to go it alone. Now he would have to take them along. They would all have to board the platform. It would be easier than trying to go it alone, anyway. But nothing about the situation made him feel any better.

There was another consequence to the turn of events, of course. When the team had set off from MI16's HQ they had all been rebels. Now they were bona fide operatives. If Stratton continued with his part of the plan *he* would be the traitor.

9

The Chinook thundered out across the ocean, a couple of thousand feet above the growing North Sea swell. Outside, it had darkened significantly, with the dropping sun masked by thickening clouds. The aircraft began to buffet as the gusting winds took hold of it.

Stratton sat on one of the team boxes studying a chart. He glanced up as rain began to pound at the glass portholes. The storm would give the team good cover. But if it grew too powerful it would affect their ability actually to reach the target.

He had serious misgivings about the approach to the platform. And if he was concerned, why wasn't London? It was part of the reason he still could not fully accept that the operation had been allowed to proceed with the scientists. Surely Jervis knew these clowns were not up to a task. Granted it was only a surveillance job, and if carried out procedurally they should never come into contact with the enemy. But it was still high risk and, even though London was not averse to taking chances, they were not usually of this nature.

Stratton got to his feet and, keeping a hand against the bulk-head, made his way to the front of the cabin. The chopper was buffeting heavily, as much as he could ever remember having experienced – with a live pilot still in control of the sticks, that was. He put on the headphones and asked for the operations room to recalculate the tidal speed and direction from the drop-off point. Heavy storms such as this one – which was only going to get worse — had a habit of shifting such things. The fast currents in the North Sea moved in long sweeping curves. If the drop-off was not accurately calculated they could miss the platform despite the speed the sub could reach.

Five minutes later the drop-off latitude and longitude were relayed back to him. Stratton gathered the team to brief them. Jackson, as it turned out, was not only a helicopter and fixed-wing pilot. Mansfield had sent him on a mini-sub operator's training course in Norfolk, Virginia, at the beginning of the year. Stratton wondered how far the MI16 boss's ambitions extended.

Stratton explained how the team would manoeuvre in and out of the tight-fitting vessel and how they should conduct themselves while it was under the water. When the briefing was complete the team climbed into lightweight dry-bags, tightened harnesses and clipped on fins, masks and the small transfer air bottles they would need when they were not connected to the sub's breathing system. Binning strapped the surveillance device securely to his side and jumped up and down a few times to ensure it was solidly attached. He had clearly seen it done on some kind of military training film since it did not quite apply to a dive operation. At least he was keen.

Stratton allowed the team to carry pistols but insisted that he alone would have a sub-machine gun, a silenced H&K to go with his pistol and two stun grenades. He neglected to mention during the briefing his own private operation: the only points he covered were the planting of the surveillance device and the move to the rendezvous pick-up location. The way he questioned Jason on all details of that last phase of the operation ought to have suggested something to them. In truth, it was blatantly obvious that he wouldn't be able to get Jordan away from the oil platform on the submarine, assuming of course that he could rescue him at all. As far as he could see the only option he had was to secure one of the platform's lifeboats: a broad enough plan — if it could be called that – for him not to have to think of it any more. First he had to locate Jordan, then separate him from the hijackers. He couldn't do much planning for that. Every stage would be a process of discovery, assessment, action and follow-on. Another reason to put it to one side.

With everyone fully rigged Stratton put them through a dry drill on the submarine, covering signals between cockpit and cabin, switching between the sub's breathing system and individual air bottles, and climbing in and out of the vessel. He questioned them on the details of every phase of the operation, the sequence of events, who would be doing what and when. He finished by explaining emergency contingency plans for anyone failing to climb the platform or falling off it – if they found themselves alone and unattached in the water their best bet would be simply to flow with the tide away from the rig and when well out of range initiate the emergency strobe lights and the SARBE emergency radio beacon that they each carried. Even in a severe storm, as long as they remained afloat there was a high chance of rescue since a good portion of the navy and air force was concentrated in the area.

Stratton did not go into great detail about climbing the platform. That would depend on their fitness and their ability to manage a caving ladder while in a dry-bag and carrying some equipment. They couldn't practise that in the Chinook – it was going to have to be done on the job.

He introduced them to the air-powered grapnel launcher, explaining how he planned to use it and how it was stowed and retrieved from inside the sub. He then secured it in the mini-sub's cabin along with the rolls of caving ladders, lines and hooks. He concluded the briefing just in time. The crewman had left the cockpit and was making his way over to them, grabbing hold of whatever part of the craft he could as it yawed from one side to the other. 'We'll be at the drop point in five minutes!' he shouted.

Stratton acknowledged him and faced the others. 'Does anyone have any questions about any phase of the mission?'

'How long do we give you?' Jason asked. 'I refer to your private mission.'

'Don't forget that's what got you this far,' Stratton replied, a little testily.

'And I appreciate it,' Jason said. 'But the question remains.'

'Soon as you've placed the device get on your way.'

'How are you going to get away with Mackay?' Jason said.

'Don't worry about that. You have your task, you have a sound plan to carry it out and you have your exfiltration options. Concentrate on them.'

The white lights went off in the cabin, to be replaced by dim red ones that barely illuminated the cramped space. The whine of an electric motor filled the air and the rear ramp began to open. A blast of wind and rain came in through the widening opening, over the top and sides of the ramp as if it was impatient to explore inside. The noise of the rotors increased, their rhythmic beating coming in on the wind. When they looked out it was pure black, impossible to see where the sky ended and the ocean began. A sheet of lightning cut through the dark and for a few seconds they saw what lay outside. The helicopter pushed on into the broiling storm. In the cockpit the faces of both pilots glowed green beneath the night-vision goggles they wore.

With the ramp locked open at a steep angle towards the water, the helicopter descended. Now they could see the sea. Every toppling white wave of it. Stratton put in earphones, tucked the loose cable behind his throat microphone and pulled on his neoprene hood to help keep it all in place. He checked that the transfer breather bottle was secure and tested his dry-suit's inflation. He looped the mouthpiece strap of his face mask over his head and tested the equipment secured to his body, including the SMG that fitted across his waist.

The rest of the team took this as their cue and pulled on their hoods, nervousness rippling between them as the seconds passed. Stratton had done this many times before. The others had never even imagined this level of adventure. They stood inside a yawing metal crate held in the air by a couple of rotors on the ends of struggling petrol-driven turbines. About to jump into the void. Into a small submarine. Into a perfect North Sea storm.

Stratton had seen their fear a thousand times before in the eyes of young soldiers going into battle for the first time. He had been assessing them from the moment they all truly knew the task would happen. He had studied their eyes as he briefed them. He knew that none of them could really comprehend the threat of confronting the armed hijackers. They wouldn't be able to get beyond the dangers of the journey to the platform and the subsequent climb. He couldn't blame them: this type of manoeuvre was one of the most perilous tasks the SBS undertook, even without the threat at the other end of an enemy with lethal intent. He suspected that despite agreeing to come on the jolly old operation they were now filled with doubt as to whether they could actually pull it off.

Jason hid his fears better than the others and would probably be the first to overcome them. He had to be frightened in some way. He wouldn't be normal otherwise. But his eyes gave nothing away, except for an occasional look at Stratton as though to assess the operative's nerve. No doubt the man knew that his ambitious plans for MI16's operational future hung in the balance.

Binning looked nervous but he seemed to be driven by something, as if his life depended on getting onto the platform. Stratton suspected an element of competion with his boss. And perhaps for more than just his job, judging by the way he eyed Rowena.

Smithy was the main concern. He seemed on the verge of snapping, no longer able to make a decision on his own, watching to see what the others were doing before he took the step himself.

He could become a liability – if he didn't back out at the last minute. Stratton wondered what effect it would have on the team's morale if he ordered the man to stand down. Jason must surely be aware of the problem. The operative decided not to step in: too many variables to worry about.

Jackson appeared to be in control of his nerves, cool enough. Stratton had the distinct feeling that the man had some previous military experience. He'd let slip a fair amount of jargon, especially when he'd been talking to the crewman, and he knew his way around the equipment. With a faulty torch from the equipment box, for instance, he'd immediately unscrewed the base, removed the first battery, reversed it and replaced the base – and it had worked. A classic soldier's trick to prevent a torch from accidentally coming on.

Rowena was the interesting one. She was nervous but didn't allow it to get in her way. She didn't seem to share Jason's enthusiasm or even agree with MI16's taking the task on. Yet she'd stayed with the team. Stratton doubted that she was there just to be alongside her lover. She was far too mature for that. He couldn't see what was keeping her on track. Stratton assumed the affair was a secret between them. They hardly acknowledged each other when there was anyone about. If he hadn't seen them embrace so passionately he wouldn't have guessed it. He wondered if Binning knew. If not, that helped to explain his sometimes overt interest in her.

'Stratton!' a voice shouted from the back of the cabin. George gave the team leader the thumbs-up and followed this gesture by raising one finger. They had a minute before the release.

Stratton stood at the top of the ramp and looked down at the rolling black water. The peaks were rising to foaming white plumes and the swell was enormous, fifty to sixty feet. In the right gear you could float on the surface, rising and falling from peak to trough. With breathing apparatus you could slip beneath the surface

142

and the storm would disappear. All well and good. The dangers came when a person in such a heavy sea came into contact with a rigid mass, such as a quayside, a ship, a submarine, or an oil platform. Bodies had a tendency to get slammed against surfaces. Like an egg dropping onto a stone floor. Nothing about the next few hours was going to be easy.

Stratton pulled on his fins and tightened the straps. 'Close up,' he shouted, tightening the thin neoprene gloves around his fingers.

The team shuffled forward in their fins.

'Stratton,' George shouted, holding one side of his headset tight against his ear. 'You have to go! Charlie's having trouble holding it. Says we'll all bloody join you if we don't dump this lot and get out of here.'

Stratton gave him a firm thumbs-up and the crewman ducked down to remove the blocks that held the sub in position on rollers fixed to the cabin deck. He gave the craft a stiff shove and the big black tube, its top at shoulder height, moved towards the rear opening like some kind of organ of death. When the nose reached the edge of the cabin George gave it another push and it dipped down onto the ramp. Stratton kept tight to the bulkhead to avoid the large flotation pack fixed to the sub's side. It tipped ungracefully off the end and dropped nose down towards the roiling water.

When it hit, Stratton stepped to the very edge of the ramp, the others following close behind. Everything that Stratton had told them about the next phase went through their minds. The seconds crammed together. The point of no return had arrived.

As the sub stabilised, the two inflation bags attached to either side of the body aiding its buoyancy, Stratton placed one fin on top of the other, leaned forward and dropped into the blackness. It seemed to take longer to fall than it should have. When he struck the water he disappeared beneath the surface. The others hesitated until he came back up.

Binning was first to follow, holding the plastic box tightly, closely followed by Jason. Rowena came next, with Jackson beside her. Smithy paused on the edge and looked as if he might refuse. Had George not given him a shove he might well have done. The skinny scientist let out a cry as he fell, arms and legs spinning like bicycle wheels, out of control.

Stratton pushed off hard with his fins to grab the side of the mini-sub. He had to release the flotation bags. Taking hold of the cable coupling, he yanked down on it. The bags drifted, the swell and the wind taking them into the darkness. The vessel dropped into a trough and Stratton pulled himself along it to the cockpit. The sub rose up the steep wall of the next wave, which broke over it, almost turning it over. Stratton was thrown into the cockpit. He struggled in the confined space to manoeuvre himself into the seat, hating how cramped the damned boats always felt when he was wearing operational equipment.

He couldn't afford to search for the others yet. The water sloshed around his chin and he ripped off the fins, jamming them in the side of the seat. He turned on the instrument panel, plugged his breathing apparatus into the sub's air outlet and put the mouthpiece in his mouth. He breathed in the oxygen, his mouth under the water more than not. The vessel leancd heavily and slid down into the next trough. If he didn't bring the nose around into the waves it would tip over. Very inconvenient. He flipped the power switch and gave the propeller full throttle, twisting the rudder hard over.

The sub responded well, then seemed to stall. Stratton could feel the powerful electric motor working, yet the nose didn't want to come around. The vessel slammed into the bottom of another deep seawater trench. As it came up the other side the nose suddenly turned as if it had been nudged by a greater power. The sub went almost vertically up the wall of water and gouged into the dark mass of the peak. It levelled out for a moment before tipping over to nose down into the next trough. He had it under a semblance of control.

Stratton looked out of the cockpit for any sign of the others. Two of them were hanging on to the passenger cabin and struggling to get inside. He twisted in his seat to look through the grille behind his head and saw movement. Something grabbed at his arm and a heavy limb struck him as Jackson scrambled unceremoniously in through the other side of the cockpit. The man's size didn't help. The tumbling rodeo-bull sub yawed at his arms as it lifted him and then dragged him under. No amount of training could have prepared him. Certainly not the bathlike waters of Puerto Rico where the US SEALs often did their initial mini-sub training. Jackson fell into the seat but then lost his fins after a wave smashed in through Stratton's side of the cockpit and ripped them from his fingers. He almost drowned when a brute of a wave filled the cockpit before he'd found the end of his breathing tube. Stratton realised that the man was in trouble. He grabbed hold of Jackson's mouthpiece, using the strap around his neck, found the end of the tube and plugged it into the panel outlet. Jackson put the mouthpiece between his teeth and coughed and spluttered as he fought to inhale. He'd nearly had it.

Stratton looked back outside the vessel to see that the bodies had gone. He hoped that meant they were all inside. He glanced up to see the rear of the Chinook, its ramp still open, a figure leaning out of the red glow. Stratton extended a thumb towards George, a gesture which looked to him as if it was returned. The huge chopper thudded away into the darkness and the sound of its rotors, a constant background noise for the past few hours, was replaced by the roar of the wind, the thrashing of the sea and the sizzle of the rain coming down in heavy sheets. Another streak of lightning lit up the sky and the rolling thunder that followed it seemed to surround them.

A hand came through the grille near Stratton's face, its thumb in the air. It was Jason indicating that everyone was on board and connected to the sub's air supply. Stratton blew the ballasts and the submarine began to sink.

The roller-coaster effect quickly reduced to nothing as the boat dropped beneath the water and away from the influence of the heavy swell. Stratton increased the throttle and the sub eased ahead under the power of its propellers.

Stratton plugged in a cable connected to his throat microphone and earplugs and looked over at Jackson who appeared to have gathered himself. He nudged the man and offered him a thumbs-up. Jackson returned the gesture, accompanied by a nod to confirm that he was okay. Stratton indicated his own mouth and mimicked talking with his fingers. Jackson searched for the ends of his throat-mike cables and plugged them into the sockets.

'Can you hear me?' Stratton asked, his voice sounding slightly strange.

'That's fine,' Jackson said.

'I can hear you both,' another voice interrupted. It was Jason in the rear cabin.

'Everything okay?' Stratton asked.

'Smithy's lost a fin. We almost lost him. Otherwise all is well.'

'Okay. Sit back and relax. The real ordeal is coming up.' Stratton checked the positioning device, a sophisticated gyroscopic motion sensor that monitored and recorded the sub's every move in every direction, constantly recalculating its position from memory. This negated the need for the sub to break the surface to get a GPS fix. He turned on the Doppler sonar, a sonic equivalent of radar, and a screen on the panel lit up, illuminating the faces of the sub's occupants in a green-blue hue. The Doppler provided a three-dimensional image of the sub's surroundings at various ranges. Stratton carried out a full scan as per operational procedure. As expected there was only one blip on the screen.

'How far from the Morpheus?' Jackson asked.

'Just over three miles. We can't get too close to the rig in these conditions or we'll hit the anchor cables. We'll drop out of the sub a klick uptide and float in. Jackson will reposition downtide. He'll wait there until he gets your signal to break surface. He should be able to hold position until first light but you will be heading towards him long before that.'

'Understood,' Jason said.

Stratton pulled up the platform's preprogrammed position and the navigation system gave the direction in the form of an arrow at two o'clock to their heading.

'It's all yours,' Stratton told Jackson.

Jackson took over the controls. He struggled at first to maintain the correct depth but it was not long before he had the hang of it.

Stratton unplugged one of the cables. 'What's it like being back in the mob?' he said.

Jackson glanced at him, suspecting that he was talking to him yet concerned at the same time. He looked down to see that the internal communications cable was unplugged and the conversation was purely between the two of them.

'My guess is air force,' said Stratton.

'How did you know?'

'A number of clues.'

'I stayed in college until I got my master's but I always wanted to be a fighter pilot. Couldn't get it out of my system. So I joined up for a few years. It was pretty fantastic – everything I'd wanted as a kid. But I couldn't help handing in design suggestions for weapons-guidance systems. One day I got a call from an office in London. The rest is history.'

'I know the feeling,' Stratton said.

'This has the new periscope system, doesn't it?'

'Yes, but it's no good in these waters. We don't need it, anyway.' Stratton checked the navigation system and the distance to the Morpheus. 'This tide is moving.' He plugged Jason's voice cable back in. 'You ready back there?'

'We're ready.'

'In one minute Jackson's going to stop the props. We'll drift with the tide and be relatively stopped. We'll have two minutes to clear the sub before Jackson will have to start the props again and get out of the track or hit the rig. I'm going to join you at the door. Hand me the grapnel launcher. You take the ladders and snag line. We'll all go straight to the surface. You happy with that, Jason?'

'Yes.'

'Jackson?'

'Yes.'

'The signal to surface on completion of the task?'

'Two thunder bombs.'

Stratton checked the navigation system again. 'Okay. Put your tail to the platform and kill the speed.'

Jackson manoeuvred the vessel while Stratton pulled on his fins, disconnected the communications cable, removed his breathing apparatus and replaced it with the breather attached to the bottle strapped to his side. He eased out of the cockpit, a far less complicated exercise than climbing in, and moved along the casing to the cabin opening. The four scientists crammed inside the dark chamber looked at him. He indicated for them to exchange their breathing systems. They felt for the portable breathing teats.

Smithy had spent every second since leaving the helicopter in a state of abject fear. The jump had been bad enough but since the scramble into the sub all he'd been able to think about in the cramped dark cabin was Stratton's comment about the climb up the platform.

When he received the signal to change from breathing off the submarine to his own air bottle he made one of the classic mistakes when it came to the procedure. He removed the sub's breathing mouthpiece from his lips, let go of it and felt around for his own portable breathing set. When he did not find it immediately he tried to find the mini-sub mouthpiece again. He failed. Panic quickly set in.

He became hysterical in his efforts to find either mouthpiece. He didn't think to find the bottle attached to his body and follow the tube from the end of it to the other end and the mouthpiece. He would soon have to take another breath, which would be all water, and he would die in that dark, cold and claustrophobic container.

When Stratton saw the stream of bubbles from the released mouthpiece and Smithy grabbing frantically at anything he knew immediately what was happening. The danger was not just to Smithy himself. His actions placed the lives of the others at risk. A drowning person had the strength of ten in their final acts of desperation and was more than capable of taking others with them. A grabbing hand would rip at anything – such as other people's breathing tubes.

Stratton did the only thing he could. He reached inside the cabin, grabbed hold of the frenzied diver by his harness and, planting his feet against the outside casing, ripped the man out of the sub and released him into the ocean. Smithy continued to kick and panic, the water's fluorescence lighting up around his beating limbs. He went into the blackness. Stratton had no idea whether he had gone up or down. But a second afterwards it no longer mattered. Not then, at least. It was done and they had their own lives to look after.

The incident had cost precious time that Jackson needed to avoid running into the rig. Stratton grabbed the grapnel launcher and beckoned the others to hurry. They were swift in their response and all three of them were soon out of the sub. As the propellers burst back into life the team headed towards the surface and the sub moved away into the gloom, the sound of its electric motor disappearing with it.

Stratton broke through to the surface first, the others a few seconds behind him. All of them stayed breathing from their air bottles, which would last another half-dozen minutes. The enormous rig stood several hundred yards away, lit up like the proverbial Christmas tree. A giant factory on legs, high above the storm waves. The sight of one of these towering structures never ceased to impress Stratton.

The others too looked in awe at the monstrous construction. They were unprepared for the sight of it so high above them in the water, in the dark. For a brief moment they forgot everything as they took in the suspended city. It looked almost alien to Jason, as if they were floating in a vast emptiness between planets and the platform was a twinkling space station.

Stratton suddenly thought of Smithy and as he rose up to the crest of the next wave he turned around in search of him. Rowena appeared to be doing the same. Neither of them could see the scientist and they forcibly removed him from their thoughts. There was too much to do to keep themselves alive.

Stratton removed his mouthpiece and slung the strap of the grapnel launcher over his head. He finned hard to keep his chin above the water. 'Where's the snag line?' he shouted.

Jason removed his mouthpiece and held up the thin, neatly coiled nylon cord that had a collection of karabiners attached to it.

Stratton took the line and hooked one of the karabiners to Jason's harness. He held another, connected by a metre-long line to Jason's, and looked for Binning who was drifting away from the group, staring up at the oil platform as if mesmerised by it.

'Binning!' Stratton shouted.

The man came out of his reverie, took out his mouthpiece and finned hard to rejoin them.

Stratton attached the karabiner to his harness. 'You two swim that way. Stretch the line tight between us. Move it.'

Jason detected anxiousness in the operative's voice but a glance at the rig revealed why. They were closing on it with surprising speed. It was getting bigger by the second. The four of them dropped down the side of a steep trough as if sliding down the side of a hill.

Jason and Binning began to fin as hard as they could away from the others.

Stratton unceremoniously grabbed Rowena, snapped the remaining karabiners to her harness and his own and swam away on his back, yanking her along. Her head went under for a moment and she surfaced coughing and spluttering. She fought to control her reaction to the swallowed water and finned hard to keep up with Stratton. The thought of being a liability to the SBS man horrified her almost as much as the possibility of drowning did.

The pairs quickly moved apart as they closed on the Morpheus's four huge black-steel piles.

Stratton singled out the leg he wanted to snag, gauging their approach. That was the tricky part, or the latest in a series of them. As the powerful tide pulled them towards the leg it became obvious to them all that if they got it wrong and missed, or even bounced off and were unable to get a pair either side, then they would sail on into the black ocean beyond. They would fail.

The current took the team in a wide curve rather than a straight line. Stratton calculated that they were too far to one side. 'Fin!' he shouted and Rowena responded. They lay on their backs and climbed the side of another huge swell and finned as hard as they could. The line went tight as the pair went over the peak. Stratton followed it to where it disappeared into the next wall of water. He hoped that Jason and Binning had made the same calculation. Suddenly the line went slack, indicating that they had. 'More!' shouted Stratton and they gave it another hard effort. They stopped to reassess their track and Rowena spat out salt water, her face cold but her body warm inside the rubber suit.

They were back on target and as they reached the peak of a swell Stratton took a second to study the levels of the platform still a couple of hundred metres away. He could see a haze of lights and not much else. If there were people outside, he couldn't see them. Yet he had the same advantage. Even an alert enemy couldn't see him. For now.

He had another advantage: the hijackers had no idea when they were coming. The enemy could watch the water constantly for any sign of a swimmer but it would be difficult to spot one. With such a large area to observe, at night in particular, it would be almost impossible to find a black-suited target in the rolling water. Night-vision goggles would reveal little unless they were trained directly on the swimmer. The same went for a thermal imager – the team's cold faces gave off hardly any heat and the rubber dry-suits masked their body warmth. A watcher on the exposed lower levels would struggle to make them out in these conditions.

But they needed to be lucky. If the watcher was there and did somehow see them he could pick them off with relative ease from one of the lower spider decks if he had a rifle.

The legs of the Morpheus loomed closer. They'd gone off track again: another adjustment was required, this time in the other direction. Together they swam towards Jason and Binning who were out of sight beyond the next peak. The line went taut again, indicating that the two men had made the same assessment.

The massive legs became dark pillars astride a vast blacked-out cave, the structure no longer distant enough to be encompassed in a single gaze. The ceiling lights in the lower decks shone so brightly down onto the water that it seemed impossible to the divers that they could not be easily seen. Stratton had thought the same the first time he'd made such an approach. But after reversing position to watch another team close in on a well-lit area he knew how difficult it was to see a blackened body unless the watcher knew precisely where to look.

They rose and fell on the rolling sea, a good fifty metres apart and rarely visible to each other, the line connecting them see-sawing as one hit a peak and the other a trough.

It grew suddenly darker as they moved into the shadow of the platform and past the perimeter of lights, heading directly beneath the overhanging balconies of the decks, the leg expanding visibly as they got closer. Rowena and Stratton passed close to another leg that was coated all the way round with a thick layer of barnacles clustered at the waterline. The waves struck the vast supports and the booming noises that they made rebounded around the platform cave.

The leg diameter was the length of a bus. Stratton's gaze darted between it and the line. Jason and Binning became visible briefly on the top of a swell and Stratton knew they would hit it perfectly.

The troughs exposed the gnarled barnacles that Stratton knew from experience were razor sharp. 'Watch out for the barnacles!' he shouted to Rowena. It was just another problem to add to the load she already had.

They rose up onto a peak as they came alongside the curved wall of steel. The wave slammed into the upright, the frothy water reaching up towards the first cross-beams. Stratton was drawn into the leg and stuck out his feet to fend it off. Solid. And sharp. The barnacles scratched his fins as he went by.

Jason and Binning went down the other side and the line wrapped around the leg. The pairs moved closer together as they slid down into another trough. The line suddenly went taut and yanked them to a brutal halt.

It was like being dragged along by a boat now. The sudden change pulled them lower in the water and it was much harder to keep breathing air. When they were at the peak of the wave they were almost dragged under and when at the trough the force was trying to yank them higher. They'd hit the leg in the middle of the line so they were held almost the same distance – its width – from it. They could hardly see anything directly beneath the platform, only a few rays of light finding their way between the girders.

Stratton lay on his back, holding on to the line. He searched the nearest girders for signs of life. The wind and rain whipped through the structure in gusts and squalls, beating tirelessly against the metal. If there was someone hiding in the darkness above they would be invisible but they would also have to be holding on tight or lashed to a span. And if they were, they could not stay there for long. Stratton felt confident that the team was not being observed.

He pulled the grapnel launcher from around his neck, took hold of the stock and trigger grip and selected the ideal spar. The air-powered device had been primed since before they'd left the Chinook and Stratton removed the bungee that held the grapnel in place, checked that the line was free to uncoil and then removed the safety catch. He put the butt against his shoulder and raised the grapnel end skyward. The heavy sea made it difficult to maintain position long enough to get off an accurate shot.

'Hold me!' he shouted.

Rowena pulled herself to him and grabbed him from behind, her hands gripping his harness, her legs finning as hard as she could. Her head went under the water and she spluttered when she surfaced but maintained her grip. She would not be able to do it for long since the difficult position kept her head under the water more than above it. Well aware of her situation, Stratton quickly aimed once again. The angle was crucial. Too high and the wind might blow it back once it had reached its full length of cable. Too low and he risked hitting the span itself or having the grapnel fly beneath it.

He felt Rowena go under but waited until they rose to the top of a wave, reducing the distance to the span by a third. As she surfaced he fired. The butt of the launcher punched into his shoulder and they both went under the water. When they surfaced at the bottom of a trough, Rowena almost choking, they could see the all-important double cable lying over the span, the ends still attached to the launcher. The grapnel had got over the spar.

Stratton let go of the gun, kept hold of the lines and pulled on them as quickly as he could. The lightweight tungsten grapnel came out of the water up towards the span and one of the claws snagged hold of a corner. He gave it a firm jerk to ensure that it was secure. 'Hand me your caving ladder,' he said.

Rowena unhooked the rolled alloy ladder from her harness and handed it to him. Stratton attached the karabiner on the end of the ladder to the end of one of the lines and pulled down on the other. The line passed through a one-way device on the grapnel and the ladder rose out of the water towards the span.

Jason and Binning watched somewhat helplessly as they rose and fell on the swell. A huge wave slammed against the leg sending water cascading over them, the boom that it made sounding like thunder. It jolted the line powerfully and as Jason traced the cable back to the leg the dropping swell exposed it. To his horror he saw that it was fraying. 'Stratton!' he called. 'The line!'

Stratton recognised the danger. He'd seen it before, a bad combination of extremely heavy seas and barnacles. They had to hurry. He released the line and it sank immediately with the weight of the launcher on the end of it. The lone caving ladder hanging from the spar was now their only way out of the water. Its end dangled in the water several metres away. It was across the tide, a high-risk quick burst away to bridge the gap. If he missed it he would float out to sea.

Stratton unhooked the karabiner that held him to the snag line, waited for the next trough and finned hard towards the ladder. As he came off the line Rowena got dragged closer to the leg by the greater weight of Jason and Binning.

Stratton caught hold of the ladder. 'Binning,' he called out immediately as he ripped his fins off and let them go. 'You. Now. To the ladder. Let's go.'

Binning did not hesitate. He unhooked himself and made a supreme effort to reach Stratton, which he did more easily than he had expected to. Stratton grabbed him at the same time with a free hand.

'I've got it,' Binning spluttered.

'If you can't carry your gear, hook it to the bottom rung of the ladder. We'll haul it up later.'

Binning shook his head. 'I'll be fine.'

The climb. Not a simple affair in calm conditions. In a storm a bad dream. Requiring a combination of iron strength and real skill. In a heavy swell the trick was knowing when to begin.

'Dump your fins,' Stratton said. 'Wait until we're at the peak, then climb as fast as you can.'

'The line's going to break,' Jason called out.

'Move your arse!' Stratton urged Binning.

As they rose up the next swell Binning unstrapped his fins, frantically wiggling them free, and at the same time struggled to grip the ladder. They went up as if they were on an escalator.

'Grab high as you can! Now!' Stratton shouted.

The wave peaked and Binning reached for the highest rung he could. When the water dropped he dangled like a fish on a hook, his hands bearing the weight of his body, suit and equipment. He fought to get a foot on a lower rung to take some of the strain from his fingers.

Some forty feet below him now, Stratton watched Binning cycling in the air. 'Climb, Binning! Climb!'

If Binning did not gain a few feet before the top of the next wave arrived it would punch him off. He climbed for all he was worth. The peak struck his legs hard but he hung on.

'Go!' Stratton urged.

Binning focused his strength and as he closed on the span

Stratton turned his attention to the others. 'Disconnect together as I start my climb!' he called out.

'You ready?' Jason shouted to Rowena.

'Yes!' she shouted.

The fraying line, however, was a second ahead of them and as Jason unclipped his karabiner the line snapped and both of them shot away from the leg.

Stratton was about to start his climb when he saw that Rowena wasn't going to make it to the ladder. He slid down as the trough dropped away, grabbed hold of a lower rung and lunged in the direction of her track. Jason made the ladder and grabbed a firm hold on it that did not help matters. Rowena finned towards Stratton as hard as she could but as they stretched out their arms towards each other their fingers barely touched. She passed him by, staring at him, finning madly even though they knew it was hopeless.

The line attached to Rowena suddenly went taut. She was yanked to a stop as Stratton lurched towards her, twisting the line that he had managed to grab with his free arm while holding on to the ladder with the other. Jason made a grab for the line and together they began to win the battle of hauling her in.

'Swim!' Stratton shouted as a heavy swell suddenly put her above them.

Binning reached the top of the ladder and hauled himself over the span in time to see the drama below.

Rowena grabbed Stratton's arm and pulled herself along it to his harness where Jason helped to hold her.

'Climb!' Stratton ordered him. 'It won't hold three of us for long!'

Jason ripped off his fins and as they went up the wall of water he grabbed the highest rung that he could reach. The swell moved on and when his foot found a rung too he climbed as quickly as he could.

'Go!' Stratton said urgently to Rowena before Jason had reached the top.

She gritted her teeth, then took a deep breath before ducking below the water to remove her fins. Stratton kept hold of her as they rose up the next wave and at its peak she surfaced, grabbed a rung of the twisting ladder and began to climb. She was strong and nimble, which Stratton was thankful for. He hung on for dear life as the water fell away beneath him. With the next swell, he followed behind her to the top.

Binning and Jason helped them onto the wide spar and when they were all secure the four of them remained seated for a moment to thank whatever gods might have helped to get them through the last hour.

Rowena looked across at Stratton, her breathing laboured. 'Thanks,' she said. It seemed difficult for her to say it.

He ignored her. There was no need for gratitude. It was what team members did for each other.

'This might be an appropriate time to spare a thought for Smithy,' Jason said.

'I suggest you stay focused on your own lives,' Stratton advised. 'You may yet join your colleague.'

The platform shuddered as the waves crashed relentlessly against the legs. Stratton eyed the upper structure that was a web of criss-crossing steel spars. Light filtered through grilles in the decking, creating shadows and dark spaces.

'Where do you need to place your device?' Stratton asked.

'The higher the better,' Binning replied. 'Especially in this weather.' He got to his feet and scanned the complex of black steel above as if looking for the ideal spot. 'I see why they call them spider decks.'

'How do we get up there?' Jason asked.

Stratton indicated the nearest leg. 'From here on we'll have to use the rungs. Not the best option but we don't have the kit for anything else. I'll lead. Beware of booby traps. Keep an eye out for taut wire or fishing nylon. If in doubt, don't touch it. Let me know.'

Stratton got to his feet and removed the bungee that secured the silenced SMG to his waist. He gave it a brief check and left it to hang from the strap across his back. He felt for the pistol in its holster at his thigh. Satisfied, he made his way across the spar to one of the vast legs and the rungs that led up into the gloom.

'Whenever you're ready,' he said, looking back at them.

Binning was right behind him.

10

Deacon sat in the control room in front of the explosive-tripped box that had contained Jordan's letter of reference. The challenge to Deacon's leadership had been an upset, despite his best efforts to reason a way through it. He knew what was behind it. It wasn't so much that he had been challenged but by whom. A former SBS twat. Just because this happened to be an oil platform on the ocean, did that make him more qualified to run the operation than Deacon? Typical of the kind of decision civilians made. Just because Mackay knew more about how the SBS operated, that qualified him to be in charge, did it? Only a military specialist would know that the terrain made no difference. A specialist was a specialist on land or sea. The only difference was a little technique when it came to certain environments. The CEO of an envelope company doesn't need to know all there is to know about envelopes in order to run it. By rights Jordan should have been hired simply as an adviser to Deacon.

He felt like calling the emergency number on his sat phone and insisting on talking to someone in charge about it. They needed to be told that you don't put an SBS bloke in charge of an SAS bloke. That sort of thing might go on these days but it hadn't in his day, or at least not to him.

Deacon picked up the sat phone to check for the number when the inner door opened and Jordan walked in, his coat and leggings soaked and dripping water. Deacon put the phone down with a frown. He put the box back in his bag.

Jordan shuffled past the technician monitoring the control panels and hung his coat on a hook. He went over to the makings corner, put a tea bag in a mug, filled it with water from the permanent heater, added a couple of spoons of sugar and powdered milk and stirred it.

He sat down at a desk, dumped the tea bag and took a sip of the hot, sweet liquid. It felt good as he warmed his hands around the mug. Jordan contemplated his situation. It had become something of a habit over the last few months, and more so since he'd taken on this task. The road to the Morpheus had been a strange one. He'd had bouts of guilt about his decisions but had managed to beat them off. He could do it easily enough. Whatever he could get out of his country, his government, he would. And he felt justified. They owed it to him, those wankers in the Ministry of Defence. His umpteen requests to stay in the SBS in any role other than as a storeman? Ignored. It hadn't been much to ask. They'd done it for others in the past. He was an invalid but not useless. It was their decision to ignore that, and so he would prove it. Give the nobs a demonstration. If they wouldn't let him stay on the team, then he would be against them. It sounded extreme at times but he had to do it to believe in himself.

The only problem that he had with this operation was the potential threat to the SBS lads themselves. They weren't to blame for anything that the MoD had done to him. If it had been up to them, Jordan would have been able to stay in the service. He was reasonably confident he could work it so that none of them got hurt. As long as he could control Deacon and his apes. It had been one of his bargaining chips with the organisers. To his surprise they had accepted this reasoning without debate. They didn't want anyone to get hurt either. This was a pure money-making task and had been planned in such a meticulous way that violence could pretty much be avoided.

Jordan had practically given up on life after leaving the SBS, with little to show for the forty years he'd been on the earth apart from a terraced house in Dorchester. He'd paid off the mortgage with his meagre medical-discharge payment. The monthly pension was all right but it was just paying him to sit around until he died. He'd been feeling dead already. When his girlfriend of ten years left him soon after the discharge he pretty much stopped believing in anything. Who wanted a civilian cripple? She'd told him that the spark had gone out of his life. It was true enough, although he didn't think that was exactly what she meant. He wasn't special any more.

When he received a call out of the blue to meet a man in a nearby pub to talk about a job that could not be discussed over the phone it was more intriguing than anything that had come Jordan's way in years. There was a time when he would have punched the man across the floor for even suggesting a task that threatened members of his former unit. But time and experiences could change a person. Into something that they would never have believed possible. He even found himself offering suggestions on how to increase the value that the planners had already attached to him. Admittedly the offer of a million dollars placed in an offshore account had been a more than attractive incentive.

They didn't tell Jordan very much about the job, other than that it was a task on an oil platform and that it could involve working against the British security forces. The man gave him a letter containing a decryption code word and a few days later he received an e-mail with an encrypted file attached that the code word opened. The attachment contained details of the promised Cayman Island bank account with half a million US dollars in it and a proposed date for the next half-million to drop. After checking that the funds really did exist he became very excited, more about the prospect of spending a million dollars than about the task itself. But as the operation drew closer the excitement about the money turned into something else: concern. About what he had to do.

About Deacon. About Deacon's men. They were a threat to his control. He had the feeling right from the start that Deacon wasn't comfortable being his subordinate. And now he could feel the man looking at him in a way that suggested the idea was eating at him.

Deacon suddenly wondered if his own expression reflected his contempt for Jordan. He looked away. 'Do we need this guy all night?' Deacon asked, wanting to get rid of the technician.

Jordan considered it, wondering what Deacon wanted. 'I can monitor things for a while.'

'Hey. You,' Deacon said to the technician who looked at him fearfully. 'I want you to go down to the cookhouse and take a break until I send for you. I'm going to let you go unescorted. But if you don't turn up, if you try and hide, when I find you I'll toss you overboard. Do you understand?'

The man nodded quickly.

'Good. Get going.'

The man headed for the door.

Deacon picked a radio off the desk and pressed a button in its side. 'This is Deacon in the control room. Technician coming down to the cook 'ouse. Let me know when he arrives.'

A moment later a squelch came from the phone, followed by a gruff foreign voice. 'Understood.'

Deacon put the radio down. He wondered again what more Jordan knew about the operation than he did, and how he might get the man to reveal any of it. Deacon's orders had been quite specific. He was responsible for the team and the prisoners, none of whom were to be harmed if at all possible. Jordan now had charge of the operation itself and the final say over strategy and policy. But the man didn't appear to be the chatty type. Yet he was an ex-serviceman and one thing ex-servicemen liked to do was talk about the years they'd spent as soldiers, Deacon reasoned, usually because civilian life was nearly always so dull and unamusing by comparison. He hoped that rule applied to Jordan. 'How long you do in the SBS?' he asked.

The question didn't particularly surprise Jordan. It was one ex-special forces guys always seemed to ask each other. A way of gauging their experience. Anyone who'd done less than eight years wasn't considered rounded enough. They might have seen a lot of action but that wasn't where the SF experience really lay. It was in the depth and variety of challenges. Jordan hadn't given much thought to Deacon's background, other than assuming the man was ex-service himself. It only then occurred to him the bloke would not have been hired without a suitable pedigree, such as SF. As they might be together for days he tried to be friendly. 'Long enough,' he said. 'What's your own background?'

Deacon's instinct was to keep his identity secret but he couldn't control his ego. Not with this individual. He wanted his top-dog status back. 'SAS.'

Jordan wondered if the man was lying. A lot of ex-servicemen in the civilian security business claimed to be former special forces. 'Which squadron?' he asked.

'B.'

'When did you get out?'

Deacon suspected that Jordan was verifying his claim. It only added to his resentment. Surely it was obvious to another soldier that Deacon had to be SAS. He and Jordan had never met but they were men of the same era. Even a shaky boat could see that. It wasn't unusual for the two services that they'd never crossed paths. Some guys had spent much of their careers cross-training between the SBS and SAS and some hardly at all. 'Just before Afghanistan.'

'You know Marvin Goodman?'

'Marvellous was my sergeant major.'

Jordan nodded, convinced. Deacon was former SAS all right.

The man's arrogance sealed it – he acted as if he'd been insulted by Jordan's doubts. It didn't matter that he'd answered the question correctly.

'You get the leg on the job?'

'Afghanistan.' Jordan felt reluctant to discuss his service history.

'I've been there but as a civvy.' Deacon felt he had little in common with the other man. 'Was it operational?'

'Yeah.'

'Something go wrong?' It was a fair enough question to ask about an SF wound. The ops were so meticulously planned that if anyone got hurt it was worth hearing about.

'Not as badly as it could've.' Other than the official debrief, Jordan had told no one about the operation in any detail. Much like Stratton. He had refrained from discussing it with SBS members because it would only cause friction. Some believed it was Stratton's fault and others felt that the incident was the price of war. He couldn't discuss it with a civilian. They could never fully understand. But another SF operator might be able to put himself in his shoes. Apply his own experiences as well as his knowledge of the system. Jordan didn't particularly trust the man in front of him but he had a sudden urge to tell him the story. Perhaps it was because he wanted to hear a qualified outsider's view. An SAS guy might give an unbiased opinion. 'It was one of those jobs that was wrong from the start.'

'Why'd it go ahead?'

'Same reason a lot of them do. Ego. On the ground as well as those up top. You know what the SBS and SAS hierarchies are like. Always competing against each other, point scoring, wanting to impress London. No offence but the regiment's been falling behind a bit of late, what with Iraq dying down. And the SBS getting all the glory in Afghanistan. And the Yanks finally starting to share the lead in SF roles . . . maybe even take it from us in places.'

This was all news to Deacon and it did not sit well with him. He had no contact with current troopers or any of his old mates from the regiment yet he had strong opinions regarding special forces. All of them. As far as he was concerned the SAS were at the top of the SF tree with the SBS several branches down and the Yanks even lower. And it had always been that way. It was only to be expected – and typical – for an SBS operator to rubbish the SAS at any opportunity. He suddenly had a good reason to dislike the other man. 'So what happened?' Deacon asked.

'The job went ahead – a hit on a Taliban encampment. We try not to arrest many these days. Ever since the media clowns and bleeding-heart liberals have been bleating on about the treatment of terrorists in prisons like Guantánamo, the only solution is to shoot them instead.'

'I like that,' Deacon said.

'Too much had been left to chance on this one.'

'I don't see why it was allowed to go on.'

'Sure you can. The SAS has had more cock-ups over the last twenty years than anyone.'

'That's because they've done nearly all the bloody work,' Deacon said defensively, feeling his hackles rising.

'That may be a part of it,' Jordan said, unaware of the hurt and venom in Deacon's reply. 'But you're missing the point. Many of those ops were damned before they started. It didn't stop 'em from going ahead, though. It's still about peer pressure and egos causing a lot of the problems.'

'So what happened?' Deacon asked, controlling his anger at the digs against his beloved former unit. His foul temper had grown worse over the years and once it turned physical he knew he was apt to lose control altogether. He had spent so long in lawless environments, where he had not been held to account for his actions, that he was no longer able to check himself. The oil platform was just such a place. The only law was that imposed by Deacon and his men, all answerable to him. The only chance of keeping him in check here was the risk of screwing up the task and losing the money.

Jordan had no inkling of his colleague's murderous intent and how his talk was eating away at the restraints on the man's madness. To him it was just a conversation, albeit a contentious one, with a fellow ex-special forces operative who was under the illusion that he was the senior figure in charge of the operation. 'As I'd expected, the hit didn't go as planned and I had to go in and hot-extract the team with vehicles. It was a mess. We were only lightly armoured and we took a lot of fire.'

'And you took one in the leg.'

'As a result I had to leave the mob.'

'What about the team leader?'

Jordan gave him a look. It was an interesting question. He hadn't intended to discuss that side of it. 'What do you mean?'

'Well, you blame him, right?'

Jordan did blame Stratton but he experienced an internal conflict whenever he thought about it. He had always liked and respected Stratton. The man was highly rated by everyone in the SBS and to accuse him of incompetence did not sit well with most of them. It felt awkward – traitorous, even. 'I suppose so,' he finally admitted.

'What do you mean, you suppose so? It was 'is fault. You got shot. Why didn't you take it out on 'im?'

'Because that's not how it's done.'

Deacon, seething inside, studied Jordan. 'Don't take this wrong – just like you said to me with your comments about my old regiment – but I think you're a pussy.'

'What's that?' Jordan asked, surprised. He hadn't seen it coming. This was one old soldier telling a war story to another.

'I've been in so many contacts, some that'd make yours look

like an exercise on Salisbury Plain. Getting shot at is all part of the big show. Listen to your crap. You know what the difference is between the SAS and the SBS? You're all a buncha whingeing pussies.'

Jordan's eyes narrowed. He felt a cross between brimming anger and confusion.

'Sorry, mate, but I 'ave to call it as I see it.'

Deacon's radio came to life. 'This is Pirate. I think there's someone on the lower spans.'

Jordan and Deacon remained staring at each other despite the significance of the interruption. Jordan was the first to disconnect. This was why he was here, in command. There were more important things to deal with.

Deacon was far more self-destructive in nature and could easily value emotional issues above practical essentials. It would have needed a similar madness from Jordan to sustain their dispute. Deacon's only respect for Jordan came from how decisively he had dealt with the Lebanese thug. That was warning enough not to give him any advantages. He suspected Jordan would not do anything to jeopardise the operation. It was the same weakness that had stopped him from challenging his team leader on that Afghanistan mission.

Jordan got to his feet. 'Tell all your call signs to go silent unless it's an emergency,' he said as he pulled on his coat.

'Why's that?' Deacon asked, remaining in his seat and looking at Jordan.

'Because if your bloke's right and someone has climbed onto the rig, it will most likely be the forward recce. It's too soon for an assault. That means in turn they'll be putting in a technical option, which means they'll be able to hear you.' Jordan felt a little better, talking down to Deacon like this. He made his way to the door. 'Where's this Pirate feller?'

'I'll show you,' Deacon said, getting to his feet and pulling on his waterproof as he stared at Jordan. He disliked him even more for the way he was talking to him.

In the driving wind and rain outside Jordan squinted beyond the rails into the blackness where the join between the sea and sky had disappeared. It was as if the platform were shrouded in a tempestuous cloak that allowed no light in from the outside world. The cold rain beating against his face was refreshing, a cleansing balm against the anger that had engulfed him back in the control room.

He wondered who might be on the platform and if he knew them. His thoughts went to Stratton, not just because of the discussion with Deacon. Bumping into him at the airport the other day had been a strange coincidence and he wondered what the chances were of him being in the first wave. He dismissed the idea as quickly as he had thought of it. If Stratton was involved in any way it would be leading one of the assault teams, not the recce. He felt grateful for it.

'This way,' Deacon shouted, walking past Jordan, his hood pulled over his head.

Jordan followed. Deacon deliberately walked too quickly. He paused at the top of a flight of riveted metal steps to wait for the former SBS operative, a mean glare in his eyes that Jordan would never be able to see in the darkness and inside his hood.

They descended to the low-blocked accommodation deck and walked across an open space in front of the cabins to another flight of stairs going down. They followed these to the lower deck and on down a set of narrower, steeper steps to the machine deck, the lowest operating deck before the spiders. There was a mixture of machine equipment, storage containers and piping of every description stacked everywhere. The thunderous boom of the powerful swell pounding against the rig's legs grew louder with each step down. The black-painted metal railings were wet and slippery.

They halted beside one of the four massive legs. A wide ladder leading down was welded to its side. Here the wind was even more turbulent, its pressure dropping and increasing alternately as it pushed between the supports.

Deacon's pace slowed and became more cautious as his concentration focused ahead. Partway around the curved surface of the huge leg he stopped and pressed himself against it. He removed his hood and slowly leaned over a rail in order to look below.

Jordan gradually closed on him.

Deacon had to search for a while before he eventually spotted the Pirate squatting on a cross-brace some twenty feet below. Only when the jet-black Somali looked up and revealed the whites of his eyes could Deacon make out which part of the dark bundle was the man's head. The Pirate pointed down and diagonally opposite.

Deacon could see nothing except shadows and shimmers of light absorbed by the white water breaking around the rig's legs. He looked around at Jordan. 'I'll bring the team in. We can ambush them as they come up.'

Deacon brought his radio to his lips but Jordan stayed his hand. 'They won't be coming up.'

'Then we'll go down and get them.'

'Bring your man up in case he's seen,' Jordan ordered.

Deacon looked at him as he yanked his hand free. 'Why?'

'Because we don't want to start a war with special forces. You know them as well as I do. If we kill just one of them they'll want revenge. Remember, there's no law out here to govern us. There's little to govern them, either. We've been there, right?' Jordan added by way of subtle manipulation.

It made sense but only to someone who didn't like confrontation. Deacon was convinced that Jordan was weak, and usurping him became suddenly a very serious consideration. The one thing stopping him from doing it, for the moment at least, was that

Jordan still held a significant ace up his sleeve. 'When are you going to tell me what this is all about?'

'You'll find out in good time.'

'This is your moment of power, isn't it?'

'Don't be so bloody childish. Now bring your man up.'

Deacon took his time going back to the rail. When the Pirate looked up, Deacon gestured for him to join them. The Somali moved slowly back along the strut to the leg and began to climb the ladder.

Jordan turned to go but Deacon grabbed his arm. 'At least tell me what our next move is.'

Jordan was beginning to get some pleasure out of squeezing the little shit. He was prepared to kill the fool if he showed serious signs of becoming a threat but he expected the man ultimately to control himself. 'They've come to do a job down there. When they're finished they'll go and I suspect it will take them minutes rather than hours. Then, if things have gone to plan, we may be able to leave too.'

'You're serious? We could be gone in hours?'

Jordan yanked his arm free and shuffled back along the gangway.

Deacon watched him go, feeling quite pleased. The prospect of getting off the platform lessened his concerns about Mackay. He had mentally prepared himself for a long-drawn-out affair. This was uplifting news, to be sure. Another half-million would be in his account in days or even hours and then he could begin the pleasant business of spending it.

Stratton began the climb up the robust steel platform ladder on the side of the massive black pile. He had removed his hood to improve his all-round senses and his SMG was slung just below his chest. The sea rolled into the structure beneath him, thumping the side of the supports as he steadily took one rung at a time. His gaze never left the dark cavernous network of girders and spars above. He felt exposed. This was ambush territory. He would have practically no control if he came under fire other than to drop and take his chances on the way down. If he hit nothing he'd still have to deal with the rolling seas. He might be able to combat the elements and to a certain extent control the fools who had come with him. But the enemy, their numbers and skills unknown, held the high ground and had the advantage. They could wait for him to come to them. It all depended on how professional and vigilant they were. If they had night-vision aids and accurate weaponry he'd be an easy target.

He made it to the next spider deck, a complex intertwining of horizontal spars that connected the four legs. Stratton paused to take a breather and a better look above. Each step brought him closer to the enemy and perhaps into the cleaner view of a sniper. He glanced down to see Binning not far below. There was movement beyond him – Jason and Rowena.

Stratton pulled himself up onto a wide span and moved along it to leave room for Binning to join him. Rowena and Jason had stopped on the level below and as prearranged would wait for Binning to secure the device and come back down.

The first operational deck came next, a dark enclosure of machinery, drilling and pumping apparatus, the humming from its engines and generators mingling with the sounds of the sea and wind. The squally rain continued to pelt them. The water ran down their faces and into their eyes and mouths as if they were looking straight into a shower head.

'Is this high enough?' Stratton asked.

'This should do fine,' Binning replied, looking around. 'I'll need to take a reading, though.'

'You happy with the procedure from here?' Stratton said.

'Do you really need to go?' Binning asked. 'You've come this far and risked so much already.'

'I'm not prepared to die for Jordan or for anyone. If I can't get him, well, at least I will have tried. Get that kit in place, go down and join the others and get going,' Stratton said. He pulled himself up.

Binning watched him go, then glanced below to see Jason and Rowena looking up at him. The black container was still attached to his harness but he made no attempt to remove it.

11

Stratton eased himself onto the gangway between several massive, noisy pumping machines and shale shakers and held the silenced SMG in his hands. It felt good to be standing on a wide floor and holding the gun. And to have got this far. He felt more confident now that he had not been watched. An ambush would have come long before he reached firm footing.

He checked the magazine pouch and the spare ammunition it held and moved forward, his rubber-soled neoprene lace-up boots practically silent on the metal flooring. After a brief pause at the foot of a narrow stairway at the end of the line of machines, he quickly made his way up the steps, crouching at the top to reduce his silhouette. Above the main machinery the area was sparsely lit, with shadows everywhere. Now he cherished the wind and rain as they whipped between the piles of equipment, finding the gaps and flapping loose tarps or lines, adding to the cacophony. He wiped his face and padded across an open section to a corner of the platform and another set of broader steps leading up to the living deck.

Stratton took the steps slowly at a slight crouch. He waited at the top. This deck was a congested area of accommodation: galley, hospital, laundry and utilities. He scanned around once again. In front of him a broad, exposed space led to an illuminated door to the accommodation block. Beams of light filtered by the griddle deck above bathed it in a yellow glow. If he walked across the space anyone who might be there would see him. Stratton chose to go around the outer edge, keeping in the shadows thrown by the bulky containers and smaller items of machinery.

He crept across the deck. He did not see the figure that stepped out a few metres behind him. Yet he heard them, even through the hum and whip of machinery and weather. Stratton's highly tuned senses picked up the out-of-place noise which sounded like a small piece of metal rolling along the metal floor. He stopped, his senses suddenly screaming but at the same time warning him not to turn around just yet.

Pirate hadn't seen the tiny bolt that he'd scuffed with the toe of his heavy boot. His stare had been fixed on the back of the figure he had seen coming up through the guts of the platform. He had moved back from his position as ordered. He hadn't engaged anyone. Yet. But he couldn't comprehend the figure's presence. He wasn't used to taking orders, or obeying any that he considered stupid. That was how he had become a commander. During the attack on a Russian ship in the Gulf of Aden a couple of years before, his boss, a man from his own village and like him a former fisherman, had ordered the men not to kill any hostages. Pirate knew the Russians to be dangerous but when he suggested they should shoot the first crewman as a warning to the others the commander chastised him.

When the Somali thugs scrambled on deck, Russian crewmen stepped out of the engine room with their empty hands held high. The pirates moved forward to capture them, signalling to the boats to come alongside. The ship was theirs. But then the Russian crewmen dropped to the floor and others carrying AK-47 assault rifles leaped from cover. Their bullets tore into the pirate ranks, cutting them down.

Further along from the fighting Pirate had climbed unseen onto the vessel. He fired his RPG at the ambushers, killing several, wounding others, and setting the ship alight. Those who could fell back into the superstructure. Pirate led the charge but this was no longer an attack for profit. It became a battle for revenge. He went through the vessel room by room, killing anyone he found. He shot the captain and officers on the bridge. He walked calmly into the communications shack to kill the radio operator.

Pirate never knew what happened to the ship, neither did he care, after abandoning it ablaze. The attack had been a waste of time and manpower. A resulting argument with his commander left the leader dead, a knife buried in his neck, the hilt firmly in Pirate's hands. And for his efforts the others made him commander.

From that day on his pirate philosophy had been to kill first, capture later. But his command turned out to be short-lived. His methods were shunned by other pirate commanders as counter-productive and he was soon forced out of his position under threat of execution.

Such was the way of his world. One's power rose and fell like the tide. Surviving was the only important thing. And so here he was again, forced to obey orders that he believed to be wrong. He had watched this man step past him carrying a gun and knew he was a threat not to be ignored. And so he decided to act. 'Move one more step and I kill you,' the African warned.

Stratton's mind raced. The fact that he had not been shot already told him the man was not quite prepared to kill him yet, for whatever reason. That gave him a narrow margin in which to negotiate. 'I'm not alone,' he said, hoping to unnerve the man.

'You will be when I shoot you,' Pirate replied.

Stratton sensed the murderous confidence in the foreign voice immediately.

'Put your gun down on the floor now or I put a bullet into the back of your head.'

'Okay,' Stratton said, trying to sound nervous. 'Don't shoot.'

As he leaned forward he used his thumb to click the selector catch on the weapon from single-shot to fully automatic and moved the barrel round so that it angled across his body instead of facing his front. With nothing to go by but the voice he estimated the man to be three or four metres behind him. The barrel of the weapon was now pointing at a head-height container forming a wall to his side. He angled the gun a little further back as he bent at the waist and lowered it to the floor. Before it touched the ground he pulled the trigger. The only sound that resulted was the click, click, clatter of the moving parts as the weapon shuddered in his grip and the bang of the bullets hitting the metal container. The silenced SMG fired low-velocity rounds: bigger bullets than the average high-powered rifle but slower and less penetrating. They couldn't pierce the skin of the container, for instance. Stratton held on to the trigger and emptied the entire magazine, the rounds striking and then ricocheting off the metal wall like billiard balls. He turned to see the figure of a man, juddering as he fell, a gun slipping from his grip.

Stratton moved to the man to look down on him. He was alive but breathing in short, rasping breaths. Stratton checked around to ensure they were alone. He couldn't leave the Somali in case he was discovered. There was too much more to be done. Under normal circumstances a follow-up team would take care of him, the details of such cases depending on the nature of the operation and its ability to absorb enemy prisoners. In most cases this would be zero. That certainly applied to Stratton's current situation.

Stratton couldn't get the man to the platform's outer edge because of the deck configuration: he'd have to drag him around the container and machinery to do that and risk exposure. The only choice he had was a gap between the narrow gangway he had climbed and the edge of the deck. A more or less unobstructed line of sight straight down to the water.

He slung the SMG over his back and dragged the man to the gangway. He heaved him up, leaned him over the top rail, picked up his heels and let the weight take him the rest of the way over.

The man fell silently into the blackness. At first. But instead of a distant plop as he hit the water, a couple of dull thuds followed by a single deeper one came back up, as though the body had struck something very solid.

Stratton had no time to worry about the man's fate. He was dead either way. The good news was that there was now one fewer enemy to fight. The bad news was that the clock had started ticking, for it would only be a matter of time before the man was declared missing and the reason for it became obvious.

He hid the Somali's weapon and moved across to the door that led into the accommodation block.

Rowena and Jason were waiting on the spider deck for Binning when Pirate's body struck the span across the gap from them and jammed awkwardly in a joint. Rowena lost her balance at the shock of it and might have fallen off the spar had Jason not been close enough to grab her.

As she steadied herself the thought hit her. Binning!

Mansfield jolted as if he'd had the same thought. 'Stay here,' he said. He shuffled to the end of the girder and climbed through an angled junction to the span where the body lay.

After a brief examination he made his way back. 'It's not Binning, or Stratton.'

'Is he dead?'

'For his sake I sincerely hope so. There's little that anyone can do for him if he isn't.'

'Then where's Binning?' Rowena asked. They peered up into the complex web of light beams and shadows.

There was nothing more for it. She had to see for herself and so she clambered up the ladder. Jason wanted to stop her but instead climbed up behind her.

'He's gone with Stratton,' she decided as Jason stepped onto the next spider deck.

'He wouldn't allow that,' Jason said.

'What other explanation could there be? Binning was supposed to set up the G43 here. Where the hell is he?'

'Maybe he had to go further up,' Jason suggested, craning to look for his colleague.

'I'm surprised you didn't go with him too. You and Binning are so keen to prove you're better than Stratton.'

'One minute you hate him, the next you're a fan.'

Rowena ignored the comment. 'What are we going to do?'

'He may be having trouble securing the device. Be patient. He'll be back soon.'

'Then what about him down there? I suppose he was just taking a stroll in the storm and slipped. Are you going to tell me you can't sense that something is really wrong here? Binning is not setting up the device anywhere here. He's gone, Jason.'

Mansfield could not ignore her or the situation any longer. She was right.

'I'm not going to wait for him,' Rowena said, taking hold of the ladder. 'I want to know where he is and that he's placing the device. You stay if you want to.' He grabbed her hand. 'Don't try to stop me, Jason, or so help me . . .' Her expression was one of pure anger.

'I'm not trying to stop you,' he replied in a deliberate, calm voice. 'We'll both go but if we simply bimble around we could end up on the news ourselves. There's no point in that, right?'

Rowena could see the sense of this.

Mansfield took out his pistol and held it firmly pointing upwards. 'Let me take the lead, please.'

She hesitated, a long-time critic of the gender-weakness thing.

'Consider it a condition of me letting you go up there at all.'

She gave in and let him go ahead of her up the ladder.

They reached the level below the machinery deck as the rain and wind whipped at them.

'He's not here,' Rowena said loudly above the noise of the weather.

'Perhaps he set up the G43 and then went off to help Stratton.'

She considered the possibility. 'How can he do this without telling us?' she said in frustration.

Jason began to have a change of heart. 'Rowena! Tell me why we're risking our lives for them. They've chosen to do this. We should go back down, get into the water and rendezvous with Jackson at the mini-sub, just as Stratton said. You forget why we're here.'

'Forget why we're here?' Rowena repeated, stupefied. 'I don't have a goddamned clue why we're here, other than to satisfy your and Binning's egos. We've lost Smithy. God only knows if Jackson's still around out there. We can't do anything about them but we might be able to do something about Binning. I can't stand him but he's still one of us.' It did not look as if she was getting through to Jason. 'If you don't know what to do, ask yourself what Stratton would do,' she shouted finally. The comment stung him, as it was meant to. 'There's another difference between you and Stratton,' she continued. 'He knows when it's time to forget what you're supposed to do and try to save the life of someone else instead.'

Rowena took out her pistol and was about to move to the narrow staircase when she paused to say something else. 'I'm too damned scared to go back down. I don't think I'll be any less a victim by jumping back into that ocean and floating off into the beyond in the hope that someone might find me.'

She walked on up towards the next level. Jason gripped his pistol, exhaled tiredly and marched on after her.

Stratton let the outer door close behind him and opened the inner one slowly and smoothly. No one. He stepped inside and allowed the door to close quietly against his back. The hum of ventilation pipes. Suppressed sounds of weather or machinery.

He padded along the corridor, leaving a line of wet footprints behind him. Doors on either side, some closed, those open revealing compact bedrooms, toilets, showers. Personal items on the floor in rooms and along the corridor signs of a hurried departure by the occupants.

He came to the end door and opened it carefully. Another corridor ran across his path.

Stratton couldn't remember the living deck too well, not having spent much time in the private quarters of the platform during his time here. He'd trained on the Morpheus, concentrating on familiarising himself with the main operations deck and on prac- tising climbing the structure. But he knew there were a couple of places large enough to keep a hundred and sixty men out of the weather. The first he planned to check was the galley. A simple diagram of the deck and its main locations was posted on the opposite wall.

He walked along a wider corridor past soft-drink machines, a water fountain, snack dispensers and cupboards of emergency equipment. Up ahead was a pair of swing doors, a clear glass panel in each of them. After them another corridor and the galley. As he approached the swing doors he kept tight to the wall.

Stratton lowered his body and placed an ear against one of the doors but he could hear nothing above the sounds of air vents and humming machinery. He decided to take a risk.

He moved his face to the corner of the glass and took a quick look, his eyes in the window frame long enough to make out a couple of figures standing ten or fifteen metres down the corridor. They were near the entrance to the galley, a strong indication that they were playing at being jailers.

He leaned back against the wall. He had to think. This was the pivotal juncture of his private task. The next point of no return. He hadn't really believed he would get here and now that he had the questions were starting. It was a bit on the crazy side, he had to admit. He could still change his mind. But Jordan had been even crazier when he'd driven into that Afghan village to rescue him. The man had been selected to be executed by the hijackers, and Stratton owed him his life, and that meant he owed Jordan a future.

Stratton put all other thoughts aside and examined the next phase. He needed to disrupt the hijackers' flow. If he could release the workers – assuming they were all in the galley – that would drastically alter the hijackers' plan. He asked himself how many of them there were, how they would react, what price they were willing to pay to succeed, and what they were willing to sacrifice when faced with failure. There were endless gambles. Endless consequences of his actions.

'Bollocks,' he muttered as he stood to face the swing doors and brought his weapon's butt into his shoulder. The gods had got him this far. He took a deep breath, exhaled, pushed open the doors and marched into the corridor. Both of the men were big. One had red hair. The other looked Slavic. They reacted slowly to him striding towards them in his black dry-bag, shoulder harness, kit hanging from hips, pistol strapped low on thigh, another weapon levelled in front just below his face, both eyes in short-range battle mode staring into theirs.

Viking and the Bulgarian began to move apart and brought their weapons up to fire. Stratton pulled the trigger. Click, click. No other sound. The first silenced bullet struck Viking in the chest, the second hit the Bulgarian in a similar spot. The initial rounds were intended to destabilise whoever they hit, the centre of the torso being a bigger and easier target than the head, which required the shooter to take a millisecond longer aiming to ensure a hit. Operatives still did this even if the targets were wearing body armour since the purpose was to disrupt the enemy's aim and increase the time they would take to return fire.

Both men rocked back as the bullets entered their bodies.

Stratton neither slowed nor speeded up his deliberate pace. He fired again, the weapon going clickety-click as two more bullets spat from the end of the silencer extension. These hit both men in the head. The life went from their limbs and they dropped as if they had been switched off, the sound of their falls the loudest noise of the firefight. But the clatter of their weapons on the solid floor had been significant relative to the quiet of the corridor.

Stratton speeded up as he approached the galley doors. He found himself in a classic hostage situation. He'd breached the first line of the kidnappers' defence and bodies had begun to drop. He knew the surviving kidnappers' choices: give up and surrender, lie down and toss their weapons aside, mingle with their captives; defend themselves and engage the attackers; or turn their weapons on the hostages in an attempt to kill as many as possible before dying themselves. It was his single responsibility to make sure he reached his objectives as swiftly as possible and kill every one of the enemy in the quickest possible time.

Stratton pushed through the galley doors and stopped dead, unable to move in further to dominate the room because of the bodies sprawled on the floor in front of him. He kept the weapon against his shoulder, looking along the top of it, analysing the panoramic image he was presented with.

Jock and Queen stood at either end of the long serving counter, weapons in their hands. They'd heard about the movement on the spider decks. The thumps and clatters in the corridor outside had snapped them out of any daydreaming. But the only way they could have been assured a fighting chance against the man who entered their space was if they'd had their weapons against their shoulders and pointing at the door.

Stratton's two targets, being at opposite ends of the counter, presented him with something of a challenge though. He would have to pivot in a wide arc to engage them both. What was more, both of them were experienced fighters and knew the first rule of engagement: move from the static position. Precisely the type of situation in which to use instinctive shooting techniques as distinct from target-shooting methods. The second option employed the weapon as a tool, the first made it an extension of one's body. One required the use of the weapon's sights, the other didn't. One needed conscious thought and deliberation, the other was all subconscious reflex and instinct. And to be effective in a close-combat situation in which the shooter was outnumbered by targets at different angles, the 'target' version undoubtedly required great skill, while the 'instinct' style demanded something extra that could not be taught.

Stratton touched his gun's trigger and the resulting click sent a round into Jock's chest just above his heart. Stratton swivelled his upper body to face Queen who was in a more advanced firing position, having had a fraction of a second longer to bring up her weapon.

Stratton squeezed the trigger a second time and swivelled back, his eyes focusing over the top of the SMG to see that Jock, although he'd been punched backwards by the force of the first bullet, was still intent on firing his weapon. The second round struck Queen in the face, below her left eye – Stratton had not risked firing a destabilising bullet at someone who was ready to fire.

Stratton fired a third round and swivelled again to find Queen still on her feet, the muzzle of her gun dropping down to aim at the men directly in front of her, her grip still strong.

Stratton fired again and twisted round to see Jock falling, his head crashing against the wall, his eyes half open, his gun slipping from his grip. The final bullet to strike Queen had hit her in the forehead and she died on her feet, dropping to the floor as if strings that had been holding her up had been cut cleanly. Jock slid on down the wall, leaving a streak of blood behind him, and crumpled on the floor in a motionless heap.

Stratton remained in the firing position to scan the room for more targets. Most of the platform workers were asleep and had remained so throughout the near-silent battle. Those awake were stunned by what they had seen and by the speed with which it had happened.

'Any more?' Stratton calmly asked a man who was sitting on the floor a few feet away and staring at him through wide eyes.

The man took a moment to gather himself and shook his head.

'You sure?'

The platform worker pulled himself together. 'I don't think so. Two outside and two in here.'

'You ex-military?' Stratton asked the man on a hunch.

He nodded. 'Green Jackets.'

'Good unit,' Stratton said, lowering his weapon and pulling his knife from its sheath. He reached behind the man and cut through his plastic handcuffs.

The men who had been awake and had seen what happened were shaking those nearby who were still asleep.

'Stay calm and keep your voices down,' Stratton said firmly, addressing everyone. 'Any more ex-servicemen here?'

Heads began nodding and affirmative answers were called out around the room. Stratton scanned each row, hoping to find Jordan there.

Stratton handed the knife to the man he had freed. 'Cut everyone free,' he ordered. 'Listen in,' he addressed the room as the man did what he'd been told. 'You soldiers take charge. I want you to stay here until I say otherwise. You've got four weapons to guard the entrances. If you go up there you'll get in the way and someone could get hurt. Is that understood?'

The soldiers nodded. Those with their hands freed got to their feet and immediately picked up the weapons that had belonged to their jailers. The atmosphere was typical of what one would expect from restrained men whose lives had been threatened and were now getting a chance to fight back. They wanted blood and were ready to take it.

'Is there a Jordan Mackay here?' Stratton asked.

Silence. The men looked to each other for an answer.

'He's the bloke that they took away,' one said.

'Aye, there was a shot outside in the corridor shortly after and I'm certain someone died,' another said.

'I heard him say it was one of their own that had been shot,' yet another offered, indicating Jock.

Stratton's hopes of a clean grab of his friend and a getaway were momentarily dashed. He was already of no further use to the men in the galley and he turned to leave.

'What'll happen now?' one of them asked.

'Are we getting off the rig?' asked another.

'Can we head to the lifeboats?'

'Where's the rest of your team?'

Stratton put up a hand, signalling silence. 'For the time being, stay here, stay quiet, get organised for a move but just wait.' He looked at the questioning faces and felt suddenly guilty. He could not tell them that he was the only rescuer, that he was all alone. They would stampede onto the deck looking for a fight and many of them could get killed. There was also the issue of the platform itself. It had a lot of highly inflammable material on board and would literally become a bomb if something went wrong. But their chances of survival had increased. Now they were at least masters of their own destiny, to some extent. Depending on the number of hijackers, theirs had become a defensible position. It all now depended on how they would react to the changed situation. 'I'll try and get back to you soon. But be prepared to wait here for several hours.'

He couldn't think of anything else of use to tell them and turned to the doors once again.

'Watch out for their leader,' a man nearby offered. 'He's a mean bastard.'

Stratton heard it and headed through the doors.

'So's he, by the look of it,' one of the old soldiers said as Stratton left. 'Right. Let's get organised,' he called out to the room.

Jordan stood at one end of the control room, preoccupied. Deacon sat studying him, noting that he had checked his watch half a dozen times since they had returned. The apparent arrival of persons unknown at the base of the platform had not worried their illustrious leader but it had certainly got him all agitated. Deacon wondered whether to press Jordan for an explanation.

The sound of the outer door opening focused both men's attentions on the inner one. It had to be one of Deacon's men. Yet all of them were currently on full alert due to the presence of the reconnaissance team below. The door opened and Banzi backed into the room, his waterproof soaked, his rifle slung over a shoulder, a pistol in his hand and aimed into the airlock. He was not alone.

Banzi urged whoever it was to come inside.

It was Binning, in assault gear minus hood, his face and hair soaking wet.

Deacon got to his feet, stupefied.

Jordan looked expectant.

'Hi,' Binning said, appearing relaxed and offering his usual under-stated smile. 'Sorry about the intrusion. I actually found this gentleman before he found me and asked him to take me to the hijackers' leader.' Binning looked between the two men, wondering who that leader was.

'He was on the machinery deck,' Banzi offered in his stunted English.

'Who the bloody 'ell are you?' Deacon asked. Then, glancing at Jordan, 'Is he one of your blokes?'

Binning had no idea what the man was talking about. 'Name's Binning. I'm a few days earlier than expected. Things are a little off schedule but all for the better, I'd say.' He beamed.

Jordan had taken a good look at Binning, noting his familiar attire, harness and accessories, including the empty holster at his thigh, the gun from which was now in Banzi's hand. 'Who are you?'

Binning held up the plastic box that had been attached to his body since leaving the helicopter. 'It's why we're all here.'

'It was supposed to be left on the spiders where I could find it at first light,' Jordan said.

'Change of plan. The SB surveillance team was going to leave it for you to pick up but I had a bad feeling about our people. Time for me to get out of there. So I've brought it along person-ally. And, of course, I'm coming along with it.'

Jordan looked unsure.

'Don't worry, old boy,' Binning said in response to the look. 'I'm sure it will be approved. Give your boss a call. Tell him that Binning is moving over earlier than planned. You see, I'm almost as important as the device.'

Deacon had been staring at the scientist with his mouth slightly open, utterly lost as to what he was going on about. He glanced at Jordan, hoping that he might enlighten him about the situation.

Jordan nodded, as if he was beginning to understand. 'I see. And that's it?' He was referring to the black box.

'Yes. Let me show you. Excuse me,' Binning said politely to Banzi as he shuffled past him.

Banzi was not sure how to take the man who had accosted him from the rainswept shadows with a polite 'Excuse me'.

Binning cleared away the cups and paperwork from a table and placed the box on it. He unclipped the latches and opened the waterproof seams, dividing the container into two equal halves. 'This is the G43,' he said, indicating a robust rubber-coated electronic device.

'The monitoring system?' Jordan asked.

'That's right,' Binning confirmed, looking between Jordan and Deacon, still unsure who was in charge. He removed the G43 from its sponge-rubber moulding, laid it down and opened a waterproof panel on its side. 'This is the battery housing,' he said. He took a small screwdriver from a pouch on his upper arm and used it to unclip several tiny catches inside the housing. He removed another cover and deftly pulled out what looked like a black ceramic tile. He placed it on the table with a reverent gesture. 'This is it,' he announced.

Jordan leaned closer to inspect the device without touching it, paying particular attention to its thin sides where there were several miniature USB-type sockets. He reached inside his pocket and took out a BlackBerry which he turned on, applying a password to start it up. He dug out a cable from the same pocket, plugged one end into the phone and the other into one of the sockets on the side of the tile. 'You know what I'm doing?' he asked Binning.

'Of course. You have a piece of software in your Rim that can input and verify the modulated output.'

Jordan was lost after 'software' but carried on doing as he had been instructed.

'You want to ensure it's the real McCoy,' Binning went on. 'Personally, I don't see the point. Why would I be coming along if it wasn't?'

Jordan didn't know or care.

'But then, you didn't know I was coming,' Binning added.

Jordan knew one thing: he wished the man would shut up.

He opened an encrypted file inside his phone's download folder. It couldn't read the file. He frowned.

Binning leaned closer to take a look. 'If you look back inside your downloads folder I suspect you'll find a new file. It's the decoded data that your phone just input through the tile.'

Jordan wasn't the most technical of people but he found the file and clicked on it. The BlackBerry's screen lit up and a few seconds later the encrypted file opened. Jordan smiled as he looked at the screen. He showed it to Binning. The scientist grinned.

'Can I see?' Deacon asked, feeling left out.

Jordan showed it to him. It was a short phrase in quotation marks: 'By Strength, By Guile.'

'What do you think that is?' Jordan asked Deacon.

'It's the poxy logo of the SBS.'

'It's also the proof that we have the decryption device,' Jordan explained. 'We need to call this in.'

Deacon was still highly confused. 'Am I to understand that all of this, this capturing of the oil platform and everything, was for this?' He pointed at the small black tile.

Jordan shrugged as if, amazingly, it was.

'This is no ordinary "this",' Binning said.

'What is it, then?' Deacon's patience was starting to wear thin.

'It's the vital part of the world's fastest encryption device.'

Deacon looked at him blankly. He might as well have said it in Albanian.

Binning persevered. 'The fastest decryption machines anywhere in the world would take between a thousand to a million years to decrypt a hundred and thirty-bit key. The different combinations would equal the number of grains of sand in the Sahara Desert. This is still in its development stage but when it's complete it will have the potential to decrypt the same data in six months to a year.'

Deacon wasn't remotely impressed. 'Six months to a year?'

Binning decided that he was talking to an unappreciative moron. He replaced the tile inside the G43 and closed the device. 'You're being paid a considerable amount for your efforts, I imagine. Somewhere in the region of a million dollars, or pounds even. Well, that amount of money is a mere drop in the ocean compared to what this is worth in the right hands.'

Deacon understood that much. Still not why, though.

'Boss,' Banzi interrupted, talking to Deacon. 'I was looking for Pirate when I found him.' He indicated Binning.

'That's nice work,' Deacon replied sarcastically.

'I couldn't find Pirate. He's gone,' Banzi said, making his point.

'You can call him on the radio,' Jordan said. 'No one's listening to us now.'

Deacon nodded. Banzi took a radio from his pocket and stepped away to talk into it.

Deacon still wasn't satisfied. 'Why go to all this trouble?' he asked. 'Why didn't you just meet up in a pub somewhere and 'and it over?'

'Where I work it's impossible to get anything out,' Binning explained. 'You couldn't get a digital watch in or out under normal circumstances. The only way it can be transferred through security is if it's required by an outside source. Impossible with this device since it's not complete. And once it is, it would no longer be in our hands anyway. Since it couldn't come out on its own, a little playing around needed to be done in order to bring it out with something else. Such as the G43.'

'Like in a Trojan 'orse,' said Deacon in a moment of unusual intuition.

'Worth every penny of all our wages.' Jordan was suddenly more cheerful than he had been in a long time.

'Boss?' Banzi interrupted. 'I can't raise Pirate.'

'Then go look for 'im,' Deacon suggested tiredly. 'Go on.'

191

Banzi held up the pistol he'd taken from Binning as if asking what he should do with it.

'Give it back to 'im,' Deacon said.

Banzi handed the pistol to Binning and left the control room.

'Where's the rest of your team?' Jordan asked. 'I suppose they think you fell overboard?'

'That reminds me. We have a rather annoying SBS operative with us. He's somewhere on these upper decks right now.'

Jordan and Deacon were both suddenly wearing similar looks of concerned curiosity.

'Why has he come to the upper decks?' Jordan asked, his stare boring into Binning.

'I don't think it's as bad as it might sound,' Binning said, attempting to reassure them. 'He's here for something specific. Give him what he wants and I'm sure he'll go away.'

'And what would that be?' Deacon asked.

'He's looking for a man, an old friend, a worker on the platform.'

'Who?' Deacon asked, becoming irritated.

Binning frowned. 'Buggered if I can remember his name. I didn't pay much attention to it at the time. You were going to execute him along with a few others. You filmed them all . . . His first name was—'

'Jordan?' Deacon said, remembering very well that they'd filmed Mackay.

'That's it,' the scientist said. 'Jordan Mackay.'

Jordan clenched his jaw as he faced Deacon. 'You stupid prick. Selecting me for the damned film shoot.'

'I didn't know you then, did I, you arse-wipe. Why would an SBS operative be looking for just you, anyway?' Deacon asked angrily.

'I can answer that,' Binning said. 'His name's John Stratton and he owes this gentleman a life.'

Jordan looked up at the mention of the name. 'Christ.'

Deacon registered his concern.

Jordan suddenly felt completely frustrated. 'I told you about him,' he said to Deacon.

'Your team leader in Afghanistan? That's brilliant,' Deacon guffawed. 'He's come all the way 'ere, risking life and limb to rescue you, thinking you're about to be executed, and all the while it's you who's doing the robbing.'

'He's dangerous,' Jordan warned.

'He's one man,' Deacon said cockily. He went over to his bag, took out a cable with a sucker on the end and stuck it to a window. 'And 'e's not the only dangerous one.' He plugged his satellite phone into the other end of the cable. 'Let's 'ope we get a connection,' he said, bringing up a number.

A moment later someone answered the call. 'This is me . . . yeah, Thanatos. We're ready to go blue . . . That's right . . . Yes, of course we've got it . . . By strength, by guile,' he said. 'Can I confirm that the obvious is ready?' he asked. 'Good. See you out there.'

Deacon collapsed the phone's antenna, unplugged the cable and put it all back in his pocket. 'We're good to go,' he said, taking the explosive-charge initiator out of his bag and extending a thin aerial from it. 'It looks like our work 'ere is done.' He flipped open a cover and pushed a button. It began to flash red. 'We've got 'alf an hour to get clear of the platform.'

Jordan could not believe his eyes and ears. 'Tell me you haven't done what I think you've just done,' he said.

Deacon squared up to him. 'Now it's *your* turn to listen to *me*. My orders were to give you command until your job was done. From what I've seen, that just 'appened. My orders were to then get us out of 'ere. That's what I'm doin'.'

'I'm curious to know how,' Binning said. 'The entire area is surrounded by Royal Navy ships and aircraft.'

'They must want that little tile of yours pretty bad,' Deacon said. 'Come on. The signal they're waiting for is the oil platform going up. Like I said, we 'ave 'alf an hour.'

'Going up?' Binning said, suddenly the one who didn't understand.

Deacon rolled his eyes. 'Catch up, genius. What do you think this is?' he said, holding up the initiator.

Binning's thoughts shot to Jason and Rowena. He could only hope they would be off the platform already.

'You bastard,' Jordan hissed, moving towards Deacon. 'What about the workers? Are you going to let them know before it's too late?'

'I'm only thinking of you, Jordan, me old mate. You see, when the rig goes up the authorities'll think that you're dead. They'll never know the part you played in it. If they thought you were still alive they'd come looking for you. You wouldn't be able to spend all that money. Bet you never thought of that, did you?' Deacon grinned.

'The escaping workers in the other lifeboats would add to our cover,' Jordan said, raising his voice. 'You need to let them go.'

'They'll only get in the way.'

The anger swelled in Jordan and although he was hampered by his injured leg he took a swing at the former SAS man. Deacon avoided the blow easily and countered viciously with an uppercut into Jordan's gut. He cocked his other hand to punch him again but Binning grabbed it. The man's vicelike grip took Deacon by surprise.

Binning smiled as he looked into Deacon's eyes. 'That's enough. We need to get going.'

Deacon pulled his arm away and stepped back, looking at the scientist with renewed respect. 'Make sure he doesn't step out of line again or I'll kill 'im.' Deacon picked his pack off the floor and went to the door.

'Where to?' Binning asked, picking up the G43.

194

'A lifeboat. I'll tell the team to close in.'

'Let's put all this behind us, Jordan,' Binning said, helping the former SBS man to the door. 'Think about the money you'll have to spend in just a few days.'

Outside it wasn't just the storm that was waiting for them.

12

'All call signs to the crane,' Deacon shouted into his radio. 'All call signs to the crane immediately!'

The wind howled over the metal deck as the three men walked across it. The energy of the storm hadn't dissipated since it had reached its peak a few hours earlier and as they moved into the light falling from the deck above everything seemed to be coming loose. Spotlights shuddered in their housings and rattled on the ends of poles. The dead worker's corpse swung from the crane's hook in the gale.

Deacon stopped beside the crane to look down at a lifeboat in its cradle suspended over the side of the deck below. 'We'll take that one,' he said. He glanced across to the stairs that led up from the accommodation block. 'Where are those blokes? You'd think they'd be 'ere like a shot.'

'Nobody move.' The voice came from the darkness.

Jordan and Binning recognised it instantly and Deacon did not take long to guess who was speaking.

'Let's have a show of hands. I have a light trigger finger.'

Binning released the G43 bag, letting it hang from his shoulder, and put up both hands. The other two men held their hands away from their bodies, palms out.

Stratton stepped from the shadows, the muzzle end of his SMG leading the way. He positioned himself where he could see each of them, his back to the rails. 'Why do I get a bad feeling about this picture? You don't look or sound much like a prisoner, Jordan.

Nor you, Binning.' Stratton looked at the third man. 'How many of you are there?' he asked.

Jordan stuck his chin up stiffly, trying to be assertive despite his feeling of extreme guilt. 'There's six more guns out there.'

Stratton wondered if they knew about the Somali or the other four he'd killed. If not, that meant only one armed man was still at large. One was enough to kill him, though. He put the thought to one side, comfortable for the time being with his back close to the rails. He needed some back-up. Flown onto the platform. That would mean he'd have to be able to contact ops. He was going to have to secure these three, and that might not be simple. 'Do you want to tell me what's going on?'

Jordan glanced at the others, wondering what they were planning, knowing that the ticking-bomb countdown would provoke an act of desperation sooner or later. 'We don't have time for talk right now.'

'Why's that?' Stratton asked, sensing a tension in all three.

A figure appeared, hurrying across the deck towards them.

'This place could get pretty crowded soon,' Deacon said, his tone cocky.

'Not with your people,' said Stratton, shrinking back into the shadows.

Deacon's smile faded. He wondered exactly what the man meant.

'I don't advise anyone to try and take advantage of any distractions. I don't need to bring any of you in alive. That goes for you too, Jordan.'

'Boss,' Banzi called out, unable to make out the individuals in the poor light. 'Something's wrong,' he said as he got to them, his assault rifle gripped firmly in his hands. 'I saw Viking and the Bulgarian on the floor. I'm sure they were dead. I think the workers have weapons. They must have the other two inside the galley.'

Banzi realised something else was wrong when Deacon and the others remained still.

'Put the gun down,' Stratton ordered. His own was pointed at the Japanese man.

Banzi turned to look at the figure emerging from the shadows.

'Put it down,' Stratton repeated.

Banzi crouched, lowered his gun to the deck and held out his hands as he stood upright again.

'You were saying,' Stratton said to Jordan.

Jordan was about to answer when two more figures moved across the deck, walking stealthily, flitting between the light and shadows.

Stratton started to shrink back once again, wondering if it was more hijackers or perhaps even workers. He suddenly recognised Rowena and then Jason. 'Over here,' he called out.

The pair recognised Stratton's voice and made their way towards the group.

'Don't get too close,' Stratton warned. 'They're still armed.'

'Binning?' Rowena exclaimed on seeing her fellow scientist with his hands out. 'I thought something had happened to you.'

'I don't think Binning's on our side any more,' Stratton said.

Rowena noticed the G43 container hanging from his shoulder. Jason stared at Binning in disbelief.

'Sorry, Jason,' Binning said. 'I meant to tell you I was leaving but I didn't have the chance.'

'What is this, Jordan? More than just a hijacking?' Stratton asked.

Jordan couldn't see the sense in keeping quiet now. As far as he was concerned, the game was up. 'A lot more. The platform was just a front.'

'That's disappointing. I came all the way here just for you, old friend.'

Jordan's feeling of guilt deepened further.

Stratton looked over at Deacon. 'Who's your mate?' he asked Jordan.

'Ex-regiment. I never met him before. He took the platform.'

Stratton kept the muzzle of his weapon trained on Deacon, sensing that he was the most dangerous. 'And you, Binning?'

Binning became his usual light-hearted self. 'Unlike your friend here, I don't think this is the time to start revealing facts and admitting guilt. There's more of this game left to play, just in case you happen to think it's all over because you currently have the upper hand. As your friend keeps trying to warn you, we don't have a great deal of time. You should think about taking him seriously.'

Stratton was not about to be manipulated. 'Before we do anything else I want you all to get down on the deck . . . on your bellies.'

'You're not listening,' Jordan pleaded. 'We don't have time for that.'

Stratton took his old friend seriously. 'Why not?'

'Charges have been critically placed. We've just enough time to get to the lifeboats. I'm serious,' Jordan assured him, seeing the doubt in Stratton's face. 'I was never in agreement with that part of the plan but it's done—'

'Don't be such a wuss,' Deacon interrupted.

'Explain the explosives,' Stratton commanded Deacon.

The man shrugged. 'Like he said. And there's an anti-lift built into both dets that'll take you longer than you 'ave just to find 'em.'

'He has the initiator,' Jordan said.

'I 'ave to say, Jordan, I've lost all respect for you.'

Stratton levelled his SMG at the former SAS man. 'Give me the initiator.'

Deacon shook his head. 'I start a job, I finish it.'

'I'll kill you in five seconds if you don't hand it to me and then he'll search you for it,' Stratton said, indicating Jason. He raised the business end of the SMG.

Deacon knew that a round leaving the gun's barrel would strike his head. And he had no doubt that Stratton was about to pull the trigger. 'It's in my pack.'

Stratton didn't move.

Deacon reached into the bag and removed the safe-box that had contained his secret instructions. 'It's in here,' he said, a smirk on his lips. He tossed the box to Jordan who caught it. 'I'll let the rat give it to you.'

Binning was the first to take advantage of the distraction by suddenly grabbing Rowena, pulling her in front of him and drawing his pistol. He held its muzzle to the back of her head. 'That's enough,' he said, stepping backwards, putting distance between himself and Stratton's lethal SMG. 'I don't have time to play these games any more. I'm going to walk down to one of the lifeboats. If anyone tries to stop me I'll kill her. Please don't doubt me. Time is running out.'

'Stand still,' Stratton said coldly. The confidence of his tone checked Binning. 'Take one more step and I'll shoot. You won't make it to the boat whether you kill her or not,' Stratton said. With finality.

Whatever Binning thought about Stratton he suddenly had no doubts that the man would kill him. He couldn't let go of Rowena but neither could he take another step towards the lifeboats.

'What's the number?' Jordan asked Deacon.

'Could take you a while to open that without it,' Deacon chuckled.

'I'm going to start shooting in three seconds,' Stratton growled.

'One, two, three, four, then the open button,' Deacon said quickly. 'I don't have a memory for complicated numbers.'

Jordan punched in the first number on the digital keyboard.

Deacon watched. He took a quick glance at Stratton, who was watching him, jaw tight and finger on the trigger. If Deacon moved he knew the SBS man would shoot him.

Binning held Rowena tightly to him, desperately wondering how to get out of this situation. Freedom was only metres away but Stratton would kill him and maybe Rowena if he moved, he was sure of it.

Deacon's stare flicked back to Jordan. There was less explosive in the box than in a hand grenade and since it was made of toughened plastic, which the heat would soften, there would be less lethal shrapnel. But the blast would be enough to injure all of them, perhaps seriously. Jordan would die, of course. All Deacon had to do was survive it, get the upper hand and escape. There was time.

Jordan touched the number three on the pad. Deacon tensed himself for four.

Jason was watching Jordan but a glance at Deacon suddenly warned him of something. The way the man's stare bored into Jordan's fingers, his body trying to lean away.

Jordan had pressed the four button. Only 'open' to go now. Deacon was trembling with the urge to dive away. If he did so too soon Jordan could stop, and Stratton would shoot him.

The operative saw the change in Deacon, the tension in his expression and the way he was leaning backwards. He didn't know whether to shoot him or shout at Jordan to stop. Either alternative would have been too late to save Jordan.

As Jordan's finger hit the final button Deacon launched himself backwards. Stratton crouched instinctively and tightened his finger on the trigger. The explosion lifted each of them away from Jordan, a wall of heat sending them reeling across the deck.

Jason came to crumpled against a piece of machinery, his head spinning, unsure of where in the world he was. All he knew was that he was in a dangerous place. He fought to pull his thoughts together. The seconds before the blast came back to him and he pushed himself up onto his hands. He realised that he couldn't see out of one eye and in a fit of panic he felt for it, expecting to find that he had lost it. The skin was sticky but the eyeball felt like it was there. He wiped it and blinked furiously. He realised blood was flowing from a cut across his forehead.

Jordan lay still, his smouldering upper body cruelly distorted by the blast. It had taken off both his arms and removed his face completely. Against the rails Stratton heaved in lungfuls of air and tried to bring his knees beneath him, to get up. Deacon was on all fours, shaking his head like a deranged drunk. The Japanese mercenary lay planted across a tool bench and, although dazed, his face peppered in bloody cuts, he was stretching an arm towards his weapon that was a foot away.

Jason could see no sign of Binning and Rowena. He got shakily to his feet and saw the Japanese man going for the weapon. If either thug regained control of the situation it would not be ideal.

Jason aimed himself at the man, put a foot on the weapon as Banzi took hold of the barrel to pull it closer, then dropped onto him. The mercenary was no slouch when it came to self-defence and with a lift of his knee somersaulted Jason over him and onto his back. Banzi got to his knees and picked up the weapon but Jason kicked him in the face from where he lay and sent the mercenary rolling.

Both men scrambled for the gun, both grabbing it at the same time, and a fierce battle for its control ensued.

Stratton had absorbed a heavy impact from the explosion. His vision was askew and he fought to control it. Oddly the blast brought back memories of other explosions that he had survived. In a strange way the memories helped him. He knew it had only been seconds since the detonation and that he had to get to his feet. If he did not gain control of himself, someone else might. He became aware of two men slamming into a piece of nearby machinery, fighting over possession of a rifle. As the rain pelted his face he saw a man on his knees a few metres away reaching for a backpack on the soaked metal deck, his hand rooting inside it. Deacon. Stratton had to get to him before he got what he wanted out of the pack.

The operative put all his weight onto his toes and hands and

202

shoved off like a sprinter. He managed to stay on track after tottering slightly and barrelled into his target, hurting himself in the process but sending the man reeling. The pistol that Deacon had in his hand clattered along the gridded floor and dropped through a gap to the deck below.

Stratton pressed home the attack with little ambition beyond smothering his adversary and controlling him. But Deacon had taken less of the blast. He flipped over and swung a punch that connected with Stratton's face. Stratton held him like a boxer hanging on to an opponent to gain breathing space. But the man fought feverishly, raining blow after blow onto Stratton and, finally freeing himself, rolled away to the top of a stairway and scrambled down the steps.

Despite the blows, Stratton could feel his senses returning, perhaps due to a combination of the cold rain and the adrenalin shooting through him. He grabbed a rail and pulled himself to his feet at the top of the steps.

Deacon had nearly reached the bottom and Stratton did the only thing he could think of: he launched himself from the top and let gravity do the rest. He hit Deacon square in the back, propelling him along the rails and into one of the lifeboat cradles. Both of them were winded but Stratton more so than the ex-SAS man. Deacon held Stratton around the neck in a powerful grip and began to force his head onto one of the guides so that the swinging vessel above might crush it. Stratton avoided the first roll but his face ended up back on the guide. Deacon held him firm and reached for the boat's release lever that if pulled would sever Stratton's head. As Stratton twisted free his harness strap got caught on a bolt-head. Deacon yanked the lever. The lifeboat swung down on its rollers along the guides and out above the water in preparation for lowering. Stratton threw himself out of the way with less than a second to spare.

Deacon was about to move in for another attack when he saw

the pistol lying on the deck between several duct pipes. He decided it was his best chance. Stratton recovered to see the mercenary grabbing a firm hold of the gun. He was too far away to charge the man. As Deacon turned to shoot, Stratton launched himself in between a dense section of piping and, bouncing between one and another, scrambled for all he was worth as the first bullet exploded from the gun and slammed into metal, ricocheting several times. A high-pressure pipe burst loudly, spurting black oily liquid in all directions. Stratton hit so much metal with his body as he ran recklessly that he could not be sure if he'd been struck by the bullet. But as long as he could still move that was what he would fight to do.

He ducked beneath spars, grabbed ahead for pipes to pull himself on. He darted between pieces of machinery, trying not to allow his pursuer a clean shot. Deacon stalked him deliberately, moving confidently over pipes, around valves, between machines, not taking his eye off his prey flitting in and out of sight and only barely managing to deny him a clean shot.

Deacon knew that he would get his man if he remained calm and controlled. He had been in similar situations before, all in the desert, following up failed ambushers or opportunist attackers who had underestimated their intended victim until it was too late. None of those past experiences would be as satisfying as this one. Not only was there more at stake but his prey was a professional like him. A man of pedigree. A member of the SBS. It would be a worthy kill.

Stratton could sense the ability of his pursuer and desperately fought through the obstacles, first one way, then another. He grabbed a steaming-hot pipe, groaned with the pain and pulled himself forward anyway. One clean shot was all the bastard would need and it would be over.

Stratton risked a glance back, only to see the muzzle flash of the gun as Deacon fired. Inches wide. Stratton searched ahead.

It was going to have to be over the side. Yet even that looked doubtful. He still had half the deck between him and the edge.

Another round slammed into a girder inches from Stratton's head. Deacon knew he had at least ten left. Another shot slammed into a storage container. Stratton suddenly emerged from the nest of piping to find himself in open space. A round sliced across his arm, cutting through his dry-suit, burning the skin.

Stratton saw his only chance: across the gap was a diving habitat, the hatch open at the end of the tube. He sprinted towards it with every ounce of strength he could muster.

As Deacon stepped out from the pipes and came up on aim, fancying his chance at a moving target, Stratton dived into the manhole-sized hatch and bounced into the tube. Deacon's shot slammed into the steel pipe. Unperturbed, he walked briskly towards the housing. As far as he could see, Stratton had run into some kind of diving bell and was trapped. The final moment was coming. Such was his confidence that Deacon paused to calculate the time remaining: he had around fifteen minutes before the charges went off. Ample time to blow this prick away and launch a lifeboat.

The habitat was basically a saturation-divers' surface-living accommodation for use between diving tasks. The entrance tube that Stratton had dived through led into a living chamber containing a couple of bunk beds and a table. A further tube led from the living chamber to another hatch that was used to connect to the actual diving bell after it was brought to the surface with the divers inside. They could remain at pressure on the platform, sleep and eat in the habitat without having to decompress, and so could go back to work the following day.

Stratton climbed from the tube into the chamber. He turned himself around and began to reach along the tube to shut the hatch, which opened inwards. As he did so Deacon appeared. Stratton knew he wouldn't make it and shuffled back into the cramped accommodation section, looking around for anything he could use. When Deacon leaned in through the hatch with his pistol gripped in his outstretched hand Stratton hit a switch on the wall and the light went out. The boom of the gun echoed loudly in the bell. The bullet struck the metal skin and bounced around inside several times before its energy dissipated.

Deacon listened for any clue that he had struck his man. 'Come on, matey. All you're doin' is delayin' the end. Let me finish you off cleanly so I can get about my business.'

The silence within the grim habitat persisted, the only sound the wind whistling past the hatch opening. Deacon checked his watch. He still had twelve or so minutes before detonation. There was time to finish the job in hand. With an irritated sigh, he lifted himself inside the tube.

He inched his way along, keeping the pistol close in front of him, confident he could get the shot in even in the darkness.

A heavy metal object flew into the tube, bounced off the side and struck Deacon hard in the face, only serving to rile the man further. 'You bleedin' twat!' he shouted, his voice echoing in the cavelike dwelling. 'Right,' he muttered, more determined than ever to get the bastard. He stopped before the end of the pipe and fired into the blackness of the accommodation. The round ricocheted across the metal room. He fired again and again in different directions, certain that he would hit the man eventually. Deacon was well aware of the risks of being struck himself but his obsession with killing Stratton was muddying his judgement. 'Come on, you little shit! The SAS are 'ere now. The boss men. The numero unos! Your betters! Accept it and take it like a man!'

Deacon fired again and as the echoes of the gun's discharge and the bullet's ricochet subsided he could hear a sound. A change in the dim light came from the opening of another tunnel at the other side of the accommodation section. Deacon squinted, wondering what it could be. He realised there was movement in the tunnel and that the light was coming from outside. Stratton was climbing out through another hatch.

Deacon fired wildly towards it and scrambled as quickly as he could. He dropped onto the floor of the habitat and ran across it to the other tube. He struck the table with his hip and cursed, lunging into the pipe. In the dim light he saw a hand reach in to grab the handle in the middle of the hatch. Deacon struggled to bring the weapon up on aim, then changed his mind and grabbed for the edge of the hatch before it closed. It was ripped from his hand and slammed shut. He lunged for the internal wheel in the darkness but it spun in his hand and bolts moved into grooves to lock the hatch solidly into place.

Deacon pulled as hard as he could on the wheel but it would not budge. The bastard had blocked it with something. The implications of his predicament filled him with panic. He had been outsmarted. But there was still the original entrance. He slid back into the living chamber as quickly as he could.

Stratton finished hammering the cleat into the hatch wheel and ran around the outside of the habitat. He paused at the control panel and quickly scanned the valves and gauges. Time was running out. He identified the valve he needed and turned it brutally several times. Something behind the panel began to hiss. He rushed to the original entrance hatch to complete the manoeuvre, reaching inside as Deacon scrambled into the tube.

Deacon raised his gun to fire and as Stratton pulled the wheel of the hatch towards himself the pistol went off. The round bounced off the inside of the hatch. Deacon lunged forward, grabbing for the wheel, this time getting hold of it before Stratton could close it. They began a desperate tug-of-war.

Stratton raised a knee up against the outer seal as Deacon hooked his feet around the edge of the tube. Stratton almost had the hatch closed but he could not pull it that last inch to turn the wheel. The gas building up inside the chamber began to escape through the hatch. Stratton put all he had into one big effort and almost managed to close the opening. It was the escaping gas that eventually worked in his favour and the hatch suddenly slammed shut like a safe door under the internal pressure.

Stratton slumped limply, hanging from the wheel in pain. He did not need to turn the handle to lock the hatch. The increasing pressure inside would ensure it remained firmly shut. Just a few pounds' difference in pressure between the inside and outside was enough to keep the door closed against the strength of a team of horses.

Stratton was in pain, his bullet wounds giving him hell after his efforts. None had penetrated deeply since all had been third- or fourth-generation ricochets. But they had done some damage.

He forced himself to his feet, all too aware of the imminence of the explosion. He checked the pressure gauges on the control panel and felt the side of his chest and dug a flattened bullet out of his dry-bag.

As he was about to set off to the main deck there came a crash nearby as a body landed from above. It was a hellish fall and if the person hadn't been dead beforehand they had to be close to it now.

Another figure scurried down a duct pipe to land nearby. Jason walked over to inspect his work, then realised the presence of someone close to him and prepared to face another attacker.

Stratton was impressed. Until then he'd considered the man to be little more than a highly intelligent stuffed shirt but it appeared that he could turn his dojo skills to some real use. He'd also clearly decided to do something about Binning. Credit had to go to Rowena for coming with him, wherever she was. But the situation for all of them was about to get much worse, Stratton was sure of it.

Jason didn't relax his stance when he realised it was Stratton before him. 'Are there any more?' he said.

Stratton straightened up, his body aching. 'I hope not,' he said, stiffly.

'Where's the other one?'

Stratton indicated the habitat. 'We need to get to the main deck.'

'Inside?' Jason asked. 'I hope I look better than you.' He looked through a glass porthole no bigger than a tennis ball on the control panel. 'He'll need to be questioned.'

'He has a gun and he's very angry and I don't think we have the time.' Stratton glanced at the gauges. 'He's also at the equivalent depth of a saturation dive. He's not getting out of there any time soon . . . We need to get the workers to the lifeboats.'

'Right,' Jason agreed, about to move away when he saw movement inside the habitat. He flicked a switch on the panel that turned on the chamber light. 'I see him.'

Stratton couldn't resist a last look at his beaten enemy. As both men peered in through the thick glass porthole, Deacon looked up at them, his face red and sweating. His lips formed into a snarl as he brought up the pistol and fired at them.

They both jerked back as the tiny window fractured but held for the moment. Yet the glass continued to crack under the pressure building inside. Deacon angrily approached the porthole to look through it.

Jason and Stratton stepped away and the porthole exploded. Pieces of shattered glass shot from the rim like bullets as the highly compressed gas blasted from the small opening. Deacon couldn't prevent himself being sucked towards the hole, his face acting like a plug. In seconds the pressure began to push him through it. The man screamed as his flesh started to protrude through the hole.

Jason and Stratton backed away in horror as a mass of flesh emerged.

'Oh my God,' Jason muttered.

They ran across the opening to a set of stairs. As they looked back the skin balloon burst and Deacon's face exploded into the swirling wind. Fine strings of mangled flesh filled the air, coming back down to coat everything on the platform, Stratton and Jason included.

They ran from the grisly spectacle up to the top of the stairway and onto the deck, hurrying towards the living quarters.

'Have you seen Binning and Rowena?' Stratton asked.

'No.' Jason went suddenly to the rail to look down onto the line of lifeboats. One of the cradles was empty. He looked out onto the black, rolling water, moving along the rail to cover a greater area as he searched it.

'There! A lifeboat!' he shouted, pointing. 'It's Binning, I know it.'

Stratton could see the orange craft rolling up and down on the heavy swell as it drifted away from the platform. 'And Rowena?'

'He wouldn't hurt her.'

'You still think you know him?'

Jason realised the stupidity of his comment.

'Why would he take her?'

Jason shook his head. 'I don't know!'

Stratton looked around at Jordan's body and as he hurried away he said, 'Go to the galley and tell the workers to get to the lifeboats.'

'Where are you going?' Jason shouted after him.

'To the control room – I'm going to call the navy, tell them to come in and pick up Binning and the rest of us. Get going!'

As Jason moved to go a massive explosion rocked the entire platform, throwing both men off their feet as the giant rig slewed to the side. A sheet of flame lit up the air beyond the furthest corner of the platform.

The deafening sound of yawing, cracking metal rent the air like satanic thunder. Seconds later there came another, lesser explosion that echoed across the sky. One of the massive steel anchor cables that held the huge platform in position snapped like a rubber band and whiplashed out to sea. Another boom was followed by a second cable snapping and the entire rig rocked once again before slowly turning on its axis and leaning heavily to one side.

The deck began to tilt. Containers and heavy machinery moved as the angle increased. Stratton got to his feet and rolled away as a section of decking buckled and snapped out of position. A crescendo of popping rivets and twisting joints joined the cracking and tearing of metal as welds failed and spars bent like sticks of licorice under the immense strain. A rack of high-pressure gas bottles spilled from their frames, rolling and dropping onto the lower decks, exploding as they smashed or roaring like rockets as their valve necks snapped and were ignited by flames.

Workers, many of them bloodied and battered, ran from the collapsing accommodation buildings. Some carried the injured, others staggered, their legs and arms mangled. Those who could sprinted for the lifeboats rocking in their cradles on all sides of the platform on several decks. A falling spar crushed one man as he reached the stairs, another fell through the deck. The section simply dropped open like a trapdoor.

A fuel-storage tank came loose from its mooring and slid down the main deck where it was punctured by a jagged girder. Its inflammable contents gushed from the hole, washed across the deck and down through the gridded floor to the lower levels and the sea, soaking one lifeboat as men crammed aboard it. The platform's exhaust flame, burning on the end of its extended gantry, turned inboard as its supports buckled. The flames roared over the fuel oil, creating an instantaneous fireball that without the storm would have been seen for a hundred miles. It incinerated the fuel-soaked lifeboat and its human load in seconds. The flames fell through the platform and set fire to the sea.

A paint-and-flammables storage bay exploded in the heat, going off like a vehicle bomb that rocked the platform once again.

Now it became impossible to stand without holding on to something. Stratton dug his fingers through the deck grille to make his way to a set of stairs. He looked up at a screeching, rending sound and scrambled out of the way as a giant shale shaker line eased past on its way to the edge where it crashed through the steel rails as if they were ribbons and plummeted into the ocean.

Another terrible sound of failing metal – the big crane leaned over the rails, the rivets at its base popping under the strain, and went crashing through the decking, flattening several men.

A lifeboat swung out prematurely, with men still scrambling into it. As a falling spar struck one of its supports the pulley connection snapped off. The nose of the boat swung down heavily, ejecting those on the outside and cramming those already inside into the wedged end.

In a calm sea the platform might have maintained its structural integrity for an indefinite period despite the horrendous damage. But the storm continued to rage and the heavy seas attacked the weakened Morpheus unrelentingly. One of its huge legs had separated from the upper structure and had fallen into the sea. The platform continued to turn and go down until the remaining anchor points took the strain. One broke at sea level under the immense pressure and the end of the three-inch-thick cable came down onto the deck like a ferocious bullwhip only feet from Stratton. Sections of the living quarters broke away, exposing rooms, toilets and offices and spewing out beds, wardrobes, cookers and fridges to fall into the water.

The central oil derrick that towered over everything buckled at its base and toppled and for a few moments described an arc through the chaos. Then came a shrieking crash as it cut through the decks. Several lifeboats managed to launch and Stratton and Jason joined a dozen workers in a combined effort to release one that had become snarled. Inspired by utter desperation, they freed the roller and the craft moved out over the water where it swung at an unhealthy angle.

Stratton grabbed the release mechanism. 'Get on!' he shouted to the remaining men. Pelted by a combination of falling metal, licking flames and rain, they scrambled across the gap to waiting arms that dragged them inside. 'Go!' he shouted to Jason.

The scientist moved to obey when a heavy spar crashed down in front of him. As he leaped over it to get into the boat the sight of Stratton, his body battered and bloody, holding his wounded side and heroically waiting to release the boat and be the last man on board was too much for him. He wanted to be that man and without a second thought he scrambled to Stratton and took hold of the mechanism. 'You go!' he shouted.

'Just get on the boat!' Stratton shouted back angrily.

'I'm not as injured as you!' Jason yelled. 'Go!'

The ridiculous argument was costing precious time. The men inside the lifeboat looked desperate enough. Stratton let go of the mechanism and jumped for it, painfully grabbing hold of the boat's side. Men pulled him aboard.

Jason yanked at the release mechanism with all his strength and it gave way. The lifeboat began to drop towards the water and Jason jumped after it. Stratton and others grabbed him as he hung over the side.

The small orange vessel dropped like a lift with its cables cut, the lines whipping through the pulleys. Men leaped off the disintegrating platform – their only chance of survival lay in the water.

Stratton's lifeboat hit hard and the men recovered to release the lines. The force of the impact threw Jason off and he disappeared below the water. Seconds later he popped back up and Stratton grabbed his harness and hauled him on board.

Yet they were far from safe as the platform threatened to collapse on top of them. The remaining legs couldn't keep it upright as the wind and tide forced the rig against the remaining anchors.

The lifeboat had come down on the weather side of the platform and the tide pushed it into the guts of the decaying structure. After the last down-line had been disconnected the rolling sea swept the boat up into the cavernous mass. A massive girder plunged into the water beside the small fibreglass boat and another struck its side.

They could only pray, well aware that one spar or chunk of machinery hitting the boat would smash it like a toy. Metal rained down. The boat struck a collection of smashed spars and for a moment was held fast. Stratton, Jason and others fought to push it off.

'Down!' Stratton shouted as the swell raised the boat and the roof slammed into a heavy beam, which split it open like an egg. A sliver of steel stabbed into the boat and passed through a man's body like a kebab skewer. The vessel dropped into the following trough that freed it from the collection of spars and it turned on its axis to sail on sideways. A couple of the men fought to start the engine and as it suddenly boomed into life Jason grabbed the wheel.

The lee side of the platform was fast approaching but the structure looked like it was going to collapse on them before they would make it. Jason pushed the throttle fully open and steered for clear water. The little boat weaved between a series of spars and rose onto a peak. As it dropped down below a hanging section of spider deck they sailed out from beneath the claws of raking spars and raining metal and were suddenly free from the jaws of the groaning beast.

Every man on the boat watched in silent disbelief as the gap between them and the platform increased. Despite the thunderous seas, the massive structure somehow maintained its unnatural position and for the time being seemed to roll with the punches it was taking from wind and tide. Chunks of it still fell away. Drill pipes clattered between the decks and down into the water. Fires burned. Thick smoke billowed. An entire section of lights flickered before going out completely while others glowed brightly.

They began to search the water for survivors. Everywhere men struggled to stay afloat, holding on to debris or swimming for their very lives. Many of the men they hauled into the lifeboat were already dead, either drowned or battered.

Stratton went over in his mind all that had happened. A single nagging thought kept returning: how much of this had he caused, how much was the consequence of his actions? Heads were going to roll for this one. He fully expected his to go on a spike at the Tower of London.

His thoughts went to Jordan and his strange involvement in it all, wondering why the man had done it. Had Stratton been the reason for his old friend's turnabout? Had he caused it? He wondered about Binning and Rowena who he supposed were not far away, awaiting their fate. It was a bloody disaster − in so many ways.

'There she goes,' someone shouted. They all looked in the direction of the Morpheus.

The great platform's end had finally arrived. The monster structure had given up the struggle and succumbed to the forces massed against it. The decks once parallel to the surface of the ocean turned vertical, levering one of the enormous legs out of the sea before it bent under its own weight and collapsed. The last of the lights went out and the fires were extinguished as the twisted wreck sunk in the black broiling water.

The storm's strength had by now lessened and the rain started to subside. Lighter skies appeared to the north. As they continued to search for survivors the sun broke over the far horizon and other lifeboats came into view.

Someone shouted and pointed at a man in the water not far away. As the lifeboat closed on him he stood up, his knees at water level. He was standing on something below the surface. Stratton and Jason realised who it was at the same time. Jackson. In the mini-submarine.

Jackson was more than relieved to see them both, having

215

witnessed the disaster himself. The mini-sub's batteries had run out of power so they tied the vessel alongside the lifeboat. Jackson was very cold and glad to get into the covered boat where he was handed a blanket. He seemed to know there was more to the story of Binning and Rowena after Jason had told him about it but he asked no further questions. As if he understood that it wasn't the time or the place.

The sound of distant rotor blades gradually came to them. Stratton got stiffly to his feet as half a dozen military helicopters flew overhead. He had a reasonably good idea how the day would unfold and resigned himself to it being a very long one indeed.

13

Stratton sat alone at a table in the windowless basement bar of the Blue Boar in Poole, eating a plate of stew. It was early evening and in the large room voices filtered through to him from around the corner. A few people stood at the bar itself.

A pretty waitress collecting used glasses came over to him. 'How's the crockpot, Stratton?' she asked, with a bright smile.

'Almost as good as mine,' he replied, returning her smile.

'Can I get you anything else?'

'I'm fine, thanks.'

'Okay. Enjoy,' she said, leaving him alone but with a parting look that did not disguise her interest in him.

He put down his fork, took a sip of wine and leaned back in thought. The bruises around the wounds on his face, those not covered by several weeks of beard growth, had mostly disappeared. The deeper cuts on his hands were now thin black lines. He looked generally gaunt and tired, his eyes dark, his skin pale.

Stratton emptied the wine glass and stretched out his legs. His body still felt stiff, particularly the healing flesh around the bullet wounds. It was time to start working out but his heart wasn't yet in it. The medic had said he was to do nothing too strenuous for another week but he knew his body better. It was his spirit that needed healing more than anything else at that moment.

He lowered his hands to his knees, continuing to bend forward slowly, stretching the backs of his legs until he could touch his toes with outstretched fingertips. It wasn't so bad. A week earlier the same exercise had been far more painful and he had reached half the distance.

He was not only disheartened but thoroughly bored.

Within hours of being picked up from the lifeboat and taken on board the operations vessel Stratton had been treated in the sickbay while being debriefed by a London suit. The debriefing had taken several hours after which he'd been returned promptly to Poole and to his home and ordered to remain in the vicinity until further notice. He wasn't under house arrest or anything like that. He could attend the camp hospital, go shopping and to the pub. But he was told that he was not to spend time with work associates and should not encourage friends to visit him. The bottom line was that under no circumstances was he to discuss any aspect of the operation. It was made very clear to him that there would be severe repercussions if he were to ignore this instruction.

It was all quite bizarre, really. Stratton hadn't experienced anything like it. He was not being admonished as such. Everyone had been cold towards him, the powers that be, but there was no official hearing, no inquiry that he had been asked to attend. It was as if he had been placed inside a box until they decided what to do with him.

Stratton hadn't seen Jason or any of the others involved in the operation since they had been rescued. He was questioned about everything and everyone but had been given nothing in return other than the news that Smithy had been picked up in the middle of the ocean and was doing fine. The futures of Binning and Rowena, however, remained a mystery to him. When he asked about them he drew a blank. They told him not to discuss the subject with anyone and that the only reason he was being allowed to police his own isolation was because of his track record with MI6.

218

A criminal mole inside MI16 was a serious situation and London would undoubtedly want the lid kept very tight on it. The television and newspapers had been full of the Morpheus disaster and had blamed the hijackers. The MoD hadn't been criticised for its lack of response to the incident. The suddenness of the destruction of the rig seemed to have struck everyone. But the press were curious about what they described as its 'premature' blowing-up. Theories abounded. All kinds of expert witnesses espoused various views, the most popular being that the explosion had to have been an accident of some kind. The hijackers had cocked it up and sunk the bloody thing by mistake. It must have been something like that since they could never have received a ransom payment in such a short time. And since none of the hijackers appeared to have survived, it was up to Scotland Yard to find out who was ultimately behind it – the mastermind behind the scenes. Another popular theory. Terrorism had not been discounted as a plausible reason for the explosion but the varied nationalities and backgrounds of the hijackers seemed to have muddied that idea. Three weeks into the investigation the police had officially uncovered very little. Of course they were divulging nothing.

The media became obsessed with one other part of the story: the mysterious individual who had released the workers after killing the hijackers singlehandedly with a silenced submachine gun. They interviewed several workers on camera, all of whom displayed deep gratitude to the shadowy stranger in black who had saved many of their lives. He had been described as darkly handsome with a chiselled jaw, a man of few words and such dominating character that his every utterance had been obeyed without question.

Several of the newspapers provided drawings, a couple of which resembled Stratton a little, but only to those few who knew it had been him. One news programme went to great lengths to create computer graphics illustrating how the special operative might have got aboard the Morpheus in the brutal storm, risking life and limb to scale the platform after having been parachuted into the ocean some distance away. And then the superhero vanished as mysteriously as he had arrived. There was mention of another two men and a mini-submarine and an effort was made to connect the destruction of the rig with their arrival. One newspaper suggested that the operative's attack had caused a last-stand action by the hijackers. The media knew when they were onto a good thing with the mysterious character and they made the most out of him that they could.

Stratton suspected that MI16 might be closed down, for the moment at least, and would be undergoing a thorough investigation. If anyone was being hammered about the corruption within its ranks it was Jason. He would obviously be a suspect too, something that would do nothing for his ego. But he had done well from the moment Jordan had been killed and Stratton had given a good account of his actions. Stratton was no longer sure how he felt about the man. The bloke had an inflated sense of his own importance and his plans to create a team of super-intelligent field operators proved it. No doubt that project had gone down in flames with the Morpheus. He hoped the man had seen the flaws in his ambitions. But then, Mansfield wasn't the type to show humility – certainly not to Stratton, at least. He couldn't see them sharing a pint.

Stratton's phone rang. An unusual sound for him at the moment. Word had spread throughout the service that he was on suspension and was not to be contacted unless it was done through the command structure. He decided to leave the phone rather than answer it and explain to whoever it was that he couldn't talk. After several rings it ceased. He took another sip of wine and went back to his stew. The phone rang again.

A persistent caller was unusual. Stratton took the phone out of his pocket and looked at the screen. There was no caller ID.

He pushed the receive button and put the phone to his ear.

'This is Mike. You're allowed to talk to me, Stratton.'

It was nice to hear a friendly voice. 'Hi. How you doing?'

'Fine. You?'

'Can't remember the last time I sat around doing nothing for so long.'

'How about that ten-day stake-out you and I did in Crossmaglen?'

'Ah. Those good old days in South Armagh. They seem like a million years ago.'

'This isn't a chatty call, John. Where are you right now?'

'Blue Boar.'

'I hope you haven't had much to drink.'

'Half a glass of the Boar's finest claret.'

'I need you to get your arse in here. You probably look like shit with a beard 'n' all.'

'I may look more relaxed than normal,' Stratton said, scratching his beard.

'You have time to get home and clean up. There's a couple people still on their way from London.'

Stratton could only wonder what it was all about. He checked his watch.

'Yes, I know it's late,' Mike said, as if reading Stratton's thoughts. 'Come straight to the ops room. Oh, and put your crockpot in the freezer this time.'

The line went dead.

The crockpot reference used to be Mike's private code for going away on an op. Perhaps now it just meant going away, as in to jail.

Stratton brushed the thoughts aside. He knew Mike well enough and could tell his mood from the tone of his voice. He'd sounded upbeat and energetic, as if he was keen to get on with something positive. Something was up. The crockpot in the freezer indicated more than a short job.

Stratton felt suddenly energised. This was good, he hoped. If it was an op, it meant he had been forgiven. Perhaps that was stretching it a little too far but it would do for the time being. He got to his feet, grabbed the old leather jacket off the back of the chair and headed to the bar to pay his bill. His favourite piece of clothing had arrived at his house from London a week before, along with the other belongings that he'd left at MI16. Stratton suspected that it had all been checked by forensics for any evidence of his involvement in the plot. They'd even examined his Jeep before it was returned by some innocuous delivery man, again from London.

Fifty minutes later he pulled into the SBS car park and climbed out of the Jeep. As he headed for the main building, fine flakes of snow began to float down from a sky the colour of wet concrete. Yet the snow refreshed him, mentally as well as physically. It conjured up memories, all of them operational in his case – days spent living in hedgerows or on mountaintops, sipping a hot drink and always watching for someone or something. He hoped that, if this meeting was all about a trip somewhere, he might be back in time to enjoy the white stuff.

He walked in through the front doors of the SBS HQ, swiped his ID card that registered his arrival as well as automatically unlocking the inner door, and headed to the ops room door. He did not have access to this one. As he reached for the buzzer the door opened and Mike stood looking at him.

Neither man moved, each studying the other, both with glib expressions. Mike's face then cracked into a smile. 'I think you're going to like this one,' he said.

Stratton didn't return the smile. 'You said that about the last job and I didn't like it much at all.'

'You only think you didn't. You'll be boring us all with your stories about it when you're retired. Let's go meet the gang.'

Stratton followed Mike through the ops room door into the

curtain cubicle. Once more they stepped through into the spacious operations room with its myriad flatscreens, charts, maps and communications systems.

The tall, white-haired SBS commanding officer stood in civilian clothes talking to the operations officer and a man in a suit who had his back to Stratton. The CO glanced at Stratton on seeing the men enter and went back to his conversation.

Mike went to the immaculate young operations officer, also dressed in civvies, taking him aside for a quiet word. Stratton stood in the room feeling self-conscious. He hadn't seen the CO since before the operation and felt something akin to shame, like the feelings he'd had years ago when he'd found himself waiting outside the headmaster's office for a reprimand.

'Stratton,' the CO finally said as he moved to a group of chairs and sat down. 'How is everything?' he asked, wearing a thin, knowing smile.

Stratton was about to answer when the suited gentleman turned to face him. It was Sumners, his operational MI6 handler.

Sumners studied him coldly. The sight of Stratton conjured up all sorts of disagreeable thoughts, and not just about the more recent disaster. The man had a track record. Sumners despised the operative. With good reason, as far as he was concerned.

Stratton didn't share the same degree of distaste for his London superior but he was well aware of Sumners's feelings. It was a private hatred, though. No one else in the room knew the history behind it. In fact there were probably only a handful of people in MI6 who knew about the potentially disastrous operation that had climaxed in Jerusalem a few years back and had caused the rift between them — and they were all senior mandarins who knew how to keep a secret. Not that Stratton and Sumners had been particularly chummy before that incident. Sumners wasn't chummy with anyone.

If Sumners had come all the way to Poole that pretty much

confirmed to Stratton there was a job on. As the main liaison between MI6 and UK special forces Sumners was usually responsible for giving the intelligence outline before someone else covered an operation's nuts and bolts.

'You know Sumners, of course,' the CO said.

The CO knew something of Sumners's responsibilities at MI6, and a little of Stratton's unique relationship with the London-based organisation. He was never privy to any operational details. But he was no fool and was aware that there was no love lost between the pair.

'Yes. How are you, sir?' Stratton asked.

Sumners gave him a very brief, empty smile and brushed his lapel, a characteristic gesture of his that implied he was marginally irritated.

'Right. Shall we get on with this?' the CO urged. 'The preamble, please, Mr Sumners.'

Stratton sat in one of the chairs beside the CO. The ops officer remained standing to one side and Mike took a seat at the back of the room. An empty seat remained at the other side of Stratton.

Sumners walked to where he was comfortable addressing everyone and took a moment to collect his thoughts. 'You all understand that what we are about to discuss is beyond secret,' he began, somewhat moodily. 'I am obliged to stress this even though it is a given . . . This operation is unique insofar as it will be a combined SBS and MI6 effort. We have always trained together, shared resources and skills. I have given many intelligence briefs to your personnel in various parts of the world. But I cannot recall the last time the two organisations actually combined operations in the manner we are proposing today. We have been joined at the hip with regards to this task, having previously been pawns in a plot that led to the destruction of the Morpheus and the theft of Her Majesty's property.

'Binning was not working alone when he removed the tile from MI16 and brought it aboard the oil platform in order to steal it. It is our belief that the hijacking of the platform was contrived entirely for the purpose of procuring the decryption device.'

'Excuse me,' Stratton interrupted, much to Sumners's annoyance, as well as the CO's. It was generally unacceptable to interrupt a briefing. All questions were usually left until the end. The sign of a good brief, in fact, was that no questions were required by the end of it, the briefer having covered all topics and contingencies. For Stratton to interrupt so soon was a surprise. An unwelcome one.

Sumners could not help taking it as a slight by the upstart. 'What is it?' he asked, frowning as he stared at his subordinate.

'Sorry, but I need to catch up on a few things. I don't know anything about a tile, or what happened to Binning and Rowena . . . if it's pertinent to the briefing.'

The CO eyed Sumners with a look of acknowledgement concerning Stratton's comment. 'He's been in information isolation since the incident. You should go back a little further.'

Sumners frowned again, even though Stratton obviously needed to know all the details. The CO coming out on the operator's side did not help soothe his animosity towards him. 'The tile refers to an extremely valuable decryption device that Binning stole from MI16, and he, along with Miss Deboventurer, escaped in a lifeboat before the platform was destroyed. During the subsequent emergency response we found the lifeboat. Empty. There was only one way they could have escaped, in our opinion at least, and that was by submarine. It would have been possible for a small surface vessel to get through the security cordon under the cover of the intense storm. But all things considered, that is highly unlikely. The destruction of the platform was calculated, a phase of the escape plan to create confusion and drain the resources of the security cordon.

But that would still have left escape by a surface vessel, even a small stealth version, a high-risk option, considering how elaborate the rest of the operation was. The planners could not have guaranteed the arrival of such a storm to mask their escape, for instance, even in the North Sea. One has to assume that they had an all-weather escape plan. A small submarine of the type we believe was used could have made it through our cordon, particularly under the prevailing conditions.

'The question must be asked, then, how the planners could justify such an expensive and elaborate operation. The answer is simple. The value of the tile is many times more than the cost involved in stealing it. I'm afraid its uses as a tool for industrial espionage are incalculable.'

'This was all about industrial espionage?' Stratton said.

'Elements of the Russian government clearly played a part in its theft – the submarine, for example – and I'm sure they didn't do it for charity. The tile is a new generation of decrypter. Hackers have successfully infiltrated the most sophisticated databases on numerous occasions – MI6 and the CIA have been victims over the years, as have many corporate and financial institutions,' Sumners explained. 'The problem they have always run into is the decryption of the stolen data. The tile has so far shown the potential of being able to crack every encryption it has been tested against. It hasn't been completed but Binning may be able to finalise the design. There are foreign governments and corporations willing to pay anything for it. To put it in perspective, imagine what the Nazis would have paid to get their hands on Ultra, the decryption device that ultimately lost them the war. Relatively speaking, the hijackers acquired the tile for practically nothing.'

'Excuse me.' Stratton felt obliged to interrupt once again. 'Was Deboventurer working with Binning?'

'We don't believe so. He took her as a hostage to assist in his escape. We can only assume that he didn't leave her on the lifeboat because she has some value. That remains unclear for now. The investigation into MI16 is intensive and ongoing. As for the other players involved in the theft, those behind the planning and funding of it, we know some of them. As I said earlier, it looks to have been a joint venture involving private individuals and elements within the Russian government. There is no evidence of direct government or FSB involvement. But state resources were clearly misused by people of influence within those organisations.'

The seated men exchanged glances.

'You may recall a certain Russian naval vessel called the *Inessa*,' Sumners said, glancing at Stratton, well aware of his failed operation on that mission. 'One of its uses is as a "stable" for long-distance mini-submarines. The operation that Stratton failed in was completed a week later by MI16.' Sumners showed no sign of revelling in the comment. Stratton knew him well enough to know how much he really was.

'The *Inessa* was monitored leaving the North Sea at a time and place that calculations indicate could have enabled a rendezvous with a submersible from the area of the Morpheus not that long after its sinking. It is also interesting to note that while Jackson was holding position in the SBS mini-sub after dropping off Stratton and the others, its Doppler sonar picked up a significant shadow about as large as a medium-sized whale. Close examination of that recording revealed that he had inadvertently registered another submarine. Since we did not put all of this together till well after the incident, nothing was done about the *Inessa* at the time.'

Sumners picked a glass of water off the table and took a sip, giving the others time to digest the information so far.

'Working on the principle that the guilty are usually far closer to home than one might expect to find them, a subsequent investigation into the owners of the Morpheus revealed some interesting facts. I won't go into all the details simply because of the time factor. But in summary, one of the major shareholders of the group that owned the platform has been in financial difficulties for years. During the last twelve months they uncharacteristically began putting money into the venture, spending it mostly, apparently, on costly improvements. That increased its insurance value. The controlling cadre is made up of four significant characters: two Arabs and two Russians.'

The men's images appeared on the sceens – the four in Abu Dhabi who had given Deacon the go-ahead by satellite phone.

'The character we're going to examine is one of the Russians: Dimitry Robalesk. He has a brother in the Russian Ministry of Trade, Vlad Robalesk. Vlad has financial interests in mining along with his brother. Vlad also has a history of industrial espionage. The pattern of relationships between businessmen and government officers grows more nefarious and complex the deeper we dig.

'Suffice it to say that it all boils down to a collection of signif-icant pointers relevant to our subject. First of all, those who owned the oil platform would not lose any money from its destruction, by natural or terrorist means, due to the insurance cover. Close friends and associates of those who owned the platform would pay a high price for obtaining the tile.

'Binning was the "operative" who succeeded in recording the *Inessa*'s data after the failed SBS operation. His disappearance after the Morpheus disaster and the theft of the tile naturally prompted an intense investigation into all his MI16 projects, as well as a closer examination of the one operation he carried out against the *Inessa*. The timings reveal that he had adequate opportunity to liaise with and board the vessel. We believe this is what actually happened and where he was able to meet representatives of the players personally and finalise the plan, and no doubt his own deal. We believe as part of the arrangement he was allowed to gain certain information about the *Inessa* and thereby succeed in his operation. The meeting was obviously prearranged. In short, gentlemen, a large portion of this highly complex and, it has to be said, quite brilliant plot was probably engineered by Binning himself. But it also has the hallmarks of government sponsorship written all over it.'

A moment was left for the clearing of throats and the exchanging of glances.

Sumners continued: 'Can you bring up the map of Russia, please? North of Plesetsky.'

The operations officer tapped several keys on his console and the large monitors came to life.

'Now,' Sumners said, clearing his own throat. 'Where does that leave us and our counter-operation to retrieve our stolen goods? Well, Vlad Robalesk owns several mines, two of them in the Plesetsky area.'

One of the monitors gave a satellite view of the vastness of Russia before zooming in on the central region.

'Some forty years ago the Russians converted an old mine into a research and development laboratory. The reason they needed something deep in the ground was, you won't be surprised to hear, not only security against prying eyes in the sky but also because it was to be a chemical and biological weapons laboratory. They needed to be able to seal the place off if something went wrong. The facility's in this area here.'

A large square graphic appeared on the screen.

'Robalesk acquired the converted mine shortly after the collapse of the communist government, apparently with the intentions of cleaning it up and reopening it as a going concern. We don't think that happened. And neither did he close the facility down. Now this is where it helps to have an intelligence organisation that knows how to cross-reference information not only by subject but also in depth and time. Two years ago, when the *Inessa* was being fitted for its current role, in our efforts to try to discover its purpose we naturally followed every lead we had, in and out of the shipyard. One of them led to the chemical warfare mine, as it became known, in Plesetsky. It was from there that we constructed our understanding of the relationship between Vlad Robalesk and certain players in the FSB and the Russian government. We have been closely observing the area for the past two weeks and there has been significant activity along the road that links the town of Plesetsky to the laboratory. Vlad Robalesk has been identified twice, along with several other significant players. This is certainly an indication that something of great interest has recently arrived at the mine.

'The surveillance photography, if you don't mind,' Sumners asked the operations officer.

Several grainy photographs appeared in layers on the screen. They were of a sedan driving along a road covered in snow. The photo zoomed in to reveal a figure seated in the back. It was difficult at first to identify him but as the pixels adjusted his features became clearer. Other similar images appeared, a time-line shot of the same vehicle moving along the road.

'A close examination of the photographs confirms it is indeed our man Binning. These photographs were taken eleven days ago. The *Inessa* arrived in Sevastopol two days before. One might be allowed to assume that Binning was on board. A day of debriefing and then to work. I think it's also safe to assume that Binning has not only provided them with the tile but that he also has a new employer.'

Sumners took another moment to allow the information to be digested.

Stratton was already thinking ahead to what the operation might be.

'We currently have a surveillance operative in the area, the person responsible for the photographs. Binning appears to commute to the town of Plesetsky where he is staying in a house. He doesn't travel every day. Sometimes he overnights at the mine. We don't know how long these circumstances will continue.

Therefore it has been decided that we should act as soon as possible.

'And so,' Sumners expressed with theatrical fatigue, as if he had finally reached the point of his presentation. 'The operation. You will of course present the details but while I'm here I'll provide the general outline. We are going to pay Mr Binning a visit. We are going to find out where our tile is. We are going to find out as much as we can from Binning about the operation, the players, et cetera, et cetera. And then we are going to terminate Mr Binning.' Sumners looked directly at Stratton as he said it.

A phone console buzzed and displayed a flashing red light. Mike quickly answered it. 'Okay,' he said before replacing the receiver. 'Your guest has arrived,' he said to Sumners.

'You can bring him down.'

Mike excused himself from the briefing.

'The task is being offered to you, Stratton,' Sumners said, examining the screen without looking at him. 'I assume you will take it and do a good job. I think you owe us that much.'

Stratton didn't respond immediately, not even with his facial expression. His crime as he saw it had been to use government property to try to rescue an old friend. He'd do it again if he had to. Binning stealing the tile and everything else had nothing to do with him. Sumners had chosen to put it in a manner that suited his own mean streak. He was being a prick as usual, and this time for an audience. Yet Stratton realised his own suitability for the operation. For a number of reasons. He knew Binning for a start. Bringing in other players would only increase the number of people who knew about it. This entire affair had to be kept as secret as possible. Yet somewhere within him he knew that wasn't enough. There had to be something else, some other, more substantial reason why he had been selected. He couldn't think of it at that moment. He might never know. But of course he would do the op. In fact, he was looking forward to it. As usual Sumners was trying to wind him up and Stratton would not dignify the attempt with any sort of reaction.

But Sumners wasn't finished yet. He had his little ace to play. 'You won't be going alone, of course. I need someone to keep an eye on you.' The MI6 man looked towards the back of the room, waiting for the visitor to arrive. As he did so Mike stepped through the black curtains and Jason Mansfield walked in behind him. There was an air of authority about him.

Stratton looked around and could not believe his eyes. He looked at the CO for a reaction. The man was far too professional to give him one.

Stratton's head was filled with questions that he couldn't ask. Dominated by one in particular: what was a civilian with no experience in this kind of operation doing here? Yet it was pointless to complain. The decision had been made at a very high level. This was an extremely sensitive operation with many potential repercussions if it went wrong. He decided to keep his mouth shut and wait for the rest of the briefing.

Jason came over to Stratton, wearing that same supercilious smile he'd worn when they'd first met. It was as if he had been cleansed of the past and everything was the same between them. 'Good to see you again, Stratton. You all healed up?'

Stratton remained sitting and looked up at the man. 'I'm fine,' he replied dryly.

Jason leaned down and spoke softly. 'You don't look pleased to see me.' He stood upright and said, as if for the room's benefit, 'Hopefully this won't be as vigorous as our last adventure.'

The man was talking like he'd been doing it for years and that they were old operational buddies.

'This is the SBS CO,' Sumners said.

Jason took the CO's hand and shook it. 'Good to meet you.

I've been looking forward to visiting Poole for such a long time and to meet the people who play with the toys I make.'

Stratton cringed. Any positive feelings he'd developed about the man after his actions on the platform withered.

'Have they sorted you out a room in the mess?' the CO asked.

'Yes, thanks. Very comfortable.'

'Good. Right, then. Shall we get on with the detailed briefing? You both have an early start tomorrow and we've got a lot to cover.'

'I'll leave you to it,' Sumners said. He took a black woollen overcoat off the back of a chair and pulled it on. 'Don't be offended if I don't wish you luck, Jason.' He wrapped a scarf around his neck. 'I never do. Don't believe in it . . . which is something of a surprise after witnessing Stratton's activities all these years.'

Jason made a poor effort of trying not to smirk, as if he was in the know.

Sumners nodded farewell to the CO and ops officer and headed for the curtains. Mike escorted him out.

The CO leaned close to Stratton. 'You have my sympathy,' he whispered. The comment had a calming effect, no doubt its intention.

'Gentlemen,' announced the operations officer. 'If you would like to be seated, we will proceed.'

Jason sat beside Stratton and took a notebook from a pocket.

The ops officer saw him scribble a couple of lines on a page. 'You can take notes of the briefing, Mr Mansfield, but nothing leaves this room.'

'I fully understand, Captain,' Jason said, with barely a glance at the officer. 'I have a photographic memory. All I need do is write down the relevant data and then I can immediately dispense with it.'

Stratton glanced round at Mike who had returned in time to hear the comment. The sergeant major grinned broadly at his friend, knowing how painful this was for him. He pointed to Jason and gave the thumbs-up, mouthing the comment 'Top man.' He then pointed to Stratton and mimicked a wanking motion.

Stratton faced the front. He felt inclined to agree with his old friend concerning the latter gesture.

14

Stratton sat in the train, looking out of its window as it clattered through a vast countryside, the view an endless portrait of winter, black leafless trees and hedges the only contrast to a frozen white backdrop. Long icicles, pointing at steep angles towards the back of the train, had formed along the outside edge of the glass. The flat and featureless land stretched to the horizon, punctuated occasionally by small rustic villages on one side or the other, some like cosy straw hamlets while others were more modern, concrete and drab. Passing through one small town, Stratton saw a man standing in the road with a goat on a leash. The man watched the train. He looked cold and hungry. It all seemed so isolated and vacant. So many miles of empty and seemingly untouched land.

He had been staring outside for hours and his eyes began to ache. He looked back inside the carriage. It was the image of uncomfortable sparseness, communist-inspired, as if nothing had changed since the fall of the Wall a couple of decades earlier. Short, stubby icicles hung from the centre of the ceiling along the length of the long carriage. A handful of people occupied the pewlike bench seats, each of them silent and unsmiling. A man snored intermittently in the row beyond Stratton's, an empty vodka bottle in his hands, although he could hardly be heard above the clatter of the wheels. He had joined the train at Moscow with a full litre and within an hour had drunk it and fallen unconscious. He wasn't the only heavy drinker on the train. Boozing seemed to be a national pastime.

Jason sat across from Stratton, in the corner, staring out of the opposite window. He had kept to himself since they'd caught the plane at Heathrow. Stratton assumed it was a reaction to being ignored since they'd left Poole. But then halfway through the flight he had leaned over and quietly apologised for his stand-offishness and explained why he'd been aloof. Jason had done some kind of one-day MI6 course on travel security as preparation. He had learned how best to act when travelling in potentially hostile environments. Stratton knew what such courses consisted of. They were pretty much advice for beginners – comprehensive but common sense and rather obvious to someone at Stratton's level. He had on occasion been asked to instruct MI6 and MI5, teaching various operational procedure lessons. Jason would have done the usual hotel, office and home security course. He might have sat through a presentation on anti-surveillance techniques by foot and by vehicle: how to detect if he was being being followed, how to prove it, and what to do and what not to do about it. The man had clearly absorbed it all and was living the role. All he needed now was the experience.

When they'd landed in Moscow his arrogance had extended to taking over the travel procedures by suggesting they move separately. It was as if Stratton had never done it before and Jason had become his mentor. They kept apart the whole time after that, except when Stratton had climbed into a taxi at the airport. Jason began some kind of pantomime for the sake of the taxi driver, asking Stratton if he minded sharing the cab. Jason said he'd overheard that Stratton was going to the railway station, which also happened to be his own destination. Stratton found himself shaking his head – mentally, at least – on more than one occasion.

After that they had separated again. Stratton didn't say a negative word about it. The separation procedures suited him perfectly. He had been wondering how he was going to ignore the other man as much as possible throughout the operation and to his relief Mansfield had come up with the solution himself. Sitting opposite each other in silence on the day-long train journey across a big stretch of Russia was apparently acceptable.

Stratton felt curious about one thing that Jason probably knew about: Rowena. Considering that she was technically a member of the British military and was now more than likely being held captive in Russia, it seemed to him that very little action was being taken to resolve the issue. Then perhaps there wasn't much that could be done about it. The Russians couldn't admit to having her without admitting their involvement in everything else. And then coming up with a sound enough reason for keeping her was equally complicated. Stratton had found her to be a most irritating, cold and obnoxious bitch, but by the time they had climbed the platform he had developed a degree of admiration for her. She'd had no doubts about the dangers but she'd gone anyway. But if she hadn't done it because of Jason and her relationship with him, why had she gone along? It niggled him. He did not sense the same level of loyalty in Jason. He wanted to understand some things a little deeper and perhaps Jason had answers.

'You've not mentioned Rowena,' Stratton said. They were the first words he had spoken to Jason in half a day.

Jason looked at him as if his mind had been on another planet and was scrambling to come back down to earth. 'I think of her all the time,' he replied eventually, looking away. 'I was thinking of her just then. Between you and me, we were quite close. Personal relationships in MI16 are frowned upon. But I knew Rowena long before I came to the organisation.

'We first met in Oxford. You think she was strong-headed when you met her. She was even worse then. And I gather that was an improvement on how she'd been as a teenager . . . Rowena was

237

adopted. I don't know anything about her natural parents. She walked out of the house when she was fourteen to join some kind of intellectual commune in Canada. She told me she was bored, not stimulated. In short, her adoptive parents were too thick.' Jason chuckled at the thought.

'We didn't see each other in college, not in any kind of carnal way. She didn't like me very much then. She said she did but I didn't believe her. She was – is – a brilliant physicist. Being beautiful and brilliant she needed to be headstrong. No one ignored her, that's for sure. She got her doctorate at Princeton and then flitted around a few places. An audio-electronics company in Japan for a few months. Then NASA for a year. Got bored there, too. Then she did something completely radical and joined MI5 – a fast track to some undercover surveillance unit that operates in places like Iraq and Afghanistan. She completed the selection and training course but didn't join the ranks. Someone up top recognised her potential and had her transferred to MI16. I suspect it was Jervis. She's never talked about that to me. I read it in her file. I think she wanted to join that unit because she had something to prove, not to anyone else but to herself. But she never got the chance. I think that's why she came on the platform operation even though she didn't approve. I have a strong feeling she's fine and well and will return safely home.'

'Based on what?'

'Intuition. I'm rather keen on mine.'

Stratton could have guessed as much. 'I need a wee,' he said, getting to his feet. The uncomfortable seats felt cold and he wanted to stretch his legs to warm up a little – the icy air had a way of finding his joints. He was well dressed against the cold, a good thing too since the carriage was an icebox. He also saw it as an opportunity to take a look at the characters on board. Paranoia was a healthy attitude, particularly in Russia. The two men had entered the country as engineers: Stratton a pipe welder and Jason a designer, naturally. A British pipe-welding company did actually operate on a gas pipeline a few hundred miles north of Moscow – not where the two men were ultimately heading but the company's books had been amended to support the cover story. However, the FSB were, by profession, a suspicious lot. Stratton would not have been surprised if they'd been tagged from the airport. The plan had taken such a probability into account, of course. But the more prepared they were, the better.

He walked along the coach, surreptitiously checking out every individual as he passed them. The unconscious drunk had vomited down his clothes. In the next row a couple sat with three remarkably quiet young children. The low temperature might have had something to do with their silence. An old couple next, sitting huddled together against the cold, woollen scarves wrapped around their heads. A couple of families in another row, eating a communal meal of bread, meat and cheese. And vodka.

The rest of the carriage was empty except for the second row from the end. Two men sat on opposite sides, one young, the other mature, both dishevelled, shifty-looking. They eyed Stratton, no doubt taking in his comparatively expensive clothing. They didn't appear to be together but Stratton sensed a common attitude between them. He pegged them more as thugs than secret service.

At the end of the carriage he could find no toilet. The door at the end had a glass panel in it but he could see nothing through the thick coating of ice. Stratton wondered if he could get into the following carriage. If that had no toilet either, well, he'd have to urinate into the freezing cold outside. He grabbed hold of the door handle and applied some pressure to push it down. Eventually the handle moved but the door wouldn't open. It was stuck solid.

He pulled on a pair of gloves and, gripping the handle with

both hands, put his weight into it. He leaned back, raised a foot up onto the frame and gave it a powerful shove. The door cracked open and the freezing air ripped inside. Stratton looked back but no one had leaned into the aisle to investigate. It was something they were no doubt used to.

Stratton tugged at the door's frosty hinges a little more, opening it enough for him to squeeze through. He knocked away a sheet of ice that had formed down one side of the door frame and stepped out onto a ledge above the linkage, the wind zipping in and out of the gap between the carriages. He felt the wind chill sharply mask his face. The ground tore along below, the shiny rails dividing the frozen gravel between the sleepers. He grabbed hold of a long horizontal bar fixed to the carriage near the door for that purpose and stepped across the coupling to plant a foot on the small platform outside the connecting carriage's door. He pulled the door to in order to give himself some privacy, at the same time wondering how on earth the ladies managed it.

It was a pleasant enough moment – the relief of emptying his bladder combined with the circumstances and a spectacular view.

When he was finished Stratton nudged the door to open it again. But it wouldn't budge. A firmer push moved it in a few inches but it immediately slid back as if it had become spring-loaded.

Stratton gave it a harder shove and this time it wedged open but a man suddenly moved into the gap. It was the older of the thuggish-looking pair.

He shouted something in Russian but Stratton didn't know the language well enough to understand him. The man repeated himself, this time gesticulating with a hand. He wanted money. But there were no guarantees that he would let Stratton back in once the exchange had been made. In fact, that was the ideal strategy.

Stratton inspected the door to the other carriage and tried to pull down the handle but it was stuck fast. The Russian said something else in a slightly louder tone, sounding angry and frustrated. He shook his open hand and held it out further in order to emphasise his demand.

Stratton would have gone a long way to avoid any kind of conflict, even paying the man had he believed he would let him return to his seat. A low profile was an obvious essential to the task. But in the middle of this freezing wilderness he couldn't risk getting stuck outside. Mansfield was unlikely to investigate before it was far too late. He had to do something decisive.

Stuff it, he decided. He reached into a pocket, pulled out a few notes and put the flapping money into the man's hand. As the Russian took the cash, Stratton twisted his wrist, at the same time kicking the door open as he yanked the man out.

The Russian thug landed on the coupling, immediately lost his balance, and with a look of terror on his face fell back and disappeared into the slipstream.

Stratton surprised himself by the ease with which he'd launched the man. It hadn't been his intention. He looked inside the carriage in preparation for an assault from the accomplice. But the younger man stood stock-still in the doorway, eyes wide at the speed with which his comrade had been dispatched. He backed away, turned around sharply and returned to his seat.

Stratton pulled himself back into the carriage and closed the door, immediately shutting out the howling, freezing wind and the noisier clattering of metal wheels on rails.

He walked back along the carriage, eyeing the young man who was now sitting tightly against the end of the bench and looking intently out of the window. He looked like he was trying to make himself invisible.

Stratton ignored him. Several people gave the operative sober glances this time, as if they knew that something had just happened.

241

There was no judgement in their expressions – or anything, in fact, other than simple curiosity.

Jason seemed to be lost in another daydream and barely acknowledged Stratton's return. Stratton checked his watch. They had been travelling for just over five hours. A couple more to go. He put his head back and closed his eyes.

It was the smell of woodsmoke that brought Stratton out of his chilly slumber. The couple with the children had lit a fire in a bucket and were huddled around it. The carriage had filled with smoke but no one appeared to have complained. At least smoke meant warmth.

He checked his watch again. The train had stopped several times at small village stations far off the beaten track and had occasionally slowed to a crawl. The seven-hour journey had turned into a ten-hour slog and Stratton was feeling hungry now as well as cold. He dug a survival bar out of a pocket and took a bite out of it. His thoughts quickly shifted to the task. But he reminded himself once again that it wasn't worth thinking about. The information he needed to progress any planning was waiting for him on the ground. Stratton had long since learned to compartmentalise such things in order to take as much advantage as possible of any down time. Rest when you can for you don't know when your next chance will come.

The train reached their destination eventually. Both men got to their feet. They each carried small backpacks containing washing gear, a change of clothes and nothing else. They kept their passports, money and return air tickets in their pockets. Stratton pulled the collar of his thick coat tight around his neck, shoved a woollen hat onto his head, rolling down the sides to cover his ears, and stepped down the carriage steps after Jason onto the snow-covered gravel. No platform. Just a couple of low brick buildings one side of the track, smoke issuing from a chimney, the only evidence of life. No one to greet the train or get aboard it. A family climbed out of the next carriage and after gathering their things huddled together and headed back along the track. The rest was tundra.

Mansfield had already set off at a brisk pace along the single road that cut the station in two: north led across the railway track into a barren steppe and south to a wooded wilderness. Jason was heading towards the trees.

Stratton marched a few metres behind, wondering when Jason was going to give up this 'We're not really together' act. The road's surface appeared to be tarmac beneath a crust of compressed snow and didn't look as if it saw much vehicular traffic. When they reached the wood it turned out to be a thick, impenetrable army of pines.

Jason left the road, turning along a footpath that traced the edge of the trees. He was following the navigational instructions to the letter, having memorised every detail from maps and satellite photographs. The rest of the journey was just as uncomplicated. At the end of the track they would come to another road where their contact should be waiting for them – the man who had taken the surveillance photographs of Binning. From there they would go to a safe house on the edge of Plesetsky and get the latest information on Binning's movements. Then it would be a case of planning his abduction. Apparently the contact would provide all they would need, including a pistol. He wouldn't get involved in anything violently physical, although he was willing to drive for them.

Once Binning had been abducted they would secure him in the safe house that reportedly had a suitable basement in which to conduct a noisy interrogation. Jason and Stratton were to play the good cop, bad cop routine – Stratton would naturally be the thug. Jason was more than confident that Binning would tell him everything. He would appeal to Binning's guilt, which he'd assured everyone the man would have in abundance, despite what he had done. Then, depending on what Binning revealed, they would come up with a plan to destroy the tile since they did not actually need the device itself – after all, MI16 had built it – the aim being to deny the technology to the other side. Ideally they would want it back but that would be impossible if it was in the mine laboratory – which was more than likely. It was the reason why Binning had to be terminated. Without him the Russians would take a lot longer, years perhaps, to figure out the other components.

Executing Binning was not going to be done in the old-fashioned way with a bullet to the head or a knotted rope around the scientist's neck. Stratton had been given a shirt with a strip of material sewn into the collar. All he needed to do was dissolve it in liquid, such as a cup of coffee. Seconds after drinking it, Binning would be dead. He would be none the wiser when his time came. The poison apparently paralysed the respiratory system in seconds.

A few metres along the track, Jason slowed to allow Stratton to catch up. He had obviously decided they could now be together since they were out of sight of anyone travelling along the road. He grinned by way of a greeting as Stratton approached and they carried along together.

'I love this kind of dry cold, don't you?' Jason said.

Stratton didn't know how to answer him. It was a simple enough question. But coming from Jason, and the way the man asked it as if he was an old sweat in the job and they were pals, it was irritating. Stratton forced a smile by way of an answer. There was no point in letting the man wind him up.

'We make a good pair, don't you think? Brains and brawn. That wasn't intended to be rude or typecasting,' he added. 'But, well, you are a bit of a thug. I mean that in the nicest possible way.'

Stratton wondered if there was any way he could convince

Jason of the need to go back to their being separated – for tactical reasons, of course.

'Seriously, though, don't you think there could be a future in both our organisations combining in this way, for certain operations? Between us we do cover all the bases.'

Something new was beginning to bug Stratton about Jason, and even more so since they'd climbed off the train. He seemed generally pleased and at ease with life. There was a chirpiness to his step and his mood. An odd attitude to have for a novice at the operational game like him. What was more, a subordinate of his had turned traitor at the expense of Jason's work and reputation and kidnapped his girlfriend, one of his staff, who was now a prisoner of a Russian crime syndicate. Stratton would have expected Jason to be upset or angry, at least nervous about the upcoming operation. He probably had no real idea of how dangerous what they were about to attempt was. Perhaps he truly was superior and able to detach himself fully from such issues. Maybe he was the new breed, his organisation the future. Stratton wasn't convinced. 'How do you feel about this operation?' he asked.

'What do you mean?'

'Well. We're going to waste your mate, hopefully find out what has become of your girlfriend, who could be dead, and if we get caught in the process we may never see the light of day again.'

'To be honest, I've not come to terms with the killing bit,' Jason said. 'Perhaps I'm in denial about that part. If it was me who had to do it, I'm not sure that I could. The man was a friend.'

'You saying that if something happens to me you won't see the plan through?'

'When you put it that way, I believe I would. But until that moment comes . . . it's hard to visualise . . . hard to think about. So I won't, if you don't mind.'

'I suppose the penalty of death just for stealing something is a bit over the top.'

Jason glanced at Stratton, suspicious that the operative might be trying to corner him. 'If we could get him back home I would rather do that. I'm only being honest. But if that's impossible, getting rid of him seems like our only option. As for Rowena, I can't think about her. I have to put her out of my thoughts. That may sound callous but to help her I must remain clear-headed. And if something bad has happened, well, I'd rather wait. Until I know for certain. As for the dangers . . . I suppose this is where ignorance comes in handy.'

'You have an imagination, though.'

Jason smiled. 'I'm with the great John Stratton. What's there to worry about?'

Stratton had the feeling that the man was avoiding the question.

A mile later the wood spilled across their path and the track carried straight on through it. As a precaution Stratton stopped to look back the way they had come in case anyone had followed them. Jason caught on to what he was doing and stood quietly until Stratton was satisfied. They continued along the track and ten minutes later stepped from the trees onto a narrow road.

A small car was parked on a verge a little way along the road, exactly where the contact was supposed to be waiting. The two men walked towards it. As they closed on the vehicle a stocky man with a greying beard climbed out and both parties stopped and studied each other.

Stratton thought he looked identical to the photograph. But that was not good enough. 'The wind is colder when it comes from the north,' he said.

'Only if you're from Smolensk,' the man replied.

Stratton smiled by way of a hello.

'Stratton. And Mansfield,' the Russian said, referring to each man accurately.

'It's good to meet you, Vasily.' Stratton immediately liked the man, who looked harmless, albeit bearlike. He was a surveillance specialist, an MI6 recruit from the Cold War era, according to the brief. It was arguably safer being a spy in Russia these days, mainly because of the vastly improved communications systems and greater freedom of travel. But agents still disappeared. Getting caught was still a very bad idea. People spied against their own for many different reasons, of course. The battle against communism had been won, or so it appeared. But to many nothing had really changed. The old spies remained loyal to the West in order to finish what the ignorant believed they had achieved when the Wall came down. And some just did it for the money. Stratton had been told little about Vasily's background other than that he was to be trusted.

The Russian got back into the car. Stratton climbed into the front passenger seat, an automatic reaction on his part. He hated relinquishing any control over his operations, particularly when strangers such as Vasily were involved. And although Jason seemed to think he was the procedural adviser on the task, when it came to a real threat Stratton would take over. In this case, he would have more influence over the driver by sitting in the front seat than he would have in the rear. Despite Jason's attitude, Stratton was the operational commander, an appointment the scientist had gracefully accepted, although there had been scant evidence of that thus far.

The car was a garbage bin on wheels, littered with empty food containers, sweet wrappers and a dozen empty unlabelled bottles. It was also as cold as a refrigerator.

'Excuse my heater,' Vasily said, firing up the engine which only started after several turns of the electric motor. 'It always stops working when the winter begins. We have a two-hour drive to town. There is a train station but I did not think it safe for you to get off there. It has been watched more closely since the increased activity at the mine laboratory. There's food in that bag. There's water and vodka. The water's frozen. Foreigners think Russians always drink vodka because we are alcoholics. That's a misconception. We're alcoholics because the water always freezes and the vodka does not.'

Vasily crunched the car into gear and eased it off the verge and onto the narrow road. He took his time getting up to speed and going through the gears. Eventually they were trundling along at a good pace, considering the quality of the vehicle and the road conditions, and the inside of the car began to warm up a little.

'I have not seen your man Binning in two days,' Vasily said. 'He left his house for the mine and has not been back. I think he's getting to like it down there.'

'Have you thought of a place where we can pick him up?' Stratton asked.

'I have an idea. You must see for yourself. Binning is always escorted by couple of guards to and from the mine. But he does not like the guards hanging around. They stay down in the lobby of his house. In the evenings he sneaks out of the back for a walk. He seems adventurous. I think he sees guards as unnecessary . . . I have the drugs I was asked to get for when you capture him. That wasn't easy. I had to get them from Moscow. They only arrived today.' He pointed at the glove compartment.

Stratton opened it to reveal a brown paper bag among several scruffy pieces of documentation. In the bag were a brown bottle and a couple of hypodermic needles. The anaesthetic should knock Binning unconscious a few minutes after he was injected with it. Stratton could see them having to hold the man down and keep him quiet and under control until the drug took effect. That was going to be the most risky point of the op as far as he was concerned. They'd need an element of luck for it to go without a hitch. He put the paper bag back and closed the glove compartment.

Stratton sat back and forced it all out of his head. This was one of those jobs where time would be on their side, within reason. They drove along endless country roads, passing only two vehicles moving in the opposite direction. They joined a highway for a few miles before leaving it to continue along yet another lonely ice road. The countryside varied little; either dense woodland or rocky wasteland coated in snow.

Vasily was a careful driver and kept to a sensible speed, mindful of the vehicle's limitations and the conditions. He played such a high-risk game yet was so cautious with everything else. Stratton dozed off a couple of times. He had not slept properly since leaving England and the rhythm of the car and the relatively safe atmosphere lulled him into the occasional slumber.

The first time Vasily thought he could see a helicopter in the distance was an hour into the journey. He hadn't been sure enough to say anything to the others. Stratton sensed a change in him after emerging from a short snooze. The man was sitting further forward than before and was gripping the wheel tightly. When he repeatedly glanced up through the top of his windscreen, trying to see between the leafless branches of the trees lining the road, Stratton became curious. 'What is it?' he asked.

'There's a helicopter up there. I've seen it a couple of times now. It seems to be moving with us.'

Stratton looked up through the crooked branches into the bright sky beyond. He could see nothing but blankness. White sky. But as he scanned further ahead he saw something. He continued to look in the same place until a gap in the trees revealed the small black object that Vasily was referring to. It was indeed a helicopter, several miles away and travelling on a parallel track.

'Helicopters are not common around here,' Vasily said. 'We're a long way from any military installation.'

The trees grew thicker but Stratton kept his gaze fixed in the general direction of the aircraft. When the trees thinned again the helicopter was still there but a little closer than before. Stratton judged it to be a sizeable craft. 'How far are we from the town?'

'Another sixty kilometres,' Vasily replied, his tone regretful.

'Any cover between here and there?' Stratton was already planning ahead.

'A tunnel would be nice,' Jason piped up from the back.

'Nothing. We are in barren lands. There's nothing but mines between here and Plesetsky.'

'We don't want to go anywhere near the laboratory mine,' Stratton said.

'We won't. I'm taking minor roads well away from it. We will pass the mine by twenty kilometres.'

'It's turning more towards us,' Jason said, craning to see the helicopter through his passenger window.

Another gap in the trees revealed that he was right. The helicopter was on a track that would eventually put it across their path.

'What shall we do?' Vasily asked, glancing nervously at Stratton.

'Why don't we just stop and see what it does?' Jason suggested.

Stratton considered it for a few seconds. 'It makes no difference,' he decided. 'If it's following this car we can't stop it.' The chopper's presence was still possibly a coincidence. If it wasn't then they had been rumbled. But then, if that was the case, why hadn't they been intercepted at the airport or on the train? He could think of another explanation. Perhaps it was Vasily who had been rumbled.

As the helicopter converged on the vehicle's path it began to take on more of a distinctive shape.

'It's a Haze,' Stratton muttered.

'Military?' Jason asked.

'Troop carrier.'

The craft began to lose height. The windows along its fuselage became clear as well as its markings. Vasily instinctively took some weight off the accelerator and the car slowed a little.

As the helicopter reached a point a few hundred metres directly in front of them it too slowed.

'They're stopping above the road.' Vasily was maintaining his composure but only just. 'It's us they're after.'

'Easy,' Stratton said, putting a hand on the dashboard close to the wheel in order to grab it should the Russian do something erratic.

Vasily couldn't bear the tension any longer and brought the car to a stop, keeping its engine running. Stratton didn't react. There was little point.

They watched the behemoth as it turned slowly on its axis to face them. After a pause it glided forward. The deep throb of its long rotors rose above the purring of the car's engine.

The fearsome-looking craft maintained a slow speed, heading straight for them. The pilots became visible and the noise of its engines grew louder. When it was less than fifty metres away it ceased its forward movement and began a slow turn, kicking up a cloud of snow from the ground. The trees caught in the down-draught shook violently.

Bits of ice dislodged from branches struck the car, startling Vasily. The Russian was white with fear. He knew only too well the penalties for being caught working for foreign intelligence services. While Stratton and Jason had a chance of living if they were captured, he had none. The only uncertainty would be the method of his death. His captors would keep him painfully alive far beyond the point where he would beg them to let him take his own life if they would only give him the chance, which they would not.

The Haze turned until it was showing them its rear and then held its position. The rear doors, like an egg cut vertically down the middle, opened like a lobster's claw. Several men in fatigues stood inside the opening looking at them. The barrel of a machine gun attached to a frame bolted to the side of the craft protruded from the door, pointing directly at the vehicle.

Vasily could bear it no longer. Something snapped inside of him. He shouldered open the car's door in a bid to climb out.

Stratton reached to grab him. 'No, Vasily!'

But Vasily's weight was already taking him out the door. He took his foot off the brake and clutch and the car shunted forward a few feet before the engine stalled. Stratton was pulled across the seat as he tried to hold on to the man. He couldn't.

Vasily fell onto the icy ground, slipped as he tried to stand, then quickly regained his footing and began to run. He was hardly past the back of the car when the door gunner opened up with a couple of staccato bursts of fire. Several rounds struck the car, puncturing it violently, passing through it like knives through icing. Glass exploded over the two men who flattened themselves against their seats.

Vasily arched his back in a violent spasm as the bullets smashed through his body. He staggered on for several paces before falling dead onto the icy road.

Stratton and Jason lay still across their seats, waiting for the next burst that would surely finish them. But it did not come. The noise of the helicopter's engines remained the same, as if it was just hovering above them, waiting for something.

Stratton raised his head enough to look over the dashboard and through the cracked windshield. The helicopter was descending onto the road where the trees on either side had given way to low hedges. Snow and ice spiralled around the craft. The door gunner remained vigilant, not taking his eyes off the car.

They were as good as behind bars. Stratton practically accepted it. He couldn't see a way out of this one. It was better than being dead, at least. They were British subjects and, even if it could be proved who they worked for, there was always a chance they might one day be freed.

As the heavy beast's wheels touched the road and it jolted to stability, men stepped down out of its dark belly and walked towards the car. They wore heavily camouflaged cold-weather fatigues, their battle harnesses and pouches stuffed with equipment and spare ammunition. They carried assault rifles in their gloved hands, wore machine pistols in black leather holsters strapped to their thighs. Stratton put up his hands as they approached, glancing in the cracked rear-view mirror at the scientist who had followed his lead. Jason looked pale with fear, his earlier chirpiness wiped away without trace.

The Russian soldiers strode confidently towards the car, their breath steaming, some wearing woollen hats against the cold. The one out in front who had short spiky blond hair wore a pair of black wraparound sunglasses. When he arrived at the vehicle he went to the front passenger window to peer inside at Stratton. He said something in Russian to his men who had surrounded the car. One of them murmured something, a couple of them chuckled in response. Another soldier kneeled by Vasily to inspect him and reported the obvious statistic.

The one with the sunglasses opened Stratton's door and said something to the Englishman in a calm voice. Stratton got the gist of the command and climbed out.

When he got to his feet the soldier shouldered his rifle on its sling and searched Stratton's clothes and body from neck to toe. When he had finished he was holding Stratton's passport in his hand. He harshly grabbed the side of Stratton's coat and used his grip on it to turn him around, pushing him against the car. Another soldier had done the same with Jason, who turned to face the car from the other side. Their wallets, passports and air tickets lay between them on its roof. The first soldier said something to Stratton and touched his watch. Stratton removed it and placed it with his possessions. Jason did the same. Another soldier pulled their small packs from the back and inspected the contents. They put everything into the packs and one of the soldiers held on to them.

Two of the men searched the car. Methodically. They looked under floor mats, through the rubbish and down the back of the seats. Beneath them. Then one slashed them with a knife. Stratton took every opportunity to assess the men and their equipment. They were certainly not ordinary soldiers. Spetsnaz, he suspected. Each was powerful-looking and well equipped. They slung their weapons rather than leaving them resting against the side of the car or on the ground, a small but significant indication of their professionalism. They had a calm confidence. Russian Spetsnaz had a habit of including martial arts as part of their regular training and it showed in these men's faces. All appeared to have had their noses broken. Any two of them would have been a fair match for Jason and Stratton. They numbered eight.

The helicopter's engines continued to turn over noisily but the soldiers didn't appear to be in any hurry. One of them held a conversation over a radio. The apparent leader, the one with the wraparound sunglasses, unceremoniously pulled Stratton away from the car and pushed him in the direction of the helicopter. Another yanked Jason in the same direction. They didn't even bother to tie their prisoners' hands. It was as if they wanted the Englishmen to try something foolish.

As the others walked away, one of the soldiers took a phosphorous grenade from a pouch, pulled the pin, tossed it into the back of the car among the bottles of vodka and then followed his comrades. The grenade popped loudly and the car burst into flames.

Stratton didn't look back as the vehicle burned. He knew precisely what had happened. The operative studied the rear entrance of the chopper as they approached it. It was dark inside the narrow cabin. The unshaven door gunner squatted by the machine gun and watched the two strangers. The gun was loaded with a belt of shiny ammunition that snaked into a feeder box attached to its side. Empty bullet casings littered the floor around the gunner's feet. He grinned, his teeth stained brown from tobacco smoke.

Stratton followed the lead soldier up the ramp and into the dimly lit cabin. In the rear section several metal war chests sat along the sides, a couple open to reveal weaponry and items of personal equipment. In the front half of the cabin basic nylon hammock seats were fixed down the sides. Opened ration boxes lay strewn about, along with empty tins and wrappings. The place certainly lacked a woman's touch.

A man sat in one of the seats, reading a file. He wore the same fatigues as the others but no weapon harness, only a pistol in a leather holster on a belt around his waist. He looked older than the rest of them. He gazed up at Stratton as they came in. A soldier took hold of the Englishman and placed him to one side of the opening, positioning him precisely as if he was a shop-window mannequin. Jason was treated the same way.

When the last soldier was aboard, the one with the sunglasses leaned close to the man sitting down and said something into his ear. The manner in which the older man acted confirmed Stratton's suspicion. He was their real leader, all right. The soldier wearing the sunglasses acknowledged something the man said and walked away to lean into the cockpit and chat briefly with the pilots.

Moments later the chopper's engines increased their revs and the heavy craft rocked from side to side as the rotors took the strain of its weight. It gradually disconnected from the earth and began to rise. A few metres off the ground the Haze tilted down at the front and lumbered forward, groaning an imaginary complaint. With the rear doors open the biting wind twisted into the back, pulling at Stratton and Jason's clothing. Stratton took hold of the bulkhead frame to steady himself while Jason, out of reach of anything else, put a hand on the operative's shoulder.

The leader put down his file, got to his feet looking as if he'd been inconvenienced and made his way towards the two Englishmen. The rest of the soldiers, other than the door gunner, congregated in the front portion of the helicopter, some taking seats, some rummaging through the rations for a snack. All watched to see what their boss was going to do.

The Russian officer eyed Jason and Stratton with disdain. Mansfield removed his hand from Stratton's shoulder and stood upright.

The Russian was short compared with the rest of his men, standing a few inches below Stratton's eye-line. His red hair was cropped, his sullen eyes grey and like the others it appeared he'd had his nose broken. More than once. 'What are your names?' he shouted above the noise of the engines and the beating rotors.

'Mark Davidson,' Stratton answered, equally loudly, the name on his false passport.

'Derek Waverly,' Jason shouted.

The Russian simply stared into the eyes of each man as he answered.

'What are you doing here?'

'We're British engineers,' Stratton said. He doubted that the Russians knew who they really worked for and why they were there. But these soldiers obviously suspected the two Englishmen of something. If they were guilty by their association with Vasily, killing the spy had not been the smartest course of action. The man would probably have revealed everything within hours. But

256

they clearly didn't care about that. The men's cover stories as engineers wouldn't hold up under scrutiny, anyway. They could be looking at the inside of a Russian prison for quite some time. Years, in fact. Stratton wondered what London's reaction would be. Their release would depend on their value. On the scale of things Stratton didn't think that he was worth much at all. And Jason not a great deal more. At the end of the day, Mansfield was a scientist and Stratton a common or garden special-forces operative. Both of them were easily replaceable. He thought of his house and envisaged the lads breaking in to clear out the perishables and cover the rest in dust sheets. It would be a long time before he saw his crockpot again. Funny how the simple things in life seemed so much more important at times like this.

The officer smiled thinly on hearing Stratton's pathetic explanation. He looked over at his subordinate in the sunglasses and gave him a nod. The blond-haired guy gestured to another soldier. The two approached the Englishmen. They grabbed hold of them firmly, pulled them harshly into the centre of the cabin and placed them side by side with their backs to the rear opening, the edge only a few feet away.

'Are you sure you don't want to tell me what you are doing here?' the leader asked loudly.

Stratton wondered how far the Russian was prepared to go with this intimidation technique. He could think of two possible options: one was to come up with a plausible explanation to appease the man, at least until the next level of interrogators took over back at the military establishment, wherever that was. The other was simply to keep quiet and call the Russian's bluff. The problem was that he couldn't think of a story good enough to cover the first option. And the second one didn't feel right. It was never a good idea to call someone's bluff when your own life was at stake.

'Don't doubt my threat,' the Russian warned, as if he was reading Stratton's thoughts. 'I have the authority to deal with petty spies like you. In any way I see fit.'

Stratton doubted the claim. It would be unwise to give a field officer that much autonomy. But he seemed confident enough.

The officer nodded to his men. They responded instantly, turning Stratton and Jason around and shoving them to within a few inches of the edge of the opening. The wind whipped more violently at their clothes but neither of them could feel the bitter cold at that moment. The operative was surprised to discover that they were already several thousand feet above the ground. The patchwork steppe was white as far as the eye could see, spotted with black blotches of woodland and the scars made by roads. The squatting door gunner to Stratton's right was looking up at him, still wearing a grin.

Turbulence suddenly buffeted the craft. Those standing splayed their feet to maintain balance. Stratton automatically reached out but he had nothing to grab. The craft's erratic movements calmed a little and he regained his balance with the help of the soldier holding him from behind. This was not a lot of fun.

'I will ask you one more time,' the Russian officer shouted close to their ears. He motioned to his soldiers who leaned the Englishmen further out of the back, their toes right on the edge now. If the Russians let go they would plummet. 'Why are you in my country?'

'I don't think he's bluffing,' Jason shouted.

Behind them the Russian officer smiled at the comment.

Stratton's mind raced to find a solution but there was none to hand. Turbulence hit the craft once again.

Stratton's lack of response was not helping Jason's growing concern one bit. 'If you kill us you'll be making a big mistake!'

the scientist shouted in desperation, suddenly convinced that the Russians intended to murder them.

The officer also found that comment amusing. 'I really don't give a damn who you are or what you're doing here. I spent many years in England. I hate you people. You have become soft! You no longer know how to rule, yet you continue to play your little games. Your day has come to an end . . . yours in particular.'

Another patch of turbulence rocked the helicopter. This time all those standing lost their balance momentarily as the helicopter dipped and juddered. Jason found himself falling to the side, the Russian behind him unable to hold on.

The soldier holding Stratton let go to secure himself. The operative stared down at the passing ground far below, managing somehow to remain on the edge yet unable to move away from it. What he did next was the result of a keen survival instinct and a belief that the Russian officer intended to kill them, one way or another. Against these zero odds of survival he could see only one wild option left to him. Even if he succeeded they would all most likely die anyway. But dying trying was better than not trying at all.

Stratton reached out and grabbed the door gunner by the collar, lifted the man out of his seat and with every ounce of strength he had threw him out into the void. Stratton looked doomed to follow the screaming gunner but as he fell he seized hold of the butt of the weapon that had turned outwards on its mounting. His feet left the edge of the ramp, his body swinging outside the craft. He hung for a second, far above the tundra, dangling in the wind, the gun the only thing stopping him from falling. Gripping the trigger guard, he swung his feet back up to find the edge of the ramp, the barrel now pointing back inside the helicopter. The soldiers went for their guns. The officer, standing a few feet away, opened his mouth in horror at the sight. Stratton couldn't stop himself from squeezing the trigger even if he had wanted to. He was holding on to it for dear life. The gun chattered to life with horrendous power and the first rounds punched through the officer, hammering his instantly lifeless body back into the craft. Stratton yawed the deadly machine gun on its axis, one side to the other. The rounds chewed up the cabin and those inside it. They tore through the bulkheads, ripped up boxes and shattered the craft's small windows. He hit each soldier with several rounds, at such close range tearing each man to shreds, the bullets passing through several of them at a time.

The machine gun ate hungrily into the ammunition belt that shuddered out of the feeder box, the empty casings flying into the air.

Rounds spat into the thin wall at the front of the helicopter and through both pilots beyond it, shattering the blood-stained windshields. Sparks flew from the holed instruments panel. The dead pilots released the controls, flopping in their seats, and the power went out of the rotors.

The weapon went suddenly quiet as the last link of rounds was consumed. The Haze's engines had ceased to scream and although the rotors still turned their power was greatly reduced. The most dominant sound was the wind rushing in through the back and out of the smashed windows on the sides and at the front of the helicopter.

Stratton had killed them all, every last one of them.

The aircraft began to rotate as the tail rotor came to a stop, the gradually increasing rate of spin making it difficult for Stratton to climb back inside. He reached along the top of the gun and pulled himself in far enough to grab the framework from where he could get onto the deck.

Only then did he think of his travelling companion. A quick scan around suggested he had fallen out of the craft but then he saw the scientist's hands wrapped around one of the door struts, the rest of his body dangling in the air, nothing below him but the Russian countryside. Stratton scrambled over to the side of the opening, hooked his arm around the bulkhead and reached down for Jason Mansfield.

The turning motion was making it increasingly difficult for Jason to hang on.

'Grab my hand!' Stratton shouted.

Jason needed both hands just to hold on. To relinquish one seemed to him to be fatal.

'Now!' Stratton yelled, his own position more than tenuous.

Jason went for it, pulling himself a little closer and lunging towards Stratton. The operative did not fail him. He gripped Jason's wrist, planted a foot firmly against the door frame and pulled back with all the strength he had left. Both men rolled into the cabin as the spinning Haze fell. Fuel came cascading down the bulkheads from bullet holes in the ceiling that had punctured the tanks. As if they didn't have enough problems, the smouldering instruments panel ignited and flames burst into the cabin from the cockpit.

Stratton could not see the ground rushing up towards them but it was clearly happening. 'Get ready to take the impact!' he shouted.

'I admire your humour!'

'If it doesn't hit nose down we can survive it!'

'Have you done this before?'

Stratton looked up at the cockpit. 'Not on fire!'

Jason's confidence was not improved by the comment.

The flames licked down the walls and the cabin began to fill with smoke. Fuel dripped onto Jason's arm and caught alight. He rolled frantically across the floor as he fought to extinguish the flames. Burning fuel splashed Stratton's boots and trousers. They might be roasted alive even before the helicopter crashed.

The sudden impact was tremendous. The wheels and under-carriage of the huge copter collapsed beneath it, crushed into

261

the ground. The violent contact ripped away the open rear doors and the tail collapsed, the smaller rotor crashing down into the hard-packed snow. A huge snowdrift absorbed a great portion of the impact. Yet the Haze had come down on the incline of a hill so it tipped and rolled onto its side. The main rotors buckled like straws and the heavy chopper's momentum took it down the slope. The two men inside it had been thrown flat by the force of the landing, then, as the cabin turned over, they had rolled up the sides and into the flames. As the rotor hub sank into the snow the craft skewed round so that the rear opening led the way downhill. It slid along like a great whale with its mouth open.

Stratton and Jason tumbled down into the snow that was being scooped inside the opening. It helped to extinguish some of the flames on their clothing but not all of them. As Stratton looked out the back he saw some kind of wooden structure covered in snow. They were going to hit it. Whatever it was. Yet right now outside was far better than in. 'Go!' Stratton yelled, clambering to his feet. He ran across the bulkhead towards the opening. Jason was up and behind him, both of them still alight. As they reached the opening the helicopter struck the wooden framework which disintegrated and the back of the chopper abruptly dropped as if it had broken through something.

The sudden fall hurled Stratton and Jason out of the back of the mangled Haze. As they braced for the ground it did not arrive. Because they had missed it. It became instantly dark and they continued to fall, both still ablaze, the wind fanning the flames on their clothing as they dropped into utter darkness. Neither of them could remotely comprehend what was happening. It was as though they had died and were accelerating straight into hell.

They could see nothing in the pitch dark by the time they struck the water like a pair of flaming meteorites. The force hit them like a hammer blow and they plunged beneath the surface, arms and legs flailing in desperation, fighting for their lives. Stratton pushed the water behind him madly, stroke after rapid stroke in the direction he thought was up. As his lungs tightened he burst through to the surface, thrashing around for something to grab. He couldn't see a damned thing. His hand brushed a rough-textured wall and he did his best to cling to it. Jason spluttered to the surface somewhere nearby, thrashing around and gasping for air.

They held on to the sides of the cave or whatever it was, panting like exhausted hounds, the flames from above providing a small amount of illumination.

'At least we're not on fire any more,' Stratton said, between breaths.

'What is this?' Jason asked.

The sides of the cavity were sheer, circular and rocky, like a vast cylindrical chimney a hundred feet high. As they looked up, the light above began to change subtly from white to orange. A sound drifted down to them, echoing off the walls, the sound of metal scraping on stone. Which was precisely what it was. The horrific reality struck them both at the same time.

'Oh my God,' Jason muttered.

The blazing helicopter was toppling into the chimney. It had nowhere else to go but down and in this narrow space that meant it would land on top of them.

Jason moved along the wall in a desperate effort to find something to hold on to as he stared up at their impending doom. He found an empty space. He felt around it quickly to discover edges on two sides and on top.

The helicopter was a tight fit in the shaft, though not quite tight enough to hold it in place. It came down towards them like a blazing lift. The increasingly loud noise it made as it scraped down the sides was horrendous. Yet the encroaching flames increased the light and Jason could see that what he took to be an indentation in the wall was a lot more. 'A tunnel!' he shouted.

Stratton had been considering diving down as deeply as he could to avoid the impact and flames and then hoping to find a way back up through or around the aircraft. But the tunnel was a far more attractive lifeline and he shot across the gap to join Jason who was already pulling himself inside. Stratton clambered in after him. The scientist stayed on his knees in the shallow water, catching his breath. Stratton did not stop and clambered ahead of Jason as if he was being pursued.

'It's not over!' Stratton shouted.

Jason didn't understand and quickly glanced back between the running operative and the tunnel opening.

'The fuel tanks!' Stratton yelled. The horizontal tunnel was barely high enough for him to run along at a crouch. The water came up to his knees.

Jason immediately understood what Stratton meant and thrashed forward in pursuit of the SBS man. It became pitch black as Stratton got deeper inside and he held a hand out in front of him for fear of bashing his head.

The sound of the helicopter's carcass scraping down the shaft increased as it closed on the bottom. When it struck the water with tremendous force the tanks did indeed rupture as Stratton had predicted. The remaining fuel ignited and the resulting giant fireball had only two directions in which to expand. The surging flames rolled into the tunnel in pursuit of the two men.

As the raging inferno reached their backs they threw themselves beneath the surface of the water that lit up around them. It lasted a few seconds before extinguishing itself.

The men broke the surface, sucking in the contaminated air and coughing and spluttering as they fought to recover from the seemingly endless sequence of near–death experiences.

The helicopter had not dropped below the surface of the water completely and flames continued to burn inside it, throwing some faint light into the tunnel.

The men looked at each other as they got to their feet, panting for air.

'Is it over yet?' Jason gasped, wondering if they would have to run from anything else in order to survive.

Stratton looked back at the burning helicopter as his breathing returned to normal. He had run out of adrenalin and the cold was creeping over him. Getting to the surface was all he could think of but he doubted they would be able to climb the main shaft. He would investigate further once the flames had died down.

He looked along the tunnel into the deep shadows, wondering where it led, if anywhere. He took a few steps, sceptical of just how useful the investigation would be in almost total darkness. The air was still and tasted dank as if it had not changed in years. His confidence that it led anywhere other than to an eventual dead end was not high. As his eyes adjusted to the dim light he thought he could see the faintest of red glows at the furthest extent of his vision.

Stratton took another few steps forward at the crouch, feeling his way by passing his fingertips along the ceiling of the tunnel. He paused to rub his eyes, wondering if they were playing tricks on him. The glow remained and he continued on towards it. It became stronger with each step and seemed not to be coming from a direct source but shining down into the tunnel from above.

As he felt his way along his hands moved higher and the cramped tunnel opened up into a small cavern filled with the red glow. He could stand upright. He had found the source of the light, a robust bulb inside a wire housing fixed to a metal box. Much more significantly, the light was fixed above a steel door set in a concrete frame that sealed off the tunnel. The door was covered in rivets and a coat of rust but it looked so thick that it would take centuries for the corrosion to eat all the way through. Encouraging though the presence of the door was, it looked like it hadn't been opened in years.

'Jason.' His voice echoed around him.

Jason lay slumped, staring at the flames and wondering what they were going to do next. He looked around to see that Stratton had gone and his voice was coming from far away. The scientist lifted his bent body and made his way into the darkness.

When he saw the red glow he speeded up, his hopes lifting at a vague possibility. A solution to their dilemma. When he reached the cavern he stood alongside Stratton and stared in amazement at the light. He could see no handles on the door. However, a line of sturdy hinges down one side indicated that it could open, in theory at least.

'Are you thinking what I'm thinking?' Jason asked.

'The laboratory.'

'Is it possible?'

'The helicopter could easily have covered the distance.'

'Do we *want* it to be possible?' Jason asked, touching the door. He was wearing a grin. 'This is too crazy.'

'It's some kind of secure emergency exit. Unless the Russians have other underground installations in the area, I'd put money on this being the lab mine.'

'Why put an emergency exit into a tunnel like this?'

'The place was a chemical and biological warfare lab. Anywhere would be better than inside if there was an accident. Maybe there's a way from here to the surface.'

'Or perhaps it's another way of getting back into the lab if they had to.'

'Whatever it is, I would like to know what's on the other side of it . . . more so in a couple of hours from now when we could be freezing to death.'

Jason climbed the wall a few feet in order to inspect the box that the light was attached to. He pulled a side of the ageing box open to look inside. 'It's a sensor,' Jason decided. 'My guess is it's a trigger. To warn if it's opened.'

It made sense to Stratton. But it wasn't much of a solution even if it was the lab. The occupants wouldn't exactly welcome them with open arms. That was assuming they could get inside at all.

Jason pushed his fingers inside the gap as if feeling for something inside. There was a spark and he yelped in shock, snatching back his hand and jumping into the water.

The light began to blink on and off in a regular rhythm. Silence fell as the men stood in the glow of the flashing light, the water up to their knees. They looked at each other.

Jason shrugged apologetically. 'I think I tripped something.'

The obvious question was: stay, or get out of there? Take the opportunity, or not? If they couldn't get out of the tunnel any other way they would die, and none too pleasantly either. Getting recaptured might not be a whole lot better but it could mean that their demise would be a whole lot later. And time allowed for opportunities.

Yet as they stood there the minutes ticked away. Nothing happened. They waited. And waited. Hoping someone would come to the door and investigate. But this was Russia, of course. And they were miles from nowhere and the Cold War was over. No one was going to come.

Then, as if to prove it, the light stopped flashing and went back to glowing normally.

Stratton could no longer feel his feet. He estimated hypothermia would set in within twenty minutes or so. They would experience a surge of energy, perhaps even a sense of invulnerability, and then fatigue would set in. Their legs would give out and they would kneel in the water. That would speed things up but by then they would be delirious. They would die soon after. Their bodies might not be found for years, if ever. Their bones would rest beneath the water. With no identity on them they would be a couple of unexplained skeletons. It would remain a mystery to London too, another Buster Crabb story.

'Would they send someone else, do you think?' Jason asked. He wasn't particularly interested in events that might occur after his death but a conversation might ease the pain of the cold a little.

Stratton didn't care.

They remained silent for another minute, hoping to hear a sound from the other side of the door. But still no one came. It was so quiet that each man could hear his own heart beating in his chest.

'I used to be afraid of the dark when I was a child,' Jason said. 'Were you?'

'No. I always knew what was out there.'

Jason looked at the operative bathed in the red glow from above. 'I'll be honest about something. Not because this may be the only opportunity to say it. Do you know why MI16 was going to take over certain operations that your lot and the SAS consider their own?'

'No.' It was something else Stratton didn't care much about.

'We're smarter than you, by a long way. We're more accomplished athletes. I'd wager we're probably all better shots than you.'

'You think that's all it takes?'

'You have military experience, I grant you that, but we're not talking about those kinds of operations. Take this one, for instance. All of it, from the beginning. None of it was a success. Your skills have only led to failure at every turn. You practically sank the platform with your arrival. Binning escaped with the tile. And we're probably going to die in this tunnel, leaving the rest of the operation a failure.'

'You would have done it differently?'

'I would have reacted differently, sure – more intelligently, less like a bull in a china shop. Rowena was right. All you've ever been in your career is lucky. And it looks like that luck has finally run out.'

Stratton absorbed the insults. He even appreciated the conversation. It took his mind off the discomfort. Jason Mansfield might even have a point, he thought. He was right about the results. 'It's moot now.'

'I don't agree. Yes, this situation has put MI16's plans back but the fundamental reasons why it's necessary remain. My place will be taken and it will eventually happen.'

'Jason, I was going to say this to you anyway. You're a wanker. It's not so much what you say, it's the way you say it.'

Jason's eyes narrowed. 'I have an idea,' he said, moving through the water to the middle of the cavern. 'Maybe we should fight it out, here and now. See who's the best. It'd keep us warm for a bit, at least. What do you say?'

Stratton simply looked at him in the glow of the light.

Jason moved closer to Stratton, shrugging his arms and turning his neck as if loosening up for a fight. 'Come on. Let's do it. To the death. Neither of us has anything to lose. None of your colleagues will know you were beaten by a mere scientist. Come on.'

Jason adopted a fighting stance and moved within range of Stratton. The operative remained still.

'Take a punch. Or are you a counter man? Is that it?'

Jason jabbed at Stratton who moved enough to avoid the strike that was only intended as a probe anyway. Jason followed it up with another blow that struck Stratton on the shoulder.

The scientist's next punch was far stronger and hit Stratton hard in the chest. Stratton lunged at him, taking only a step, his heart not in it.

Jason kept his side-to-side stepping routine going, sloshing around in the water. 'That's it. Come on. Now hit me.'

Stratton was growing more irritated than angry but still not enough to be drawn in.

Jason dummied with one hand and struck Stratton in the face with the other, hard enough to send his head back. Stratton's mounting anger went up a couple of notches.

Jason danced left and right. 'You're going down if you don't defend yourself,' he warned. 'I sincerely plan on killing you. It's something I often contemplated, ever since I began karate. What would it be like to kill someone using my bare hands? What better subject than you?'

Jason came in for another series of punches and outmanoeuvred Stratton's unskilled defences, striking him with several hard blows. Stratton lunged forward again but Jason surprised him with a vicious kick to his ribs.

Stratton dropped to one knee in pain and glared at Jason. The scientist was grinning at him but did not waste any more time gloating. He came in with a low blow. Stratton moved back with it and grabbed the clenched fist, at the same time back-handing Jason across the mouth so viciously that it sent him back.

Jason stopped to feel the cut that had opened up on his lip. He felt the blood with the back of his hand and broke into a grin again. 'That's more like it.' His eyes narrowed and he looked suddenly dangerous as he came forward to get stuck in.

Stratton stood against the door, poised to respond to Jason's next attack. The idiot was serious about fighting to the death. Stratton didn't know if he had flipped or what. The scientist's issues clearly went a lot deeper than anyone knew.

As Jason moved to prepare for his attack, Stratton heard

something other than feet moving through the water. 'Quiet,' he said, his voice lowered, his eyes looking up.

'Not going to work,' Jason said as he tensed.

'Quiet! I heard something.'

Jason suddenly suspected that the other man might be telling the truth. He kept his distance but stayed alert as he listened.

A faint clanging sound came from beyond the door. Stratton turned to face it, ignoring Jason completely.

A heavy clunk was followed by the sound of an electric motor. A gear engaged and the door jolted. Bits of rust and debris fell from seams around the door.

Stratton stepped back.

The electric motor laboured heavily. The door jerked again and more debris fell from the hinges. The motor was beginning to sound as if it might fail when the entire door shuddered and then cracked open. The motor picked up and as the gap widened a bright light flooded the rock walls.

The two men instinctively moved out of the immediate view of anyone who might emerge from the opening. The water rushed in through the gap to fill a space on the other side and when the door was open wide enough to let a man through the motors went silent.

Stratton and Jason remained still, their senses straining to detect what if anything was on the other side of it.

A gloved hand reached around the door frame followed by its owner wearing a heavy-duty one-piece boiler suit and waders. He turned on a flashlight and aimed it up at the sensor as he backed out of the doorway. Stratton grabbed the hand holding the torch, almost giving the man a heart attack. As he cried out, Stratton covered his mouth. The frightened man shut up instantly.

Stratton released his grip and gestured for the man to stay quiet. He obeyed. Stratton stepped through the doorway into a brightly lit landing at the foot of a narrow concrete stairwell. His instinct suddenly warned him and he faced the steps to see a young Russian soldier partway up them aiming an AK-74 down at him. The soldier was as surprised to see the stranger as his engineer colleague had been but it did not divert him from his task. He pulled a radio from a pouch, put it to his mouth and talked quickly into it.

Jason stepped through the door and raised his empty hands in the air. 'Well, at least I won't freeze to death. And you've been saved from an embarrassing thrashing.'

15

Stratton and Jason stood in a large room that housed several noisy pieces of heavy equipment. Their hands had been chained around a thick metal bracing, part of a steel structure that supported a large pumping machine. Two sides of the rectangular space had been hewn out of solid rock, the other sides were constructed from cemented concrete blocks. The young soldier stood on the far side of the room by a wooden door, calmly watching, his gun in his hands. Puddles of water had collected around the feet of the two prisoners. They had been there for over an hour but at least the room was warm and they had stopped shivering.

The young soldier had made them wait at gunpoint at the foot of the emergency stairwell until half a dozen reinforcements had arrived. The response from the mine's guards had been enthusiastic due to the novelty of such a visit. Every soldier not at a duty post had answered the call to action. They promptly led the bedraggled pair up and down several levels and through a labyrinth of corridors, their walls made of bare rock or brick, to the pump room, the nearest thing they had to a dedicated cell at the facility.

The mine, or laboratory, appeared to be a series of interconnecting halls dug out of the rock. A hundred miles of piping and conduits of all sizes wound along the ceilings and through the walls. Some halls housed pumps and generators while in others sat collections of weird-looking storage vats and drums of differing sizes and colours. The entire place had a feel of decay, as though it was in serious need of reconstruction, with chipping paint, broken fixtures and mildew everywhere. At intervals along the connecting tunnels between many of the halls stood airtight steel doors like those in a bank vault, so heavy that they could only be moved by hydraulic rams.

The wooden door to the pump room opened and Stratton and Jason looked up to see a grim-faced Russian officer in casual uniform walk in. He glanced at the soldier and then at the two Englishmen before stepping aside from the doorway to allow the man behind him into the room. Binning.

Stratton and Jason weren't entirely surprised. During the time they had spent waiting they'd wondered if such a meeting might take place.

Binning wore a white technician's coat and a smarmy grin as he put his hands on his hips and planted his feet astride. 'Well, well, well. This is a surprise. I can't tell you how stunned I was to hear the descriptions of the men they had found lurking in the tunnels. How the hell did you end up there?'

Neither man answered.

'I just know you had something to do with the helicopter that crashed almost right on top of us. I can't wait to hear how that all came about . . . Major,' he said, addressing the officer. 'This is John Stratton, British special forces. And this is Jason Mansfield, my boss, or should I say former boss, from MI16.'

The officer looked at the men with a hint of satisfaction in his eyes.

'I suspect they came here to take back the tile,' Binning mused. 'Or kill me. Or both. What do you say, chaps? Does that about sum it up?'

Both prisoners remained stone-faced as they stared at the traitor.

'Major, would you be good enough to unchain this one?' Binning asked, indicating Jason.

A frown formed on the officer's brow. 'By what authority?' he asked.

'Can I remind you I have been given the equivalent rank of lieutenant colonel? Okay, it's not yet official but that's just a matter of procedure.'

The major still didn't move.

Binning sighed. 'Major, all I have to do is make a phone call and someone whose rank you *do* respect will simply order you to do it. Now do we have to go through all of that, and get someone annoyed with you? You have guards, you have guns. He doesn't. Just do it, please.'

The officer gave a brief order to the soldier who handed him his weapon and walked over to Jason Mansfield. He took a key from his pocket and unlocked the padlock connecting the chains that secured Jason to the bracing.

The chains dropped to the concrete floor and Jason rubbed his wrists where the metal had chafed them. He looked into Binning's cold eyes as the man walked slowly towards him.

'A few tense and interesting moments but we got there in the end,' Binning said, his face cracking into a broader smile.

Mansfield's face broke into a matching grin and the two men embraced, hugging each other strongly as they laughed heartily.

'You look well,' Binning said, moving back to take a look at Jason. 'Bit cold and wet but in good shape, considering.'

'You have no idea,' Jason said. 'I tell you, there's the easy way of doing things and then there's Stratton's way. Dear God, it was utter madness at times. Between that damned platform and getting here I think I used up all my spare lives.'

'Let's get you a change of clothes and a hot meal.'

'Tell me you had the decency to procure a fine malt,' Jason said, taking a step with Binning towards the door.

'Part of the deal, old boy.'

They both laughed out loud as they walked.

Halfway across the room Jason stopped to look back at Stratton. 'Shocked, Stratton?'

The operative was stunned but did not show it.

'Come on, man. Say something. Your face is almost worth the whole caper.'

'You've been planning this a long time, I suppose,' Stratton said.

'A couple of years. It was complicated. Binning and I play three-dimensional chess. We're practically unbeatable. This was every bit as complex. You see, it's all about calculating the opponent's next move in respect of yours and then his next, and yours and so on. We must have gone to about twenty moves ahead,' he said, looking at Binning for acknowledgement.

Binning raised his eyes in appreciative agreement.

'Who were your opponents?' Stratton asked.

'London. Your people. Never saw that damned helicopter coming, though. But then, that's why we chose you. One of the more interesting aspects of the plan. We needed one of the best to get us through the tougher physical issues. You were perfect. Thank you.'

'Why?'

'You wouldn't understand. Something beyond your paltry intelligence's ability to grasp. In simple terms, the Russians could give me what our side wouldn't. Head of MI16 was all I was ever going to be. A brain for hire. The Russians offered me power, and business opportunities.'

'Money?'

'That's a given. This plan alone is evidence of our genius. I have to admit there were a few times when I thought it was perhaps a little too ambitious. You see, it wasn't just about handing over the tile – you'll notice I said "handing over" as opposed to stealing it: it belonged to us, the copyright is a minor issue. But the essence of the plan was about succeeding without London knowing of my involvement. You see, I'm going back. My handover's not quite complete. There's more to be had.'

'Your recording device at Sevastopol wasn't faulty, you'll be relieved to know,' Binning said.

'You needed to discredit me to allow you to do the job and complete the arrangements with the *Inessa*,' Stratton said.

'And then get you to MI16 in order to carry out the platform task,' Jason added.

'Chaz never brought anything into the airlock,' Stratton surmised.

'No. I thought we'd blown it trying to get the helicopter to drop us off with the mini-sub. That was a big hurdle, London allowing us to continue to the platform. Once again you tipped the scales in our favour.'

'Jordan was Jason's idea,' Binning said proudly. 'A real stroke of genius, on top of superb analysis.'

'Thank you,' Jason said to his friend. 'It was all about finding the right pieces and then fitting them together. Much the same thing we do every day with our designs,' Jason bragged. 'It was a complex mathematical problem. That's how we laid it out in the theory room.'

'Was destroying the platform a part of it?'

Jason smirked. 'Of course, we have partners who have interests of their own that they threw into the calculation. I understand the owners needed the insurance money. London has its suspicions about that but it doesn't affect our operation.'

'The Russian government is in on this?' Stratton asked.

'Elements are aware, of course. Sumners was quite correct. But at the end of the day it's a matter of all's fair in love and espionage. There are winners and there are losers.'

'And Rowena?' Stratton asked.

Jason smiled. 'A pawn, like you. She's being kept in another part of the complex. I need her for the next stage of the plan. You see, you die. I succeed in our task. I go back to London with Rowena, who will think I rescued her. Her innocence will improve my credibility. I will of course say wonderful things about you, and probably more wonderful things about myself. That's the advantage of winning, Stratton.' Jason came closer to the operative to look deeper into his eyes. 'I wish we'd finished that fight. It would have been a perfect climax. The great John Stratton. Beaten by a civvy.' He chuckled. 'You've never come up against anyone like me before. Rowena was right about you. You've always been lucky. But brilliance doesn't need luck. In fact, I can't afford it.'

Jason lingered long enough to gloat before turning away.

'Jason,' Stratton called out.

Mansfield paused at the door to look back at him.

'I was right about you. You *are* a wanker.'

'We won't be seeing each other again,' Mansfield said, continuing through the door. 'I'm going to insist they get rid of you right away. Chain him up well, Major,' he shouted. 'He's very lucky.'

Binning took a moment to look back at Stratton, his grin apparently ineradicable. He raised his eyebrows as if to say 'That's life', and padded after his boss.

Before he followed the others, the major glanced at the guard in a way that conveyed his need to remain alert.

Stratton stood there in stunned silence. This was a bloody mess. He slid the chains down the bracket, sat on the wet floor and went over the situation. One aspect of it had apparently changed. He wouldn't be spending years in a Russian jail after all.

Stratton remained where he was for many hours. At one point he drifted off to sleep, the long hours and violent events of the day getting the better of him, despite the grim prospect of his impending end. He woke up at one point after hearing a sound close by only to discover that it was the young guard holding a cup of water out to him. Stratton drank it as the man held the cup.

During his conscious moments, Stratton considered every possible avenue of escape, one of which included getting back down into the emergency tunnel and taking his chances with the vertical shaft. But no matter what he came up with, while he was chained so heavily to the bracket and with a guard seated at the door holding a gun and watching him, the opportunity for any kind of escape attempt looked highly unlikely.

He had no accurate sense of the passing time and how long he had dozed off for. The only clue that it had been several hours since his capture was that his clothes had practically dried on him. The lights remained the same and the only sound was the constant hum of machinery. After another period of pondering a variety of dead ends he fell back into a fitful half-sleep, his bottom aching on the cold concrete floor, his back uncomfortable against the rock wall, his wrists chafing against his chains, his bruises and burns combining with the other pains and discomforts.

As Stratton dozed he was distantly aware that the lights had gone out and although he heard the door open it was not enough to drag him fully out of his slumber. Even the sound of a dull thud followed by the clatter of something metallic on the concrete floor came like a distant echo and could easily have been part of a dream. But something deep inside his mind called to him to wake up and it was eventually a rush of fear that startled him into consciousness.

He opened his eyes to a room in near darkness, the only light coming through the open door and from the glowing bulbs on the pumping machine's control panel. A figure crouched by another that was lying on the floor. As his eyes adjusted to the dim light Stratton realised the guard was lying prone and the other figure was searching his pockets.

The figure stood up and walked towards him. The red and green lights on the machine beside him revealed its identity: Rowena, in a boiler suit a few sizes too large for her. She crouched beside him, holding a couple of keys.

'Are you injured?' she asked calmly as she tried the first key in the lock.

'No,' Stratton replied, getting to his knees.

'That's good. I suspect we're going to have to run at some point. And maybe more than that.'

He could only stare at her as she fitted the next key and twisted it in the lock that then popped open. He removed the chains and got to his feet.

She stood up in front of him, looking into eyes that were full of questions. 'I always suspected Jason,' she said. 'Not of being a traitor, though. A woman knows when a man is hiding something from her. I thought he was cheating on me. But my digging only led to him and Binning. I even wondered if they were gay. I was almost relieved when I found out. Female ego.'

'How long have you known?'

'Couple of hours. I thought you'd all perished with the platform. I watched it sink from the lifeboat. Then the Russian mini-sub arrived and took us away. I've been here a week, kept in an office with a bunk bed.'

'How did you get to me?' Stratton asked as he walked over to check on the young guard.

'I wasn't always a scientist.'

Stratton glanced at her, remembering what Jason had said about her.

'I did a selection course for a military undercover unit. I got pulled out after I finished it. We covered hostage situations,' she explained. 'I learned a few things. From the moment they took me from Binning I played the pathetic frightened child.'

'That must have been a challenge.'

Rowena was not offended by the remark.

The young guard remained unconscious but Stratton decided he would live.

'The guards took to locking me in the office. They felt sorry for me and stopped checking on me every few hours. After a couple of days I only saw them at mealtimes. I worked out how to pick the door lock open as well as how to relock it. At night I had a look around. I found diagrams of this place, inventories, files. They still have literally tons of chemical and biological concoctions here.'

Stratton picked up the guard's AK-74, checked it was ready to fire and went to the door to look into the empty corridor.

'Today I heard voices outside the room. It was the laughter I recognised. I couldn't believe it was them together again. That's when it all began to make sense. Their conspiratorial meetings. The things I thought were strange. They went into a nearby room. I rigged the intercom phone so I could listen in.'

Stratton looked at her, for a moment wondering if this was some kind of set-up, another piece of the three-dimensional chess game. But he was free, from the chains at least, and he had a gun in his hands. Not that that seemed to make a difference to the kind of plans these characters conjured up.

Rowena took his look as one of disbelief. 'Rigging a simple intercom phone is child's play, literally.'

He looked away, believing her.

'Jason wants you dead by tonight. They mentioned the pump room, and so here I am.'

'I don't suppose you've figured out how to get out of here.'

'Of course I have.'

He looked at her again, more doubt in his eyes.

'I'm a nuclear engineer. I have an IQ forty points above genius.'

'And a photographic memory, of course.'

'Live with it. You doubt me, don't you?'

Stratton thought carefully about his answer. 'No, I don't.'

She looked thoughtful. 'I wouldn't blame you if you did. You've been royally screwed. By two of the best.'

'Well, I've got you on my side now, haven't I?'

Rowena wanted him to know that he did. 'There are two lift shafts. One for cargo and everyday use by the soldiers. The other is in one of the labs for executive use only. There is a single stairwell to the surface, two hundred and fifty feet above us. Since Binning got here the guard force has doubled. But there aren't many of them down here in the complex. They stay up top, stopping people from getting in. They don't like being down here, anyway.'

He waited for more of the plan to materialise. So far she had given him hardly anything.

'I can see only one way out,' Rowena said. 'And that's to create a situation where everyone else down here needs to get out too.'

That interested him. 'An emergency?'

'Right.'

But Stratton's interest began to fade without more info. 'So we get to the surface along with everyone else. That's not an escape.'

'That depends on what kind of emergency. If there's a serious bio leak, every safety door in the complex automatically seals the place tight and cannot be opened without an executive order from Moscow. The safety doors are between each chemical and biological storage hall and at the top of both lift shafts and the stairwell.'

'I still don't see it.'

'This place is old. The door seals are shit. Everyone knows that if there was a serious bio leak it wouldn't be contained. Those who managed to get to the surface before the place shut down wouldn't stop at the surface. They'd keep on running for as far as they could get, just like at Chernobyl.'

Stratton perked up. But there were still holes in the plan. 'How much time to get to the surface before the place seals?'

'None. Everything shuts down as soon as the alarms are triggered.'

He looked at her with raised eyebrows.

'Certain death? That's also what the scientists who worked down here thought when they first came. They didn't like that idea much either so they built a delay mechanism into the executive lift only. Anyone working in the labs or offices might make it to the surface. The lift's big enough. Everyone else who didn't make it . . . well, tough. When a leak sets off the alarms, all the doors seal within two minutes. The executive lift stays live for five minutes more. The door that seals the surface exit to the exec elevator stays open for another minute.'

Stratton was beginning to see something of a plan. 'So, we create a fake leak and get out using the executive lift.'

Rowena shook her head. 'Not that easy. The only way to fake-trigger the system is by using the test circuit. But the guards up top will be able to see that. They won't run away because they'll know it's just a test.'

'Then we need them to believe it's real.'

She nodded.

'How?'

She shrugged. 'Only one way. It has to *be* real.'

He looked at her. 'Real?'

'I don't see any other way.'

'That *would* be another Chernobyl!'

'Maybe worse. You won't believe some of the shit they have down here.'

Stratton contemplated the idea. 'You really are a cold-hearted bitch, aren't you?'

'You have a problem with surviving?'

He shook his head. 'You are in the wrong job . . . How does it work?'

'There are dozens of sensors around the place but several different locations need to detect the leak in order to trigger a full shut-down. A small leak won't work. We need to be at the lift when

283

the sensors trip, otherwise someone might beat us to it. Once it goes up it will not come back down.'

'Have you figured that part out – how we set the leak and get to the lift before the sensors trip?'

'No.'

'Some genius.'

Rowena clenched her jaw. 'I thought I'd leave something for you to figure out.'

Stratton ran his fingers through his hair as he pondered their next move. 'You know where the exec lift is?'

'I can see the map in my head.'

'And the storage rooms?'

'Yes.'

He gripped the AK-74 and took another moment.

'What do you think?' she asked. 'Too crazy?'

He wasn't entirely sure but there were no other options. 'It sounds like my kind of plan.'

She fought back a smile. She had gone from despising the man to seeking his approval. He had something about him.

The guard moaned as he began to come around.

Stratton indicated for Rowena to lead the way along the corridor. 'After you.'

She took a breath, focused her mind and moved ahead.

A wooden door at the end led into another, broader corridor running left and right. She did not hesitate in selecting a direction.

A short distance along it they came to one of the huge emergency doorway seals. They paused to check beyond it and Stratton took a moment to inspect the huge steel door that had a thick rubber seal lining the inside frame. An electric motor behind the door operated a hydraulic arm that closed it. It was covered in rust and when Stratton grabbed hold of the rubber seal a piece of it broke away.

Rowena saw the rubber crumble in his hand. 'Good old Soviet maintenance under a new name,' she muttered.

Beyond the doorway a metal gantry extended mid-height through a cavernous hall that housed several large and noisy machines. The hall was hewn out of the bare rock and reinforced with concrete and steel bracing.

Stratton leaned onto the gantry to look below and saw a couple of engineers in hard hats working on one of the machines. He gave Rowena a gentle nudge. 'Go for it,' he said.

Rowena was no less committed than when she had climbed the oil platform and she did not need any further encouragement. Leaving the safety of the doorway she crossed the gantry. Stratton followed close behind and they reached the other end without attracting any attention. They passed into a short rock tunnel with another emergency door seal halfway along it. Beyond lay a cavern of the same size and construction as the previous one.

Rowena crouched on the edge of the gantry to look down into the hall as Stratton joined her. 'This is the first of three bio-storage rooms,' she said.

Stratton leaned further out to take a look for himself. Halfway along the gantry a metal staircase led down to the floor. Two huge vats the size of shipping containers were on one side. A web of various-sized piping led from valves on the faces of the vats and threaded their way to yet more valve systems before disappearing into the walls.

'What's inside them?' he asked.

'The serials mean nothing to me,' Rowena replied, referring to the Cyrillic stencilling on the faces of the containers. 'Some of these concoctions are probably unknown outside of here.'

'How far are we from the lift?'

'Through there.' She indicated ahead on the same level. 'First right, next left, down a long corridor past several offices and into a large room, which I think is a laboratory. Do you want to check it out first?'

'The longer we hang around the more chance we have of being busted.' He studied her. 'If you're right about all you said then we should just get on with it.'

Rowena looked him in the eye. 'I'm right about what I said.'

Stratton believed her. He suddenly ducked back, pulling her with him as a man in a bright yellow chemical-hazard suit moved into view on the floor below. It was difficult to hear any sounds above the noise of the machinery from the hall behind them. 'You ready to do this?' Stratton asked her.

'We haven't worked out how to cause a leak, never mind how to delay it.'

'We're past the point of no return,' he said, looking back the way they had come. 'We either give up or go for it.' He knew what her answer would be as she gritted her teeth.

He gripped the assault rifle and walked casually along the gangway to the steps. Rowena followed as he walked down them. Another engineer in a chemical-hazard suit was joining his colleague when they both saw Stratton and Rowena and stopped what they were doing.

Stratton indicated that they should move back to the wall, an instruction which they eagerly obeyed. 'Tie them,' he said to Rowena, indicating a coil of rope.

She quickly secured the men's hands to a large pipe. Not particularly adept with knots and having an ample supply of rope, she overdid the bondage, but at least the men were going nowhere.

The soldier and the scientist joined each other in the middle of the hall to inspect the massive vats of death and figure out how they were going to open them.

'Why don't we just set a fire?' Stratton suggested.

'Not reliable enough. They have sprinklers,' she said, indicating them. 'If they work they could put out the fire before it burned through the skin.' Rowena turned on her heels, scanning every inch of the room. In a corner lay a collection of gas bottles. She walked over to examine them. 'Oxygen,' she announced. The discovery inspired her and she hurried across to the other side of the room to a stack of metal piping. After a brief examination she got to her feet. 'I have it,' she said.

'Tell me.'

'We make a thermic lance.'

Stratton knew what a thermic lance was, having used miniature versions in the SBS to cut through steel bulkheads. He looked between the pipes and the gas bottles and nodded. 'How do we get the delay?'

'We run the pipes beneath the two vats. We'll have to connect a couple of them. We attach an oxygen bottle to one end. We turn on the gas and ignite the other end of the pipe. It'll burn like a fuse wire beneath the vats and at twenty thousand degrees will melt through on its way.'

Stratton looked suddenly unsure.

'What?' she asked, seeing his doubtful expression.

'We make a hole in the vat, sure – but what if that's not enough?'

Rowena saw his point and was suddenly unsure herself.

'What if we put an oxygen bottle under each vat on top of the pipe?' he suggested. 'The lance'll cut into the oxy bottle and it will explode.'

'And burst open the vat. I like it.' She looked impressed with him. 'You're starting to turn me on.'

He winked at her. 'Let's get on with it.'

The pair set to work, Stratton lifting and shifting the heavy oxygen bottles into position. Rowena threaded the pipes below the vats but paused to think how she was going to connect them together as well as seal the end to the gas cylinder.

She scanned around the room again, saw what she wanted

hanging from the belt of one of the engineers, walked over and pulled a roll of heavy-duty tape off its hook. 'Thanks,' she said as she made her way back to the pipes.

The engineers watched with growing concern as they followed the couple's progress.

The Russian major walked along the narrow corridor towards the pump room, curious about why the lights were off inside. When he walked in the door the first thing he saw was his guard sitting on the ground, holding his head. Then his eyes flashed to the bracket where he had left Stratton and saw the empty chain around the base of it. He kicked the guard brutally in the back, took the radio from his belt and talked rapidly into it as he pulled out a pistol and hurried out of the room.

Half a dozen scruffy soldiers lounged in an untidy guardroom on the surface of the Plesetsky mine, soiled bunk beds along one wall, a cast-iron pig oven stuffed with burning coal glowing in the centre, a pan of potatoes bubbling on top. When the officer's excited voice boomed over the main communications console they burst into life, grabbed their rifles from a rack by the door and hurried outside.

The major ran along a rock corridor and burst in through the doors of a large laboratory. Jason, cleaned up and wearing a boiler suit, stood with Binning and two Russian technicians. The tile lay on a glass table in two halves with some of its components removed and set beside it.

'Your man has escaped,' the officer shouted.

Jason flinched in anger. 'I warned you! Damn it. Where is he? Is he still in the complex?'

'There are only two exits on the surface and my guards are there. Nobody has been in or out since I left him.'

'Make sure it stays that way.' Jason was livid.

'Rowena,' Binning exclaimed.

'Have you checked with her guard?' Jason asked the officer.

The Russian looked vexed as he reached for his radio. 'No one can leave here. Don't worry. She is locked in her room.'

'Locked?' Jason shouted.

'But she's—' the officer stammered.

'If you say she's just a bloody woman I'll shoot you,' Jason growled as he walked towards him. 'Get your men down here and search the place. Do it. Now.'

'They're on their way.'

'You find him and you kill him. Immediately. No questions. Just shoot. I warned you about him.'

The officer understood. 'And what about her?'

Jason glanced at Binning though he had already decided what had to be done.

'She can't go back with you now,' Binning said.

Jason looked at the Russian. 'Kill her.'

'I'll have to get authority.'

Jason's expression darkened and he put his face closer to the major's. 'If they get out of here, I promise you, you will die.'

The Russian officer swallowed hard and ran from the room.

'Idiots.'

'I don't like the thought of that man running loose around here,' Binning said.

Jason's expression changed to one of cynicism. 'You've had nothing but contempt for him up until now.'

'I've never underestimated how dangerous he could be.'

Jason had to agree. He took a pistol from a holster hanging on a hook. 'Then we'd better ensure he doesn't do any more damage. We've beaten him before. Let's do it for the last time.'

Stratton lowered the last oxygen cylinder into position beneath the biochemical vat on top of the pipe and took a breather as he watched Rowena tape up the pipe connection. She found some wire wool, taped it around the opposite end of the pipe and walked back to the gas bottle that would be used to feed the lance. He saw her secure the pipe over the valve nozzle, using up the rest of the tape and wrapping it around continuously to ensure a good seal.

As a final test she turned the gas bottle's valve fully open. The hissing gush of high-pressure gas filled the room. The taped joints held and she turned off the valve. 'It doesn't matter if there's some leakage,' she said, studying the simple but deadly system. 'There's enough pressure. It's ready.'

'How do we light the wire wool?'

'The Russians'll have a lighter. They stink of cigarette smoke even in their suits.'

Stratton walked over to the two men, dug into one of their breast pockets and pulled out a pack of cigarettes and a lighter.

'Could you light me one of those cigarettes?' Rowena asked. 'And please, no quips about it being unhealthy.'

Stratton removed one of the cigarettes from the pack and gestured to the engineer to ask if it was okay. The man nodded enthusiastically. Stratton put the pack back into the man's pocket, lit the cigarette and went over to Rowena.

He handed her the cigarette and walked over to the other end of the pipe that had the lump of wire wool attached. 'How long do you think the pipe will take to burn down to the first vat?' he asked, studying its length.

'A minute, more or less.'

Stratton ignited the lighter and stared at the flame. He racked his brains for anything they had forgotten.

'What about them?' she asked.

He extinguished the lighter and looked at the frightened engineers who had clearly worked out that something very bad was going on.

'Untie them.'

Rowena walked over to the men and untied the rope.

'Don't run until I say.' Stratton gestured to the men, trying to convey the message.

They didn't appear to understand but remained where they were. He had the gun and they could sense that he was a dangerous individual.

'You happy where the lift is?' he asked Rowena.

'Yes.'

'You ready?'

'Yes.'

'Turn on the gas.'

She went back to the bottle, crouched to grip the valve and looked over at him.

He lit the lighter.

Rowena turned on the gas and it began to hiss. But then another sound echoed around the hall from behind her. The sound of boots running along the gantry. She looked to see half a dozen soldiers spread out on it, aiming rifles down at them.

The Russian major marched smartly from the tunnel, holding his pistol, and stood between his men, looking smug. 'Put down your weapon!'

'Which one?' Stratton asked.

The officer looked confused. 'The rifle.'

Stratton laid the rifle on the floor and stepped back, close to the vat that offered some cover from view. He was still within reach of the wire wool that quivered as the oxygen passed through it. 'What about this one?' Stratton held out the lighter.

The Russian couldn't make out what Stratton had in his hand.

'With this I can open up this,' Stratton said, placing a hand on the side of the large vat.

The officer did not comprehend the threat. He took a rifle from one of his men and aimed it at Stratton. As soon as he did, the engineers began shouting and waving their hands as they hurried from Stratton to the officer. One of them quickly explained the significance of the oxygen cylinders beneath the vats as well as the dangers of a bullet zooming around the room. He capped off his elaborate description with a simplified 'Boom!' that everyone could understand.

The officer looked concerned, as did his soldiers, who began to grasp the situation. One of them was the young soldier who had guarded Stratton. He had a bump on the side of his head. He was the first to lower his rifle without receiving a command to do so and the others followed his lead.

The officer realised that he had been checked. 'Okay,' he said, lowering his own weapon. 'You turn off the gas and nothing will happen to you.'

Stratton rolled his eyes. 'Who are you trying to kid? This is it for us. We're dead. But it's the end for you too. We're going to take you with us.'

The officer was unable to hide his nervousness. 'It . . . it doesn't have to be that way.'

'It's the only way. I would rather die like this than in one of your prisons.' Stratton looked over at Rowena who nodded and looked up at the Russians.

'Me too,' she said.

One of the soldiers could speak enough English to understand what had been said and relayed the suicide threat to his colleagues in Russian. A ripple of fear ran through them.

Stratton ignited the lighter and lit the wire wool. It glowed as it burned as quickly as hay and when the pipe itself ignited, the steel, acting as a fuel encouraged by the oxygen, sparked furiously and glowed bright red and roared loudly as smoke and flames issued from the end of it.

The two engineers could stand it no longer and scrambled to the stairs and up them. As they passed the soldiers their panic infected them and every man immediately took flight, except the officer. He stood his ground for a few seconds before stepping back and breaking into a sprint after the others.

Stratton and Rowena looked at each other as the pipe burned swiftly towards the vat.

'Turn it off,' he called out.

Rowena obeyed, screwing down the valve until the gas was cut off. The roaring ceased and the flames spewing from the end of the pipe subsided. 'What now?' she asked.

Stratton picked up the gun. 'Get going. Hopefully the guards'll keep running when they get to the surface. We'll have to take our chances.'

'You weren't serious about wanting to end it here rather than in a prison?'

'Not while there's some hope. Go!'

Rowena made her way to the stairs and jogged up them. As Stratton reached the bottom steps she was hurrying along the gantry to the connecting tunnel. When he reached the top of the steps he stopped in his tracks. Jason Mansfield stood in the tunnel, his arm firmly around Rowena's neck, the muzzle of a pistol pressed against her temple. Binning stood beside them with the Russian officer and a couple of his men.

Stratton brought the rifle up, ready to aim it.

'Easy, Stratton. Pretending to destroy a chemical container had these idiots fooled – for a moment.'

The Russian officer felt a mixture of embarrassment and anger as he gripped his pistol tightly by his side. He wanted to shoot Stratton for making a fool out of him but resisted taking aim while the dangerous Englishman still had a gun in his own hands.

'Put the gun down, Stratton,' Jason urged him. 'This time it's really over . . . You've had a good run but this is as far as you can go now.' He pressed the weapon still harder against Rowena, who stiffened angrily in his grip.

Stratton went over his options as he looked into Jason's eyes.

'Always contemplating options, Stratton. You are insufferable. Shall I try to take the mad fool with me with a quick shot, and hope he doesn't kill the girl? Or do I concede this phase and hope there will be another opportunity?'

'There's another,' Stratton said.

Jason's smirk wavered. What other options could the man possibly have?

As she looked into Stratton's eyes Rowena suddenly realised what he was considering. 'Do it,' she said.

Jason remained at a loss to figure out their plan but instinctively tensed himself for something.

Stratton continued to stare into her eyes as he imagined the potential consequences of his next action. And what they needed to do to survive.

Rowena swallowed and did the same.

Stratton turned and aimed the gun at the oxygen bottle beneath the container. He fired.

The rocky cavern magnified the deafening explosion. Chunks of the oxygen cylinder flew in every direction. Stratton, exposed where he stood, fell back to the floor, the weapon clattering away. The expanding blast caught Binning and the Russian officer and his men as they dropped to cover themselves.

Rowena had braced herself for the detonation and as Jason tensed in reaction to it she grabbed his gun hand and slammed him hard with her elbow. He dropped the gun and she followed up with a palm thrust to his heart that threw him back against the rock wall and onto one knee where he fought to catch his breath. He reached beyond his momentary haze and snatched hold of her arm, his grip vicelike, flashing a look up at her. She saw the terrible threat in his eyes but could not get free.

The full force of the exploding gas cylinder had punched through the belly of the huge vat and ripped it open. Tons of bright green sludge gushed out and a heavy gas issued from it, rapidly expanding to cover the floor like a smoky liquid as it rose up the walls of the hall.

Stratton looked through the grille floor of the gantry to see the gas rising up towards him. He sprang to his feet and ran fast towards the tunnel, hurdling over Binning and the Russians.

Jason was about to strike Rowena when Stratton steamrollered into him, delivering a crunching blow to the side of his head that sent him sprawling. At the same time the operative grabbed Rowena and tumbled into the next hall with her.

The green gas began to bubble up through the gantry as Binning got to his feet and ran from it like a man possessed. The Russian officer and one of his men were hot on his heels but the remaining soldier stayed dazed on his hands and knees, a cut across his forehead. The gas seeped through the gridded metal and over his hands. He felt immediate excruciating pain and instinctively pulled his hands away from the terrible vapour. It had already exposed his finger bones, had simply melted the flesh from his hands. The gas rose up his body and he screamed as the flesh literally fell from him and he collapsed beneath the devouring mist.

Jason looked around to see the gas heading into the tunnel towards him and he was up and running faster and more recklessly than he had ever run in his life.

Stratton and Rowena also ran for all they were worth along the corridor.

Binning and the two Russians were not far behind.

The gas accelerated through the connecting tunnel and flowed like a living liquid into the next hall.

Sensors picked up the deadly vapour and klaxons began to sound throughout the complex, accompanied by red flashing strobe lights above all the doors.

The electric motors beside the heavy steel barriers burst into life and large hydraulic arms began stretching out to close them. The doors shuddered as the old hinges cracked and complained as they were brought into use after so many years. The massive doors began to move.

Rowena led the way to a corridor junction and without hesitation selected a turn. They passed through a closing steel door and ran on.

A few seconds later Binning and the Russians jumped through the same narrowing gap.

Jason ran hard around the corner and caught sight of the men up ahead. He leaped through the door with some room to spare and sprinted on.

Stratton and Rowena hurtled down the corridor. As they passed a door an engineer hurried out from it just in time for Binning and the major to slam into him. They all went sprawling except for the young soldier just behind them who jumped over the pile-up and carried on.

Binning got to his feet as Jason arrived and together the scientists ran on. The officer stood up and looked back. The gas had reached the corner. Eyes wide, he ran for his life.

The dazed engineer, unable fully to comprehend what was happening, looked in the direction of the fleeing men. He heard something behind him, a growing sizzling sound. As he turned, the gas, which filled every inch of the corridor from floor to ceiling, enveloped him, disintegrating his body inside his clothing in seconds.

Jason and Binning reached a junction and took the right turn without hesitation.

The officer arrived a second behind them and paused, looking in both directions. He made a decision, choosing the left corridor, which he ran along as fast as he could. Up ahead the young soldier reached a heavy steel door as the hydraulic arm was reducing the gap and dived through. But his rifle got caught and he fought to pull it free. The officer saw the closing gap and screamed, his arms outstretched towards it. The soldier let go of the weapon as he saw the gas and fell back into a brightly lit stairwell that spiralled up before him.

The officer lunged for the door but he couldn't get through the dwindling gap. He grabbed the barrel of the gun and frantically tried to lever the door open. But it was useless. The hydraulics moaned as the door crushed the weapon's wooden stock and it came to a hissing halt.

The Russian turned to look back along the corridor as the green gas rolled towards him. He reached for his holster only to find it empty, remembering that he had dropped the gun when the gas cylinder exploded. He looked at the rifle jammed in the door, placed his heart against the muzzle, reached for the trigger and pushed it. The gun fired, killing him instantly as the gas engulfed him.

The green mist seeped through the door that was now wedged slightly open by the gun. It slowly filled the bottom of the stairwell. Several spirals up, the young soldier saw the gathering green death. He hauled himself up the stairs.

Rowena and Stratton reached the laboratory door, flung it open and ran into the room, pausing only to slam the door behind them and locate the lift before racing to the far side of the lab and ripping open the sliding door of the lift cage.

The lift, like everything else in the complex, was old and basic. Large enough to fit a grand piano inside, the ceiling and floor were made of gridded metal connected by struts and wire-mesh walls.

Binning, a little ahead of Jason, reached the lab door but as he slowed to open it Jason ran into him and callously propelled his colleague further along the floor of the corridor. It had become a race for personal survival.

As Jason barged open the lab door and sprinted across the room towards the lift Binning rose to his feet. He saw the approaching gas, scrambled back to the door and threw himself inside before the gas could touch him.

Stratton and Rowena closed the door of the lift cage but not before Jason managed to jam an arm inside.

In his desperation Binning fell over chairs and tables as he tried to get to the lift, spilling the encryption tile to the floor as the green gas rolled into the room.

'It won't move unless the door's closed!' Jason shouted.

Stratton had no choice and slid aside the lift-cage door. Jason leaped into the lift and looked back at Binning pulling himself across the room, the gas right behind him. Jason slammed the cage shut, pulled the lever and the lift jerked as it began to ascend.

'No!' Binning yelled. He leaped for the rising lift and tugged at the cage. He grabbed the cable attached to its underside and stuck his fingers up through the grille of the floor. As he went up, the poisonous gas crept into the opening and down into the shaft.

Stratton and Rowena stood on the side of the creaking lift opposite to Jason as it rose slowly. They looked down at Binning through the floor, his life entirely dependent on the strength in his fingers.

'Help me!' he screamed.

Stratton stared at Jason across the small space, unsure how to handle the man. The scientist's game plan could only continue if Stratton and Rowena were silenced. Jason was a dangerous man and could not be given another opportunity.

But Stratton wasn't the only person in the lift with a grievance against Jason. In fact Rowena arguably had a greater one. Mansfield had duped her, used her, lied to her and tried to kill her. Worse still, as far as she was concerned, he had taken her as his lover purely to further his traitorous ambitions.

Staring at him, face to face for the first time since discovering how evil and low he was, she could not contain herself. 'You piece of shit!' she screamed, throwing herself at him.

But Jason was fully prepared for an attack from either of them, and he was far too strong and skilful for her. He sidestepped her punch and struck her savagely on the side of her neck, a blow that sent her near unconscious as she dropped to the floor.

Stratton was quick to follow through on her effort, deciding that his best strategy was to get hold of the man in order to counter his superior martial-arts skills. But it was never going to be easy. As Stratton dived at him, Jason blocked the move and delivered a vicious kick. Yet Stratton was nothing if not determined and after absorbing several blows he countered a punch and slammed a fist into Jason's face.

Binning let out a scream each time one of them stepped on his fingers. His grip began to weaken, his legs swinging beneath him in a desperate effort to find a purchase.

Rowena knelt on the floor, looking down through the grille. She saw the green mist in the darkness of the shaft rising silently towards them. The sight was enough to bring her fully out of her daze and on to her feet.

Jason and Stratton had drawn apart briefly but were ready to go at it once more.

'It's coming,' Rowena said.

All thought of conflict paused as they realised they might not have the time to worry about anything else.

The mist reached Binning's feet and he screamed insanely as he felt his flesh bubbling. The pain was intense and his grip weakened.

The gas reached above his knees and Binning trembled violently, his face a pathetic mask as he stared up at them. His fingers suddenly lost their hold on the grille and he screamed for less than a second before he disappeared.

Stratton looked up through the grille of the lift's ceiling to see light coming from the square opening at the top of the shaft. Their exit.

Rowena kept her stare fixed on the gas, trying to calculate if they would make it.

Then the lift jerked to a stop.

As one they ripped open the cage as the gas came up through the floor and then they were running for their lives down a broad whitewashed corridor. At the end of it a huge steel security door had begun to close slowly, to seal the exit, to shut out the daylight.

Jason grabbed at Stratton to pull him back. Stratton lashed out and struck him. Jason staggered back a little with the blow but managed to clip one of Stratton's feet with an aimed kick and trip him up. The operative went sprawling but as he fell he reached out a hand and grabbed Jason's ankle.

It was Mansfield's turn to go sprawling on the floor and as Stratton got to his feet and sprinted on he planted a powerful kick into the scientist's lower back to keep him down a second longer.

Rowena ran through the ever-decreasing gap as the massive hydraulic arm pushed relentlessly to close the heavy door.

Jason got up quickly and, fleeter than Stratton, was soon right behind him. But Stratton was first into the gap and flung himself through it. With Rowena's help he sprang free. As Jason pushed his way through behind him, Stratton turned and grabbed the man by the throat, holding him firmly in the closing gap.

Jason grasped Stratton's hand in a desperate effort to force himself free but the operative held him fast.

'Not this time, Jason,' Stratton said, his arm and body shaking with concentrated effort.

The door closed on one of Jason's feet. He screamed as it broke the bones inside his boot. The hydraulics struggled to seal the door completely but eventually the closing process ground to a halt. The security door was almost closed but not quite.

Stratton released Jason and stepped back.

The scientist fought to get free but it was useless. He was caught like an animal in a trap.

After a herculean effort Jason suddenly stopped, realising it was in vain. He would never release himself in time.

'Never underestimate luck,' Stratton said as he stepped back.

Jason looked at the pair of them as the green gas slithered around his ankles.

Rowena looked on in horror as Jason's feet began to bubble.

The gas seeped out along the length of the door seal and Jason Mansfield started to shudder. As it enveloped him, Stratton and Rowena turned and ran. Jason's pitiful scream became a choking gurgle as his flesh melted and the gas reached out across the ground.

They sprinted through the unmanned main gate and along the road that cut across barren moorland.

As they ran they heard footsteps behind them. Stratton looked back over his shoulder to see his young Russian guard gaining on them. The youngster was swift of foot and went pounding past the couple with hardly a glance at them.

Stratton and Rowena did not pause or let up their speed until they reached a highway.

Stratton stopped briefly to check the wind direction. 'This way,' he said and they broke into a brisk jog.

'What do we do now?' Rowena asked as she ran alongside him, their breath steaming in the chilly air.

'Get to Moscow and our embassy.'

A truck appeared, coming along the highway from behind them, and Stratton practically threw himself in front of it in order to get it to stop. The driver pulled the vehicle to a halt and they scrambled into the cab. Moments later it moved off.

'*Spasibo*,' Stratton said to the driver, who gave them the once-over but otherwise seemed only a little annoyed with his hijackers.

Rowena regained her breath, huddled against the operative on the passenger seat. She looked back through the window to see if the gas was following. There was no sign of it. She stared ahead again and sighed.

'You okay?' Stratton asked.

She had to think about it for a moment. 'I've only met you twice and both times I've quite literally had to scramble for my life.'

'How do you think I feel? I have to live with me.'

Rowena lost the fight with herself to stop smiling.

Epilogue

Attracting looks of curiosity from a couple of Customs officers, Stratton and Rowena walked out of the baggage hall at Heathrow Airport. Neither of them had any luggage. They were dressed in cheap clothes that had been bought from a Moscow store near the British Embassy by a young aide who lacked taste and a memory for size. They were clean, pale and bore the marks of their brutal fight to escape the mine, with cuts and bruises on their knuckles and faces.

'Excuse me, sir,' one of the officials said, moving in front of Stratton to block his path.

The other officer moved to where he could stop Rowena if she decided to run. He looked her up and down suspiciously.

'Where have you travelled from?' the official asked Stratton.

Stratton exhaled tiredly and took a small plastic wallet from a pocket, opened it and showed it to the official. Inside was a small, ornate, circular, gold-inlaid enamel royal coat of arms.

The official looked at it, then back at Stratton as if he did not understand its meaning.

Stratton flipped up the badge on its neat leather hinge to reveal an inscription that read: 'MI6: The bearer of this badge will receive all assistance on request from British Crown authorities in the course of their duty on behalf of Her Majesty the Queen.' The badge had been given to Stratton by the British ambassador in Moscow on instructions from London as he was leaving.

The Customs official reached for the wallet.

'No need to touch,' Stratton said. 'Just read it.'

The official frowned a little but studied the badge. He had seen photographs of it although he had never seen one in real life before. He also remembered that he was to obey the inscription without question. 'Is there anything I can do for you, sir?' he asked.

Stratton shook his head.

The Customs official nodded, bid his colleague step back and moved away himself to allow the couple through.

Stratton and Rowena walked into the cavernous arrivals hall where the operative stopped as if weighed down by indecision.

Rowena gave him his space. They had hardly talked throughout the journey back and had not exchanged a single word about the operation. It was not so much because the subject would be thoroughly hashed-out over the coming days, more a case of unwinding and returning to earth after such a psychologically and physically depleting experience. But there was something else. It was unfinished. There were unanswered questions and the more Stratton thought about them, the more uneasy he had grown.

As Rowena watched him she became concerned for him. She suspected there was a lot more to the plot than she knew and she wanted to help somehow, though she didn't know how. 'What are you going to do?' she asked.

Stratton felt unsure about confiding in her. He looked at her bruised face and into her tired eyes and decided that she was more of a partner to him in this business than anyone else had been. She had been a reluctant member of Jason's team, had been betrayed by him and Binning and had shown great courage and fortitude when most needed. 'One thing has been bothering me since I've had time to think about all that's happened. But I'm not sure how to go about solving it.'

Rowena stepped closer to him, curious to know, hoping she could help.

'I don't believe that Jason and Binning accomplished all they did on their own.'

'They didn't. They had the help of powerful Russian officials and wealthy businessmen.'

'I mean they must've had serious assistance from heavy players on our side too. Getting onto the platform, for instance. And Jason going to Russia with me. He said he didn't believe in luck, that everything he did was meticulously planned. Yet he had no control over some of the most important leaps in the series of events.'

'That would mean someone pretty high up?'

'Someone with direct influence on the operation. There's only one person it could be.' Stratton walked over to a public phone.

He picked up the receiver and dialled a number. It was the SBS HQ operator's freephone number. 'This is John Stratton. Put me through to Mike Manning.'

Stratton looked at Rowena as she came up to him, her hands in the pockets of the cheap coat with its matted synthetic fur-lined collar.

'Mike? Stratton. No time right now. I need something. It's important. I want to know where Jervis is. Sumners'll tell you if you make it sound operationally important. I'll wait for your call back . . . You have the number? Roger that.'

Stratton put the phone down.

'What are you going to do?' Rowena asked again.

'I'm going to find Jervis and ask him.'

'Just like that?'

He shrugged. 'Unless you have another suggestion?'

'You have a very direct style, don't you?'

'I need answers. All I can think of is to ask the person who I think has them.'

A man walked over to the phone kiosk and reached for the receiver. Stratton put his hand on it. 'There's another one over there,' he said.

'I'd like to use this one,' the man said. He was bigger than Stratton and looked as though he could handle himself.

'Are you deaf?' Rowena asked him from behind. 'Go and use that phone over there before I put your head through it.'

The man looked at the pair of them, taking in their bruised complexions. But it was their stone-cold, unblinking eyes that gave him pause for thought. 'Okay,' he said, stepping back and turning away.

The phone rang and Stratton quickly picked it up. 'Yes . . . Thanks. Yeah, I'll see you tomorrow.'

He put the phone back down and looked at Rowena. 'He's in the City, having dinner.'

'Can I come with you?'

Stratton considered the request. 'Why not?' He put his hand in his pocket and took out the money that the embassy aide had given him. 'Let's grab a cab.'

They headed across the hall and into the cold night air.

The taxi pulled to a halt in St James's Place, just up the road from The Mall. Stratton and Rowena climbed out. The well-lit street was empty of life. They walked along a short cul-de-sac and up the flight of steps to the entrance of Duke's Hotel.

The compact, well-appointed lobby had an empty reception desk in one corner. Stratton heard laughter nearby and walked through a narrow opening that offered a choice of directions to either the cocktail bar or several rooms.

Voices came from the bar. Stratton moved to the door and eased it open. It was a small, tastefully furnished, cramped room with a handful of little tables and a small yet grand bar. The bartender wore a white jacket and a bow tie. Two tables had been pushed together by a window with its curtains drawn. Seated around them were the bar's only customers. Stratton recognised all four of the men.

Rowena moved to his side. 'You see a lion's den, you just walk right into it.'

Sumners was the first to see Stratton, his weasel-like, self-preserving and unsmiling eyes staring at him. The others caught on to their colleague's distraction. Nevins, Jackson and Jervis all looked round to see who it was. Jackson appeared to be the only one surprised to see the two of them.

'Ah. The adventurers return,' Jervis said. 'Come on in and join us. 'Ave a glass of claret. I think you've earned one.' Jervis always lost control of his fake posh accent after a few drinks, his true South London mongrel quality shining through.

Stratton stood in front of the group.

Rowena eyed Nevins as he pulled on a cigarette. 'Do you mind if I have of those? Russian cigarettes give me heartburn.'

'Help yourself, my dear,' Nevins said, offering her a packet as well as his lighter. 'We've classified the bar as a private room for the evening.'

She lit one up and sat down at the next table.

'I wasn't expecting to see you so soon,' Jervis said. 'You must've just stepped off the plane.' Jervis noted Stratton's dark expression and the way he looked at him. 'Something on your mind, old boy?'

Stratton wasn't sure where to start, despite having thought it through while in the taxi. 'A couple of things.'

'Why don't I tell you what they are, and you tell me if I'm right?' Jervis offered.

Stratton was always wary of Jervis. He was one of those completely unapproachable individuals, habitually deceptive and secluded. It was the strategy of his rank and position but also embedded in his character. Stratton could not imagine him having a single close friend and wondered if he had a wife and children. There was no evidence to suggest that he could possibly get close to anyone. And Stratton could not see Jervis sharing a single idea with anyone unless he expected to get something in return.

Stratton nodded.

'Why did I let Jason and his mob continue to the platform when I could have ordered the helicopter to land? That's one, isn't it?'

Stratton nodded again.

'And why did I let 'im go to Russia with you when he was as bent as Binning?'

'You knew?' Stratton asked, unsure whether to believe him or not.

'Not exactly,' Jervis admitted. 'That's why we 'ad to flush 'im. To tell you the truth, I quite liked the idea of MI16 having an operational licence. You thick bastards are all right when it comes to breakin' down walls with your 'eads. But those boys 'ad brains as well as muscle . . . Problem is, they also 'ad too much ambition.'

'You risked the decoder.'

'Everything we do's a risk, laddie. You should know that much by now. It's all about values and exchanges. The tile was not the complete item and I was confident we'd get Binning. It had to be the real thing or they would've rumbled the game. That's where Jackson came in.'

Jackson forced a smile and gave Stratton a respectful nod.

'He thought you'd rumbled 'im when you sussed him in the sub.' Jervis paused to take a sip of wine. 'Jackson did a little number on the device. It worked normally but it was obvious they'd want to strip it down and duplicate it so he put a clever little anti-tampering thingummy in it. When they put it back together it wouldn't work. But you took care of all that, anyway. The tile is in the mine and no one's going back into that place for a bloody millennium. They've sealed off the whole complex with a million tons of concrete . . . Does that about cover it?'

Stratton looked at the faces staring back at him: Nevins with a thin smile, Jackson apologetic, Sumners uninterested and Jervis like the cat that got the cream. 'I suppose it does.'

Jervis moved his gaze to Rowena. 'What are we going to do about you, young lady?'

Rowena took a long draw on the cigarette. She'd been wondering the same thing. By agreeing to go on the platform operation she had displayed a level of disloyalty to London. She expected to get kicked out and although she tried to be philosophical about it, looking forward to doing something new, deep down she was disappointed by the thought. She had never been completely comfortable working in MI16 but had never fully identified why. But then, she had never been comfortable anywhere. She suspected that was because she had always been under others. Perhaps the only answer was to find something she could do by herself. The question was what.

'You fancy 'eading up Sixteen until I can find someone more intelligent?'

Rowena was quite taken aback by the offer but tried not to let it show. A feeling of relief flooded through her, quickly overtaken by an excitement and boost to her confidence. 'Sure,' she said, poker-faced.

'Good. Stick around. We need to talk. You've got a bit of clearin' up to do first.' Jervis looked up at Stratton. 'Well, if you're not going to 'ave a glass, Stratton, sod off back to Poole and write your post-op report.'

Stratton was satisfied with Jervis's explanation. And the last thing he wanted to do was have a beverage with that lot. He nodded a farewell and headed for the door.

As he stepped outside the hotel into the chilly air Rowena walked out behind him.

'Stratton.'

He stopped to look back at her.

She took a final drag on her cigarette and dropped it to the ground as she approached him. All hostility and coldness had gone from her face. 'I want to say thanks.'

'We never thank each other afterwards. We all owe the same.'

She smiled softly and nodded her understanding. 'You bothered Jason. Even before he met you. He couldn't accept that you might be better than him. I wouldn't be surprised if it was the last thing he thought. You'd beaten him. That would have been even harder for him to accept than dying.'

Stratton didn't particularly care what Jason had thought. 'See you around,' he said as he turned and walked away.

'You *are* a lucky bastard, though!' Rowena called out.

Stratton didn't look back. He continued walking, a smile growing on his face.